# VAINGLORIOUS

## A CIAPHAS CAIN NOVEL

# VAINGLORIOUS

## A CIAPHAS CAIN NOVEL

**SANDY MITCHELL**

BLACK LIBRARY

## A BLACK LIBRARY PUBLICATION

First published in 2023.
This edition published in Great Britain in 2024 by
Black Library,
Games Workshop Ltd.,
Willow Road,
Nottingham, NG7 2WS, UK.

10 9 8 7 6 5 4 3 2 1

Produced by Games Workshop in Nottingham.
Cover illustration by Jan Drenovec.

See Black Library on the internet at

# blacklibrary.com

Find out more about Games Workshop
and the world of Warhammer 40,000 at

# games-workshop.com

Printed and bound in the UK.

*For Hester and Rebecca – apples not far from the tree.*

For more than a hundred centuries the Emperor has sat immobile on the Golden Throne of Earth. He is the Master of Mankind. By the might of his inexhaustible armies a million worlds stand against the dark.

Yet, he is a rotting carcass, the Carrion Lord of the Imperium held in life by marvels from the Dark Age of Technology and the thousand souls sacrificed each day so his may continue to burn.

To be a man in such times is to be one amongst untold billions. It is to live in the cruelest and most bloody regime imaginable. It is to suffer an eternity of carnage and slaughter. It is to have cries of anguish and sorrow drowned by the thirsting laughter of dark gods.

This is a dark and terrible era where you will find little comfort or hope. Forget the power of technology and science. Forget the promise of progress and advancement. Forget any notion of common humanity or compassion.

There is no peace amongst the stars, for in the grim darkness of the far future, there is only war.

*Editorial Note:*

*Although Cain encountered the necrons on relatively few occasions throughout his decades of service to the Imperium, he did so far more frequently than most – especially given that the vast majority of sentient life forms who have such an experience do so only once, and not for very long. Unsurprisingly, these incidents seem to have made quite an impression on him, and none more so than his first encounter, which he refers to in passing many times over the course of his memoirs. (The fact that he lost two fingers to a glancing hit from a gauss flayer probably went some way towards lodging it in his memory.) Since his activities on Interitus Prime make up one of the shorter fragments of those already edited and disseminated to the gratifyingly large number of my fellow inquisitors who have expressed an interest in perusing them, I see no reason to reiterate them now.*

*Instead, I've chosen to devote the current volume to a much later incident, in the closing years of the last millennium, shortly before his retirement from active service to take up the post of tutor to the commissar cadets at the Schola Progenium on Perlia. Those of my readers who have already seen the volume detailing his activities there during the Black Crusade may find it a little odd, as did I, that he makes no reference therein to the events of this newly prepared tranche of his memoirs – but since he is no longer around to ask, I can only speculate that the circumstances at the time reminded him more strongly of his earlier encounters with the ambulatory metal horrors on Interitus Prime and Simia Orichalcae than the more nuanced interaction he describes here.*

*With that in mind, I turn to his typically idiosyncratic account of the founding of the forge world Eucopia, and the part he played in uncovering a hidden threat there which, left unchecked, would have had incalculable consequences for the entire sector. It's probably no exaggeration to say that without his intervention, our beleaguered little corner of the Imperium would be in straits even more dire than they currently are – if, indeed, it had managed to survive this long at all.*

*As usual, I've tried to leave Cain's account of events as close to how I found it as possible, apart from the interpolation of other material to add context to his typically self-centred narrative, dividing it into chapters for ease of reading, and the addition of footnotes to clarify the odd reference or correct the occasional inaccuracy.*

*Amberley Vail, Ordo Xenos*

# ONE

I've seen a fair few worlds in my century or so of rattling around the galaxy, though few indeed could be described as 'fair', bearing in mind how close I came to losing my life on most of them. For the most part these visits were as short as I could manage, given that wars or other unpleasantness were the main reasons for my presence, and being where people or other things aren't doing their best to shoot or dismember me is, on the whole, more congenial.

It's hardly surprising, therefore, that return visits to any of them have been few and far between, and with the exception of Perlia, where I've finally found some semblance of a home,[1] distinctly unwelcome.

---

1  *From which we may infer that this portion of his memoirs was composed shortly after his arrival there, before his relatively peaceful retirement was interrupted by the second siege, in which he was to play so pivotal a role.*

The other exception, of course, was Coronus,[2] through which I passed so often I lost count of the number of occasions quite early on in my career. Given the number of regiments typically quartered there, not to mention the plethora of warships floating about the system,[3] I felt as safe on Coronus[4] as anywhere in the galaxy – which is probably why I let my guard down at a crucial moment, with almost fatal results.

Ironically, I was in a particularly good mood at the time, which doubtless went some way towards blunting my habitual paranoia. I'd recently arrived back from Fecundia, where my single-minded attempts to preserve my own skin had somehow been interpreted as crucial in preventing a strategically and logistically vital forge world from disappearing down the gullet of a tyranid hive fleet, and had reported in to the office of the Commissariat with my usual sense of vague trepidation. The trouble with having a reputation like mine is that people tend to believe it, with the unenviable result that every time a particularly foolhardy or suicidal assignment cropped up, my name was at the top of the list of gung-ho idiots to try and palm it off on. As the official

---

2    *An Imperial Guard garrison system, devoted entirely to the resupply and redeployment of Astra Militarum assets.*

3    *The task forces being assembled there typically included a number of Naval vessels, for escorting troop ships or engaging whatever spaceborne assets the enemy might have available wherever they were going.*

4    *By which he means the primary planet, which, in common with practice throughout the Imperium, is regarded as synonymous with the system as a whole. In reality, many of the facilities are located on other planets, asteroids and void stations, particularly those tending to the swarms of starships arriving and departing constantly, and those specialised assets best kept as far away as possible from the ordinary line troopers, such as sanctioned psykers, penal battalion holding pens, abhuman auxiliaries and the like.*

commissarial liaison officer to the lord general's staff, I was able to sidestep most of these attempts at giving a Hero of the Imperium a suitably glorious and messy demise, of course, regretfully citing the pressure of my diplomatic duties, but I was uncomfortably aware that that particular excuse was going to wear pretty thin before very much longer.

'Cain. Welcome back.' The familiar, faintly querulous tones of Lord Commissar[5] Mavin greeted me as I entered, and my heart made a distinct shift in the direction of my boots. I knew him of old: an unimaginative plodder well into his second century, who would probably be found in a quiet corner of the office one day by someone wondering why they hadn't spoken to him for a couple of weeks, and where the smell was coming from. Which isn't to say that I didn't envy him a little too – fortune had favoured him with an undemanding desk job about as far from a combat zone as it was possible to get, which had been my overriding ambition since the day I first tied my scarlet sash.[6]

'Lord commissar.' I arranged a smile on my face, and shook a hand which felt like a desiccated sparrow's corpse. 'A pleasure as always. Still minding the fort, I see.'

As usual, the flattery sparked an answering twitch which might have been a smile, or perhaps a sign of dyspepsia.

'Someone's got to keep the files in order while you youngsters go gallivanting around the sector putting the fear of the Emperor into the unholy,' he responded, in what, for

---

5  *A courtesy title bestowed on particularly long-serving or otherwise notable members of the Commissariat. Cain was, of course, entitled to use it himself, but disdained to do so – either out of genuine modesty, or because seeming to be so bolstered his reputation more than accepting the honour would have done.*

6  *The symbol of a commissar's office.*

him, was quite a friendly fashion. Resisting the temptation to point out that I was almost a centenarian myself, despite the odd juvenat treatment over the years leaving me looking considerably younger, I took the proffered chair. As I sat down, Mavin pottered over to one of the filing cabinets lining the walls and extricated a thick wodge of documentation. He dumped it on the cheap flakboard table between us with a resonant thud, and began leafing through it. 'The Quadravidia thing went off all right?'

'I got diverted,' I said, wondering how much of it he was actually reading. 'To Fecundia.' Throne help us, if he really needed bringing up to speed on my activities since the last time I was on Coronus we'd be here for hours. I began to regret turning down the hot grox bap my aide, Jurgen, had offered me that morning – typically, it had vanished into one of his webbing pouches 'for later' as soon as I'd finished shaking my head, although I suspected when it emerged again only one of us would find it even close to palatable.

'Indeed.' Mavin paged on. 'Quite a coup for you, it seems. Got the t'au to withdraw, formed an alliance against the encroaching tyranids, saw them off with no help I can see from the little grey heathens, and it seems the truce is still holding.' A remarkably succinct summation which missed practically everything significant. 'And got the cogboys[7] owing us a favour into the bargain.'

'I can hardly take much credit for that,' I said, knowing that refusing to do so would simply make whatever kudos was going round adhere more tightly to me.

'Nevertheless.' Mavin closed the file with an audible snap.

---

7  *A faintly disparaging term for members of the Adeptus Mechanicus common among the Imperial Guard, derived from the cogwheel symbol of their calling.*

'We feel that a success on this scale leaves you perfectly placed to take on another challenge. One which, in its own way, you might feel is even more daunting.'

And here it came, the fool's errand guaranteed to crown my career with a glorious last stand and a hero's death – although a coward's life had always seemed a far better option from where I was sitting. No point panicking before I even knew what I had to weasel out of, though, so I plastered an expression of polite enquiry across my face, and raised an eyebrow.

'We?'

'Our entire complement,' Mavin said. 'We've discussed it at length, and everyone feels you're the perfect man for the job.'

'How gratifying,' I said, my last hope that at least some of my colleagues might be persuaded that I wasn't the right man after all vanishing as fast as the contents of an unattended smorgasbord while my aide was around. 'And this job would be?'

'You've been to Perlia, I believe,' Mavin said, changing direction as abruptly as Jurgen at the controls of a Salamander. I nodded confirmation, trepidation beginning to give way to bafflement.

'Not for a long time. About sixty years, give or take.' A disquieting possibility occurred to me. 'The orks aren't back, are they?' Because if they were, who better to see them off again than the man everyone believed[8] had ensured our victory the last time.

'Not that we're aware of,' Mavin said, looking faintly surprised at the question. 'No more than usual, I suppose.'

Pretty much anywhere the creatures had once infested was prone to the occasional outbreak of marauding warbands,

---

8  *Not without some justification, it must be said.*

but I'd have thought the local planetary defence force would be more than capable of dealing with them without calling for Militarum assistance; one thing the experience of a full-scale invasion would certainly have left them with would be an almost Valhallan level of expertise in killing greenskins.

Malin paused, inserting a dry little cough, probably for dramatic effect. 'The job we have in mind would be a vital one, ensuring the future of Imperial rule in the Eastern Arm for generations to come.'

In other words, a suicidal foray against overwhelming odds, which probably meant some desperate attempt to head off a newly detected tendril of the tyranid hive fleets. Unless the t'au were already taking advantage of the instability to further their own agenda, in spite of the assurances they'd given – Throne knows, we'd do the same in a heartbeat if we thought we could get away with it. Or perhaps the Great Enemy was up to something, which never ended well, particularly if daemons were involved.

Such speculation was pointless, though, so I suppressed it firmly, before I pitched myself into an even greater funk.

'My duties to the lord general's office–' I began, adopting a tone of polite regret, in an attempt to prepare the groundwork for a plausible excuse when the time came to deliver one. To my surprise, however, I got no further before being interrupted by a wheezy chuckle.

'I told them you'd dig your heels in,' Mavin said, in the faintly smug manner of a cantankerous pedant who'd just been proved right. 'Retirement's never going to sit well with a man like Cain, I said. We all know you'd rather go down swinging a chainsword when the Emperor calls you to the Golden Throne at last, but perhaps you'll at least hear me out?'

'Retirement?' I said, blinking like Jurgen trying to assimilate some strange and alien concept, like the possibility that socks could be changed before they were capable of standing up by themselves. 'What do you mean, retirement?'

I must have spoken a little more forcefully than I'd realised, because Mavin looked quite disconcerted, and the tone of his voice became almost excessively conciliatory.

'No one's doubting your fitness for active service, far from it, and we all appreciate your reluctance to lay down your arms while you're still capable of wielding them so effectively. But sometimes the path of duty takes us in directions we've never considered, or would prefer not to go.'

'That's certainly true,' I agreed with feeling, because I'd spent most of my life being taken in directions I'd rather have run away screaming from. Then, conscious of the sort of thing the sort of man he thought I was would probably say at this juncture, I added, 'No offence taken, I was just somewhat surprised. I've never shirked my duty before' – which was one of the most barefaced lies even I've ever told – 'and I've no intention of starting now by ignoring the advice of a colleague whose counsel I've always valued.' The fact that I hadn't valued it particularly highly was neither here nor there; the implied flattery smoothed over any lingering awkwardness, and if he felt he'd done a good job of persuading me when I took him up on the offer, that would be no bad thing either.

You have to remember, I was quite genuinely astonished at the proposal: retirement was something I'd literally never expected to live to see, not least because it so seldom happens to anyone in the Astra Militarum. No one ever asks for it themselves, because the Inquisition tend to regard such a request as shirking one's duty to the Emperor, and therefore treasonous,[9] so it's an honour, or privilege, which tends to arrive entirely out of the blue, invariably with some kind of price tag attached. Since the price was unlikely to include being shot at so often, or spending quite so much time in a state of bowel-freezing terror, I adopted an expression of polite interest and waited for him to continue.

'Perlia has changed a good deal since you saw off the orkish invasion,' Mavin said, giving me far too much credit – although since that was pretty much everyone's impression of the incident, I'd long since learned to live with it. 'A huge amount of resources have gone into the reconstruction effort, and the Munitorum has reinforced its defences considerably.'

'That seems prudent,' I said, doing my best to recall where the hell the system was in relation to us, and, more importantly, the 'nids and the t'au.[10] To the best of my recollection it was comfortably far from the tyranid line of advance, and sufficiently removed from the t'au border, to be as safe from either as anywhere was.

'Quite,' Mavin agreed, doing a pretty poor impression of actually caring. 'But of more interest to us is the establishment of several new Imperial institutions on Perlia, to improve its strategic and tactical value at a subsector level.'

'I see,' I said, nodding politely and wishing he'd get to the point. 'From which I'm to infer the Commissariat intend to establish a presence there?' An administrative posting to a relative backwater would suit me down to the ground,

---

9    Not quite, though many of my colleagues are of such a mind, and given the number of existential threats to humanity needing suitably qualified servants of the Imperium to combat, it's not an impression we're particularly keen to dispel in any case.

10    The two most pressing tactical problems in the Damocles Gulf at the time; although other xenos threats, such as the orks and aeldari, couldn't be lightly dismissed either.

although I couldn't for the life of me see why they'd bother; any Imperial Guard units in-system would bring their own commissars with them, and local militias don't need supervising that closely.

Mavin chuckled again. 'Not as such,' he said, 'although we do have need of a commissar willing to take up residence there for the foreseeable future. One, as I said, not afraid of a challenge.'

'Challenges go with the job,' I said, still trying to fathom what he was driving at, 'and I doubt anything there now will be quite as daunting as the one I had to deal with on my last visit.' Which just goes to show how much I knew.

'This would certainly be different,' Mavin agreed. 'One of the new Imperial institutions I mentioned is a Schola Progenium. Which means we will, of course, be needing a dedicated commissar with an impeccable service record to take charge of the commissarial cadets, and prepare them for service in the field.'

'I'd hardly call my service record impeccable,' I said, masking my astonishment behind the sort of show of modesty he'd probably be expecting. 'I'm immensely flattered to be considered, naturally, but surely someone a little more by-the-book would be more suitable?'

'The book's one thing, ducking las-bolts quite another,' Mavin said. 'And, to be blunt, your proven ability to do the latter counts for a great deal more than being able to quote the litanies of command verbatim. If you can pass on a bit of your knack for surviving the battlefield to our successors, everyone will benefit.'

'I can't argue with that,' I said, having had no intention of doing so in the first place. The Emperor, it seemed, was finally buying me a drink for doing His work for so long, albeit reluctantly, and I certainly wasn't about to turn it down. But on the other hand, it probably wouldn't do to seem too eager. 'How long do I have to consider it?'

'How long do you think you'll need?' Mavin responded, reasonably enough. 'We'd like you to start by the turn of the year, but if you decide against it we'll have to start considering other candidates. So the sooner the better, really.'

'Well,' I said, doing a fair job of feigning indecision, 'it's a tremendous honour, and I'm bound to say the chance to leave a lasting legacy of service to the Imperium is tempting, to put it mildly. But I wouldn't feel right about accepting without speaking to the lord general first. We've served together for a long time, and I owe him that much at least.'

'I'd expect nothing less,' Mavin said, no doubt thinking he had me convinced, and could afford to show a little forbearance. 'I'll look forward to hearing your answer.'

'I'll let you know tomorrow,' I said. 'I happen to be dining with him this evening, and, as you say, it's in no one's best interests to spin these things out.'

Mavin's face twitched again in another probable smile. 'Until tomorrow, then,' he said.

# TWO

I'd seen Coronus from orbit so often the sight barely registered any more, but this evening, through the viewport of the shuttle bearing me towards a convivial interlude aboard the lord general's flagship, the vista seemed altogether new and delightful. Zyvan and I had been as close to friends as our respective positions in the Astra Militarum allowed for several decades by this point, meeting whenever we could to enjoy one another's company; and, apart from being shot at a good deal less frequently, being able to get together over the dining table or the regicide board more often was the thing I most appreciated about my attachment to his general staff.

Coronus Prime was not, I have to say, a particularly prepossessing world, being devoted almost entirely to the needs of a transient population merely catching their breath before being plunged back into the never-ending maelstrom of warfare which constituted life in the Imperial Guard. Most of the dayside was hazed with dust, raised by the constant arrival and departure of shuttles and drop-ships without number, obscuring a surface almost entirely covered by installations of one sort or another.[11] Conversely, the night hemisphere glowed softly from innumerable luminators, only a few dark lesions marking the position of wilderness areas reserved for training and live-fire exercises. On this occasion, however, I found myself quite charmed by the prospect, noticing subtle graduations of colour and shading which had quite escaped me before.

In short, I was in a remarkably good humour, a sensation I have to say I found both unfamiliar and faintly disquieting. Having lived with the prospect of imminent death for so long, and having escaped from it so narrowly on so many occasions, I was finding my unexpected good fortune almost too good to be true; try as I might, I couldn't quite still the nagging little voice in the back of my head insisting that something was bound to go wrong sooner or later.

And, of course, I was right about that, although even in my most pessimistic imaginings I hadn't expected things to go ploin-shaped quite so quickly.

My first intimation of trouble was the laconic voice of the traffic controller aboard the *Ocean Orchestra*,[12] which echoed faintly in my comm-bead. Out of long habit, and because I've

---

11   The oldest Imperial records list Coronus as a desert world, with no substantial bodies of water to speak of, although it was officially reclassified as garrisoned in the middle of M39, since when the amount of infrastructure has expanded exponentially.

12   The Armageddon-class battle cruiser serving as Zyvan's flagship at the time. His habit of commandeering whichever vessel seemed most suitable for a given campaign, rather than having a vessel permanently assigned for his personal use, probably accounted for his remarkable longevity in the role of highest-priority target for whichever enemy was currently being engaged; by the time they worked out where he was, he'd already moved on to a different ship.

never liked surprises, I'd been monitoring the exchanges, and something about the words sent a faint, premonitory tingling through the palms of my hands. *'Shuttle two-seven-niner, correct course by one decimal three degrees x, zero decimal zero-four degrees z.'* I was no expert in three-dimensional navigation, but it seemed to me that it was quite a severe course adjustment over such a short distance; we could only be a handful of kilometres from the starship by this time, and on my previous visits the servitor manning the flight controls had remained nailed to the correct trajectory like a bead on an abacus.

Telling myself I was being overly cautious, even though that was a habit which had kept me alive against almost impossible odds for decades, I rose from my seat and made my way towards the cockpit, my boot soles seeming to sink almost ankle-deep in the pile of the carpet. One of the perks of being given most of the Militarum resources of the Eastern Arm to play with[13] is that your living arrangements can be made a good deal more comfortable than those of the average line trooper, and Zyvan had certainly learned that lesson well. (Though since he'd done more than his fair share of mud-slogging in his younger days I certainly didn't begrudge him the odd luxury now, especially as he was more than happy to share them with me.) His personal shuttle was, accordingly, as well appointed as that of the average planetary governor, although in rather better taste, its utilitarian bulkheads hidden behind carved wooden panelling (along with a selection of amply stocked decanters and other such aids to whiling away a tedious journey), into which lacquered

---

13  *Something of an exaggeration, as the Eastern Arm contains a great deal more than the Damocles Gulf and its adjacent subsectors, which marked the limits of Zyvan's remit.*

Imperial aquilae and images of the more martially inclined saints had been carefully inlaid.

As I reached the icon of the Emperor concealing the doorway leading to the flight deck, the traffic controller tried again, his voice as calm and measured as anyone trying not to betray a rising sense of alarm. *'Two-seven-niner, correct your course at once. Confirm.'*

*'Course confirmed, trajectory nominal,'* the uninflected tones of the servitor in the pilot's seat responded, with the mechanical obstinacy of its kind.

That definitely wasn't comforting, so I shouldered the door open and hurried into the cockpit, dropping into the co-pilot's seat next to the one currently occupied by the amalgam of metal and flesh currently in charge of the ship. Typically, it took no notice of my presence, its gold-plated fingers immobile on the control lectern in front of it.

*'Shuttle two-seven-niner, I repeat, correct course by one decimal three degrees x, zero decimal zero-four degrees z. At once.'*

To my immense lack of surprise, the servitor simply responded by parroting back the same assurance that we were following the preprogrammed course we quite clearly weren't.

'This is Commissar Cain,' I voxed, seizing the initiative, since no one else was going to. 'The bucket of bolts flying this thing seems to be malfunctioning. What can I do to reset it?'

*'Commissar.'* The air of relief infusing the traffic controller's voice was far from reassuring – he obviously felt that my mere presence had averted the problem, which I suppose it would have, if I'd had the faintest idea of how to fly a shuttle. Unfortunately, I'd always left that sort of thing to the Navy or, at a pinch, a suitably qualified servitor or civilian, and although I'd been in the cockpit of one a number

of times I'd usually been too preoccupied by incoming fire or an imminent impact to pay much attention to whatever the pilot had been doing. *'Can you take the controls?'*

'I wouldn't know what to do with them,' I said, biting back the more pithy rejoinder which first came to mind. At that point, you understand, I was still more irritated than seriously worried, the starship we were approaching little more than a brighter point of light among the myriad hanging in orbit, or burning steadily in the firmament beyond them. It seemed to be growing brighter and larger by the moment, though, so if I was going to do anything, it would have to be fast.

*'We're getting a pilot up here to talk you through the landing procedure,'* the traffic controller said. *'And a tech-priest.'*

'I don't think I'll have time for a ritual of maintenance,' I jested, to mask the sudden flare of apprehension I felt. Bringing a shuttle into a landing bay is a job for an expert, or a dedicated machine-spirit, and I was by no means confident in my ability to handle it.

*'You'll need to take the servitor offline,'* the unmistakable drone of a voxcoder cut in, indicating that at least the acolyte of the Omnissiah had arrived promptly. *'Otherwise it'll continue to follow the course you're on.'*

'Which is what, exactly?' I asked. 'Am I going into an independent orbit?' The question I really wanted to ask being, 'Am I going to get incinerated in an uncontrolled re-entry?' of course, but I didn't want to think about that possibility too much.

*'You can bring the course up on the pict screen to your left,'* a new voice informed me, a woman this time, her brisk manner somewhat undercut by slight breathlessness. *'Just select "trajectory" from the on-screen playbill.'*

After a moment's fumbling I did as I was bid. 'Oh,' I said.

'*Oh indeed,*' the woman agreed. '*You're on a collision course with the flagship. So we'd best get this done, right?*'

'Right,' I said. 'Otherwise everyone's day gets a crimp put in it.' The projected impact point was some distance from the docking bay we were supposed to be heading for, and a maddening sense of familiarity nagged at me for a moment, before I forced it aside. This was no time to be getting distracted.

'*Mostly yours,*' the pilot said, with the forced cheeriness of someone trying to take the edge off bad news, and knowing it's not going to work. '*You've got about three minutes before the point defences[14] tag you as a threat and open fire.*'

'*Incorrect,*' the tech-priest interjected. '*The targeting auspex array has been taken offline for routine maintenance and recon-secration. Leaving you seven minutes to avoid the impact.*'

'Then let's not waste them,' I said, adding, 'You'd better get everyone you can to the saviour pods to be on the safe side,' because people expected me to say that sort of thing.

'*That would be futile,*' the tech-priest droned, '*as they too have been–*'

'Fine, then let's just get to it,' I interrupted, wondering if there was a void suit aboard – but if there was, I probably wouldn't have time to even find it, let alone clamber into it before we hit, and suffocating slowly adrift around Coronus didn't strike me as a particularly pleasant way to go in any case. 'How do I deactivate the servitor?' A couple of ideas occurred to me even as I spoke, and I found my hands drifting to my laspistol and chainsword, but checked the impulse before drawing them. Using weapons

---

14   *Close-range gun batteries, intended to shoot down fighters and incoming missiles before they get close enough to inflict any damage.*

in a confined space rammed with delicate equipment essential to my survival wasn't likely to end well, even leaving aside the vast amounts of nothing at all on the other side of the viewport.

'*There should be a data-entry port on the nape of the neck,*' the tech-priest instructed. '*Remove the interface cable from the socket.*'

'Right.' I half stood, leaning across the thing, and grasped the block into which a tangle of wires led. 'You want me to pull the plug.' I yanked it out in one swift movement, bracing in anticipation of friction or resistance, but it slid smoothly from the socket, leaving me feeling momentarily unbalanced. 'Got it.'

'*That should have exposed the main power unit.*'

I squinted at a large red switch, which had previously been concealed by the cabling. 'It has.' I flicked it to the opposite setting. 'And it's off.'

'*Wait!*' The voxcoder drone took on what in a human voice would have been a distinct tone of alarm. '*You need to-*'

The servitor rose smoothly from its seat, and turned in my direction. 'Unauthorised system access,' it said. 'Maintain the integrity of the unit.' Gilded metal hands reached for my throat.

'*–isolate the secondary powercells first,*' the tech-priest finished.

I ducked under the reaching hands, and drew my laspistol, all my earlier qualms at using it in so confined a space vanishing in an instant. I pulled the trigger, hoping to find a vulnerable system, although in my experience most servitors in military service were armoured against just such a contingency. As it happened, though, the Emperor seemed to be with me for once, as the thing staggered backwards, leaking ichor, smoke and lubricants in roughly equal measure. I followed up with a further double tap,[15] and it fell, half-slumped against the bulkhead.

'Right, it's deactivated. More or less.' I ducked back into my seat. 'Now what do I do?'

*'You'll need to access the guidance system,'* the pilot said, taking over the conversation with almost indecent haste. Under the circumstances, however, I was hardly about to chide her for a lack of vox etiquette. *'The same lectern you used to bring up the trajectory data.'*

'Got it,' I said, after a few random pokes at the controls in front of me. 'Now what?' The projected course on the pict screen was still about to end somewhere amidships, probably among spreading clouds of debris. The starship would almost certainly survive the impact, albeit with several decks gutted, but the shuttle definitely wouldn't, and neither would I.

*'There should be a bank of four switches to your right,'* the pilot said. *'Can you see them?'*

'I can,' I confirmed, on the point of reaching for the nearest, before remembering what had happened with the servitor and resolving not to mess about with anything I didn't understand without getting clear instructions first. I glanced up at the viewport ahead of me, and immediately wished I hadn't; the *Ocean Orchestra* was clearly visible in the distance, still too far away to resolve in much detail, but undeniably big and disconcertingly solid.

*'They control the attitude thrusters. You push them forward to make a burn, release the pressure to cut the thrust. The switch will return to neutral as soon as you let go. Clear?'*

'Pellucid,' I assured her. The starship was filling nearly a quarter of the viewport by now, and I hoped she was going

---

15   *Two shots in quick succession.*

to get to the point before too much longer. 'Which ones do I need?'

'*All of them, but that's not the point right now. You need to slow your approach. The retros should be next to your left hand – a large lever, looks a bit like a heavy weapon trigger.*'

'Got it,' I said, wondering why they couldn't just label these things in plain Gothic.

'*Make a three-second burn.*'

I squeezed the trigger, and felt an answering vibration hum through the fabric of the ship. After my best guess at the right amount of time, I let go and peered hopefully at the pict screen. The projected impact point had shifted a little, drifting slightly towards the stern, but there was no doubt about it, I was still going to hit. 'Done,' I reported, with as much confidence as I could inject into my voice. Then, a little more hopefully, I added, 'I don't suppose I could just slow to a stop and wait for the recovery team?'

'*Not a chance,*' the pilot assured me, with what sounded like genuine regret. '*You've got too much momentum to k– dissipate.*' At least she'd been tactful enough to bite off the word 'kill', which I appreciated. '*You'd just hit the fusion converters instead of the lord general's stateroom.*' Which would likely vaporise the entire ship. No wonder they all sounded so nervous.

'So what do I do now?' I asked, conscious of every passing second. The view ahead of me was almost entirely composed of metal by this point, a jagged landscape of protruding turrets and auspex arrays, interspersed with the lights leaking from viewports and the utility pods accompanying the hulljacks carrying out their arcane rituals on the surface of the ship.

'*Bring up the docking procedure on the pict screen,*' the pilot instructed. '*It should be the third item on the playbill.*'

'Got it,' I said, doing as I was bid, and the image changed
to one that looked almost familiar: a targeting crosshair, like
the display of a vehicle-mounted heavy weapon. I wasn't a
trained gunner by any means, but I'd taken the controls of
a Chimera's primary turret often enough when there was no
one else left to do so, and always appreciated a pintle mount
on the Salamanders I habitually commandeered for my personal use whenever I could get away with it.[16] I felt the first
faint stirrings of renewed confidence. 'I take it I'm supposed
to shift the reticule over the docking port?'

*'We're redesignating your entry point,'* the traffic controller
cut in, much to my surprise; I'd been so caught up in what
I'd been doing I'd almost forgotten he was there. *'The heavy
shuttle bay will be easier to access.'* By which he clearly meant
harder to miss; the average heavy cargo lifter would need
hangar doors several hundred metres wide to negotiate safely,
instead of the much smaller bays normally used by passenger vessels like the one I was on.

*'Updating the course data now,'* the tech-priest added, and
a rune appeared at the corner of the screen. *'Can you see the
red icon yet?'*

'I can,' I confirmed, wondering how I was supposed to
use the information. A glance through the viewport showed
me nothing but canyons and outcrops of metal now, tiny
moving dots of light marking the positions of utility pods
and void-suited hulljacks scrambling to get out of the way
of what, to them, must have seemed like the wrath of the
Emperor about to descend. Then I noticed a red, blinking
light, half obscured by a vox-antenna, in a position which
seemed to correspond to the location of the rune on the pict.

---

16   *In other words, most of the time.*

'*Good.*' The pilot was back. '*You need to use the attitude thrusters. As you fire them, the ship will turn, and the reticule will move across the screen. Once the icon is centred, you'll be heading straight for the hangar bay. Easy, right?*'

'If it were that easy you wouldn't be on your current stipend,' I said, hoping to keep everyone focused by showing some respect for their skills, 'but I'll do my best.' I reached out for the quartet of switches. 'Here goes.'

'*Port, starboard, ventral, dorsal,*' the pilot interjected hastily, '*front to back. Got that?*'

'I hope so,' I said, holding the second switch down for an experimental second. The rune began drifting along the bottom of the screen, almost agonisingly slowly, so I flicked the fourth one too. This time the icon began a leisurely rise up the screen as well, moving diagonally towards the outer ring of the reticule. 'It seems to be working.' A brief memory of playing games on a data-slate after lights out at my old schola floated to the surface of my mind, and I dismissed it abruptly. I'd never been much good at them, and the last thing I needed to do now was dent my confidence.

'*Good,*' the pilot said, '*but lining up a bit faster would be better.*'

'Faster it is,' I replied, feeling somewhat on top of things, and returned my attention to the switches. The icon moved across the screen a little more rapidly, clipping the edge of the target, and drifting past. 'Frak.'

'*You need opposite thrust to slow or stop,*' the pilot said, an unmistakable sense of urgency beginning to suffuse her voice, in spite of an obvious attempt to suppress it. '*Nothing to slow you down in space.*'

'Apart from the *Ocean Orchestra*,' I said, stating the obvious before anyone else could, and hoping they'd think I was joking. I could see the entrance to the hangar bay through the viewport now, the shuttle approaching it at an oblique angle that meant I'd either miss it altogether or collide with the side wall or the deck as soon as I was inside. I juggled the switches again, moving the icon around, my frustration rising by the second; a couple of times I actually managed to centre it, only to see it drifting away from the crosshairs as I overcorrected or mistimed a steadying thruster burn.

'*Retros again,*' the pilot instructed, and I triggered them, slowing my approach, although the vast slab of metal in front of me still seemed to be increasing its proximity with worrying speed. Red lights began to flash, and alarms blare, but I had no time to think about those, or even acknowledge how annoying they were. The entrance to the hangar bay oscillated wildly across the viewport, and I gave up entirely on the pict display, concentrating completely on the external view. '*Full retros, now!*'

I squeezed the trigger again, my other hand still darting from one switch to another, and by luck or the Emperor's grace I managed to get more or less lined up in the nick of time. With a sound not unreminiscent of someone hitting a cathedral bell with a sledgehammer, the shuttle caromed off the starboard rim of the external door, bounced a couple of times on the deck plates, and slithered to a halt against the far wall.

'I'm down,' I said, trying not to sound too winded from the impact of my sternum against the console, and realising a little too late that the seat had been fitted with crash restraints. The massive doors behind me began to grind closed, and void-suited crew members swarm into the hangar. 'How do I turn these bloody alarms off?'

The tech-priest responded with a series of instructions that seemed to work, and sudden silence descended, broken only by a faint and worrying hissing sound. After a moment of panic reason reasserted itself, assuring me that any breaches in the hull couldn't have been enough to vent my atmosphere into the near-total vacuum of the hangar bay or I'd already have been too busy being dead to notice, and I started to breathe a little more easily. A few moments of blissful quiet later I began to notice a rising swell of bumps and clanging from outside, as the damage control party got on with controlling the damage, which meant the atmosphere in the hangar was getting thick enough to breathe. I popped the hatch, sucking thin, chill air gratefully into my lungs.

'Thank you all,' I voxed, 'you did a magnificent job,' which was no more than the truth, as well as being the kind of thing I'd be expected to say.

Ignoring the inevitable protestations that it was nothing, they'd only been doing their duty to the Throne, the Omnissiah and the Navy, I looked around the hangar, taking in the deep gouges in the deck where the shuttle had hit, and shuddering at the thought of how close I'd come to death. Exposed conduits were emitting sparks and foul vapours in roughly equal proportions, and though everyone around me seemed to know what they were doing, that was a combination which I was understandably keen to get as far away from as possible. Gathering my dignity and straightening my cap, I made for the nearest exit as fast as I could manage without appearing to hurry.

'Ciaphas.' To my faint surprise, Zyvan was already waiting for me on the other side of the airlock, what I could see of his face behind his luxuriant beard undeniably troubled. 'You've certainly lost none of your flair for the dramatic entrance.'

'Much as I'd like to take the credit,' I said, 'I can't for this one. Purely an accident, I'm afraid.'

'I'm sure it was meant to look like one,' Zyvan conceded, while his personal guard formed up around us, their gold-plated hellguns at the ready.

'If it wasn't an accident,' I said, the palms of my hands beginning to tingle again, as they so often did when my paranoia kicked in, 'then what was it?'

'An assassination attempt,' Zyvan said, as though merely remarking on the weather.

# THREE

'I'm still not convinced,' I said, a couple of hours later, feeling greatly fortified by the culinary expertise of Zyvan's personal chef. I swirled the dregs of a post-prandial amasec around the bottom of my goblet, and stared thoughtfully at the gently rotating bulk of the planet below us. 'Most of my enemies are dead, and the rest are a long way from Coronus.' Not much of the *Ocean Orchestra*'s superstructure was visible from here, but I've always had a reasonable knack for orientation,[17] and I found it faintly disconcerting to realise I was sitting almost exactly where I would have died if the malfunctioning servitor had continued on its original course.

'A fair point,' Zyvan conceded, leaning forward in his armchair to proffer a refill. I held out the goblet, and drew it back

---

17   *Particularly in complex tunnel systems, a legacy of his early life on an as yet unidentified hive world.*

comfortably replenished. 'Assuming you were the intended target, of course.'

'Meaning that you were,' I said. That, at least, was comforting, if a little insulting – if I ever do meet my end at the hands of the Emperor's enemies, I'd like to at least know they meant it, rather than considering me nothing more than collateral damage.

'Throne knows it wouldn't be the first time,' Zyvan said, with a glance at the stuffed heads of several previous would-be assassins adorning the walls of his private sitting room. Not all of them were present, of course, having been left in too many pieces to be worth preserving, but it was a respectable haul none the less. I'd even contributed a few to the collection myself, most notably the Slaaneshi cultists who'd rudely interrupted a strategy meeting at his headquarters on Adumbria not long after our association had begun, and an ork kommando who still wore the same expression of stupefied astonishment it'd adopted at the moment my chainsword had sheared through its neck.

'Nor the last, probably,' I agreed, savouring the drink. 'But why would anyone take the risk of coming after you here?'

Zyvan shrugged. 'I'm sure we'll find out. Unless you're right, and it really was an accident.' Since finding out one way or the other wasn't my job, and there were people on his staff for that kind of thing, I decided to move the conversation to safer ground before it occurred to him that I might be able to offer some assistance in getting to the bottom of the matter.

'So,' I said, after pausing just long enough to look as though it had been weighing on my mind despite the conversation moving on to other topics in the meantime, 'what do you think of the Perlia job?'

Zyvan laughed heartily, clearly as mellowed as I was by good food and better drink. 'I think it's a terrible idea. I'll never find another commissarial liaison officer with half as much common sense as you, or fighting spirit come to that.' Which made him half-right, I suppose. 'You'll leave a big hole when you go. But of course you should take it. If anyone's earned an honourable retirement, it's you.'

'I am inclined to take them up on it,' I admitted. 'But if it leaves you in the lurch...'

For a moment I feared I'd overplayed my hand, but the lord general simply laughed again. 'See, that's typical of you, Ciaphas. Always letting your sense of duty have the upper hand. We'll manage.'

'I'm sure you will,' I said. For what it was worth, I had enough clout among the Commissariat for my recommendations to be listened to when it came to appointing my replacement, and I'd be able to make sure he wasn't stuck with the sort of overly enthusiastic meddler who'd question his decisions and generally get in the way. There were more than enough of those, naturally, but they tended to get assigned to line regiments, where they either learned better very quickly or died heroically in the name of the Emperor, sometimes at the hands of the enemy.

'How soon will you be leaving?' Zyvan asked, in the manner of someone trying to appear as though the answer weren't particularly important, and not quite succeeding.

'Apparently they'd like me in post around the turn of the year,' I said, quietly flattered that he was obviously going to miss me, and making it clear that I'd still have time for a few more raids on his dinner table before we finally parted company. But, of course, that wasn't his real reason for asking.

'So you'd have time for a small side trip on the way?' Zyvan leaned forwards a little in his chair, a habit he tended to fall into when confiding in someone.

'I might,' I agreed, wondering what he was driving at. 'Where did you have in mind?'

'Eucopia.' He paused, expectantly.

'Never heard of it,' I said, my sense of bafflement increasing. 'Should I have?'

'Not unless you've been playing cards with the local tech-priests,' Zyvan said, with a hint of amusement. My skill with a tarot deck was not entirely unknown to him, which, I suspected, was one of the reasons he preferred regicide when we found time to socialise.

I shook my head, acknowledging the jest. 'No fun when they don't have any currency,' I replied, not entirely truthfully, although I'd certainly found being able to supplement my stipend by sitting down with a few suckers who still thought games of chance had something to do with luck more than a little handy over the years. I'd even found enough acolytes of the Cult Mechanicus who sufficiently relished what they thought of as an interesting practical exercise in probability theory to give me a pleasant evening or two's diversion now and again, although, as Zyvan had intimated, the pickings had been slender in the extreme.[18] Their skitarii, on the other hand, were soldiers as much as they were cogboys, and a fair few of them retained a soldier's fondness for losing what little money they had in the name of recreation.

'It's a forge world,' Zyvan said, clearly noting the raising of my eyebrow as he spoke. Forge worlds were strategically vital to the Imperium, and correspondingly among the most

---

18  *Since the Church of the Omnissiah provides for most of the needs of its adherents, very few of them go in for much in the way of personal property.*

well-known systems in the sector. This one, however, I'd never heard of before. 'Or, at least, it's going to be.'

'I see,' I said, thinking I did. 'Just been tagged by an explorator fleet, has it?' I was vague on the details, but I knew the Mechanicus had scout flotillas out all the time looking for resource-rich systems to pillage. But that didn't make a lot of sense, now I came to think about it – if Eucopia was between here and Perlia it had to be well within the borders of the Imperium, not somewhere out on the fringes which would probably need a small crusade to annexe; not to mention fending off interlopers with an eye on the planet's bounty for themselves, like the jokaero or the squats.

'Quite recently,' Zyvan said, with a hint of amusement. 'It's been on their to-do list since just before the turn of the last millennium,[19] but recent events have rather forced their hand.'

I nodded, catching his drift. 'The hive fleets,' I said. Despite the best efforts of the Astra Militarum, Astartes and Navy alike, not to mention our somewhat shaky alliance of convenience with the t'au, the tyranids were driving ever deeper into the Eastern Arm, and that was playing havoc with our supply chain. More than one forge world around the Gulf had fallen to the scuttling horrors in the last decade, not to mention a double handful of Imperial manufacturing worlds, whose bustling hive cities had no doubt struck the encroaching fleets as the 'nid equivalent of an all-you-can-eat smorgasbord. 'How soon can they start cranking the weapons out?'

Zyvan chuckled. 'Straight to the point, as always. But that's the problem. They should have begun full-scale production over a year ago.'

---

19  *In fact the formal declaration of purpose, and granting of an Imperial Charter to the Adeptus Mechanicus for exclusive rights to the system and all it contained, was dated 79.872.M39, but I suppose he was near enough.*

'So why haven't they?' I asked, reasonably enough under the circumstances.

The lord general's brow furrowed. 'Your guess is as good as mine. All we're getting is a few token shipments and endless excuses. Even the magi here are getting fobbed off whenever they try to look into it.'

'Sounds like tech-priests,' I said, trying to lighten the mood. 'Put two in a room and you get three schisms. They're probably still arguing about which incense they need to burn over the on button.'

Zyvan shook his head. 'It's nothing like that. At least not this time.' He pushed a data-slate across the abandoned game board between us. I glanced at it, seeing the image of a typical mid-ranking member of the order, which is to say more metal than flesh, their original gender indeterminate. 'The archmagos sent this fellow, Tyron Clode, to make some discreet enquiries on-site.'

'So what did he find?' I asked, with a faint presentiment of the negative answer to come.

Zyvan shrugged. 'Your guess is as good as mine. No one's seen or heard from him since he got off the shuttle.'

All of a sudden the evening's meal seemed to double its mass in my stomach.

'And you want me to pick up where he left off?' I was no stranger to covert activities, of course, generally at Amberley's request, but they'd never sat particularly well with me. That sort of thing generally made enemies, and I'd far rather face mine on a battlefield, where I at least had some idea of who was out to get me and which direction they were likely to be coming from, than have to periodically check my shoulder blades for a dagger hilt.

'Not exactly,' Zyvan said. 'But I don't need to tell you how badly the Militarum needs the weapons we've been promised. Not to mention the Navy and the Adeptus Astartes, who my sources tell me are having similar problems. Perhaps a goodwill visit from someone of your reputation will persuade them to stop frakking about and get the job done.'

'Perhaps it will,' I agreed, although privately I rather doubted it. In my experience cogboys seldom even listened to one another, let alone outsiders with most of their original organs intact. I could hardly refuse, though, not if I wanted to continue enjoying the lord general's hospitality until my departure, so I merely nodded judiciously and helped myself to another goblet of amasec while I still had the chance. 'I'll poke around a bit, see what I can find.' Although if I'd had the faintest idea of what was waiting for me there, I'd have headed in the opposite direction as fast as the warp could take me.

*Editorial Note:*

*Since Cain glosses over the details of his journey to Eucopia, picking up his account of events shortly after his arrival in orbit around the embryonic forge world, this seems like as good a place as any to add some background information to supplement his own comments about conditions there (which, typically, are largely confined to complaints about those aspects of it he finds personally inconvenient).*

*As my usual source for such additional information, Sekara's well-known travelogue* A Wanderer's Waybook, *has nothing to say about the place, having been published approximately a millennium and a half before initial attempts at colonisation commenced, I've fallen back on a rather less readable substitute – Appendix 47(b) of the* Initial Report on Potential Exploitation of the Resources of the World Eucopia and of its Associated Planetary System, *paragraphs 2,416 to 2,418 inclusive.*

The world itself is technically within the habitable zone surrounding the system's primary, but only just. Given the freezing temperature, the thinness of its atmosphere and the lack of photosynthesising organisms capable of altering its composition to something breathable, substantial augmetic modification would be required to any and all potential colonists to enable their survival on the planet's surface. Accounting for the density of population required by a functioning forge world, the diversion of manufacturing resources on the scale required to achieve this option would be prohibitive.

Accordingly, it is recommended that initial settlement should take place entirely within sealed enclaves, allowing the first wave of colonists to live comfortably while commencing the construction of the required manufacturing facilities and the planetary engineering infrastructure necessary to render the wider environment capable of supporting life unaided. Initial estimates would indicate that this could be achieved within a timescale of approximately two millennia, with full terraforming completed by the third or fourth century of M43, unless unexpected difficulties are encountered.

Preliminary cost/benefit analysis [see Appendix 69(a–c, f, k–m) and associated footnotes] would indicate efficiency savings of three hundred and forty-nine per cent over the mass augmentation option should this course of action be chosen, and terraforming is therefore recommended in this case.

# FOUR

I've seen a great many forge worlds from orbit over the decades, their all-enveloping clouds of effluvia making them
look pretty much of a muchness, and was expecting more of
the same – but my first sight of Eucopia came as something
of a surprise. As our shuttle emerged slowly from its hangar
bay into the harsh light of a sun unmediated by any trace
of an atmosphere, the swell of the planet became gradually
visible behind the vast wall of metal behind us, growing to
dominate the view as the blocky little utility vessel moved
around the hull of the starship[20] which had brought us here.

'Doesn't look too bad,' Jurgen said, craning his neck to peer
through the viewport, and favouring me with a quick burst

---

20 The Mechanical Perfection, *an Adeptus Mechanicus vessel
on which Cain had taken passage. From the fact that he says nothing
about the voyage itself we can safely assume that it passed without incident, or indeed amusement, something acolytes of the Omnissiah place
a very low priority on.*

of halitosis, before returning his attention to what looked like a bag of caba nuts retrieved from somewhere among the collection of webbing pouches with which he was habitually festooned. Since the Emperor Himself probably had no idea how long they'd been there, I refused the proffered handful with perfunctory thanks, and devoted rather more of my attention to our destination than my aide had.

My first impression was one of desolation, stark plains of drifted sand in muted browns and greys, from which hills and mountain ranges grew like barren reefs. Faint wisps of cloud swirled in the air below us, but barely enough to floss your teeth with; certainly the likelihood of any of them coalescing sufficiently to squeeze out a raindrop or two was low in the extreme.

As we descended into the tenuous upper atmosphere, and my aide adopted the familiar queasy expression which usually accompanied any form of air travel, I began to make out the topography of the world that awaited us in a little more detail. Gullies and crevasses appeared in the areas of naked rock, apparently scoured by the wind or ancient geological processes, since water appeared to be entirely absent. Far in the distance a vast structure loomed several kilometres into the air, too smooth and regular to be a natural formation.

'Is that a hive spire?' Jurgen asked, no doubt pleased to have something to distract him from his sensitive stomach.

I shook my head. 'One of the atmospheric engines, I think.' Eucopia was newly settled, after all, and had nothing like the population required to support a hive complex – although give it a few millennia and it would probably be just as crowded as any other forge world.

Jurgen's brow furrowed, dislodging a few particles of grime in the process. 'Sorry, sir, you just lost me.'

'Part of the terraforming effort,' I said, knowing little more than he did, since I'd paid only the most cursory attention to the briefing slate. 'I'm told this miserable rock was completely unliveable before the Mechanicus started work on it.' As opposed to being only mostly unliveable now. As we drew even closer to the surface, I began to make out patches of lichen mottling some of the hillsides, and wondered idly if they were native to Eucopia or had been introduced by the environmental enginseers. 'They're breaking down the minerals to release the gases we need to breathe.'

'Blimey.' My aide contemplated this for a moment. 'They must have some really small chisels.'

'I expect they do,' I said, any other response being unlikely to bring the ensuing conversation to an end before we reached the ground. Our shuttle changed course by a degree or two, slotting neatly between two mountain peaks, and our destination came into view at last. Not a hive, by any stretch of the imagination, but sizeable enough nonetheless: a sprawling conglomeration of manufactoria and their associated hab-units filling a valley surrounded by scarps and tors, across which building-sized mineral harvesters were trundling. Craning my neck as we passed over one, I could see the load hopper was only half full, instead of stuffed with raw materials as it should have been.

'That must be it,' Jurgen said, his voice suffused with relief as the noise of the engine increased in pitch, and the shuttle began to descend towards a landing pad on the roof of the largest and most ornate structure in the complex. Unlike almost every other Mechanicus manufacturing facility I'd ever seen, it lacked a coating of grime, the devotional icons of the Omnissiah and the sacred cogwheel encrusting its surface gleaming brightly in the setting sun. 'Do you think that's the welcoming committee?'

'Probably,' I said, catching sight of a small group of tech-priests waiting by the edge of the pad. I couldn't make out much at this distance, apart from a vaguely defined melange of russet robes and gleaming metal augmetics, but they seemed quite senior, judging by the metal to flesh ratio and the amount of it which appeared to have been gilded. I found myself wondering if the bafflingly absent Tyron Clode had been similarly honoured, and felt my hands drift to the hilt of my chainsword and the butt of my laspistol for reassurance, before reason reasserted itself. Whatever had befallen him, it was hardly likely that anyone would make an attempt on my life quite so soon, or so publicly, come to that. On the other hand, it never hurt to be prudent, and I made sure the weapons were loose enough for a quick draw if that turned out to be necessary.

We grounded with a faint bump, a tribute to the skill of our pilot, and waited a moment while the engines powered down. Feeling the sturdy little vessel sink a little lower on its landing gear, I stood and checked the angle of my cap and the hang of my sash almost by reflex. Heroes of the Imperium were supposed to look the part, and making a good first impression on my reluctant hosts would undoubtedly aid my endeavours on the lord general's behalf.

Not that I had much of an idea what I was actually supposed to be doing, other than asking a few discreet questions while dispensing the usual diplomatic platitudes, but that would probably suffice for the present – Throne alone knew, I'd had enough practice at that sort of thing.

Leaving Jurgen to sort out our kitbags, I strode to the hatch and waited for the boarding ramp to descend. The seals broke with a faint hiss, and a bone-chilling cold immediately swept into the passenger compartment, accompanied by a few faint wisps of mist as the air around me began to condense. I gasped reflexively, my lungs straining, and a wave of dizziness swept over me.

'Commissar. Welcome to Eucopia.' The delegation of tech-priests was waiting for me at the bottom of the ramp, the most metallic and ornately robed at their head. His voxcoder sounded unusually faint and high-pitched for such a device.

'A pleasure to be here,' I lied, the words constricting in my throat, and tottered down the ramp to meet them, trying to ignore the black, swirling clouds which suddenly seemed to be encroaching on my peripheral vision.

'Are you functioning within normal operating parameters?' the gnat-like whine enquired, the tech-priest's head inclining in a manner I took to be indicative of concern.

'I'll be fine,' I said, my own voice sounding peculiarly attenuated as well. A memory dredged itself up from the depths of my subconscious, of the air gushing from Amberley's suite on one of the highest levels of a hive spire on Chyroprase after a couple of stray bolter rounds weakened the armour-crys window,[21] and the precise nature of my predicament suddenly became clear to me. 'Just need a bit more air.'

'I've got you, sir.' Jurgen materialised at my elbow, having abandoned our luggage, offering the support of a grubby but nonetheless welcome arm. He seemed surprisingly unaffected by the conditions here, although I suppose that at least the cold didn't bother him unduly,[22] leaving him better able to cope with the tenuous atmosphere. 'This way.' Ignoring the

---

21   *That sort of thing being something of an occupational hazard for a roving inquisitor, especially when you try to flush out the heretics by letting them think you're on to them already.*

22   *Jurgen was an ice-worlder, serving originally with the Valhallan 12th Field Artillery until being assigned as Cain's aide.*

disconcerted delegation, he led the way across the pristine rooftop to an open access door in the side of a higher out-crop of the main building, faced with a vertigo-inducing mosaic of interconnected cogwheels.

'My most profound apologies.' The senior tech-priest scurried after us, a comet tail of his subordinates trailing out behind him. 'We so rarely get unaugmented visitors the thinness of the atmosphere quite slipped my mind.'

'Don't mention it,' I gasped, my vision greying; then a door slammed to behind us, a burst of artificial light assaulted my retinas, and welcome air surged into my lungs.

'Only a temporary problem, I assure you,' the magos went on, looking and sounding about as embarrassed as it was possible to with a face composed almost entirely of ironmongery and a voice which resembled nothing so much as a large insect trapped inside a box now that I was able to hear it properly. 'The atmosphere will be perfectly adequate for the unaugmented within seventy to eighty standard years.'[23]

'I don't imagine I'll be taking advantage of your hospitality for quite that long,' I said, taking another surprisingly welcome draught of Jurgen's unique aroma, and held out a hand to shake. 'But if I go out to admire the scenery, I'll remember to take a breather mask.'

After regarding my hand dubiously for a moment my host appeared to remember the appropriate social ritual, and took it in one of his own, which, to my distinct lack of surprise, had very little of the organic about it. 'Magos Vorspung,' he said, 'Omniprophet of Eucopia.'[24] He broke off, loosening

---

23   As opposed to the local year, the period of Eucopia's orbit.
24   The most highly ranked tech-priest on the planet.

his grip and studying my hand with intense interest. 'Your fingers would appear to be of exceptional workmanship.'

'Master-crafted, I believe,' I said, peeling the glove off to allow him a closer look. Not something I'd normally do in public, but you know me – anything to make a favourable impression, and this seemed as good a way as any to get him onside. 'By a Techmarine from the Reclaimers Chapter of the Adeptus Astartes.'

'So I've heard.' He stared at the digits in question for a moment, while his hangers-on milled around trying to pretend they weren't as fascinated as he was, then returned his gaze to my face. 'We're aware of the connection between you, of course.'

'Of course,' I said, wondering briefly how he knew, before remembering that the Reclaimers had something of a special relationship with the Adeptus Mechanicus. Space Marines weren't exactly inclined to gossip, but I suppose my name would have come up from time to time, especially after the recent unpleasantness on Fecundia, in which the acolytes of the Omnissiah hadn't been entirely uninvolved themselves. 'Been a while since I've served with them on a more formal basis' – given the Astartes' predilection for charging in with bolters blazing at the first sign of trouble that was a good thing too, if you asked me; although if push comes to shove, a genetically engineered superhuman in ceramite power armour's a lot better to hide behind than the average Guard trooper – 'but it was certainly a memorable experience.' Especially the part where I'd got dragged along on the suicidal boarding of a space hulk we'd spent several months tracking through the warp.

'I'm sure it was,' Vorspung agreed.

'Begging your pardon, sir,' Jurgen interjected, 'but would now be a good time to go back to the shuttle for our kit?'

Vorspung and his companions were, for the most part, unable to muster the expression of vaguely horrified bemusement most people adopted on first encountering my aide. I had no doubt they would have done had they still possessed enough flesh in their faces to be able to, now they'd been reminded of his presence.

'My aide, Gunner Jurgen,' I said, making the vague hand gestures common to perfunctory introductions throughout the galaxy.

Vorspung rallied with commendable speed. 'I'll have your belongings collected,' he said, 'and transferred to your quarters. I trust that would be satisfactory?'

'Eminently,' I agreed, before Jurgen could object. Knowing him, he'd consider it a point of honour to take care of my possessions himself, regardless of the consequences, and I really didn't want the only other person on the planet I trusted incapacitated unnecessarily.

Vorspung nodded, a faint air of relief settling around him like another layer of over-ornamented fabric. Which I could hardly blame him for; having lost one envoy already, he could hardly be expected to relish explaining to Zyvan that the Astra Militarum representative had gone the same way as the Adeptus Mechanicus one. Which reminded me, I might as well start as I meant to go on...

'At least your last visitor won't have been quite so incommoded on his arrival,' I said, inflecting it like a casual pleasantry.

'Young Clode, you mean?' Vorspung didn't miss a beat, although I suppose I'd have had better luck spotting any signs of unease or evasion in someone less thoroughly augmented. 'I wasn't aware that you were acquainted.'

'We're not,' I said, pretending to take the remark at face

value. 'But I gather we're here on similar business, so it might be helpful to compare notes if the opportunity arises.'

'A most rational conclusion,' Vorspung agreed. 'I look forward to your combined input.' He began to walk down the corridor, clearly expecting Jurgen and I to follow, so we did, continuing the conversation as we went. 'No doubt the Militarum is as aware as our counterparts at the shrine on Coronus that we're experiencing some unforeseen complications in the commissioning of the manufactory here.'

'It's come up in the conversation,' I conceded. 'And since I was on my way to Perlia anyway, the lord general suggested I might like to drop by and learn enough about the situation to reassure him that you're on top of things.' I've never been averse to dropping names if they're likely to be caught, and it wouldn't hurt to make it absolutely clear that I was acting on behalf of the highest authority. Especially if something really had happened to Clode, and Vorspung knew about it; that way I was much more likely to be fobbed off than assassinated. Which worked for me.

'We will be happy to assist you in any way we can, of course,' Vorspung said. 'But if I might suggest that you rest and consume nutriment before commencing your enquiries? It would hardly be conducive to them if you were still operating at suboptimal levels of efficiency.' Which was as close as the average tech-priest was ever likely to come to suggesting a meal and a decent night's sleep before getting to work. A sentiment I found myself in full agreement with, as it happened, since I was still feeling the effects of having been exposed to the tenuous atmosphere.

So much so, in fact, that our surroundings barely registered with me, beyond the gleaming metal surfaces and examples of particularly revered techno-theological junk being protected from the sticky fingers of the unhallowed by the dusty glass cases common to corridors in Mechanicus shrines. Most of the hangers-on from the welcoming party drifted away en route to the guest quarters, leaving only Vorspung himself and a couple of aides too junior to have said anything[25] still with us by the time we reached the rooms set aside for our use.

'That was quick,' Jurgen said, a note of approval entering his voice as a servitor plodded up to us, carrying our kitbags. He took them and disappeared into our quarters, leaving me alone with the tech-priest.

'I look forward to resuming our conversation tomorrow morning,' Vorspung said, in the faintly stilted manner of someone for whom small talk might just as well have been a dialect of the aeldari language.[26]

'As do I,' I agreed, with more politeness than sincerity. Then I added, as an apparent afterthought, 'Will Magos Clode be joining us?'

'I couldn't say.' There was no doubt about it, Vorspung was noticeably disconcerted by the question. 'He hasn't been in contact for some time.'

'Forgive me,' I said, feeling distinctly apprehensive all of a sudden, but hiding it with the ease of a lifetime's practice at dissembling, 'but I was under the impression that you were monitoring pretty much everything that happens on Eucopia.'

'In the abstract, yes,' Vorspung said, manifestly happier to be back on surer conceptual ground. 'But the aggregated data points to wider trends in production, material flow and

---

25    At least in a fashion overhearable by Cain – they could quite easily have been communing with one another, or the shrine's machine-spirits, through inbuilt vox-units the entire time.

26    In other words, pretty much any tech-priest in the Imperium.

usage of resources. The whereabouts and activities of a single individual would be well below the granularity of the information we normally process in the analyticae.'

'I see,' I said, pretending I did. 'A planet's a pretty big place for one man to get lost in.' Not a thought I found particularly comforting, under the circumstances.

'Quite so,' Vorspung agreed. He paused for a moment, as though waiting for me to continue the conversation, then inclined his head in a manner I took to be formal. 'Until tomorrow, then.'

'Pleasant dreams,' I said, the first reflexive pleasantry to spring to mind.

Vorspung looked surprised, then faintly confused. 'I don't dream,' he said. 'That would be an inefficient use of my cortical processors. But thank you for your good wishes.'

'Don't mention it,' I said, and went to turn in.

*Editorial Note:*

*Though Cain mentions in passing the importance of Eucopia to the Imperium, just how pivotal a role in shaping the future of the entire Eastern Arm his intervention was to play appears to have escaped him. With this in mind, I append the following extract, which may go some way towards emphasising its importance.*

From *In Blackest Night: The Millennial Wars Appraised*, by Ayjaepi Clothier, 127.M42.

Even prior to the resurgence of the Great Enemy, presaged at first by the greatest and most destructive of the so-called Black Crusades, which was itself to pale into insignificance next to the cataclysmic opening of the Great Rift, the Imperium found itself hard-pressed across much of the Eastern Arm. To the expansionist ambitions of the t'au, the wanton destruction of the orks and the piratical raids of the drukhari was added the inexorable advance of the Great Devourer as the tyranid hive fleets bore inexorably onward, leaving naught but desolation in their wake. This last, perhaps, took the greatest toll, as every Imperial world consumed ceased its contribution to the whole; the furnaces of forge worlds and manufactory hives fell silent, their supplies of weapons and ammunition denied to the Astra Militarum and the Space Marine Chapters who stood firm in their resolve to defend what was left of the Emperor's demesne, but were weakened by every such loss. So too the agri worlds, whose looted provender could no longer sustain those who stood against the Emperor's foes, or the populations of the industrial worlds working desperately to make up the ever-increasing shortfall.

Thus, the establishment of the new forge world of Eucopia was more than a simple colonisation project. Put simply, the military supplies it was primarily intended to produce could make all the difference between the maintenance or collapse of Imperial rule, both in the Damocles Gulf and, potentially, as far afield as the adjacent sectors. The importance of this enterprise can be judged by the fact that the Imperial Guard representative sent to liaise with the tech-priests in charge of Eucopia was none other than Ciaphas Cain, the celebrated commissar, whose fortitude and resolution in the face of the Emperor's foes was legendary.[27]

As events turned out, Cain's presence was to prove fortuitous indeed, as treachery, heresy and an unsuspected enemy threatened the future of not only the enterprise itself, but also the entire Eastern Arm.

---

27   *Though possibly more in the literal sense, of being widely believed but without foundation, than Clothier intends to convey.*

# FIVE

To my faint surprise, the quarters we'd been assigned turned out to be a great deal more comfortable than I'd expected, and I slept soundly throughout the night. They were pretty basic by most standards, of course, but laid out and furnished with the convenience of the non-augmented rather more in mind than I was used to finding in Adeptus Mechanicus facilities. The bed, which could easily have held two of me, and was so high I had to clamber up onto it, had a thin, firm mattress covering the slab of polished steel forming its base, and the adjoining balnearia boasted a bath large and deep enough for me to have submerged myself in it entirely had I felt so inclined.

The rooms themselves were airy and bright, the rising sun beyond the window which made up most of the wall of the living area imparting a warm glow to the burnished bronze walls and the scattered furnishings. The carpet was grey, inevitably, the weave incorporating a cogwheel motif echoing the one I'd noted adorning the exterior of the building, and though the furnishings were sparse, they were at least reassuringly solid.

'Morning, sir,' Jurgen said, glancing up from the rudimentary cooking facilities in one corner of the main living area, where he was pushing something which looked as much like food as anything we were likely to find in an Adeptus Mechanicus facility around a pan with a spatula. 'Comfortable night?'

'A lot more than some we've had,' I said, with an appreciative sniff at the aroma of frying food, which was currently masking my aide's more robust bouquet.

Jurgen nodded. 'Haven't we just,' he agreed, mercifully without elaborating, since reliving some of the horrors of my past wasn't exactly the best way of commencing a new day. He poked hopefully at the mush in front of him, and decanted it onto a plate. 'I've done what I can with this, but I wouldn't get your hopes up.'

'I'm sure it's fine,' I said, realising for the first time how hungry I was, and seating myself at the dining table. The chair seemed both higher than usual and too low for the tabletop, but right then I was too focused on eating to think about that, simply bundling up my greatcoat to form a makeshift cushion on top of the seat. 'Aren't you having something?'

'I've already eaten,' Jurgen said, plonking the plate down in front of me, along with the utensils. 'The first batch was a bit iffy, and I didn't want to waste it.' He placed a steaming, fragrant mug on the tabletop, beside the plateful of food. 'At least we've got some tanna[28] to wash it down.'

'Excellent,' I said, my spirits rising with the first sip, as the aromatic liquid warmed its way down to my stomach. Thus

---

28 *A Valhallan beverage to which Cain was inexplicably partial – I've heard it described as an acquired taste on many occasions, but still have no idea why anyone would wish to do so.*

fortified, I turned my attention to the plate, and began plying my fork. I chewed thoughtfully for a moment. 'And this isn't half bad.'

'Thank you, sir. Luckily I found some seasoning before we left the ship.' I let that go, knowing better than to ask where he'd found it, or who might still be looking for it. I knew the Mechanicus of old, and if we were going to have to subsist on soylens viridiens for the duration of our stay, any assistance in rendering it palatable would be more than welcome. So far as most tech-priests were concerned food was just an inconvenient way of refuelling their biological systems, although I had encountered a handful of them over the years with a healthier attitude to the ingestion of nutriment, even though their colleagues considered them eccentric at best.

I was just chasing the last remnants of foodoid substance around my plate, and wondering vaguely how best to begin tackling the commission I'd been given by Zyvan, when the decision was made for me. A small section of wall, which I'd taken for a decorative panel embossed with some arcane techno-theological rune, hinged aside, and a CAT[29] about the size of an obese sump rat trundled out into the centre of the room. There, it wandered around in circles for a moment before eventually working out where I was sitting and coming to a standstill facing me. After whirring and pinging to itself for a moment, a small pict screen rose jerkily from a slot in its back, like the galaxy's most indigestible slice of toast.

---

29  *Cyber Altered Task unit, a small, self-propelled mechanical device generally used for a single specialised function too simple to require the services of a dedicated servitor. They tend to proliferate around Adeptus Mechanicus shrines, as many magi seem to construct or modify them as recreational projects, with finding a useful task for them to do once they're completed being something of an afterthought.*

'*Commissar.*' Vorspung's face appeared, his voice sounding even tinnier than usual through the CAT's tiny speaker. '*I trust you slept well?*'

'Very comfortably,' I assured him, tilting my neck a little awkwardly to look down at the device, and hoping the conversation would be a short one. 'Just finishing breakfast.'

'*Commendably efficient,*' Vorspung said. '*Then we may begin our tour of inspection forthwith. Unless you have any further biological requirements to attend to beforehand, of course.*'

'That might be prudent,' I said diplomatically. In my experience Mechanicus shrines weren't particularly well endowed with plumbing. 'And I think I should get some trousers on. Don't want to scandalise the workforce.'

'*No.*' Vorspung looked faintly confused, no doubt thinking of the people who actually ran things as little more than integral components of the production line – which probably worked fine until they started getting ideas of their own and began pilfering, rioting or otherwise entertaining themselves. Not my problem, though, so no point thinking about it. '*I'll be waiting for you in the central command chapel when your preparations are complete.*'

'Fine,' I said, before realising I had no idea where the central command chapel actually was – or anything else around here other than the landing pad we'd arrived at the previous evening, come to that. 'How do I find it?'

'*Just follow Rolo,*' Vorspung said, and cut the link, before I had a chance to ask, 'Who?'

'Oh, I get it.' Jurgen nodded, a faint half-smile flickering on his face for a moment before it returned to its habitual blankness. 'Who knew cogboys had a sense of humour?'

'A few of them do,' I said, although in my experience it wasn't likely to be the kind that thinks starting an anecdote with 'An ork, a t'au and an inquisitor walk into a bar...' automatically guarantees you a hilarious pay-off. I still couldn't see what my aide was driving at, though, until I'd hopped off the oversized chair and skirted the patiently waiting mechanism on my way to the balnearia. At that point my eye was caught by the serial number *R010* stencilled on its polished metal posterior. 'And it seems Magos Vorspung has a whimsical streak, at least.'

The CAT was still sitting patiently where it could most conveniently create a trip hazard, awaiting my return, when I'd completed my ablutions and returned to the living area. Almost as soon as I reappeared it emitted a couple of rattles and clicks, and began trundling towards the door, which slid open at its approach.

'Here we go then,' Jurgen said, accurately but unnecessarily, and fell into place at my shoulder.

Whether by coincidence or design, the ambulatory mechanism trundled along the corridors at a comfortable walking pace, which enabled me to get a better feel for my surroundings than I'd managed the previous evening; given my condition at the time, of course, that was hardly surprising.

Some of my first impressions of the place turned out to be accurate: the gleaming metal walls and glass display cases were just as I remembered them from last night, and from previous visits to Adeptus Mechanicus facilities. The thing which struck me most forcefully, though, was the general sense of brightness and spaciousness I'd first noticed in our living quarters. As so much else of what I saw seemed to fit the standard Mechanicus template, however, I was initially nonplussed as to why this particular shrine should feel so different.

Only when I saw Jurgen squinting as we crossed a patch of sunlight, striking in through one of the many large windows set into the side of the corridor we were traversing, did it dawn on me that it was the first time I'd ever seen the interior of a major Mechanicus shrine illuminated entirely by natural means. Not all the others I'd visited had been underground, naturally, but the amount of effluvia in the atmosphere around their manufactories had plunged them into such stygian gloom that, for the most part, they might just as well have been. In fact, now I came to think about it, I could barely recall if I'd seen any windows at all on the forge worlds I'd previously visited.

For that reason alone I found the landscape beyond the vast sheets of armourcrys strangely compelling, slackening my pace a little to take it in as we crossed a high, enclosed bridge between two jutting outcrops of the main habitat. The sky was almost clear, a delicate translucent blue, smeared with faint wisps of high cloud, like the ones I'd noticed on our approach from orbit; indeed, one, a particularly long narrow streak, was probably not natural at all, but a shuttle either threading the same path back into the atmosphere or on the verge of shrugging its way free of it. Though much of the surrounding landscape was obscured by the bulk of the complex, I could still make out the slopes of the highlands enclosing it, and, through an occasional cleft in the rock formations, caught glimpses of a vast, featureless plain beyond, merging almost imperceptibly into the horizon.

The clear, bright sunlight revealed a bewildering number of colours and shades among the towering cliffs and tumbled rocks surrounding the site. These were muted browns and greys for the most part, with occasional streaks of more vibrant hues: reds, yellows and the odd greenish tinge, which, had I not known better, I might have mistaken for patches of vegetation. The overall effect was strangely peaceful, despite the throng of augmented humanity passing us in both directions, and the swarm of servitors and vehicles of one sort or another clambering[30] over the hillsides on errands I could barely guess at.

I didn't have long to contemplate the view, however, as Vorspung and a handful of the hangers-on from last night were waiting for me on a wide, echoing mezzanine above a hall full of bustling functionaries and even more venerated ironmongery under glass[31] at the far end of the bridge.

'Commissar.' The magos greeted me with a stiff nod of the head, like someone for whom social interaction had previously been little more than a theoretical exercise.[32] Having delivered me safely to my destination, the guiding CAT veered away, disappearing through a flap which opened suddenly in a nearby wall, and which snapped to behind it so abruptly I half expected to hear a mechanical belch. 'Ready to commence our inspection of the facility?'

'By all means,' I assured him, dismissing the fleeting impulse to proffer a hand to shake. Since we'd been sort of introduced the previous evening, it would probably only have confused him. 'Where would you like to start?'

'I thought perhaps the control chapel,' Vorspung said, clearly pleased to be focusing on his specialist subject, and turned to lead the way through a wide, high set of double doors, inevitably embellished with interlocking cogwheels

---

30  *Presumably this only refers to the servitors, unless some of the vehicles in question were walkers, like the Imperial Guard Sentinels Cain was familiar with.*

31  *Possibly a museum, or a chapel of some kind; a distinction not always immediately obvious in Mechanicus facilities.*

32  *Something not entirely confined to the Adeptus Mechanicus, in my experience.*

in burnished bronze. Jurgen and I followed, finding ourselves in a gallery overlooking a space which immediately
put me in mind of the command centres we'd set up in
commandeered warehouses back in my days with the Valhallan 597th,[33] though on a far larger and more complicated
scale. The serried ranks of control lecterns, pict screens and
hololithic displays – all of them manned by at least one
russet-robed acolyte of the Machine-God – receded away
beneath me, to a distant armourcrys wall, through which
the vista of the surrounding landscape could be discerned
once more. To my distinct lack of surprise, though, no one
was bothering to admire the view, intent on the instru-
ments they tended, or scurrying between them on arcane
errands of their own. One or two even seemed to be physically connected to their consoles, although whether they
were wrangling data directly or merely recharging their
powerbanks I had no idea. (Nor, if I'm honest, interest.)

The main thing which struck me about the activity below,
however, was the silence it was being carried out in. Had it
been an Imperial Guard post, everything would have been
marinaded in sound: the constant hum of voices exchanging
information, demanding refills of tanna, or swearing about
something someone else had done (or, troopers being troopers, something the swearer had done but hoped to deflect the
blame for onto somebody else). Here, though, the hush was
profound enough for the constant footfalls of the purposeful
scurriers to echo around the vast space like surf on a distant
beach, overlaid with the mechanical clickings, tweetings and
hummings of the devices being ministered to.

---

33   *The Imperial Guard regiment with which he had the long-
est and closest association, prior to his attachment to the general staff.*

'Do you control the entire complex from here?' I asked, and after a moment Vorspung remembered how to nod.

'We do,' he confirmed. 'But not only that.' He drew my attention to a bank of monitoring equipment almost immediately below us, in the centre of which a hololithic display was projecting an image of almost incomprehensible complexity. 'We also collate the data flows from outlying installations, to create an immediate overview of resource management and expenditure. That node, for example, is observing the atmospheric engine to the south-east of here, and managing its energy flow as required.'

'Impressive,' I said, as I suspected I was supposed to. 'And you do this for every installation on the planet?'

'Precisely so,' Vorspung agreed, the merest trace of smugness managing to insinuate itself into the even tones of his voxcoder.

'So what if it all goes paps up?' Jurgen asked, with his usual ingenuous directness. 'Sounds like one accident down there and you're frakked.'

'Such an occurrence would be completely impossible,' Vorspung assured him, while my aide and I exchanged glances of mutual disbelief – we'd heard similar sentiments expressed far too often in the past to put much credence in them. 'But if it did, the backup systems would kick in at once.'

'I'm pleased to hear it,' I said, prepared to take the reassurance at face value, rather than run the risk of precipitating a long and tedious monologue by asking for more detail. Jurgen, however, ploughed on, oblivious to the imminent danger of extreme boredom.

'But what if they didn't?' He gestured towards the transparent wall at the far end of the echoing chamber, where the streak in the sky I'd noticed before was further elongated, and beginning to curve in our general direction. 'What if that shuttle missed the pad and crashed in here?'

'It wouldn't make any difference,' Vorspung said, a hint of *froideur* injecting itself into his even monotone. 'The data is shared with other shrines around the planet, and constantly updated.'

'Very reassuring,' I said hastily, before Jurgen could pursue the point. Once he had an idea in his head, rare as that was, he could chew on it like a kroot with a bone. 'Though I imagine it would make a considerable difference to us.'

'The probability of a mishap of that kind is vanishingly small,' Vorspung said, before it dawned on him that I was joking. 'The automatic guidance system is extremely reliable, and the pilot of that particular vessel exceptionally skilled. As one might expect.'

'Indeed,' I said, trying not to think of my eventful trip to meet Zyvan aboard the *Ocean Orchestra*. Though at least it sounded like they employed (mostly) flesh-and-blood pilots around here, which under the circumstances was fine by me.

Vorspung turned, leading the way towards the door by which we'd entered.

'Perhaps you'd like to see the production facilities themselves next?' he asked.

'It sounds fascinating,' I lied, trailing in his wake.

# SIX

After leaving the control chapel we ambled along another of the enclosed bridges, exchanging remarks of little substance and no value, although years of sifting small talk for nuggets of information to pass on to Amberley kept me subliminally alert for anything which might prove of interest to Zyvan – or, for that matter, the magi back on Coronus, who seemed equally concerned about the situation here.

'They all seem busy enough,' Jurgen muttered to me, in a *voce* he seemed to imagine was sufficiently *sotto* to escape the attention of our hosts. 'If anyone has been slacking off, they're not making it obvious.'

'Everything seems in order,' I agreed, wary of the possibility that Vorspung, or any of his retinue, might have augmented hearing. I wasn't entirely convinced that he wasn't responsible for the problems we'd been sent to investigate, but I was prepared to keep an open mind, and if it turned out that he was, it wouldn't hurt to let him think he'd got us fooled.

'Everyone here is mindful of their duties and responsibili-ties,' Vorspung assured us, thereby confirming that his hearing was indeed a great deal better than the human average. 'To the Imperium, and the Machine-God alike.'

'I'd expect nothing less,' I said, more to keep the conversa-tion going than anything else, but Vorspung took the remark at face value, and nodded, a trifle smugly.

'The greatest reward of service is the service itself,' he quoted.[34] My surprise must have been obvious to him, as he rather spoilt the effect by adding, 'I inloaded the volumes you have stored in your recreational reading files to facilitate social interaction.'

'Very thoughtful of you,' I said, not bothering to wonder how he'd obtained access to the contents of my personal data-slate – he was a magos after all, and I'd taken the precaution of making sure there was nothing sensitive in there before leaving Coronus in any case. I'd had dealings with the Mechanicus before, and was well aware of their propensity for considering any data in the vicinity to be public property; trying to restrict access to it was like trying to lay personal claim to the air we were breath-ing, and any encryption or security protocols would simply be taken as a challenge. I fleetingly wondered if he'd done the same for Jurgen's usual choice of reading matter, and its asso-ciated illustrations. If so, he'd probably be discovering a great deal more about the unmodified human anatomy and the uses to which it could be put than he'd ever thought possible.

'We always attempt to put our guests at their ease,' Vor-spung said, 'although the unmodified are often difficult to understand.'

'Not only for the augmented,' I conceded. 'Pretty much

---

34  *From* The Precepts of Saint Emelia, *a work which, rather sur-prisingly, Cain was familiar enough with to have transcribed several of its passages into his commonplace book.*

everyone has their own quirks and foibles. I should know, it's my job to stop them getting in the way of winning battles.' Which was sort of true, and sidestepped the possibility of making any potentially embarrassing comments about the augmetically enhanced.

'Which way are we going?' Jurgen asked, peering down through the armourcrys wall of the bridge to the blocky manufactoria filling most of the valley below. The hab-units surrounding them[35] were smaller overall, but their position ranged about the lower slopes raised many of them to a similar roofline, giving the impression that the cleft in the rocks sprawled further than it actually did.

'To our closest production facility,' Vorspung replied, with a gesture which took in about a quarter of the complex on that side of the bridge. No doubt deducing that this was of little help in getting orientated, he pointed at the structure almost directly below us, which was seeping vapours in various unhealthy-looking colours from a number of vents. 'It, at least, is functioning at optimum efficiency.'

'And producing munitions?' I asked, thinking I might as well remind everyone of why I was here in the first place. The distant contrail was definitely heading in our direction, but still too far away to make out anything of the aircraft generating it; if it was indeed making for the complex, it wouldn't be arriving for some while yet. Dismissing Jurgen's dire prognostication in the control chapel with rather more of an effort than I would have liked, I squinted at the manufactorum as though the answer to my question ought to

---

35   *Though it seems clear from Cain's description of his walk to the command chapel that, as an honoured guest, his quarters were in the heart of the shrine itself rather than the living area set aside for the general workforce.*

be obvious. And maybe it would have been if I were a little more familiar with the iconography of the Cult Mechanicus. As it was, though, the sigils decorating the roof and walls meant nothing to me.[36]

'For the most part,' Vorspung said, a little uncomfortably, 'although only a modest proportion of its current output is destined for the Imperial Guard.'

'Then who gets the rest of it?' Jurgen asked, with his usual lack of diplomacy.

'Our own skitarii, of course,' Vorspung said. 'As our output increases, this world will become of ever greater strategic value, and therefore a higher-priority target for every enemy of humanity in the sector. Bolstering our defences to keep pace with the increasing threat level is the only rational course of action.'

'I'm delighted you think so,' I said, quite truthfully. The last forge world I'd visited had relied almost entirely on the Imperial Guard to defend it, seeing the maintenance of their own forces as an unnecessary diversion of resources given the number of regiments usually in-system for resupply at any one time, and that had almost proven to be a fatal miscalculation. 'Although there's no denying the Astra Militarum needs all the ammunition it can get at the moment.'

'We are aware of the difficulty,' Vorspung assured me, gesturing towards the opening doors of an elevator at the far end of the bridge. 'Perhaps we can put your mind at rest.'

---

36   *They probably wouldn't have been all that much help even if he had been able to read them, given the propensity of tech-priests to replace their original eyes with augmetic ones capable of seeing much further up and down the spectrum; at best the unmodified see only about a third of the signage in most Mechanicus facilities. Which can be rather inconvenient if you've drunk too much recaff in the early stages of a visit.*

The first thing to strike me as we entered the factory floor was the noise. Vorspung and his retinue seemed entirely unaffected by it, as did the tech-priests bustling about the place, herding servitors and the artisans tending to machines of staggering size and complexity. The things they spat out onto conveyor belts were picked up, attached to other things, and dropped into hoppers or thrown onto fresh belts which whisked them away to be packed, sorted or fed into still more machines.

'Most impressive,' I said, or, to be a little more accurate, shouted. We were standing on a mezzanine over the main work area, an architectural quirk the Mechanicus seemed particularly fond of, looking down at a seething hive of activity.

'Everything is functional,' Vorspung agreed, leading the way towards a large metal door at the end of the gallery. 'Perhaps you would care to inspect the finished output?'

'Very much so,' I replied, and followed him through the portal, which swung closed behind us, cutting off most of the noise. After descending a set of metal mesh stairs, we reached the floor of a warehousing area which looked pretty much like any other storage facility I'd ever been in. Cargo containers with Munitorum loading codes stencilled across them were neatly stacked, awaiting collection, and I glanced at the nearest with interest. 'Lasgun powercells?'

'And the weapons themselves, of course.' Vorspung indicated a nearby pallet, laden with familiar rectangular cases, and glanced at the battered longarm slung from Jurgen's shoulder. 'Feel free to obtain an upgrade should you so wish.'

'Thanks, but I'll stick with the one I know,' Jurgen said, as I expected. Though bearing the marks of long and hard use, the weapon was still reliable, and he was familiar enough with its weight and feel to aim and fire it without any conscious thought – something the subtly different balance of a new one would make more difficult. I felt the same about my laspistol, come to that, having steadfastly refused to replace it on several occasions when the opportunity arose, even though the proffered alternatives had had greater range and stopping power. Neither of which would have been much good to me if I'd missed the target in the first place.

'These all seem satisfactory,' I said, exhuming a lasgun from a nearby crate, and slotting the powercell into place with a satisfying click. I aimed it at the wall and pulled the trigger, adding a small, charred blemish to the general patination of scuffs and grime. One of Vorspung's retinue hurried forward to take the weapon as I lowered it, removing the power pack and restowing both in the box I'd taken them from with a muted binharic benediction. 'What else have you got?'

'Plasma guns,' Vorspung said, heading off at an angle between the nearest group of containers. He glanced back in my direction. 'Although I would advise against confirming their operability in quite the same fashion, given the nature of the materials surrounding us.'

'Point taken,' I agreed. Plasma guns are one of the most dangerous man-portable weapons in the Imperial Guard arsenal, almost as much to their operators as to the enemy.[37] This accounts for their relative rarity on the battlefield, most regimental commanders preferring their troopers not to be reduced to a cloud of greasy smoke if that can be avoided.

'That's something you don't see every day,' Jurgen said, in tones of grudging approval, as the magos opened a cargo container to reveal a dozen or so of the bulky weapons.

---

37  Only the t'au seem to have mastered the ability to mass-produce plasma weapons light and reliable enough to be issued to their ordinary line troopers as a matter of course.

'Indeed it is,' I said, lifting one cautiously from its cradle. It was heavy, more so than I'd expected, the plasma vents hissing in a faintly sinister fashion and emitting a faint smell of ozone as I flicked the activation rune. Mindful of Vorspung's admonition, and my own disinclination to accidental self-immolation, I switched it off again almost at once, returning it to the packing material with a vague sense of relief. 'And they seem in excellent condition.'

'Again, feel free to avail yourselves if you wish,' Vorspung said.

'Thank you, but I think we'll pass,' I said. I had no use for anything so bulky, even if it weren't so dangerous, and Jurgen was far too fond of the melta he'd scrounged decades ago for those occasions on which we needed a bit of extra firepower to give it up for an untried replacement. I indicated a cargo door in the nearby wall, large enough to have accommodated a utility truck, and from behind which more sounds of industry were echoing. 'What's through here?'

'The supplies for our skitarii garrison,' Vorspung said, 'and the workshops which keep them functioning at peak operational efficiency.'

'They certainly sound busy,' I said. If anything the noise had increased while we'd been talking, the intermittent thudding of heavy machinery now loud enough to be sending faint tremors through the floor. I felt a vague sense of disquiet beginning to build, although I couldn't really have said why.

'Our mechwrights are–' Vorspung began, then broke off suddenly, staring into space for a second or so. 'We should leave. At once.'

'What's going on?' Jurgen asked, his hand straying instinctively towards his lasgun.

'A malfunction has occurred,' Vorspung said, turning back

towards the staircase, which suddenly seemed a lot further away than it had done. The loudest thud yet shook the floor, raising a faint pall of dust, and the coin belatedly dropped: I'd been hearing explosions, not distant industrial processes. 'It is being contained, but...'

This time the detonation was unmistakable. The wall crazed, chips of masonry flying everywhere, and a ragged crack appeared in it next to the thick metal portal.

'Doesn't look very contained to me,' Jurgen said, unslinging his lasgun and aiming at the steadily widening breach. Something metallic was moving beyond it, too large to make out clearly. A gigantic hammer blow struck the crumbling wall, smashing it to rubble, and he squeezed off a burst at the Dreadnought-sized figure thus revealed.

'What the hell's that?' I asked, as the tech-priests scattered. The looming figure ducked a little, and began to force its way through the breach it had made.

'A Kastelan,' Vorspung said, making for the stairway at a pace demonstrating beyond any lingering doubt that the dignity of his office was now the farthest thing possible from his mind.

'Which is what?' I asked, matching his pace, Jurgen at my heels as always, if my nose could be relied on. 'Some kind of combat servitor?' Those were tough, true, but I'd bested them before.

'A relic,' Vorspung said, no doubt grateful that his voxcoder still let him pontificate while he was using all his breath for running, 'from the dark times before the light of the Omnissiah. It has no organic components.'

'So it's like a giant CAT,' Jurgen said.

'Which will try to kill us,' Vorspung added.

'So how do we stop it?' I asked, focusing on the essential.

'We cannot,' Vorspung said. 'Our only recourse is to retreat, while the datasmiths attempt to regain control.' His eyes unfocused again for a moment. 'Which may take some time, as the one assigned to this unit is dead.'

'Then we'll have to take care of it for ourselves,' I said, veering off towards the still-open container of plasma guns. Standing and fighting was never my favourite course of action, but the thing bearing down on us, scattering containers as it went, would be on top of us before we even reached the stairs. Twin power fists sent a parked cargo-6 bouncing across the warehouse, toppling stacks of crates as it went, and I found myself fervently petitioning the Emperor to have seen to it that none of their contents were too volatile.

'Easier said than done,' Jurgen opined, sending another burst at the towering metal monstrosity. His shots raised a few sparks from its carapace, but did nothing to slow it down. 'Las-bolts won't stop it.'

'But these will,' I said, hoping I was right, and grabbing the nearest plasma gun from the batch Vorspung had shown us as I spoke. The tech-priest was halfway to the staircase by now, putting on an impressive turn of speed, thanks to the augmetic legs pistoning away beneath his flapping robe. His retinue had scattered, trying to find whatever refuge they could among the crates and cargo containers, but given the trail of damage the rampaging automaton was leaving in its wake, I doubted that would be much of a long-term survival strategy. An impression confirmed a moment later by another resonant thud and a choked-off scream from somewhere in its immediate vicinity.

'If you say so, sir,' Jurgen said, slinging his lasgun and seizing another of the heavy weapons. He activated it, and raised it to aim with a halitosis-laden sigh of exasperation. 'But I'd have preferred the melta.'

'You weren't to know you might need it,' I said, bringing

my own weapon up, and thumbing the activation rune with a faint tingle of apprehension. A towering stack of crates was unceremoniously swept aside, revealing our target, and we both fired almost simultaneously. Two beams of ravening star-stuff ripped through the air, lashing the thing's torso, but to my astonished horror having little visible effect.

'The repulsor grid is still active,' Vorspung informed us helpfully, his voice buzzing in my comm-bead. 'It will absorb copious amounts of incoming fire.'

'Then how do we hurt it?' I asked, falling back in the face of the thing's implacable advance. My skin was tingling from the thermal backwash, like a mild case of sunburn, but at least we were still in one piece.

'You cannot,' Vorspung said pedantically, 'since it is incapable of feeling pain. But prolonged intense fire might overload the grid, allowing you to inflict damage on it.'

'Great,' I said, prolonged intense fire being just the kind of thing guaranteed to make the weapons we were holding overload and blow up. But under the circumstances, it seemed like the only plan we'd got. Then I noticed something else that made my blood run cold. 'Is that a flamer it's got on its shoulder?' I began to look for some refuge which looked relatively uninflammable, but that seemed to be in short supply. Not to mention pointless, as the whole idea of incendiary weapons is to negate hard cover by flowing around it.

'Not exactly,' Vorspung said, 'but the principle is close enough. However, while it is executing the Conqueror Protocol, it will be incapable of firing.' Which was not exactly good news, given how efficiently it was tearing the place apart, but the best we were going to get.

'Make for the stairs, sir,' Jurgen said, with grim determination. 'I can hold it off.'

'I don't doubt it,' I said, strongly tempted to take him up on the offer, I have to admit. But if I made the attempt, I'd barely get halfway there before the thing tore my aide apart and ran me down like a rodent on a highway. 'But let's take the magos' advice. Fire together.' This time the back-wash felt less like sunburn and more like opening a bake oven.[38] The automaton staggered for a moment, then came on again, crushing the container we'd grabbed our weapons from underfoot. An alarming number of sparks and electrical discharges rose around its legs.

'Get behind those containers!' I commanded, a desperate idea beginning to form. 'And shoot at its feet!'

'That would be highly inadvisable,' Vorspung began, 'as the plasma coils of the damaged weapons are liable to–'

'Fire!' I yelled, as Jurgen joined me in our makeshift refuge, and the air thickened perceptibly. Flash burns seared my skin, the light of the plasma streams almost blinded me, and then we were picked up and thrown through the air by a detonation which seemed to fill the world. I hit unyielding rockcrete and rolled instinctively, the unwieldy weapon clattering across the floor to Emperor knew where, and good riddance to it. I regained my feet, reaching by reflex for my laspistol and chainsword, which would have been next to useless, of course, and stared back in the direction of our erstwhile antagonist.

'Did we get it?' Jurgen scrambled to his feet, looking even more dishevelled than usual, which was quite a trick when you thought about it.

'I think so,' I said. The automaton stood immobile for an

---

38  *Not something I imagine he'd have done as a matter of course, but no doubt he'd inspected more than his fair share of field kitchens in the course of his career.*

interminable second or so, then toppled, with a sound like the galaxy's biggest ration kit hitting the floor. I turned to face Vorspung, who by now was halfway down the staircase again. What little I could read of his face registered stupefied astonishment. 'And I suppose at least I can report that the weapons you're producing are effective.'

# SEVEN

'So, where to next?' I asked, as the lift doors squealed closed, cutting us off from the bustle of emergency workers and a belatedly arriving squad of skitarii, who'd seemed vaguely disappointed to find nothing left to shoot at. Judging by the size of it, the elevator was intended primarily for shifting cargoes in bulk, which at least meant we weren't too crowded now most of Vorspung's entourage had caught up with us; the ones still missing, I strongly suspected, never would.

'To the landing pads,' Vorspung said, with an air of faint surprise. 'Although if you would prefer to suspend your tour of inspection in the light of the recent incident, that would be acceptable. I am told the unaugmented often require time to process a traumatic and unexpected event.'

'Many do,' I replied diplomatically, 'but for Jurgen and I this sort of thing is a frequent occurrence.' Despite my best efforts to the contrary. 'We won't need time to recuperate.' Because if the rampaging automaton had been set to malfunction in a plot to kill us, then handing the initiative to our enemies would be a very bad idea.

'Why the landing pads?' Jurgen asked.

'Because an aircar has been placed at the commissar's disposal for the duration of his visit.' He turned back to me. 'Our manufactoria are widely dispersed, so it was deemed more efficient to assign you your own transportation.'

The elevator doors opened again, to reveal a familiar bustling concourse, across which he led the way. Tech-priests and artisans were scurrying about their business as though nothing untoward had even happened.

'Most appreciated,' I replied, digesting this unexpected development. If Vorspung did have something to hide, he'd be extremely unlikely to hand me the ability to go poking around wherever I pleased on a whim. On the other hand, the vehicle would be just as tied in to the sea of data immersing the world as everything else around here, so it could just be a subtle way of keeping tabs on whatever I was up to. Then another thought struck me. 'I trust breather masks are available today?'

'That won't be necessary,' Vorspung said, in a manner he clearly imagined to be reassuring, although his synthesised voice remained as devoid of inflection as ever. 'The vehicle in question is parked in a pressurised hangar, for your continued wellbeing and convenience.'

'Besides which, the main surface pad is required for something a great deal larger today,' a new voice cut in, and I turned, surprised, to find another Mechanicus acolyte approaching. Like all of them she was more metal than flesh, red robes swirling around her as she strode confidently forward on augmetic legs, but the thickness of her ferrous carapace and the barely concealed offensive systems incorporated within it made it abundantly obvious that she was a high-ranking skitarius rather than an ordinary tech-priest. To my surprise, she proffered a hand to shake as she came within arm's reach of me. 'Kyrus Norgard, praetor[39] of the skitarii.' She smiled, as much as was possible given the limited amount of flesh remaining on her face, and, to my vague surprise, carried on speaking in normal colloquial Gothic instead of the stilted manner most acolytes of the Omnissiah affected. 'My apologies for failing to meet you last night with the magos. I had a small riot in the protein reclamation plant to deal with.'

'Duty before pleasure,' I agreed, shaking the proffered hand, and finding, as I'd expected, unyielding metal beneath the covering glove. 'Besides, I wasn't really feeling well enough to be sociable.'

'So I heard,' Norgard said, falling into place beside me. Either she still retained some idea of sociability from before her extensive upgrades, or she'd absorbed the briefing far more effectively than Vorspung. 'We'll try to do better in future.'

I pretended not to hear Jurgen's sceptical sniff.

'Thank you for making the time now,' I said, determined to be diplomatic.

Norgard inclined her head, in a fair simulation of polite interest. 'I've been eager to make your acquaintance,' she said. 'Your reputation precedes you.'

---

39 *Nomenclature of rank within the fighting forces of the Adeptus Mechanicus varies at least as much as it does within the Astra Militarum, pretty much every forge world or significant shrine having their own ideas on the subject – not to mention force organisation. Though Cain doesn't go into much detail about the military assets of Eucopia, it's safe to assume Norgard was responsible for at least a legion, or the rough equivalent of an Imperial Guard battalion.*

By this point we'd begun to traverse another of the enclosed bridges, the vast majority of the installation laid out below us, smoke, steam and particulates in an interesting variety of colours seeping from the manufactory sections. The only points I could see higher than our current position were the section we'd just left, and an even higher outcrop of masonry into which the other side of the walkway disappeared, its shadow rippling away across the rooftops at an oblique angle from where we were standing.

'I wouldn't believe much of it,' I said, truthfully enough, although it was the sort of thing people expected me to say, and, in my experience, generally made them even more credulous.

'I wouldn't,' Norgard said, 'except that I've accessed your service records.' Some of them, anyway – my avocation as an occasional, and invariably reluctant, agent of the Inquisition was known to very few, and some of my other exploits were so highly classified even I wasn't allowed to read them.[40] 'I look forward to hearing your personal account of the pursuit of the *Spawn of Damnation*. If you feel inclined to revisit it, of course.'

'I'm flattered by your interest,' I said diplomatically, although 'staggered' would probably be a more accurate description. Of all the experiences I've had in my long and discreditable career, tagging along with the Reclaimers Space Marine Chapter[41] in their obsessive attempt to follow a space hulk through the warp, not to mention the nearly suicidal attempt to board and loot it once they'd found the damn

---

40   *Clearly exaggeration for humorous effect, as his position on the lord general's staff, not to mention his status within the Commissariat, gave him almost unlimited access to whatever files he wished. The inclination to peruse them, on the other hand, was very rarely evident.*

41   *Or a few members of it, to be more precise.*

thing, was one of those I'd be least inclined to relive given the choice. I wondered fleetingly why this particular incident had caught her attention, before remembering the Chapter's unusually close ties to the Adeptus Mechanicus; no doubt they'd passed the story on while handing over some of the archeotech Drummon and his battle-brothers had recovered from the wreck. 'Although as it's been so long, you'll have to forgive me if I seem a bit hazy on some of the details.'

'Of course.' Norgard looked out across the artificial landscape and the mountains beyond, her augmetic eyes emitting a barely audible whirring sound as they focused on the airborne shuttle, which was now aiming straight for the complex, skimming over the surrounding peaks on an unmistakable approach trajectory. I squinted, trying to make out more detail, but at that distance all I could discern was a fast-moving dot, rendered indistinct by a nimbus of reflected sunlight. She picked up her pace a little, the rest of us unconsciously lengthening our stride to keep up. 'If you'll excuse me, I have only three minutes and seventeen seconds to reach the pad before our other guests arrive.'

'Other guests?' I asked, but by this point she'd accelerated to a pace I couldn't match without exerting myself more than would appear seemly under the circumstances, so I let her go and turned back to Vorspung. 'Another delegation from Coronus?' It seemed the most likely explanation, as the last envoy from the shrine there had apparently evaporated shortly after his arrival, and the Adeptus Mechanicus could generally be relied on to react to a problem by trying the same thing a few more times in the vague hope that the result would be different.[42]

---

42   *Not entirely fair: according to Yanbel, the tech-priest attached*

'Not this time,' Vorspung said, without elaborating further. 'But since our destination is directly below the landing pad, an introduction may be effected if you so wish.'

'If it's not too inconvenient,' I said. I've often observed that the more you know, the better prepared you are for the worst, so I was understandably keen to find out what lay behind this unexpected development – but I'd played enough tarot to know when not to reveal my hand, so I kept my tone casual, as if my interest in whoever else might be about to join us was merely a matter of etiquette.

'Not at all,' Vorspung assured me. 'The hangar is only three levels below the rooftop, so we can easily divert to the portal there with minimal loss of time.'

'Excellent,' I said, my attention once again caught by the approaching spacecraft. It seemed to be heading for the section of the complex on the other side of the bridge, where, according to my usually reliable sense of direction, the pad we'd so memorably disembarked at the previous evening would be somewhere on the roof. It was a great deal closer now, the shape of it more distinct, the blocky silhouette somehow familiar, a faint rumble from its engines becoming audible even through the attenuated atmosphere and the intervening armourcrys.

'That's a Thunderhawk,' Jurgen said, an instant before I recognised it myself, the huge dorsal cannon and the racks of wing-mounted missiles unmistakable even from this distance.

'From the Reclaimers,' I added, its yellow-and-white livery

---

*to my personal staff, they vary some of the parameters each time in an attempt to isolate the cause of a problem, such as a burned-out relay or the wrong kind of votive candle being lit on a control lectern. Though to the uninitiated, I suppose, it does look as if they're just going through the motions.*

sparking uncomfortable memories of having flown in a couple of identical vessels during my eventful secondment to the Chapter early on in my career. They'd been quite spectacularly uncomfortable as I recalled, not least because Space Marines tend to keep their helmets on when en route to potential trouble, so soundproofing wasn't exactly a priority for their passenger compartments.

'Quite so,' Vorspung said. 'We have a great deal to discuss with them, but I can assure you that your presence here will not go unforgotten or neglected.'

'I'm delighted to hear it,' I said, sifting his mechanical monotone for any hint as to whether that was meant as a veiled threat, or merely another attempt at politeness. Since I couldn't tell one way or the other, I let my paranoia urge caution, concealing my unease behind the inflection of a reflexive pleasantry.

By this time we'd reached the end of the bridge, and followed our host into a broad concourse as crowded with cogboys, servitors and scuttling CATs as the rest of the complex. He made straight for a bank of lifts on the far side, and only as Jurgen and I joined him and the doors rattled closed behind us did I realise that, by accident or design, we'd given his entourage the slip. Definitely the latter, judging by his next words, almost muffled by a faint squealing of ungreased metal as the elevator cage jerked into motion.

'Should you discover Magos Clode's whereabouts in the course of your inspection, I would earnestly recommend discretion in disseminating that data,' Vorspung said.

'You would?' I enquired, trying, and probably failing, to conceal my surprise.

'Emphatically,' Vorspung replied, in what would probably have been melodramatic tones if his voxcoder had been capable of much in the way of inflection. 'In his last inter-action with me, he expressed doubts that the production delays were entirely systemic in origin.'

Jurgen's brow furrowed as he tried to disentangle the syntax of that, and I responded hastily, hoping to head off a typically blunt remark about people who couldn't just come out with things in plain Gothic.

'He suspected deliberate interference,' I said, noting my aide's sudden comprehension out of the corner of my eye, while keeping the bulk of my attention on the tech-priest, mentally cursing the inscrutability a mostly metal face conferred on him.

'He did,' Vorspung said. 'A conclusion I dismissed at the time, but in the light of recent developments feel compelled to reconsider.'

'What developments?' Jurgen asked, forthright as ever.

'His disappearance, of course,' I said, before returning my attention fully to Vorspung. 'You suspect foul play?'

'It would be logical not to rule it out,' Vorspung admitted, 'just as rational analysis would indicate that human activity is more probably responsible for the production delays than...' Here he hesitated, before vocalising a thought close to heresy for most in his vocation, '...some kind of mechanical failure.'

I nodded agreement, to his evident relief. 'Have you shared this suspicion with anyone else?' I asked, my innate paranoia immediately jumping to the more pressing question of how big a target he might have painted on his back by doing so, and, by implication, that of anyone else he might have confided in. Which now included me.

'Not as yet,' the tech-priest assured me. 'If I have indeed drawn the correct inference, then doing so would hardly be prudent, given that such interference could only be perpetrated by a heretical group within the Cult Mechanicus itself. Such things are rumoured to exist, although until recently I had dismissed them as wildly improbable.'

'Then I appreciate your decision to confide in us,' I said, though I was far from happy about it. Cogboys were hard enough to deal with at the best of times, let alone when they had something to hide, and if Vorspung was right about a heretical conspiracy on Eucopia they'd no doubt be willing to take direct action against anyone they suspected might be on to them. I had no time to quiz him further about his suspicions, or what kind of heresy might be found in the murkier corners of the Machine-God's realm,[43] however, because at that point the lift shuddered to a halt and the doors wheezed open, admitting a draught of freezing air and a murmur of conversation.

---

43   *Even the Inquisition has very little idea about this, beyond whatever clues the Ordo Malleus may have in their records of the abominations unleashed by the corrupted magi in the service of the Great Enemy, although doctrinal differences are no doubt as pervasive and bitterly contested in the Adeptus Mechanicus as they are in the Ecclesiarchy.*

# EIGHT

The voices grew louder as I followed our host round a couple of turns in the by-now-familiar tangle of identical-looking corridors, until I found myself in one I most definitely recognised – just next to the airlock by which I'd entered the complex the night before. Which I supposed explained the chill still lingering in the air, as the local environmental systems laboured to bring the temperature up to the ambient one of the rest of the complex.

Not that anyone else seemed to be bothered by the freshness of the air; Jurgen was an ice-worlder, the tech-priests were mostly metal anyway, and the only other people present were Space Marines, still enclosed within their suits of power armour, which seemed to me to be in imminent danger of dislodging the luminators from the ceiling with the crests of their helmets. Even if I hadn't been so recently and unexpectedly reunited with my old comrades in arms,[44] I would have recognised the yellow gauntlets and faceplates of the Reclaimers at once. Norgard was conversing with their leader, a veteran sergeant if I was reading the heraldry on his pauldron correctly.[45]

'Commissar Cain.' The Space Marine broke off the conversation at once, the beak of his helmet[46] tilting down to look at me as we approached the group. I'd be lying if I didn't admit to finding the effect somewhat intimidating, even though I was pretty sure he meant me no harm, but then I'd defy anyone being loomed over by a superhuman giant in power armour not to feel a faint stirring in the bowels as the full effect of the spectacle kicked in. 'Your association with our Chapter honours us both.'

'Me rather more than you, I suspect, brother-sergeant,' I said, accurately enough, though I knew he'd simply take it as an expression of modesty. To my relief he reached up to remove his helmet, which came away with a faint hiss of equalising pressure as the seals broke, revealing a face which seemed to consist mainly of scar tissue, but which I could at least read. To my complete lack of surprise I didn't recognise him, but since I'd only been personally acquainted with a relative handful of his fellows in the Chapter, that was only to be expected.[47]

---

44   *During the defence of Fecundia, to which he's already alluded.*

45   *Cain's period of secondment to the Chapter left him acquainted with their iconography and practices to a far greater extent than most non-initiates.*

46   *The Reclaimers seem to possess an unusual number of the ancient Corvus-pattern helmets, conferring them on members of the Chapter who distinguish themselves in some way as visible marks of honour.*

47   *Like most Space Marine Chapters, the Reclaimers probably have almost a thousand battle-brothers under arms at any given moment, although since they're widely dispersed in units ranging from companies down to individual detached squads, often operating independently for years at a time, their exact numbers are hard to determine – even by their own Chapter Master.*

'And I suspect otherwise.' To my genuine surprise he smiled, an expression I'd rarely seen on the faces of his comrades, apart from my old friend Drummon on occasion, and held out a yellow-gauntleted hand which could have enclosed and crushed my entire head should he have felt so inclined. 'So perhaps we'd better agree that the honours are even, in the interests of amity.'

'I'm all for amity,' I said, extending my own for a pre-dictably awkward handshake, given that I could barely have grasped one of his ceramite-encased fingers in earnest. Out of the corner of my eye I caught a glimpse of Norgard looking gratifyingly impressed, and Vorspung as astonished as it was possible to with a face composed almost entirely of metal. Retrieving my hand before it could be entirely engulfed, I used it to gesture towards my companions. 'Magos Vorspung I'm sure you know, and this is my aide, Gunner Jurgen.'

'Sir.' Jurgen nodded a formal greeting, apparently remembering that Space Marines weren't much given to saluting, although, since being assigned as my aide and therefore technically attached to the Commissariat, he'd tended to regard that kind of thing as more or less optional in any case.[48]

'Of course.' The towering Space Marine echoed the gesture, to Jurgen's unconcealed satisfaction, and Norgard's barely concealed astonishment; if the skitarius' jaw hadn't been soldered in place it would probably have dropped halfway to her

---

48  *Jurgen was technically still a serving member of the Imperial Guard, but his ambiguous status as a de facto representative of the Commissariat as well allowed him a degree of discretion as to which code of conduct he was required to follow under any given set of circumstances. Having a fairly straightforward approach to most areas of uncertainty, he generally resolved the paradox by adhering to whichever protocol seemed the most advantageous to him at the time.*

knees. 'Your name is also known to the Chapter. I'm gratified to find you still serving the Emperor.'

'What else would I do?' Jurgen asked, in genuine surprise.

'What indeed?' He seemed to have said the right thing anyway, though more by luck than judgement if I knew Jurgen, as the half a dozen or so Astartes accompanying the sergeant nodded formally too, the beaked helmets most of them wore making them look like a flock of birds suddenly spotting a fresh spillage of seeds.

I found myself a little taken aback at this – for someone so distinctive, Jurgen tended to be overlooked more often than not, and it seemed a little surprising that the Reclaimers still remembered his presence more than half a century after we'd parted company with them.[49]

'Yours isn't to us, though,' Jurgen said, in his typically forthright manner. I wasn't sure any of the cogboys were physically capable of inhaling sharply, but I could have sworn I heard a faint, shocked susurrus in any case.

To my astonished relief the towering sergeant unleashed a bellow of laughter which rattled my fillings, and reverberated through the confined space of the corridor like a grenade going off.

'Of course.' He inclined his head again, towards me this time, in accordance with protocol. 'Toba Morie, of the Eighth Company.'

'Sergeant Morie.' I inclined my head again too, partly for the look of the thing, but mainly because I was beginning to develop a crick in my neck from trying to keep his face in my eyeline. 'A pleasure to make your acquaintance.'

---

49　*Or perhaps not. The number of outsiders who have spent a prolonged period of time aboard a Space Marine vessel isn't particularly large.*

'A pleasure I trust you'll prolong by accompanying us?' Morie said, to Vorspung's evident discomfiture. The magos took a couple of paces forward, not quite edging between us, but clearly intent on reminding everyone who was supposed to be in charge here.

'If you're certain such a contravention of protocol is warranted,' he said. 'Our discussions were supposed to be confidential.'

'And will remain equally so with Commissar Cain present,' Morie said, in tones which brooked no argument. (Which, to be fair, was true of pretty much anything a Space Marine said.)

'A reasonable inference,' Vorspung conceded. Accepting defeat, he turned to Norgard and initiated a short conversation in the chirruping argot of the tech-priests.[50] At its conclusion, the skitarius turned to Morie's companions and gestured for them to follow her.

'Our facilities are entirely at your disposal,' she said, leading the rest of the squad away in the rough direction of the living quarters Jurgen and I were currently occupying, the cyclopean scale of their furnishings suddenly making a great deal more sense.

'As are the manufactoria,' Vorspung added, taking a couple of steps in the opposite direction, clearly expecting the rest of us to fall into place behind him. His head turned in my direction. 'Though I'm afraid our visit to the nearest will have to wait a while.'

'Not a problem,' I assured him, lengthening my stride a little to keep up, although Morie had shortened his so much he seemed to be practically ambling, not a gait I normally

---

50 *A dialect known to its speakers as binharic, which, despite centuries of determined, if not obsessive, study by the Ordo Dialogus, remains utterly and frustratingly opaque to outsiders.*

associated with a member of the Adeptus Astartes. 'So where are we going to now?'

'A different shrine.' He glanced up at Morie, as though wondering how much it would be prudent to say, and the brother-sergeant inclined his head, giving his tacit approval. 'Where we produce weapons and other necessities for Sergeant Morie's Chapter.'

'Should be producing them, anyway,' Morie said. He smiled at me, with little humour. 'I assume from your presence the Imperial Guard have been equally disappointed?'

'You assume correctly,' I assured him, wondering for a moment whether to mention the suspicions Vorspung had confided in me, before deciding to hold my tongue for the time being. There was no telling who else might be listening, or how for that matter, in a place like this, and Vorspung might react badly to having his confidence breached. 'But I'm sure between us we can get to the bottom of the problem.' I glanced meaningfully at the tech-priest as I spoke, but if he took my meaning he was in no hurry to act on it. Instead, he led us down a wide stairwell,[51] which brought us, after negotiating a couple of airlocks, to the hangar we'd set out to reach in the first place.

'Is that the aircar you mentioned?' I asked, indicating a four-seater gravitic sedan, decked out in the usual red livery of Mechanicus vehicles,[52] the silver cogwheels emblazoned on the driver's and front passenger doors putting its

---

51   *Presumably intended to accommodate visiting Space Marines, as if Morie had found it too cramped to traverse comfortably Cain would almost certainly have had something trenchant to say about the matter.*

52   *The more comfortable ones, anyway. Most, in fact, are utilitarian in both nature and design, tending to plain dark colours, or simply bare metal where exposure to the local environment is unlikely to result in significant corrosion.*

ownership beyond any possible doubt. A brace of cargo haulers, roughly double its size and far less sleek and shiny, were parked nearby, being poked and prodded by enginseers, but other than that we appeared to have the place to ourselves.

A couple of servitors plodded past, laden with equipment for the work parties, ignoring our presence completely, their feet ringing loudly on the metal grilles covering the floor. Glancing down, I noticed the void between the mesh and the rockcrete beneath it was stuffed with utility conduits and faded prayer slips, the latter presumably having been discarded during the routine maintenance and reconsecration of the vehicles passing through the facility.

'It is,' Vorspung confirmed, leading us across the open space towards the aircar, performing an impromptu arabesque to avoid a scuttling CAT as he did so, and entirely failing to look as though he'd meant to do that. He threw out a hand towards the vehicle, as if hoping to pass off the momentary loss of balance as an extravagantly proprietorial gesture. 'Yours for the duration of your stay.' He paused, as if struck by a sudden thought. 'Can you pilot it yourself?'

'At a pinch,' I said cautiously. Normally I left the driving to Jurgen, on the entirely reasonable grounds that if I was going to die in an embarrassing tangle of metal at least it wouldn't be my fault (and with my aide in the driving seat any danger to life or limb would be rendered much greater to everyone else in the vicinity, thus tilting the odds of survival further in my favour). But his entrenched antipathy to aerial travel of any kind meant that his almost uncanny ability to persuade ground vehicles to perform far beyond the limits envisaged by their designers would definitely not be replicated in this case. I had a passing familiarity with the controls of a standard aircar, not to mention some hastily acquired expertise in not crashing them while being shot at, but, if I'm honest, decades of being ferried around by under-lings had left my piloting skills rudimentary at best. 'I have to admit I'm a bit out of practice, though.'

I glanced at Jurgen, who'd already gone a paler shade of grimy, and decided it would be better to not even ask.

'I can pilot a Land Speeder,' Morie offered unexpectedly. 'An aircar seems to be more or less the same.'[53]

'There are one or two similarities in their handling charac-teristics,' Vorspung agreed diplomatically, 'but under the circumstances, perhaps I should be the one to take the controls.'

Jurgen muttered something which might have been 'works for me' but, judging by his pallor, probably wasn't.

'Then we should proceed with all due dispatch,' Morie said, taking a step or two towards the aircar, then coming to a halt as it suddenly dawned on us that, having been designed for passengers of normal stature, its roof was roughly level with his hips.

'Or perhaps not.' Vorspung turned his head, and gestured at the little knot of enginseers clustered around the nearest of the utility vehicles; like the aircar, it was floating a few centi-metres above the deck plates, a faint and irritating humming emanating from its repulsor arrays. One of the enginseers poking at it responded with a wave of his mechadendrites and came trotting towards us, with a chirrup of binharic as he approached.

'Please communicate in Gothic, for the benefit of our guests,' Vorspung admonished him, and the young tech-priest, who

---

53   *Other than it not being a heavily armoured gun platform intended to be flown with near-suicidal recklessness, of course.*

was still low enough in the Mechanicus hierarchy to have more flesh than metal showing above the neck, actually blushed visibly.

'My apologies.' He made the sign of the cogwheel, which Morie returned, to his evident surprise.[54] 'How may we be of assistance?'

'Are either of those cargo haulers ready to fly?' I asked, edging a little further away from Jurgen, whose nervousness at the prospect of getting airborne was beginning to thicken the air around both of us already.

'That one is.' The young tech-priest indicated the blocky utility vehicle closest to us, on which he and his fellows had been focusing their efforts. The others, I noted with some amusement, had stopped whatever they were doing to peer curiously in our direction, making only the most token attempt to pretend to be engrossed in the vehicle's inner workings. 'We've just completed the preflight checks, and renewed the votive seals of airworthiness.'

'Then we'll take that instead,' Vorspung decreed, setting off towards it. I followed, seeing no reason to delay our departure any further, my nose giving me all the assurance I needed that Jurgen had fallen in behind me as usual. Nor, for that matter, did I need to see Morie to know he'd joined us, his footfalls shaking the deck plates with every stride.

'Of course, magos. But...' The young man hesitated, his unmodified voice rising a little, in spite of his best attempts

---

54  *Cain remarks elsewhere in his memoirs that the Reclaimers seem to venerate the Omnissiah to a far greater extent than most Space Marine Chapters, but whether the Machine-God is the main focus of their faith, or seen simply as an aspect of their primarch or the Emperor Himself, only their initiates really know. The Ordo Hereticus may have their suspicions, but so far have seen no reason to act.*

to maintain the unemotional delivery expected of a member of his calling.

'Is there a difficulty?' Vorspung asked, in a manner calculated to convey that there'd better not be, without actually saying so.

'Not with the conveyance itself,' the young tech-priest hurried to assure him. 'But it has been scheduled to deliver replacement capacitors to the atmospheric engine in sector three-sigma-tethra. Without them, the efficiency will be reduced by–'

'Then take the aircar instead,' Vorspung interrupted, displaying a degree of testiness unusual in one of his calling. 'The internal volume will be sufficient, will it not?'

'I believe so, magos,' the young man said, glancing at the sleek and shiny aircar with an expression that suggested his birthday had come unexpectedly early. He returned his voice, which had risen noticeably in pitch, to the even monotone expected of him with a clearly audible effort. 'The crates are sufficiently small to fit on the passenger seats.' He pointed to a stack of boxes against one of the walls, the same shape and size as the ones lasgun powercells generally came in.[55]

'Then I suggest you commence loading with all due dispatch,' Vorspung said. 'Those capacitors won't deliver themselves.'

'Of course.' The young tech-priest gestured to his companions, who immediately stopped whatever they were doing, and moved away from the utility vehicle they'd been clustered

---

55   *Hardly surprising, as the Adeptus Mechanicus tend to standardise pretty much everything they can in the name of resource management… before their most senior acolytes proceed to tinker with it in a variety of inventive and life-threatening ways.*

around.[56] The servitors abandoned their toolkits and plodded over to the pile of boxes, which they began moving methodically to the aircar, where a couple of the junior tech-priests presided over the process of stowing them.

'This looks more suitable,' Morie said, ducking only slightly as he squeezed in through the double doors at the rear of the larger vehicle. The cargo hauler wobbled a little as the gravitic emitters tried to compensate for the sudden addition of his weight, then stabilised as he stopped moving and sat on a metal bench running fore to aft along one side of the hold, evidently intended to do double duty as either a shelf for cargo or makeshift seating as required. The metal groaned audibly but barely deformed, leaving him perched a little awkwardly on the narrow bench, his knees level with the aquila embossed across the chestplate of his armour. Jurgen followed him inside, taking the opposite bench, propping his lasgun upright between his knees and leaning against it as though in need of support; which, with the immediate prospect of taking to the air, he probably was.

'Commissar?' Vorspung took a couple of steps towards the cab at the front, obviously expecting me to join him, then hesitated. 'Unless you would prefer to ride with your companion?'

'And leave you on your own when you've been such an attentive host?' I said, with every appearance of affability I could summon up. 'Wouldn't dream of it.' Not when the alternative was spending an indeterminate amount of time in a confined space and close proximity to an airsick Jurgen,

---

56 *Presumably in response to his instructions over an internal vox-link – an augmentation favoured by many tech-priests, which the rest of us find distinctly unnerving, since it's impossible to overhear whatever they might be saying about us behind our backs.*

anyway. I felt a fleeting moment of sympathy for Morie, before the reflection that a veteran Space Marine had probably had a great deal worse than that to put up with in the course of his career elbowed it aside, and I swung myself up into the passenger seat of the cab with a passing display of enthusiasm. 'Besides, it's an excellent opportunity to remind myself how one of these things is supposed to work.'

'A commendably efficient use of the journey time,' Vorspung said, settling into the driver's seat and pulling a toggle on the dashboard which closed the doors behind us. A couple of runes flashed green, assuring us that the passenger and cargo compartments were both sealed and pressurised, and the magos began running through a brief checklist of the systems he was powering up.

'Atomic batteries to power – turbines to speed…' He glanced in my direction. 'Fastening your seat belt would be advisable.'

'Of course,' I said, tugging my chainsword around so that the scabbard wedged more or less comfortably between the door and the thinly padded seat. 'Safety first.'

'Taking precautions against avoidable injury is always prudent,' Vorspung agreed, feeding power to the gravitic emitters; a couple of the tech-priests who'd so recently been working on the vehicle leapt for their lives as it lurched half a metre forward, before coming to a sudden halt again. Taking the point, and ignoring the sudden explosion of Valhallan profanity in my earpiece, I buckled the crash restraints with almost indecent haste.

'Ah,' said Vorspung. 'Forgot the inertial dampers.'

'Easily done,' I said, already beginning to wonder if we should have tried to squeeze Morie in here after all and let him have a go. But Vorspung seemed to be gaining in confidence, so I held my tongue and memorised the position of the door latch in case I needed to bail out in a hurry. 'Just for the sake of conversation, when was the last time you flew one of these?'

'Forty-seven years ago,' Vorspung said. 'But I can assure you my memory files remain completely uncorrupted.' He poked at a rune or two, with a disconcertingly hopeful air. 'There, that should do it.'

'It would seem so,' I agreed diplomatically, as something went *pleep!* and the vehicle rose a little on its repulsor field. 'But perhaps we should wait for a moment?'

'That would be prudent,' Vorspung said, with a glance to our left, where the great bronze door sealing the pressurised hangar from the outside world was grinding slowly open, to reveal the ridgeline beyond. The tech-priests and servitors were moving away from the aircar, which was already heading towards the portal with an alacrity that struck me as distinctly unwise in such a confined space, their robes and purity seals fluttering in the gush of escaping air. 'A collision this early in our progress would be extremely embarrassing.'

'Indeed it would.' I nodded, suppressing the impulse to ask by which point he felt one might become acceptable.

The young tech-priest we'd spoken to waved to his compatriots from the driving seat of the aircar in a manner rather more exuberant than I normally expected from a wearer of the russet robe, and hurtled out into the open air, almost leaving a layer of paint on the still-opening door as he went.

Vorspung emitted an odd sound from his voxcoder which might have been a tut. 'The impetuosity of youth,' he commented, with a shake of his head.

'No doubt he'll grow out of it,' I said, as we began to glide smoothly forward, following the aircar out into the open skies beyond. He was clear of the complex perimeter already, banking in a smooth arc above the enclosing hills to head out across the plain, and Vorspung began to gain altitude as well, taking us over the landing pad still occupied by the Reclaimers' Thunderhawk.

'Provided he is sufficiently cautious in the interim,' Vorspung agreed, as the bank turned into a barrel roll. No sooner had he finished speaking than the hurtling aircar was ripped apart by a suddenly erupting fireball, the remaining cloud of debris slamming into the valley wall a handful of metres below the ridge crest.

'Emperor on Terra!' I expostulated, thoroughly shaken by the thought that had it not been for the bulk of Morie's armour derailing our plans, we would have been aboard the vehicle ourselves. 'What just happened?'

'A very good question,' Vorspung said, his eyes unfocusing for a moment as he inloaded the data, which I have to admit to finding faintly alarming given that he was in the pilot's seat at the time. 'According to the telemetry feed, there was a systems failure in the secondary power coupling.' He looked at me significantly as he came back to himself. 'It has every indication of being a regrettable accident.'

'Which means it probably wasn't one,' I said, never having been slow to pick up a hint when the most paranoid interpretation seemed possible.

'It was widely known that that particular vehicle had been assigned to your exclusive use,' Vorspung said. 'And such a mishap, while possible, is extremely unlikely.'

'That's what they said about the lord general's shuttle,' I said, feeling a faint chill at the base of my spine. I didn't believe in coincidences, at least not when they followed hard on the heels of one another, and I found myself wondering if

Zyvan had really been the target of an assassination attempt aboard the *Ocean Orchestra*.

What if it had been me all along?

# NINE

'A reasonable inference,' Vorspung agreed, when I voiced the thought aloud. He slowed the cargo hauler, and turned, bringing us around in a wide arc to begin following the ridgeline towards the plume of smoke and pulverised rock marking the site of the crash. Quite what assistance he expected to be able to render was beyond me, though: both explosion and impact had clearly been unsurvivable.[57] 'Particularly given the suspicions I confided in you earlier.'

'But how could someone from Eucopia have tried to have me killed on Coronus?' I asked, in some bemusement. I glanced back at the complex below us. A double handful of flyers were already swarming into the air from hangars and landing pads scattered around the tangle of buildings, their

---

57  Clearly, perhaps, to a man who had spent most of the preceding seventy years either in, or in close proximity to, a warzone; Vorspung, having spent most of his life in the service of the Machine-God, may have retained the pious hope that most things could be fixed.

airframes festooned with lifting gear and fire suppressants. There were figures moving on foot as well, scrambling up the steep slope towards the wreckage of the aircar, though from this distance it was hard to tell whether they were tech-priests or servitors. Probably a few of both, I thought. 'Or why, come to that.'

'Heresy spreads,'[58] Vorspung pointed out. He came to a halt, hovering over the crash site, gazing down at it with a faint air of bemused hope, which gradually flickered out as it became obvious the only things still moving amid the wreckage were flames and smoke. 'Messages and personnel have been travelling between shrines in both systems for decades, members of our hypothetical cabal no doubt among them.' Giving up the search for survivors as self-evidently futile, he started the cargo hauler moving again. 'And as for your second question–'

*'Commissar,'* Jurgen's voice interrupted, buzzing slightly in my vox-bead as usual. *'Are we turning back?'* The tone of hope in his voice was so pronounced I felt a little guilty about disappointing him.

'I'm afraid not,' I said. 'Just a slight delay.'

*'Is the situation serious?'* Morie asked, cutting in on the same frequency.

'Not for us,' Vorspung assured him, returning his attention to the controls. He seemed to have been right about not having lost the knack of piloting over the last few decades, as the vehicle responded smoothly, taking us up and over the ridgeline, out of the way of the approaching salvage parties. I'd expected him to give our companions a succinct

---

58   *Indeed it does. Ask any inquisitor. Just be sure you're prepared for the answer, as some think actions speak louder than words.*

summary of the accident, and its aftermath, but instead he resumed his conversation with me as though it had never been interrupted. 'It's not exactly a secret that you have the ear and full confidence of the lord general. The probability of him selecting you to make discreet enquiries here once the Imperial Guard began to take an interest would be well in excess of eighty per cent.'

'I see,' I responded reflexively, while I thought about the implications of that. The only reasonable inference was that I'd been targeted simply as a precaution, which spoke volumes for the ruthlessness of whoever was behind all this. In my experience, conspiracies spanning more than one world were never good news, especially when they seemed to have it in for me personally. It was why I tended to pass any indications of that sort of thing I came across to Amberley at the earliest opportunity. My chances of being able to do that undetected on a planet full of tech-priests, any one of whom might be a heretic with access to the comm-net, however, seemed remote in the extreme. What's more, any attempt would almost certainly redouble their efforts to do me harm (not to mention reveal my avocation as an occasional, and invariably reluctant, agent of the Inquisition, which I was certain[59] Amberley would take rather a dim view of). Better, then, to bide my time, affect to write off the incident as a regrettable accident, and keep my wits about me until I got off this Throne-forsaken rock and could report it in relative safety. On the plus side, I supposed, at least my hurt feelings about being merely collateral damage in an attempt on Zyvan's life had been soothed.

I just wished that had come as more of a comfort.

---

59   *Quite correctly.*

The shrine we were heading for was almost exactly what
I'd been expecting – a small satellite manufactory, several
leagues from the main complex, which loomed up out of
the desert like a misshapen outcrop of wind-eroded sand-
stone as we got closer to it. In actual fact, of course, it was
composed of far more durable rockcrete, its irregular shape
the result of decades of accretion rather than weathering –
a fabricatory here, a chapel there, and the inevitable landing
pad for the use of shuttles arriving with supplies and departing laden with lethal toys for the Reclaimers to play with.
Vorspung and I had lost no time in bringing Morie up to
speed about the crash of the aircar we should have been in,
with the heartening result that the Thunderhawk, and its
complement of Space Marines, had beaten us to it.[60] The
heavily armed gunship was already settling onto the slab of
'crete next to the wide, high loading door set into the sloping
side of the artificial escarpment as we began our approach,
the localised sandstorm raised by its engines obscuring the
highway connecting our destination to the shrine we'd just
left. The few vehicles traversing it slowed, no doubt to the
accompaniment of appropriate comments from the inconvenienced drivers, which we were mercifully spared by their
absence from our comm-net. Even before the Thunderhawk's
engines had powered down, gradually revealing the familiar
blocky fuselage through the settling cloud of dust enveloping it, towering figures in yellow-and-white power armour
could be seen disembarking, fanning out to secure the pad
and the surrounding area.

'Commendably prompt,' I commented, taking heart from

---

60　*Hardly a surprise, as if there's one thing the Adeptus Astartes
are good at, it's responding to an unexpected threat.*

their arrival; I knew their Chapter's fighting spirit of old, and, even though it seemed to me to be untempered by much in the way of caution,[61] their presence would throw up an insurmountable barrier to anyone intending to take another crack at me. Unless the conspirators included a cabal of skitarii, of course, but even if that were so (and by now I was in no mood to take anything for granted), I doubted they'd be willing to show their hand quite so blatantly. That did raise a rather disquieting prospect, however, and I turned to Vorspung at once, hoping to discount it. 'How much do you think we can trust Norgard?'

'That would depend on how you quantify trust,' he replied helpfully, steering our conveyance towards an opening portal in the side of the shrine, taking my question as literally as I suppose I should have expected from a tech-priest. 'As a straight percentage, the variables–'

'Would you feel comfortable confiding your suspicions to her?' I asked, getting straight to the point. Vorspung hesitated for a moment before replying, apparently preoccupied with steering us inside the hangar, where a couple of similar vehicles and a rather battered-looking Aquila were parked, plugged in to servicing umbilicals of one sort or another. He swung us around, rotating the cargo hauler almost on the spot, and settled it down on the 'crete next to the spacecraft so smoothly I barely felt the movement stop. Unlike the hangar we'd departed from, there were no ground crews or servitors visible; nor, for that matter, could I see any cargo containers stacked against the walls. Bright as the luminators were, I found the lack of bustle I would normally have expected to find in a place like this more than a little

---

61   *Well it would, wouldn't it?*

disconcerting. In my experience, apparently deserted installations generally concealed an unpleasant surprise or two,
like a lurking genestealer infestation or aeldari pirates intent
on looting everything movable, including the inhabitants.[62]
As the magos powered down the repulsors, and our vehicle
settled firmly onto its undercarriage, he nodded judiciously.

'More so than most,' he conceded. 'But I would rather not
do so until absolutely necessary.'

'And Sergeant Morie?' I enquired, unfastening the seat
restraints as I did so.

'Like you, he is outside the Cult Mechanicus, and therefore
unlikely to be a party to any conspiracy within it,' Vorspung
said.

'Fair point,' I agreed, scrambling out of the passenger door
and rearranging my sidearms into a more comfortable position – by which, of course, I mean where I could draw them
with the minimum of delay.

The clang of the rear door opening, and a sudden thicken-
ing of the air in my immediate vicinity, drew my attention
to the reappearance of my aide, who regained the solid floor
with an air of intense relief, looking even less healthy than
usual. (Which, for a man who once walked through a sentry line of Nurgle cultists unchallenged, was something of
an achievement.[63]) Morie followed, unfolding himself from

---

62   *As I've had occasion to remark in other parts of his memoirs,
Cain seems never to have noticed, or cared about if he had, the difference between craftworlders and their webway-dwelling kin, only the latter
being known to raid for slaves as well as resources. Although, to be fair,
since both were equally keen to kill him in most of his interactions with
them, it may well have seemed to him to be a distinction without a difference in any case.*

63   *Cain is, perhaps, being a little unfair here, since, as one of the
incredibly rare individuals immune to psychic influence, Jurgen would*

the cramped conditions he'd travelled in like a particularly lethal deckchair. I nodded to him, and returned my attention to the tech-priest, who had finished ministering to our vehicle and joined us on the stained 'crete of the hangar floor. 'Where are we, exactly?'

'One of the most sacred spaces on Eucopia,' Morie cut in unexpectedly, his expansive gesture taking in the parked flyers, the shabby-looking Aquila, and a number of interestingly shaped stains on the walls and floor. Any impulse I might have had to laugh in response, though, was pre-emptively quelled by the resonance of his voice, and the way it echoed in the wide, high chamber. His face, too, was completely serious.

'Then I'm honoured to be here,' I said, more politely than accurately.

'The honour is ours,' Morie said, with a perfunctory genuflection in the direction of the icon of the Omnissiah dominating the far wall – the only feature of note in sight.

'And ours,' Vorspung agreed, echoing the gesture, and turning to lead the way out of the hangar. The exchange surprised me, I don't mind admitting, but the reason for the Space Marine's strangely proprietorial attitude towards what I'd assumed to be an Adeptus Mechanicus shrine became clear as soon as we'd gained the corridor beyond. Instead of the throng of tech-priests and servitors (not to mention scuttling CATs getting underfoot) I'd expected to find there, fully half the people I saw seemed to be relatively unmodified, the few augmetics I could see presumably the results of old injuries, like my right fore and middle fingers. They stood

---

*be effectively undetectable to anyone tainted by the warp; indeed, many of the so-called 'blanks' are afflicted with something akin to negative charisma, rendering them less likely to be noticed even by the rest of us.*

out among the russet-robed tech-priests sharing the space, the white and yellow trim of their robes and tunics identifying them instantly, even if their deferential attitude to Morie hadn't marked them out at once.

'Chapter-serfs,' Jurgen said, his surprise clearly at least as great as mine. 'Haven't seen any of those in a while.'

'Indeed not,' I agreed,[64] nodding courteously to one of their number, who was evidently equally astonished by the sight of us.

'This facility produces materiel entirely for the Reclaimers,' Vorspung said. 'Though fully integrated with the Eucopian infrastructure, by treaty it's ceded to them as part of their Chapter demesne.'[65]

'Which the Adeptus Mechanicus continues to operate for us,' Morie concluded, which seemed fair enough to me. After all, the Cult Mechanicus guarded its holy lore jealously, and would undoubtedly be reluctant to leave its manufacturing processes in the hands of outsiders, however close the pact between them and the Reclaimers' Techmarines might be; while, for their part, the Adeptus Astartes take little interest in anything which doesn't involve slaughtering the Emperor's enemies.

'Though not, at the moment, as effectively as either of us might wish,' Vorspung added, receiving a nod of confirmation from the brother-sergeant.

---

64   *If any had been present in support of the Reclaimers on Fecundia, the fact had evidently slipped his mind.*

65   *Most Chapters of the Adeptus Astartes are responsible for the guardianship of their home worlds and associated systems, which are considered under their jurisdiction rather than that of the usual Imperial institutions such as the Administratum, the Adeptus Arbites and the Ecclesiarchy. A few have holdings somewhat greater in extent, encompassing several inhabited worlds, stellar systems or both, the largest and most famous of which is, of course, the Realm of Ultramar.*

'How badly are your production schedules being affected?' I asked, feeling bold enough to speak a little more freely now. It was still possible that one or more of the tech-priests milling around us on errands of their own were party to the conspiracy Vorspung so strongly suspected, of course, but highly unlikely – only candidates of the highest calibre and probity would be trusted to even enter a Chapter holding, let alone work there, and the Reclaimers had centuries of experience in detecting the subtle signs of heresy.[66]

'About as badly as yours, I suspect,' Morie said, leading the way into a quieter side room. No stranger to the Reclaimers' taste in interior decoration, after spending far more time than I'd been comfortable with as a guest on one of their battle-barges,[67] I recognised the briefing room for what it was the moment the door slid to behind us. It had plainly been prepared for us in advance, as a hololithic image was flickering and sputtering over the conference table in the middle of the room.

'Tanna, sir?' Jurgen asked, making straight for the samovar in the corner, from which the unmistakable aroma of the beverage was emanating, along with some mildly alarming hissing and bubbling sounds. More proof, if I needed it, that my presence here had been anticipated; my fondness

---

66 *For Cain, this is a remarkably trusting assumption; most Space Marines' ability to recognise signs of heresy is limited to sticking their heads up to see where the bolter rounds are coming from. Which, to be fair, is pretty much the only indication they actually need.*

67 *Actually a strike cruiser: although given the rarity of battle-barges themselves, even the most lavishly equipped Chapters only being able to maintain one or two of these gigantic transport and assault craft, Cain can be forgiven for mistaking their name for a generic term for Space Marine vessels – an error he makes on more than one occasion in the course of his memoirs.*

for that particular drink had been known to the Reclaimers I'd served with, and they must have gone to some trouble to prepare it in advance of my arrival.[68]

'Thank you, Jurgen,' I said, dropping into a comfortably padded seat at the central table. It was the right size for me, Throne be praised, although the table surface was roughly level with my chin. Everyone else remained standing, which was precisely as I'd expected (I'd hardly ever seen a Space Marine sit down, apart from in a transport vehicle), and Vorspung made a beeline for the hololith projector, where he immediately began muttering incantations, flicking switches and hitting the casing with his fist. The ritual had its desired effect: the image stabilised, revealing a complex tangle of interconnected data lines which meant nothing to me, but were vaguely reminiscent of a disembowelled carnifex. Jurgen bustled over and handed me a tea bowl full of the fragrant liquid, the steam of which I inhaled appreciatively – partly because the scent put me in a more tranquil frame of mind, which I rather suspected wouldn't last for very long, and partly because it masked the more earthy aroma of its bearer. 'Better get one for yourself,' I told him. 'This could take some time.'

'Very good, sir,' my aide rejoined, and complied with alacrity, snagging a drink from the side table before placing himself firmly in front of the door, his lasgun slung where he could ready it for use in an instant. Not that we were likely to be interrupted by intruders in so secure a location, but we'd only reached the age we had by never taking anything for granted, and I must confess I felt distinctly cheered by his evident readiness for trouble. Punctuating his vigil

---

68   *Not to mention obtaining it in the first place.*

by occasional slurping noises, he did his best to fade into the background, although his grubby fatigues and battered body armour didn't exactly match the decor.

'What exactly are we looking at?' I asked, returning my attention to the image in the hololith, which continued to resemble nothing so much as abstract art in an abattoir.

'A visual representation of the flow of resources through the Eucopian infrastructure,' Vorspung told me, completely unhelpfully, 'graded by colour for ease of interpretation. Puce, for instance, shows the distribution of fissionables, taupe data flow through the cogitator nodes, cyan the allocation of personnel, ultraviolet raw materials currently in transit, viridian those available for processing–'

'Quite fascinating,' I said, before he could run through the entire spectrum, including the parts invisible to my unaugmented eyes, 'but a little too detailed for a layman like me to interpret. Can you just narrow it down to the most probable cause?'

Vorspung stopped speaking abruptly and turned back to us, glancing at Morie as if hoping for some show of support. 'The variables are extremely complex–' he began.

'Evidently,' Morie said. 'But, like the commissar, I lack the expertise to interpret such a comprehensive analysis.' Or the patience, if I was any judge. 'Just the bolt points, please.'

'But…' Vorspung appeared to take several deep breaths, no mean feat for a man who I suspected had long ago dispensed with anything so inefficient as lungs. 'Of course. It's a gross oversimplification, but the proximate cause of the manufactories' lack of output would appear to be a lack of raw materials. Why this should be remains puzzling, however, as Eucopia is unusually abundant in the required minerals.'

'Which is why it was colonised in the first place,' I put in, to show I wasn't completely out of my depth. 'So why's no one digging them out?'

'They are,' Vorspung said. 'But it appears the flow has diminished.' He poked at the hololith's controls again, and another diagram appeared, this one a good deal easier to follow, to my great relief. 'As you can see, the actual yield from our mining operations are considerably below those projected for this stage of the colonisation process.'

'Considerably,' Morie agreed. Space Marines were notoriously hard to read, of course, although my months spent accompanying the Reclaimers had left me better equipped than most to interpret the subtle shifts of their normally impassive features, and if I was any judge he was as unimpressed as I was by the size of the gap between the two lines on the graph. 'And the reason for this unfortunate shortfall?'

'Is not entirely clear,' Vorspung admitted, looking as unhappy about that as it was possible to for someone with so much metal in his face that expressions were generally something which only happened to other people. 'The aggregated data is clear, but the choke points far harder to identify.'

'And why would that be?' I asked. 'Could someone be falsifying the data?'

Vorspung was silent and motionless for so long after that, I began to wonder if he'd short-circuited something. I was just on the point of standing up and poking him to check, when he snapped out of whatever fugue state he'd been in, and nodded slowly.

'It is possible,' he said, about as enthusiastically as an ecclesiarch being asked to consider whether Horus might have been well intentioned but a trifle misguided. 'But the idea of a tech-priest deliberately corrupting information...'

'Is disconcerting in the extreme,' Morie agreed. 'But it

would explain a great deal. And after what happened to the aircar, I would hardly rule it out.'

'Neither would I,' I said. I turned to the tech-priest, with all the sincerity I could counterfeit. 'Especially after our conversation earlier. Perhaps...' I let my voice tail away, confident that he'd take the hint.

'You are, of course, correct.' Vorspung nodded. 'We should confide in Sergeant Morie. If our suspicions are correct, the Reclaimers will be invaluable allies.'

'I was under the impression that we already were,' Morie said, without much heat. He turned to me. 'What is occurring here?'

'Precisely what I was sent to Eucopia to find out,' I said. 'And if the magos is right, the corruption of data's the least of it.'

# TEN

Morie listened impassively as Vorspung set out his suspicions, in rather more detail than he'd done with me – but then a briefing room in a Space Marine facility was a lot more secure than a lift in a crowded Mechanicus shrine. The gist of it was still the same, though: that the lack of output from the manufactoria on Eucopia was most likely to be the result of the machinations of a shadowy cabal hell-bent on crippling the Imperium's efforts to defend itself from the enemies surrounding us on all sides.

'Who, though?' Morie asked. 'And, more to the point, why?'

'Answer that,' I said, 'and you answer the first question too.' I'd been on more than my fair share of heretic hunts with Amberley, and though I was a long way from being able to think like an inquisitor, I'd picked up a rough idea of how they go about things.[69] 'Find the motive, and you're well on the way to identifying the guilty.'

'That's the conundrum,' Vorspung said. 'The conspirators are evidently working against the efficient use of resources and the interests of the Machine-God, but only members of the Cult Mechanicus have the expertise required to do so while remaining undetected. That is a paradox which I find myself unable to resolve. Blasphemy against the Omnissiah by consecrated tech-priests is so unthinkable I must confess to doubting my own sanity on several occasions since I first began to suspect such a thing.'

'Then they are deluded, misguided or corrupted,' Morie said simply.

'Or genuinely believe they're serving the Omnissiah in some higher fashion,' I said. I coughed delicately, aware I was about to tread on Vorspung's iridium replacement toes. 'Are there any, ah, doctrinal disputes in that area?'

Vorspung's voxcoder emitted a short burst of static, which, had I believed him capable of such a thing, I might have taken for stifled amusement. 'Techno-theology consists of practically nothing but doctrinal differences,' he said. 'But all concur that the true path is towards the perfectibility of humankind in the Omnissiah's image.' He paused, a little awkwardly. 'And the name of the Emperor too, of course.'

'Are they not one and the same?' Morie asked, a trifle sharply it seemed to me.

'Without a doubt,' I put in hastily, although to be honest I had no idea, both in my experience tending to come to the aid of whoever had the biggest gun at the time. 'Which

---

69   *The subtler ones, anyway – there are always a few who'll kill every-thing in sight just to be on the safe side, even in the Ordo Xenos, let alone the Hereticus, who like to be thorough, and the Malleus, who don't dare not to be.*

rather begs the question, what kind of tech-priest would turn their back on so fundamental a principle?'

'The traitor kind,' Morie said, his face twisted with loathing. 'Those who turn away from the light of the Omnissiah to throw in their lot with the Great Enemy.'

'We do not speak of them,' Vorspung said, the volume of his voxcoder suddenly seeming a good deal louder, 'still less traffic with thrice-damned heretics.'

'I've fought Traitor Space Marines,' I said mildly to Morie, 'as, I'm certain, have you. Their existence in no way tarnishes the glorious deeds of the Adeptus Astartes.' I braced myself for a sharp rejoinder, if not worse, but to my carefully concealed relief, Morie was nodding.

'A point well made,' he said. 'The Dark Mechanicum are equally abhorrent, but equally no true servants of the Omnissiah.'

'Indeed not.' Vorspung appeared to have accepted the implied apology, his voxcoder back at its usual volume. 'Their allegiance is entirely to the Dark Gods.'

'That's always been my impression,' I said, trying not to think about the daemon engines I'd done my best to avoid on a number of battlefields over the decades. Whoever was capable of even conceptualising such abominations, let alone calling them into being, would have to be corrupt beyond even my worst imaginings. 'I can't see anyone that tainted being able to escape detection for long, let alone further their plans while doing it.'

'It wouldn't be the first time the Great Enemy had infiltrated an Imperial institution,' Morie persisted, 'but your point is a reasonable one. You've had more experience with such situations than either of us.'[70]

---

70  *Because by the time a hidden Chaos cult became enough of a*

'True,' I said, although none of that experience had exactly been from choice. I couldn't rule out a Chaos cult entirely, but in my dealings with such things, they tended to crop up either amid the wealthiest stratum of society, where the search for novel diversions could lead down dangerous paths, or among the detritus at the bottom – those desperate enough to hazard their souls to upend the social order, as they felt they had nothing to lose in any case. Tech-priests didn't fall into either category, having little interest in personal possessions and more than enough to occupy their time. The manufactory serfs were another matter, of course, but in my experience would probably be more inclined to vent their frustrations in more direct ways. Nevertheless, I made a mental note to ask Norgard about the riots she'd mentioned at our first meeting: whether anyone had been mucking about with suspicious-sounding chants, or daubing graffiti that made your eyes bleed to look at on the commissary walls, that sort of thing. 'But if we are looking for a hidden cult, my money would be on genestealers rather than heretics.'

'Genestealers could never infect tech-priests, surely?' Vorspung demurred. 'And the indentured labourers would lack the influence and resources to disrupt output as comprehensively as we suspect.'

'I've known at least one tech-priest who carried the taint,' I said, which must have come as an unwelcome surprise to him, given the length of the silence which ensued. 'And it would make sense on a strategic level too.'

'Indeed it would,' Morie agreed. 'The war against the hive fleets is the most pressing threat to the Imperium in the entire

---

*nuisance to attract the attention of the Adeptus Astartes, it wouldn't be so much a shadowy conspiracy as a planetwide insurrection.*

Eastern Arm. The materiel Eucopia has promised us, and the Imperial Guard, could make all the difference between survival and annihilation.'

'The lord general is of a similar mind,' I said. 'But on the bright side, our alliance with the t'au against the 'nids seems to be holding across most of the sector, at least for the time being.' Although neither of us trusted the little blue blighters not to cut and run the moment they thought it expedient, leaving us to bear the brunt of a tyranid onslaught while they annexed a few Imperial worlds left relatively undefended. (No doubt they felt exactly the same about our intentions, probably with equally good reason.)

'Which means the t'au are hardly likely to be working against us,' Vorspung said, while Morie and I exchanged pitying glances at his naivety. 'Not to mention the fact that their techno-sorcery is unhallowed. Any tech-priest associating with it would face instant excommunication as a heretek.'

'Well, I doubt they'll be working with the orks,' I said, feeling it was time to move the discussion on to more practical matters. Morie smiled at the jest, but, predictably, Vorspung took it at face value.

'Indeed so,' he said. 'Their mechanisms are crude in the extreme, and of no conceivable interest to a disciple of the Omnissiah.'[71]

'Which might incline them to value the services of more competent enginseers,' I said, unable to resist pulling his

---

71  *Of no interest to most of them, anyway. The few exceptions are eccentric, to put it mildly, perhaps because many of the products of a mekboy's foundry only appear to work because the wielder believes they will, which does interesting things to the sanity of a tech-priest determined to unravel their secrets.*

leg. 'Though what they might offer in exchange would be hard to imagine.'

'It would indeed,' Vorspung said. 'Rare materials, or archeo-tech, perhaps? They might stumble across either in the course of their depredations.'

'They might,' Morie replied, 'but if so they would be instantly claimed by one of their mekboyz, not traded to Imperial traitors.'

'I'm inclined to agree,' I said. 'Orks aren't noted for their willingness to share, and they definitely don't do covert.' Apart from their kommandos that is, who were as good at infiltration and sabotage as anyone else in the galaxy, but definitely too focused on blowing things up to bother with negotiating secret alliances.

'Then the most reasonable assumption would appear to be that we're dealing with an infestation of genestealers,' Vorspung conceded. His voice remained as uninflected as ever, but I couldn't help fancying I detected a certain air of relief about him now that we believed we'd identified the nature of the shadowy enemy we faced. We were completely wrong, as it happened, but perhaps that was just as well; if I'd realised what we were actually facing, I would proba-bly have dissolved into gibbering panic on the spot, which would hardly have consolidated my reputation with our Space Marine hosts. 'The question now is what we should do about it.' He looked hopefully at Morie and I, and even glanced briefly in Jurgen's direction, apparently under the impression that we'd have an answer for him.

'I think,' I said, after the ensuing silence had just passed the point of tipping from dramatic into awkward, 'that it's time we spoke to Norgard.'

\* \* \*

Who was, of course, predictably disgruntled at being summoned to a facility which, as an Adeptus Astartes Chapter holding, was outside her jurisdiction anyway. She was, however, diplomatic enough to disguise her irritation as best she could, surprise replacing it almost at once as she climbed out of an aircar unnervingly similar to the one that had detonated in the skies over the Mechanicus shrine a few hours earlier.

'Commissar.' She grasped the hand I was holding out, and shook it, with every sign of genuine goodwill. Morie and Vorspung had readily agreed to my offer to meet her in the hangar bay, which still looked disconcertingly sterile to me, as the high regard she evidently held me in should go some way towards mitigating her understandable annoyance at being dragged out here in the first place. 'This is a most pleasant surprise.'

'Kind of you to say so,' I said, relinquishing my grip, and beginning to lead the way out of the echoing chamber. As I did so, she turned aside to genuflect briefly in the direction of the icon of the Omnissiah on the wall, which I felt was an encouraging sign. It appeared to be a genuine reflex, rather than a performance for my benefit, so perhaps Vorspung's confidence in her probity was merited. 'Although after this morning, I'm just relieved to be here at all.'

'Quite so,' Norgard agreed, as we passed through the main doorway and gained the corridor, where we paused for a moment to let a covey of Chapter-serfs hurry past on some urgent errand. Several of them were now carrying autopistols holstered at their waists, something I couldn't recall ever having seen aboard the *Revenant*,[72] and evidence that Morie

---

72    *The Reclaimers strike cruiser aboard which he'd spent some time during its eventful voyage in search of the space hulk* Spawn of Damnation.

had lost no time in raising the alert level of the entire instal-lation.[73] 'Our investigations are proceeding, of course, but I regret I have very little to go on at this stage. Or for the inci-dent with the Kastelan, come to that.'

'But you suspect sabotage?' I asked, as casually as I could.

Norgard blinked, the non-ferrous portions of her face a picture of astonishment.

'It can't be ruled out,' she said after a moment, 'but I've been working on the assumption of a systems failure in both instances. The data seems to support that.'

'Well it would, wouldn't it?' I said, turning aside to let a servitor plod past, dragging a trolley with an annoyingly squeaky wheel. 'The question is whether the failures were assisted or not.'

'Who by?' she asked, rising a good deal in my estima-tion: no prevaricating or bleating about the impossibility of a tech-priest being party to such infamy, just straight to the point.

'We have a working hypothesis,' I said, holding the door of the briefing room open.

'We?' She entered ahead of me, taking in the presence of Morie and Vorspung, ignoring Jurgen as most people seemed to do whenever the opportunity presented itself, and turned

---

73    *Given the secrecy most Adeptus Astartes Chapters maintain about their traditions and practices it's hard to be sure, but this would seem to be somewhat unusual. Most Chapter-serfs appear to be aspirant recruits to the ranks of the Space Marines themselves (those who failed to make the grade during the selection process while still distinguishing themselves sufficiently to be offered the chance to serve the Chapter in a supporting role) so would certainly be familiar enough with most weapons to use them effectively. Very few instances of them being routinely armed by their patron Chapter are on record, however, other than the serfs of the Bone Knives, who carry weapons openly, and often get the chance to use them while carrying out their logistical support duties just behind the front line.*

back to me as I closed the door behind us. 'What exactly is going on here?'

'Commissar Cain suspects that our recent difficulties are the result of genestealer infiltration,' Vorspung told her, 'a suggestion which I'm inclined to agree merits further investigation.'

'As am I,' Morie rumbled, before the praetor could voice an objection.

'I see.' Norgard looked at me with manifest scepticism. 'And your evidence for this assertion would be?'

'Scattered across the hillside,' I said, before remembering tech-priests generally didn't do sarcasm.

'It's a simple matter of probabilities,' Vorspung said, stepping in hastily. 'The pattern of disruption to the manufactoria output is significantly greater than could be explained entirely by random factors.'

'Not to mention the fact that our aircar exploded shortly after Magos Vorspung confided his suspicions to me,' I added. 'Discreet as he was, it's not impossible we were somehow overheard. Any conspirators worth their soylens would have realised he was the most likely man on Eucopia to have deduced their presence, and kept him under observation.' A suggestion which left the senior tech-priest looking both flattered and somewhat disconcerted.

'I, too, would have been slain,' Morie reminded us. 'Anyone acting against the interests of the Imperium must have realised that the Reclaimers' garrison here would be a formidable obstacle to their plans.'

'Very much in their interests to silence the magos before he could enlist their aid,' I said, to show I was still paying attention.

'In theory, yes,' Norgard conceded. 'But you still have no hard evidence to back up your claims.' Jurgen emitted a phlegm-laden snort of derision, which I pretended not to have heard. Norgard continued, equally diplomatically deaf. 'If the aircar accident was a deliberate attempt to assassinate you all, how would the conspirators have known you'd be travelling together? And why would they have chosen to strike then, instead of picking you off one by one?'

'Opportunity,' I said. I smiled, without much humour, in Morie's direction. 'And I suspect that the brother-sergeant would be more than a little difficult to pick off in any case.'

'As would you,' Morie agreed, nodding his agreement at what he no doubt regarded as a compliment.

'It would hardly have been difficult to infer that we'd be sharing a conveyance,' Vorspung said. 'Sergeant Morie and I had much to discuss, and Commissar Cain is an old and valued associate of the Reclaimers.'

Norgard nodded, clearly taking all this on board with some difficulty. 'Assuming you're correct about this,' she said, still sounding far from convinced, 'we should take immediate measures to safeguard the most critical systems of the Eucopian infrastructure.'

'The which of the what?' Jurgen muttered, as he handed me a fresh bowl of tanna.

'Posting guards on anything the 'stealers might want to blow up,' I translated for him, and my aide nodded, his hand straying absently to the safety catch of his lasgun, before diverting to scratch his buttocks. I made a mental note to avoid accepting a refill.

'The first thing we need to do is arrange gene scans for the four of us,' I said.[74] I expected Norgard to object to that,

---

74　*Morie's extensive genetic modifications making him immune to having his DNA overwritten by the 'stealers.*

but she simply nodded, apparently mollified by me having included myself on the list of potential suspects. Having had rather more experience of genestealer infestations than the praetor, I knew that was precisely the kind of bluff I would have attempted to execute if I really was a member of the broodmind, but felt it wouldn't be politic to mention that.

'A sound suggestion,' Morie said. 'Then every serf and tech-priest in the Chapter holding.'

'That would take some time,' Vorspung said, 'but I'm inclined to agree. If there's anywhere on Eucopia we're certain of being able to keep free of taint, it would be here.'

'Then, I would suggest, we move on to the skitarii,' Norgard said, sounding as enthusiastic about that as could reasonably be expected. 'One maniple at a time. If any are compromised, the sooner they're neutralised the better.'

'Quite,' I agreed. 'You and your legion are the best line of defence this world has.[75] I pray to the Throne I'm wrong, but if not we may need you sooner than we expect.' Something I was right about, unfortunately, but in a manner none of us could have predicted at the time.

---

75  *If Morie disagreed with this assessment, Cain doesn't mention the fact; although given the handful of Space Marines actually present on Eucopia, he may simply have concurred.*

# ELEVEN

Although I would have been surprised to say the least if any of us had turned out to be carrying the genestealer taint, I have to admit to a profound sense of relief as the Reclaimers' Apothecary glanced up from the screen of his genecode reader and shook his head.

'None of you appear to be compromised,' he said, as though failing to detect any trace of our subversion had been vaguely disappointing.

'As I'd expected,' I said, only exaggerating a little. I'd already been as certain as I could be that neither Jurgen nor I were secret agents of the broodmind.[76] My real concern

---

76  *A superficially flippant observation which may well have a grain of truth in it; the question of how aware those unfortunate enough to have been implanted with 'stealer genetic material actually are of being a part of the broodmind remains an open one. The current working hypothesis of the magi biologis studying the question on behalf of the Ordo Xenos essentially boils down to 'your guess is as good as ours', but with rather more polysyllabic jargon.*

131

had been that Vorspung or Norgard had been subverted. The commander of the local skitarii would have been a prime target, and a valuable potential ally, for any hidden infiltrators, while Vorspung, as I'd already pointed out, would be the most likely person to unravel the conspiracy; having him under the broodmind's control would not only neutralise that threat, but also place Eucopia's considerable resources at their disposal into the bargain. Of course, he'd been the one who'd drawn my attention to the potential threat in the first place, but for someone as paranoid as I am that didn't really prove anything – it could have been an elaborate double bluff, or an attempt to lure me into an ambush. Little surprise, then, that he looked as relieved as I felt as we took our leave of the apothecarion, pretending not to notice the pair of Terminators loitering in the corridor outside, their storm bolters seeming even more ominously large and deadly than usual. (Which, given the size of the average Space Marine, not to mention their heaviest armour, was saying quite a lot.)

'So, we can be sure of ourselves, at least,' Norgard said, taking the only comfortable seat at the briefing room table, leaving me to lean casually against it as though taking a keen interest in whatever she had to say. True to form she didn't include Jurgen in the appraising glance she shot around the room, which suited my aide; he made a beeline for the samovar instead, tutting in disapproval at the state of the tanna remaining within it.

'Stewed, I'm afraid, sir.' He made for the door again. 'I'll find you some fresh. And a hot grox bap or something.'

'Thank you, Jurgen,' I said, as he disappeared, leaving only a faint aromatic reminder of his presence. I had no doubt that if there was any refreshment to be found in the shrine

Jurgen was the man to find it, his talent for scrounging bordering on the preternatural.

'If you require sustenance, we can provide it,' Morie said, looking a little discomfited at the implied slur on his Chapter's hospitality.

'Not at all,' I assured him, despite feeling a trifle peckish now my aide had reminded me of quite how long it had been since breakfast. 'Jurgen likes to feel useful, and perhaps we can talk more freely now everyone here has a sufficiently high security clearance. I'm sure we can trust him to find some tanna while we do.' Not to mention any little snippets of information he might come across in the course of his scrounging which our hosts might be reluctant to share with us. It goes without saying that if you can't trust the Adeptus Astartes, who can you trust?[77] But no one likes to play their cards face up, least of all me, and it never hurts to have someone easily overlooked making sure the deck isn't stacked while the dealer's attention is otherwise engaged.

'An excellent point,' Vorspung agreed, displaying a degree of relish at being able to use phrases like 'security clearance' with a straight face most unusual in a tech-priest; members of his order generally considered showing enthusiasm for anything which didn't emit sparks or drip lubricant as distinctly undignified. I've often noticed the same sort of thing among civilian representatives of the local authorities sitting in on security briefings, who do like to think their opinions matter, even though they're noticeably absent when the las-bolts start to fly. Norgard looked a little more sceptical, no doubt realising that anything Jurgen wanted to know

---

77  Ha!

about our deliberations in his absence he'd find out soon enough anyway.[78]

'I would suggest we return to the Nexus as soon as we can,' Norgard said, glancing at Vorspung and myself as she spoke; after a moment I realised she must have meant the shrine we'd set out from that morning. 'If we remain absent for too long, our adversaries may realise we're aware of their existence.'

Morie nodded. 'I'll remain here while we complete the screening process, and produce whatever stocks of wargear we can with the materials currently to hand.' He looked at Vorspung a trifle ruefully. 'Though it seems we'll still be producing the traditional patterns for a while yet.'

Vorspung nodded. 'The preliminary designs we've had for the new bolt rifles look promising, but retooling is taking longer than we expected. We hope to be able to commence full production once the supply issue has been resolved.'

'Standard bolters will be more than sufficient,' Morie said. 'Our faith in the Emperor will always be our strongest weapon in any case.'

'Well said,' I agreed, because it was expected of me, even though in my experience it didn't matter how much faith you had if that was the only thing you were armed with and the enemy had guns. 'How long until you're sure no one here's been infected?'

Morie looked distracted for a moment, presumably consulting the Apothecary through the vox-gear built into his armour.

---

78   *Technically, as the aide of a commissar, Jurgen had access to anything which fell within the Commissariat's remit. In practice, he had access to anything which wasn't nailed down, and a few things which were if something had been left lying around to remove the nails with.*

'Two to three days,' he said, 'to be absolutely certain. Two if all goes well, three if we uncover some evidence of the taint among the serfs or the priests of the Omnissiah working here, and they attempt to make a fight of it.'

'Then we should turn our attention to the Nexus,' I said. 'How long will it take to screen the personnel there?'

Norgard looked distinctly unhappy. 'Too long,' she said. 'There are at least ten times as many people permanently assigned to the site as there are here, plus an average of two hundred and seventeen transients arriving and departing each day.'

Vorspung nodded. 'And the majority of those are logistical support specialists, who visit shrines and manufactoria all over the planet. Any one of whom could spread the taint elsewhere, or bring it back to the Nexus if the genestealer cult is embedded in another installation entirely.'

'Then that complicates things,' I said, doing the maths in my head, no doubt a lot more slowly and inaccurately than either of the tech-priests. 'The best part of a month to be sure the Nexus is clear, assuming no more hybrids or implants arrive in the meantime.'

'At least we can be sure the Chapter holding will be free of taint,' Morie said, with a faint air of smugness. 'We have minimal contact with the rest of Eucopia, apart from the deliveries of raw material. It will be easy enough to insulate the logisticians accompanying those from the interior of the shrine.'

'If you can do it discreetly,' I said, uncomfortably aware that discretion wasn't usually high on the list of requirements for elevation to one of the Emperor's finest.[79]

---

79  *Yes and no. Some Space Marine commanders value subterfuge and diplomacy at least as much as their bolters, although superior firepower still tends to be the first solution they think of to any given problem.*

'We'll cite an outbreak of mirepox among the serfs,' Morie said. 'That should persuade most visitors to keep their distance.'

'Allowing you to coordinate our efforts from here,' Norgard agreed.

'Unfortunately a similar subterfuge will be far less easy to perpetrate in the Nexus,' Vorspung said. 'Too many of the residents will have access to the primary data, and attempting to falsify it would draw too much unwelcome attention.' He shuddered, barely perceptibly. 'Not to mention the ethical and theological issues such a course of action would entail.'

Norgard nodded. 'Compromises must sometimes be made in the name of expediency,' she said, 'but one of this magnitude...' Her voice trailed away.

I nodded, feigning a sympathy I didn't feel. In my book you did whatever you needed to do to confound the Emperor's enemies, and telling a few fibs was the least of it; but to a tech-priest the truth was sacred, and pressing the point wouldn't help us maintain a united front against them.

'That wouldn't help anyway,' I said, to the visible relief of both tech-priests. 'If everything is as interlinked as you explained to me in the control chapel, the moment we start general genescans, pretty much everyone on the planet will know. Including the 'stealers.'

'Then what do you suggest?' Morie asked.

'Begin with the skitarii,' I said, 'and pray to the Throne none of them are compromised.' I turned to Norgard. 'There must be some pretext you can use to isolate them from the rest of the Nexus for as long as it takes to screen them.'

Norgard nodded. 'I'm sure our honoured allies from the Adeptus Astartes are eager to observe their performance in a live-fire exercise. Which will mean moving all those currently assigned to the Nexus to the proving grounds to prepare.'

'In small enough groups to test discreetly,' I added, in tones of approval I didn't have to cultivate. 'Once you've cleared a squad or two, they can keep an eye on the others while they wait for their turn.' Because if there were any 'stealer infiltrators among the skitarii, it was inevitable they'd try to shoot their way out the minute they realised we were on to them.

'We'll start with the command staff,' Norgard said, 'and their close-protection units. Once they've been cleared we'll have enough firepower to contain any little surprises.'

'As will we,' Morie put in. 'The Reclaimers delegation will include an honour guard of Terminators.' He smiled, in a slightly forced manner, in the praetor's direction. 'As protocol demands when dealing with so exalted a host.'

'I would say I'm flattered,' Norgard said, 'but under the circumstances I'll just be happy to see them there.' Which was hardly surprising; I'd seen skitarii in action before, and a few turncoats among them would be guaranteed to make a considerable mess before being subdued. She glanced at me. 'And the Imperial Guard liaison, of course. It would be unusual not to have you attend the demonstration on behalf of the lord general, would it not?'

I nodded reluctantly. This was a development I'd failed to anticipate, but she was absolutely right; if I wasn't there, we might just as well hold up a sign saying *You've been rumbled and this is a trap* for any subverted skitarii in her legion. 'I look forward to seeing your troops show what they're capable of,' I said diplomatically, which was sort of true, unless what they were capable of turned out to be treachery and my attempted murder.

'But won't that leave the Nexus undefended?' Vorspung objected.

'Technically, I suppose so,' I conceded. 'Although there doesn't seem to be any clear and present military threat to it at the moment.'

Norgard nodded. 'The proving grounds are close enough to respond from if the orks decide to invade while our backs are turned,' she reassured the magos, who still looked distinctly unconvinced from where I stood. 'And the probability of that is low in the extreme.'

'On the order of zero point zero-seven per cent,' Vorspung agreed, having taken a moment to work it out.

'For an ork invasion specifically?' I asked, partly out of genuine curiosity, but mostly from a sense of mischief. Vorspung's eyes unfocused momentarily again.

'Specifically,' he said, as incapable of most of his brethren of recognising sarcasm when he heard it. 'The probability of an invasion of any kind would be zero point one-five, of which the tyranids would be the most likely aggressor, the chances of an attack by them being zero point–'

'Low enough,' I said hastily, regretting the impulse to pull his leg almost at once, and determined to move the conversation in a more productive direction as quickly as possible. I turned back to Norgard. 'What about the skitarii assigned elsewhere on the planet?' Or in the rest of the system, come to that. The colonisation effort here might be concentrated primarily on the world we were standing on, but there were bound to be orbitals and void stations in its immediate vicinity, to service the starships transporting the bounty of its manufactories to where it was needed. Whenever it started producing enough to begin attracting more than a handful of starships, of course. In a few more generations there would probably be outposts looting the other planets, moons and asteroids of their own raw materials as well, which would have made our task even more difficult, but for the moment, thank the Throne, we'd be able to concentrate our efforts on Eucopia alone.

Norgard nodded, as though pleased I'd brought the matter up. Perhaps she even was.

'Spread fairly thinly,' she said, 'and only a fraction of the strength of a mature forge world.' Which could be good or bad news, I supposed, depending on how strong a foothold our shadowy enemies had managed to secure among their ranks. 'In terms you're familiar with, one regimental equivalent assigned to the main legion facilities at the Nexus, one primarily concerned with the other shrines and manufactories in this hemisphere, Impi Tertius maintaining security of the other,[80] and a handful of maniples seconded from each of the other three to form the nucleus of a fourth when population, resources and strategic requirements permit. Most of those currently being deployed among the off-world facilities.'

'And therefore of no immediate concern,' Vorspung put in, oblivious to the glances exchanged by Norgard, Morie and I, all three of us under no such illusion. In my book, out of sight meant very much in mind, unless you were willing to risk a shot in the back.

'I would appreciate the details of their disposition,' Morie said, and I nodded my agreement, certain that the Reclaimers would be drawing up contingency plans to neutralise every skitarii unit on the planet with a higher threat rating than latrine orderly[81] before the day was out.

---

80  *Which was less populated, with correspondingly fewer installations to secure.*

81  *Not a military specialty much in demand among the forces of the Adeptus Mechanicus, it must be said.*

'By all means,' Norgard said, no doubt intending to do precisely the same thing in case, against all likelihood, the Reclaimers turned out to be infested with turncoats after all.

As we were shortly to discover, though, the threat was far more insidious, deeply hidden and dangerous than any gene-stealer cult could possibly be.

*Editorial note:*

*Since one of the many lacunae in his memoirs during which nothing happened that Cain deems worthy of recording, at least from his singularly self-centred perspective, now occurs, this seems as good a time as any to interpolate another, more dispassionate, assessment.*

From *In Blackest Night: The Millennial Wars Appraised*, by Ayjaepi Clothier, 127.M42.

Though Commissar Cain and his allies soon became aware of the presence of a hidden enemy on Eucopia, thanks to a botched assassination attempt, their initial efforts to uncover and eliminate the threat were far from successful. Their plans were meticulous, and followed through with all the efficiency expected from the Adeptus Mechanicus, but no trace of the genestealer infestation they had at first suspected was ever found.

Perhaps emboldened by the lack of an effective response, the true conspirators risked moving more openly against the

Imperium – an act which, with hindsight, may well have precipitated their own downfall.

# TWELVE

As I'd expected, but never quite dared to hope, everyone at the Reclaimers' citadel turned out to be completely free of taint, which was the one piece of good news I got that week. Morie's message was, of course, both cryptic and brief, since there was no telling who among the thousands of tech-priests in the Nexus might be capable of intercepting it,[82] or might be a part of the shadowy cabal working so diligently against us, but it left me comfortably reassured that the Chapter holding was a potentially safe refuge should I require one.

Which, nice as it was, left me no further forward in my commission from Zyvan. Vorspung and I had conferred on a few occasions, as discreetly as we could, but of necessity our discussions were brief, and as casual seeming as we could contrive. Even for someone as habitually paranoid as I am,

---

82   *Most of them, probably, though few would have any interest in doing so.*

the possibility that any one of the red-robed acolytes of the Martian deity surrounding us could be eavesdropping, or, rather more pertinently from my point of view, preparing to slip a knife between my ribs, was profoundly disturbing; all the more so the longer it took for the other boot to fail to drop.

So, to put it mildly, I was feeling more than a little wary as Jurgen and I set out for the proving grounds, where the weapons produced by the manufactories of Eucopia were tried out before being shipped to whichever battlefront most desperately needed them.[83] Since they were wide open areas of nothing at all, existing solely for their topography to be rearranged by heavy weapons fire, Norgard's skitarii maintained a small facility there to which only they had access. Not quite as secure as the Chapter holding, but a great deal more so than the Nexus, which probably accounted for the feeling of relief which swept over me the moment I got word that it was time to set off.

'Thought you'd rather keep your feet on the ground this time, sir,' Jurgen said, swinging himself up into the cab of the cargo-8 Ridgehauler he'd evidently found unattended in a loading bay somewhere.

'You thought right,' I assured him, with an appreciative glance at the angular cab and the blocky cargo compartment behind it. Dented and rust-streaked by long, hard use, the metal bodywork looked thick and robust enough to shrug off a las-bolt or two, and might even be proof against the odd bolter round; in the absence of a Salamander[84] the vehicle

---

83   *Or, equally likely, were mislabelled, dumped in storage facilities and forgotten about, or sent to the wrong system entirely, with all the logistical expertise the Munitorum is famous for.*

84   *Cain's preferred mode of transport, the light scout vehicle having*

would get us where we needed to go in relative safety. Not that I wouldn't have appreciated something with a heavy weapon mount as well, but I suppose that might have been a bit of a giveaway if anyone really was watching me for signs that their plot had been rumbled.

Using the tread of a tyre which rose as high as my sash for a foothold I clambered in through the passenger door, which swung closed behind me with the reassuring sigh of an airtight seal, and fastened the crash webbing of the seat nearest to it. There were three in all, the centre one occupied by Jurgen's personal weapons, and, Jurgen being Jurgen, a large flask of tanna and a scattering of ration packs, the contents of one of which had already been converted into a scattering of crumbs adhering to his facial hair.[85] Everything had been lashed into place by the seat restraints, although his lasgun was, as always, close enough to the driving seat for him to lay a hand on in a heartbeat. Which left the butt of the melta he'd neglected to return to stores several decades ago nudging me rather uncomfortably in the ribs, until I unclipped and restowed it with the stock resting in the footwell next to my leg. As I did so, I raised an enquiring eyebrow.

'Do you really think you'll need this?'

---

*both a powerful enough engine to outrun most trouble and sufficient armour to offer some protection against the rest.*

85 *Jurgen always maintained that he had a medicae dispensation to grow a beard, due to his comprehensive collection of skin diseases – a claim no Imperial Guard officer ever appears to have disputed, either because of his ambiguous status as a commissarial aide, the fact that the random eruptions of facial hair between patches of psoriasis seldom formed anything cohesive enough to be described as a beard in any case, or understandable apprehension about what the application of a razor might reveal.*

Jurgen shrugged. 'If there are 'stealers about,' he said, 'it'd
be just our luck to run into the bloody patriarch.' Sure I was
settled, he fired up the engine, and started us rolling towards
the massive doors of the Titan-sized airlock[86] ahead of us.
'And I'm not leaving it lying around where some cogboy
might decide he needs some spare parts.'

'Good points,' I agreed, unable to fault his logic on either
count. I leant forward a little as the inner doors ground
closed behind us and the outer ones began to part, revealing a slowly growing sliver of the outside world. 'Let's hope
this trip's a bit less eventful than the last one.'

Jurgen shrugged again. 'It'll take a bit longer,' he said, 'but
I can live with that.'

As could I. Vorspung had, naturally, offered me the use of
another aircar, which I'd politely declined, as my aide and
I had both had more than enough of that particular mode
of transportation to be going on with – though possibly for
different reasons. The Ridgehauler would be slower, but I
trusted Jurgen to handle its controls a good deal more competently than I could pilot an aircar, and the simple, robust
promethium engine was operated entirely by mechanical
linkages – nothing a hidden cultist could exploit remotely
to blow us to pieces or divert us off the edge of a cliff. The
unexpected detonation of our old flyer was still being officially treated as a regrettable accident, despite none of its
putative passengers believing that for a moment. Norgard's
diligent enquiries had failed to find a shred of evidence as to
who might have been responsible for an act of sabotage – or,
for that matter, how they might have gone about it. I made

---

86  *Something of an exaggeration, since even the largest mineral
harvester would barely have come up to the knees of a Warhound, let
alone something like a Reaver.*

the mistake of asking only once, finding not a syllable of the answer intelligible.

So, as the harsh sunlight of Eucopia fell on us through the windscreen, I found my spirits lifting, despite the prospect of some time to come in a pressurised cabin in close proximity to Jurgen. The Nexus still loomed over us, but at least I was no longer surrounded by augmetically enhanced potential assassins, quite possibly capable of whistling up a concealed genestealer or two into the bargain. As we edged out of the shadow of the gargantuan building, it dawned on me that this was the first time I'd seen the barren landscape of Eucopia from ground level, and I found myself scanning it as much from simple curiosity as wary anticipation of a potential threat.

The transitway we joined was broad and relatively smooth, although several decades of use had eroded the rockcrete surface in places – not enough to impede our progress, but sufficient to send an occasional jolt through the suspension and the worn seat I occupied. Our elevated position in the cab afforded us an impressive view of our surroundings, and the other traffic sharing the road with us: utility haulers like ours, for the most part, crewed by relatively unaugmented lay brethren or indentured artisans, who glanced at us with varying expressions of indifference, surprise or hostility (in a few cases all three as Jurgen overtook slower-moving vehicles with his usual disdain for anything in the immediate vicinity which might technically have had the right of way). Occasionally larger vehicles, laden with prefabricated components for something under construction elsewhere, or cargoes shrouded in tarpaulins which somehow managed to look both quotidian and vaguely threatening, loomed up out of the dust clouds raised by every passing conveyance only to vanish again as quickly as they'd appeared.

The dust, I soon realised, was ubiquitous. Though too tenuous to breathe, the atmosphere was thick enough for winds to blow, and with no rain to wash them out of the air the fine particulates abraded from the mountains by aeons of erosion drifted everywhere, raised from wherever they'd settled by the passage of every passing lorry. As Jurgen swung us off the main road, however, onto the less travelled one leading to our eventual destination, the haze began to clear. The only dust plume now visible was the one we were raising ourselves. Trying not to reflect that this would make us a sitting target for anyone intent on ambush, I turned my head to look directly out of the passenger side window.[87]

The landscape was just as barren as it had appeared from our descending shuttle, the narrow road we followed threading its way through a broken panorama of jutting outcrops and steep ravines, the plains we'd flown over proving to be riven with fissures and scattered boulders. I was put in mind of a sun-baked lake bed, though this world had never seen open water, and likely never would; however successful the terraforming effort eventually became, the Adeptus Mechanicus would be loath to render any of its resources more difficult to extract by inundating them. On several occasions we crossed surprisingly deep canyons on bridges barely wide enough to accommodate our vehicle. True to form, Jurgen never slowed, steering us between uncomfortably fragile-seeming guard rails centimetres from our wheels with his usual insouciance. Knowing better than to show any signs of concern, which would only leave him feeling aggrieved at the implied slur on his competence, I glanced

---

87 *Always a good idea when in an enclosed vehicle with Jurgen in the driving seat.*

down into their shadowed depths, where dust, driven by the winds channelled through them, flowed like arid streams, obscuring whatever lay beneath.

'Looks like company, sir,' Jurgen said at last, pointing through the windscreen at a dust plume heading directly towards us.

I squinted, trying to discern the outline of the shapes moving inside it. They seemed vaguely familiar, though somehow wrong. 'Sentinels?' I asked, not quite sure whether I could trust my eyes or not.

'Looks like it,' Jurgen agreed. 'But not like any I've seen before.'

As my view of the approaching walkers became clearer within their cloud of enveloping dust, I found myself forced to agree. For one thing they moved more fluidly than any Astra Militarum equivalent I'd ever seen, or even a t'au battle-suit come to that; only the wraithbone constructs of the aeldari surpassed their apparently effortless locomotion. For another, they seemed far more lightly armoured. Through the thinning murk I could make out what I first assumed was a pilot sitting in an open cockpit embedded in the thing's torso, only realising my mistake[88] as the trio of ambulatory weapons platforms fell into formation around us. A gunner, perched somewhat precariously on top in what looked remarkably like a Rough Rider's saddle, behind a pair of autocannons, waved a casual greeting. I waved back, concealing a sudden flare of unease. All the skitarii at the proving

---

88  *Adeptus Mechanicus walkers, generally dubbed 'Ironstriders' for reasons which ought to be obvious given the average tech-priest's lack of imagination, have a servitor embedded in their bodywork to take care of the routine piloting chores, allowing the exposed gunner riding them to be shot by the enemy as efficiently as possible.*

grounds had been tested and cleared, but even so, their sudden appearance was unnerving.

'That must be it,' Jurgen said, pointing to an outcrop in the distance too smooth and regular in its dimensions to be a natural formation.

'Indeed it must,' I agreed, and keyed my comm-bead to the frequency Norgard had instructed me to use. 'Approaching your outer perimeter, Bunker One. ETA…' I glanced at my aide, who shrugged.

'About ten minutes, sir. If this bucket of bolts doesn't get in our way too much.' He gestured, somewhat derisively, at the walker jogging ahead of us; as if aware of his comment, it moved off the carriageway, continuing to parallel it without any diminution of speed.

'Seven minutes,' I said, eliciting the faint smile from my aide I'd expected in response. As I'd anticipated, he seized on the implied challenge eagerly, accelerating to a speed that would no doubt have induced apoplexy in the engineer normally assigned to minister to the truck he was driving. 'And thanks for the escort.'

'*Escort?*' There was no mistaking the tone of puzzlement in the voice of whoever was on the other end of the vox-link. '*No escort was dispatched.*'

'Turn!' I yelled, and Jurgen took me at my word, yanking the wheel hard over an instant before both the Striders behind us opened fire. A blizzard of tracer rounds, all the more intimidating for the knowledge that each one was accompanied by four times as many[89] equally lethal companions we couldn't see, howled through the space we'd

---

89   *Assuming skitarii followed the same loading practice as the Adeptus Astartes and the Imperial Guard.*

so recently vacated. I just had time to brace myself against the door frame before the entire hauler shook, the clang of impact reverberating through the empty cargo compartment behind us like a cathedral bell, as Jurgen rammed the walker which had been pacing us.

It staggered sideways, the whine of its gyros rising to a pitch which seemed to strip the enamel from my teeth even through the bodywork of our truck, its rider clinging to his weapon mount for dear life. I just had time to hope he'd fall and break his augmetically enhanced neck before the servitor controlling its systems made the appropriate corrections, and the wretched mechanism regained its equilibrium. The rider didn't exactly glare at us, what with his face being composed almost entirely of metal and all, but the way he crouched over the weapon mount and lined up a second salvo was eloquent enough: he really didn't like us. He triggered both autocannons, but we were too close for him to be able to target the cab, even though he'd depressed the barrels about as far as they could go. The rounds howled just over our heads, and the cathedral bell tolled again as they ripped through the bulkier cargo compartment behind us.

'*Commissar.*' Norgard's voice echoed in my vox-bead. '*What's going on?*'

'We're under attack,' I told her. 'Three walkers with autocannons.'

'*Reinforcements have been dispatched,*' she assured me.

'They'll be too late,' I said flatly. The numbers spoke for themselves. We were at least five minutes out from the bunker, even at the speed Jurgen could probably wring out of the vehicle we'd commandeered, which meant whatever forces Norgard had sent to help us would take at least that long to get to where we were. Even if, by some miracle, we were able to keep moving flat out and meet them halfway, that was still two to three minutes I doubted very strongly that we had. One good burst from any of the autocannons surrounding us would rip our truck apart like a ration pack spotted by Jurgen, and even he couldn't evade all three walkers for that long. The cab juddered and shook as the abused suspension bounced over the uneven ground, and I silently blessed whichever of the saints had guided Jurgen to an off-road vehicle.

'Hold on, sir,' Jurgen said, as though I hadn't been whitening my knuckles already, and swung the wheel again. As before he timed it to a nicety, the barrage of fire from the two walkers behind us ripping through the air where we no longer were. To my elated surprise they clipped the third one, still turning to try to follow us, blowing out one of its knee joints. It went down hard, still kicking, raising a cloud of dust from the hammering of its single functional leg against the ground.

'Well done,' I said grimly. We'd been damned lucky, that was for sure, but I was all too aware that our luck wouldn't last. Right on cue the entire truck shook as a renewed barrage slammed into the rear compartment. A faint, ominous hissing sound made itself heard over the cacophony of impacting cannon rounds, the roaring of our overstressed engine and the juddering rattle of our abused suspension.

'Cabin breach,' Jurgen remarked, as though I hadn't been able to work that out for myself. A compartment in the dashboard, surrounded by red and yellow chevrons, popped open to reveal a couple of breather masks, and I grabbed the nearest. Instinct demanded that I don it myself, but I overrode the impulse with a positively Macharian act of will, holding it out to Jurgen instead; if he passed out at the controls of the hurtling vehicle, neither of us would survive in any case. He glanced at it and nodded. 'Just a moment, sir. Bit busy.'

He slammed the brake on, and the loudest *clang* yet reverberated through the abused cargo compartment, even attenuated as it was by the thinning atmosphere in the cab. The truck lurched and bounced forward, almost pitching me through the windscreen, then my aide accelerated again.

'Thank you, sir.' He took the mask and donned it one-handed, the other continuing to work the controls. 'You might want to hold on for this bit.'

Though the impulse to make a grab for the other breather was almost overwhelming, my lungs beginning to labour as they sucked at the thinning air in the cab, I took the hint and followed his suggestion – decades of being driven by Jurgen made hanging on and hoping for the best pretty much second nature in this sort of situation, in any case. The cargo-8 lurched again, spinning almost on the spot, to face more or less back in the direction we'd come from. Jurgen kicked up a gear, and we began accelerating towards the road we'd bounced off a moment or two before.

The nearest of the walkers was marching steadily away from us, the servitor controlling it reduced to a mangled mess of flesh and augmetic components by the impact, still stirring feebly in an attempt to steer the thing. The gunner perched on top of it was working feverishly to try bringing his auto-cannons to bear, but couldn't swivel it far enough, blocked by his own body from being able to target us. Serves him right, I thought, rummaging for the second breather unit through the faint wisps of grey fog beginning to cloud my vision. My fingers closed on it, and after a second or two of fumbling with the fastenings, I felt my lungs inflate again.

I glanced round, looking for the enemy. 'Two down,' I said, more in hope than expectation.

'Looks that way,' Jurgen agreed, bouncing us back onto the carriageway. The damaged walker was still plodding relentlessly towards the horizon, but looked unlikely to make it that far, on account of the ravine between us and the proving grounds, over which a long, narrow bridge soared. To my surprise the other one was pacing its fellow rather than coming after us, but under the circumstances I'd take whatever respite the Emperor was kind enough to throw in our direction.

'What's he doing?' I wondered aloud, the gunner on the sole undamaged Strider leaning towards the other, reaching out a hand to his compatriot. Their hands touched, clasped, and the gunner of the walker plodding blindly towards the precipice stood up in his saddle.

'He's not going to make it,' Jurgen opined, as the gunner, red robes flapping around him as he rose from behind the shelter of the autocannons, made a stumbling jump towards the other walker. He almost did, but just as he took off, the Strider's leading foot came down hard on the edge of the cliff. Rock and sand gave way, and the plodding mechanism pitched forward, tearing his hand from the other skitarius' grasp.

As the stricken Strider toppled into the depths, its erstwhile rider plunged after it, scrabbling desperately at the lip of the precipice for traction as he slid downwards, arresting his fall at the last possible moment.

Jurgen shrugged. 'My mistake.'

The surviving Strider turned, apparently just on the brink of following its crippled fellow, and its foot slammed down on the struggling gunner. Blood and lubricants sprayed the sand, and then he was gone, following his mount down into the depths.

Jurgen and I winced in unison, then turned our attention to the war machine sprinting vengefully towards us.

'Fast would be good,' I remarked, and Jurgen nodded, the overstressed engine whining pitifully as he fought to wrench a few more kilometres an hour out of it. We were almost at the bridge now, and rising dust in the distance indicated that Norgard's promised reinforcements were on their way, but another burst of autocannon fire from our persistent pursuer soon put paid to any hope I might have been beginning to feel that they'd be with us in time.

'Fast it is, sir,' Jurgen agreed, jinking just in time to send the shots wild, where they chewed up the ground, adding a fresh flurry to the pall of dust hanging in the air around us.

'Frak this,' I said, popping the door and squirming around in my seat as far as I could while still constricted by the crash webbing. I could have got a better angle on the mechanism sprinting after us if I'd unfastened it, of course, but given the speed we were going and the violence of Jurgen's evasive manoeuvres I'd almost certainly be pitched out of the truck within seconds if I tried. I squinted through the miniature dust storm being whirled up by our progress, and cracked off a couple of shots from my laspistol, which whined off into the distance in the general direction of the enemy without any discernible effect.

'Just coming up on the bridge, sir,' Jurgen assured me, as another fusillade of autocannon rounds ripped into our vehicle, which leapt and juddered as though being electrocuted. Only the steady grip of my augmetic fingers kept me from losing the laspistol, and I clutched at it convulsively, thanking the Throne for the solidity of the seat restraints. Our suspension had evidently taken some damage, which I suppose was hardly surprising under the circumstances, as the shuddering through the chassis continued, and Jurgen was wrestling with the steering wheel, which seemed determined to rip itself out of his hands. His brow furrowed. 'Can you smell something?'

'Promethium!' I yelled back, after a glance behind us. The last burst of autocannon fire had ruptured our fuel tank, and a slick of it was spreading out behind us, turning the dust into thick, foul-smelling porridge. If a tracer round hit us now, we'd go up in a fireball Norgard would be able to see from her command bunker. 'Time we were leaving!'

'Very good, sir,' Jurgen said, as though I'd simply asked for another bowl of tanna. 'I'll slow down a bit.' Which we didn't exactly have a choice about, if we wanted to avoid breaking our necks when we made a jump for it. He slammed on the brakes, yanking the wheel hard around as he did so. The lorry slewed sideways across the road, began to tilt, then, just as I was bracing myself for it to fall over entirely, wobbled back to slam its wheels hard down on the transitway, blocking the approach to the bridge.

'Nicely done,' I complimented Jurgen, smacking the quick release of the crash restraint as I did so, and cracking off a few more shots in the direction of the war machine still charging down on us. This time my aim was a bit better, a couple actually impacting against the bodywork, but doing no discernible damage as they did so. They achieved what I set out to do, though: the gunner ducked back behind his gun shield, which kept him occupied for the few brief seconds we needed to bail out. Jurgen was already out of the driver's door, his lasgun in his hands, and I made to follow him, squirming across the intervening seats as he opened up on full-auto from behind the cover of our wounded transport. Finding the melta getting in my way, I seized it and thrust it ahead of me as I dived out of the open driver's door.

'Good idea, sir,' Jurgen said, slinging his lasgun and taking the weapon from me as I emerged. 'That'll give the rust-licker something to think about.'

'And us,' I said, with an expansive wave at the pool of promethium still spreading from our ruptured fuel tanks. 'One spark here and we're done for.' I gestured towards the bridge behind us. 'Just run.'

To his credit, Jurgen needed no further urging, falling in behind me as I sprinted for the viaduct. We were only a score or so metres from it, and the abyss it spanned, and I glanced up at the approaching dust cloud in the distance. Norgard's reinforcements were so close now I could distinguish moving dots within the murk. For a moment I dared to entertain the hope that the rogue unit behind us would see the game was up and make a run for it, but I'd underestimated the single-minded tenacity of the augmetically enhanced. No sooner had the thought occurred to me than another burst of autocannon fire chewed up the ground around us.

'Down!' I yelled, fitting the action to the word. Trying to cross the bridge would be suicidal, the flat decking offering no cover at all, but there were rockcrete piers at either end, anchoring the structure to the solid ground on both sides of the chasm. Jurgen and I scurried behind the nearest, throwing ourselves flat as a fresh fusillade of autocannon rounds ripped through the air. The shells gouged craters into the rockcrete in front of us, so close I felt my eyes stinging from the pulverised residue.

'Come on then,' Jurgen muttered, adding a couple of orkish oaths for good measure, as he snuggled the stock of the melta into his shoulder. The walker had reached the abandoned truck by now, mostly hidden by the mangled bodywork, its rider appearing to bob up and down behind the wreck like a target in a fairground shooting gallery. Now I'd got a good look at our erstwhile transport, I was astonished it had made it as far as it had – it resembled nothing so much as a wheeled colander, the metalwork of its cargo compartment ripped and shredded. Fortunately there seemed to be some cargo still left in the back, which Jurgen had apparently missed in the course of acquiring it, and which had absorbed a lot of the incoming fire. What it might have been before the Striders started using it for target practice was anybody's guess, but, I supposed, it accounted for the fact that we were still here at all. Without the protection it offered, the cab would almost certainly have been penetrated, which would have done my aide and I no favours whatsoever.

'Steady,' I cautioned, quite unnecessarily given the number of times we'd been in situations like this over the decades, but Jurgen didn't seem to resent my interest, if he even noticed it at all, simply slowing his breathing and tightening his finger almost imperceptibly on the trigger. 'Wait for it to move into the open.' I had no doubt that it would, the rider circling wide to get a clear shot at us, without the wreckage intervening.

I was right. Emboldened by our lack of response, and likely thinking we had nothing to defend ourselves with apart from our lasweapons, which had so far failed to have any effect on the Strider's armour plate, the rider directed it into the open with an almost casual air, not even bothering to put down a bit of suppressive fire to keep us pinned. Not that I could blame him for that; with the cliff edge right behind us we had nowhere else to go in any case, and moving into the open ourselves would be instantly fatal. He probably thought he had all the time in the galaxy to line up a killing shot, so why hurry?

'Cocky gretchin-fondler,' Jurgen said, and squeezed the trigger. Forewarned, I closed my eyes against the weapon's actinic glare, which, as ever, punched through my eyelids, leaving vivid green after-images dancing across my retinas when I opened them again. He'd aimed for the servitor, clearly visible dangling from the thing's chest like a monstrous infant in a parental baby sling,[90] reducing it instantly to charred meat and shards of fused mechanica. The Strider staggered, now bereft of even the most rudimentary direction; bizarrely, though, it continued to trot towards us, wavering slightly from side to side like a trooper returning to barracks after a two-day bar crawl. To my great relief the gunner seemed too preoccupied with hanging on to be able to shoot at us again. His resultant contortions meant he was no longer completely protected behind his gun shield, though, so I lined up a shot with my laspistol, hoping I'd be able to get in a lucky hit before he regained his balance.

Then I had a better idea, and switched aim at the last minute to send the las-bolt straight into the wreckage of our gallant cargo-8. The vapour rising from the spilled promethium erupted in a fireball, ignited by the spark of impact.

The battered truck converted itself instantly into a more than serviceable bomb, the smaller fragments of bodywork

---

90  *Although, according to the official records, he left no known descendants, Cain occasionally employs turns of phrase which suggest he wasn't entirely unfamiliar with the existence of small children – possibly a result of the time he spent as the regimental commissar of the Valhallan 597th, a mixed-gender regiment, where it's safe to assume that human nature resulted in the inevitable ensuing welfare issues crossing his desk from time to time.*

becoming a lethal blizzard of shrapnel, while the larger pieces of wreckage battered the staggering mechanism like a pugilist's fists. The gunner's flapping robes caught fire, although I suppose that didn't inconvenience him too much considering his metal to flesh ratio, the flickering flames appearing like highlights on the russet weave. After a few more frantic attempts to cling to his mount, the shockwave from the blast pitched him to the blazing sand beneath, where he vanished from our sight among the flames.

'That's right, run away,' Jurgen muttered, though that was probably the last thing on our assailant's mind. As his erstwhile mount waddled mindlessly over the cliff edge, joining its fellow in the canyon below in a cacophony of rending metal and a plume of smoke, the renegade skitarius staggered from the depths of the fireball, the lenses of his optical implants glowing a dull, vengeful red (although I suppose that just might have been the reflection of the flames). He plodded determinedly towards us, malfunctioning mechanica embedded in charred and blackened flesh sparking erratically, and I found myself grateful for the breather mask, which blocked the inevitable stench. Throne alone knew what he expected to achieve by taking us on unarmed,[91] but he never got the chance. Jurgen triggered the melta again, reducing most of our would-be assailant to greasy vapour, and staring at the steaming residue with undisguised contempt. 'Some people just can't take a hint.'

'Well, he got it in the end,' I said, getting cautiously to my feet. A shadow swept over us, and I raised my sidearm again, tracking the target, before relaxing with a loud exhalation

---

91   *Of course he may not have been, many skitarii being equipped with implanted weaponry to enhance their effectiveness in close combat.*

of relief. A speeder in the distinctive yellow-and-white liv-ery of the Reclaimers was banking sharply round the plume of smoke rising lazily from the wreckage of the truck, and a moment later grounded nearby in a cloud of dust which mingled with it in an excessively eye-watering fashion. The pilot waved as his boots hit the sand, his bolter at the ready, even though there was no further sign of a threat in our immediate vicinity. 'Brother-sergeant. This is an unexpected pleasure.'

'For me as well,' Morie rejoined. 'I expected you to be dead by now.'

'So did he.' Jurgen lifted his breather just long enough to spit, surprisingly accurately, at the sizzling remains of our would-be murderer.

'Life's full of little disappointments,' I said, turning back to Morie. Another speeder was circling overhead, and a yellow-and-white Rhino rumbling towards us across the bridge, and I felt reasonably safe in relaxing my guard a little now. 'What the hell was that all about?'

'Some of the skitarii have mutinied,' he replied soberly. 'Why, we have no idea.'

*Editorial Note:*

*Though the reason soon became clear enough, it was not one which the wider galaxy needed to know. Hence the following, which was hastily disseminated among the general populace of Eucopia, in a variety of forms. The binharic files exchanged among the tech-priests will, of course, be incomprehensible to most of my readers, not to mention myself, so I've settled on this, fairly typical, iteration, intended for the largely unaugmented man-ufactory workforce.*

From the *Eucopian Annual Almanac*, printsheet edition, 993. M41.

The Proving Grounds Massacre, 487.992.M41

Tragedy struck on this date, when scheduled training exercises between the Eucopian skitarii and an off-world delegation of the Reclaimers Adeptus Astartes Chapter resulted in several deaths due to the erroneous issuing of live ammunition to the participants. How the wrong information was delivered is still under review, although the mistaken installation of an unconsecrated relay in the data network is believed to have been responsible. Altogether, twenty-seven skitarii perished before the mistake could be rectified, and several Space Marines are reported to have sustained minor cuts and bruising in the unfortunate encounter. Brother-Sergeant Morie, the senior representative of the Reclaimers present, expressed his regret, and reaffirmed the pact of amity between his Chapter and the Adeptus Mechanicus.

> *Rather more illuminating is this account, from Tysus ap Cathode, a junior tech-priest specialising in rituals of communication, who was on duty in Norgard's command centre at the time of the incident. Fortunately his testimony was given to the subsequent enquiry in Gothic, as a courtesy to the Reclaimers' observer, and is therefore comprehensible to the rest of us.*

At 487.23.65 I observed an anomalous data pulse in the skitarii command net, notified my task coordinator in accordance with standard procedure, and began routine diagnostic measures in an attempt to isolate the cause. Such incidents are not uncommon, and usually due to misrouted messages or systems failure in redundant relays.

On closer examination the data pulse appeared encrypted, to a level beyond my ability to decipher, so I forwarded my findings to the appropriate authorities and returned to work.

Shortly thereafter Commissar Cain reported his approach, and subsequently came under attack from renegade Ironstriders. At the same time Brother-Sergeant Morie of the Reclaimers was fired upon by a squad of skitarii rangers assigned to perimeter defence. The brother-sergeant repelled the attack, aided by several of his brethren and a second squad of skitarii, who had witnessed this act of treachery and immediately come to his aid.

Unable to determine which of her subordinates could be trusted, Praetor Norgard ordered all skitarii in the proving grounds to stand down at once, placing the entire installation under the jurisdiction of the Reclaimers until the matter could be resolved. This triggered a more widespread mutiny, as other renegade units turned on their clade mates and the visiting Space Marines, who, between them, swiftly neutralised the threat.

I have no idea why the anomalous signal had the effect it did, but thank the Omnissiah that it affected so few of the garrison here. Though it is hardly my place to do so, I would urge great caution in the analysis of its datanomes, as it may continue to exert a baleful influence on those assigned to study it.

# THIRTEEN

'Bit of a mess,' Jurgen remarked, peering through one of the firing ports as the Rhino rumbled into the command centre of the proving grounds. I nodded, glancing down at him from my perch in the command cupola; an odd place to elect to ride, you may think, if you've read much of my previous ramblings, and, truth to tell, the temptation to stay securely behind the protection of the vehicle's armour plate was very strong. However, as I'd observed before when serving with Space Marines, secure as they were, Astartes Rhinos weren't exactly comfortable for the genetically unmodified. The solid metal benches were too high for humans of normal stature, which left Jurgen and I sitting with our feet dangling like children on adult-sized seats, and neither soundproofing nor much in the way of suspension seemed to have been high on the list of design priorities. Not to mention the fact that although I've never gone looking for trouble, I've always felt happier being able to see it coming, which makes it so much easier to hide until it goes away again.

'It is,' I agreed, thankful for the reassuring bulk of the gunner next to me, whose armour had acquired a mottled coating of the ubiquitous dust during his vigil, but who'd kept the twin barrels of his storm bolter clean enough to have earned a grudging nod of approval from even the most fastidious of Imperial Guard gunnery sergeants. Evidence of heavy fighting could be seen everywhere, not least the scattered bodies of dead skitarii, whose robes were no longer red entirely from their dye. Living ones were moving around recovering the cadavers, darting quick, suspicious glances at any other squads they encountered, but, so far at least, no one seemed jumpy enough to grab a weapon. Which of these corpses had been traitors and which ones loyal I hadn't a clue; nor, if I'm honest, did I care. It was the Emperor's job to sort them out now, and I wished Him joy of it.

The main command bunker stood out clearly from the rest of the buildings, both by its size and solidity and the relative lack of damage it had sustained. It was, of course, bearing the stigmata of heavy weapons fire, pockmarks the size of my head disfiguring the rockcrete facade, and the ubiquitous votive cogwheels plastered on every available surface, but the 'crete was evidently thick and dense enough not to have been breached. The smaller structures surrounding it, barrack blocks, workshops and storage sheds for the most part, had fared less well, looking considerably better ventilated than they had been hitherto. A few had even been reduced to little more than tumbled ruins, and fires still smouldered here and there, sending thick plumes of smoke to mingle with the ubiquitous dust clouds.

To my faint surprise, although I have no idea why that should have been given I was riding in one of their vehicles, I spotted several Space Marines standing sentry watch around the compound, no doubt keeping a close eye on the skitarii still upright in case any more harboured thoughts of sedition – though bearing in mind the firepower the Reclaimers were carrying, it would have been a very foolish traitor indeed who'd have reached for a weapon anywhere within their line of sight. There were even a handful of Terminators plodding about, brandishing storm bolters and power swords, one with an additional pair of shoulder-mounted missile racks which would have made even a Baneblade commander think twice about taking him on.

'You seem to have everything under control,' I voxed, as Morie swooped low over the trundling Rhino, and he took a hand off the speeder's controls for a moment to raise in response.

*'We have successfully secured the compound,'* he replied. *'Norgard thought it best to cede authority to us. At least until she can be sure which of her own men she can trust.'*

'Damn few of them at the moment I'll be bound,' I said, and the Space Marine sergeant laughed, without much humour.

*'I do not envy her,'* he agreed, banking around in a wide spiral, before grounding the speeder in front of a massive door in the side of the bunker, which began to grind open to admit the Rhino. The metal was almost as thick as the length of my forearm, although a determined effort seemed to have been made to crack it, judging by the blast and scorch marks marring its surface. That job would have taken a Titan, though, or at the very least a Demolisher or two; fortunately for all of us, except the mutineers I suppose, they'd lacked that kind of firepower. Which raised the question of what in the warp they thought they'd been playing at.

* * *

This was, of course, the main topic of conversation as soon as Morie, Norgard and I found ourselves alone. We were in an extravagantly secure conference room which had been diligently searched for listening devices by three separate teams of tech-priests, then again by a Techmarine from the Reclaimers in case one of the earlier search parties had planted something under the guise of looking for it. As I'd expected, it was as utilitarian as most rooms in an Adeptus Mechanicus facility, but even so I found it a little more comfortable than its counterpart in the Reclaimers' Chapter holding. The table and chairs were normal height, for one thing, and once Jurgen had obtained a couple of cushions from somewhere to mitigate the hardness of the plain metal seat, tolerable enough to spend as long sitting in as I fully expected our deliberations to take. The floor was carpeted in a plain russet weave, which had probably been chosen to evoke fond memories of their Martian home[92] in the acolytes of the Omnissiah, but which reminded me rather too much of the stained robes of their fallen fellows for comfort, while the inevitable icons of the Machine-God dominated the wall at the head of the room and its reflection in the polished metal table.

On the other hand, the samovar the Reclaimers had provided to ease the process of discussion during our earlier meeting in their holding was noticeable by its absence, a deprivation I resolved to face stoically, once fortified with a mug or two of recaff and a couple of blocks of soylens viridiens.

So, all in all, I was feeling quite positive by the time the thick steel door swung closed with a reassuring *thunk!*, Jurgen settling into a seat in the corridor outside, his melta across

---

92  *Which the vast majority of their order never actually saw for themselves.*

his lap and a ration bar in his hand, flanked by a couple of bolter-toting Space Marines who seemed vaguely bemused at his presence.

It was only then that something occurred to me which has no doubt struck you already, but please bear in mind that I'd recently been shot at, and until a few moments before had been in urgent need of a meal.

'What about Vorspung?' I asked. 'Is he all right?' The treacherous skitarii had certainly had it in for Morie and I, going to some considerable trouble to fail to kill us, and had clearly been keen to get at Norgard judging by the damage to the bunker I'd noticed on the way in, so it was a reasonable assumption that Vorspung was close to the top of their to-do list as well.

'On his way to the Chapter holding,' Morie assured me, 'in a Rhino with an escort of speeders. Purely as a precaution, of course.'

Norgard nodded. 'No attempt seems to have been made on his life, but he'll certainly be safer there than back at the Nexus.'

'Odd, that,' I remarked, 'given that he seems an obvious target.'

Norgard nodded again. 'Assuming he was one of the intended victims of the aircar and the Kastelan incidents. But seeing as both you and the brother-sergeant were targeted here, perhaps he would only have been collateral damage.'

'Or perhaps we're just lucky all the skitarii from the Nexus were moved here,' Morie demurred. 'If any had been left behind, a few of them might well have proved equally treacherous.'

'Indeed.' Norgard didn't exactly flinch at the brother-sergeant's choice of adjective, even the most militant of the Omnissiah's servants not being much given to displays of emotion, but I had no doubt it would have stung nonetheless. No commander in my experience would have taken such flagrant disloyalty by the troops under their command as anything other than a personal failing, even if exonerated by a subsequent court of enquiry, and there had hardly been time to even begin such a process. She must have been wondering if Morie and I still trusted her, which I'm bound to say I did, insofar as I ever trusted anyone apart from Jurgen;[93] after all, if Norgard had been allied with our unseen antagonists she would hardly have stood down the surviving skitarii and turned over command of the proving grounds to the Reclaimers. On the contrary, there were more than enough of them concentrated here to have put paid to the lot of us if the entire garrison had risen in open rebellion. 'We should certainly proceed on the assumption that all four of us have been targeted.'

'I concur,' Morie said, tactful, or more likely pragmatic, enough to conceal any reservations of his own he might still have been harbouring. 'The question now is by whom.'

I shrugged, equally at a loss. The obvious assumption we'd been working under, a genestealer cult, had been comprehensively ruled out: all the skitarii rebels had been genescanned and cleared before they arrived here. Which left another possibility I was loath to even think about, let alone voice.

'The Great Enemy?' Norgard said, a faint edge of hesitancy entering her voice. 'There are certain highly classified files...' She trailed off, in a most un-tech-priestly fashion, glancing uneasily at both of us.

'The Dark Mechanicum,' Morie said, looking as though he

---

93   *I might resent the implications of that, given our personal connection, if it weren't for the fact that I'm honestly grateful I never had to choose between it and my duty to the Emperor.*

was fighting the impulse to cleanse his mouth by spitting. 'We have encountered their abominations more than once.'

'As have I,' I said, trying not to recall any in too much detail. 'But only on the battlefield. They don't seem to go in much for infiltration and subversion.'

'That's true,' Norgard said. 'But they have allies who do. Who better to suborn a fledgling forge world and bend it to their foul purposes?'

'I've encountered Chaos cults before,' I said, immediately trying to suppress another flood of unwelcome memories, 'and in my experience they're far more indiscriminate in their methods.' Morie nodded, encouragingly, so I went on. 'They wouldn't have simply subverted a handful of skitarii. They try to spread their influence as widely as they can.' I turned to Norgard. 'How much contact would the average skitarius have with the wider civilian population?'

'Practically none,' she confirmed.

'Then it doesn't make sense,' I said. 'Chaos cults lure in as many members as they can, from as many walks of life as possible.' Which was something of an oversimplification, of course – I'd encountered small, discreet ones as well, but they'd all been embedded among the most influential citizens of a planet, like the court of the governor, or, at the other end of the social scale, gangsters and corrupt arbites,[94] who, in their own way, were equally well placed to gnaw away at the fabric of society. 'Your mutineers simply don't fit the pattern.'

'Could they have been part of a wider network regardless?'

---

94    *By which he means local law enforcers, rather than members of the Adeptus Arbites itself, a colloquial usage common among those who've spent their lives hopping from world to world; which, given the bewildering variety of local names for such functionaries, is hardly surprising.*

Morie asked, clearly reluctant to discount the possibility entirely.

'I don't see how,' I admitted, after another moment's thought. 'For one thing, the Ruinous Powers corrupt their victims by preying on innate human weaknesses, like hedonism, anger and fear. Hardly widespread traits on a planet full of tech-priests, whose reason overrides their passions.'

We both looked at Norgard, who nodded slowly. 'For the most part,' she conceded. 'But if it's not agents of the tyranids or the Ruinous Powers walking among us, then who?'

An uneasy silence settled across the conference room, which, eventually, I felt compelled to break.

'In all honesty?' I said. 'I haven't a clue.'

# FOURTEEN

Oddly enough, it was Vorspung who was to provide one, and a great deal more rapidly than any of us would have dared to hope.

'How sure are you about this?' I asked, my attention still partially on the data-slate he'd presented me with, before belatedly realising what I'd said, and instantly regretting my choice of words.

'As certain as all the variables allow,' he replied instantly. 'Given that the data was readily accessible, uncorrupted in any manner immediately discernible, even after careful examination for signs of' – his voxcoder stuttered almost imperceptibly over the heretical word – 'falsification, and my own capacities appear unimpaired, I would say that is so close to one hundred per cent that any statistical variation is too insignificant to be worth factoring in.'

'Then I am prepared to trust your judgement,' Morie said,

glancing up from a slate of his own, which was almost engulfed in the palm of his gauntlet. How he managed to manipulate the settings without crushing it was beyond me, although I supposed he must have had plenty of practice at that sort of thing over the years.[95]

'Me too,' I agreed, looking out at the westering sun, casting kilometre-long shadows across the plain beyond the Chapter holding as it slid inexorably behind the range of hills on the horizon. We were in a long gallery in one of the upper storeys of the main habitat. The room was walled with armourcrys, allowing natural light to flood onto a large mural depicting the Ascension of the Emperor, the sunset hues deepening the splashes of blood a trifle overdramatically in my opinion. The composition had been executed with rather more enthusiasm than flair, the fleeing Horus having more of the air of a man ducking out of a restaurant without paying than a thwarted regicide, while the facial expression of Him on Terra as He mounted the Golden Throne seemed to suggest that He'd found a hair in one of the canapes. I could hardly fault the piety of its artist, though, and the Reclaimers garrisoned here clearly found it of spiritual comfort, judging by the number of candle stubs and incense burners scattered around the place. I suppose, given their calling, it was quite remarkable that one of the battle-brothers had chosen to express himself in such a manner at all.[96]

---

95  *Personal equipment intended for the use of Space Marines is large and robust enough to be commensurate with their physiques, although their fine motor skills, as superior to those of common humanity as pretty much everything else about them, renders this not strictly necessary. Presumably this particular data-slate had been handed to him by Vorspung a few moments before.*

96  *Or perhaps not. Some Chapters place a high value on artistic endeavour, reasoning that a truly accomplished warrior should balance*

'I'm gratified to hear that,' Vorspung said, displaying as much smugness as a tech-priest ever did, which was rather more than they tended to realise.

I took another look at the slate, which continued to display a dense block of text interspersed with diagrams that meant nothing to me, and braced myself for the inevitable.

'Perhaps a short verbal summary?' I asked, uncomfortably aware that for most tech-priests the two concepts were completely incompatible. Morie evidently felt the same, because he nodded hastily.

'As concisely as possible, in the interests of operational efficiency,' he added.

'Concise, of course. Efficiency is to be commended in all matters,' Vorspung agreed. I half expected him to expound on the topic for several minutes before getting to the point, but it seemed Morie had found an effective way of prodding him in the right direction, because his voxcoder emitted the short burst of static I'd begun to equate with a preparatory clearing of the throat he no longer possessed. 'The origin of the signal which precipitated the erratic behaviour of the skitarii remains unknown, although forensic examination of the communications system continues.'

Morie nodded again. 'Praetor Norgard has already informed us of that.'

'She has?' I asked, as this was news to me. Morie looked faintly surprised.

'While you were in transit from the proving grounds.' A short hop in a lumbering cargo plane, which I'd spent asleep – partly because narrowly escaping death is surprisingly

---

*destructiveness and creativity to better serve the Emperor, or that it cultivates a more flexible mind, thus enhancing their effectiveness on the battlefield. Or possibly both.*

fatiguing, but mainly as a way of avoiding Jurgen's inevitable airsickness, which could easily become as distressing to anyone in the immediate vicinity as to Jurgen himself. 'Your aide assured me he would pass on the message at the earliest opportunity.'

'And I've no doubt he will,' I said. Jurgen had been even more subdued than usual on our arrival, due to some unexpected turbulence en route, hurrying off behind a stack of promethium drums as soon as the hangar bay pressurised. Under the circumstances I'd felt it prudent to afford him a few moments of privacy. Where he was now I had no idea, and rather suspected I didn't want to, particularly if anything edible, portable or both had gone missing in the hour or so since our arrival.

'Precautions are also being taken to harden the data systems against any further intrusion,' Vorspung went on, pointing to something on the slate that might have been a snowstorm but probably wasn't. I nodded, to give the impression I appreciated its significance.

'We discussed that before I left,' I said. Norgard hadn't been jittery, exactly, but had certainly been showing more signs of agitation than someone so metallic normally did. The idea that another tranche of her skitarii might suddenly turn traitor without warning could hardly have been comforting. 'She seemed to think that that, at least, was fairly straightforward.'

'But we still don't know what the data pulse contained,' Morie pointed out. 'Let alone why it had the effect it did.'

'Or why it only affected those particular skitarii,' I agreed. That, more than anything, was what seemed to have Norgard spooked, and I could well understand why. Until that particular question was answered, there was no guarantee that it might not happen again. 'There didn't seem to be any connection between them at all.' We'd already discovered that the affected skitarii had come from a number of different units, almost all of them grouped in single squads or the equivalent, and, prior to turning on their comrades, none of the formations had served with any of the others.

'Not an obvious one,' Vorspung replied, doing the *not-smug-at-all* thing again. 'But there is one factor they all have in common.' He fiddled with the data-slate again, pulling up a map of Eucopia's southern hemisphere. 'All have been assigned to the security detachment at one particular shrine in the last eight years.' A dot glowed red, marking its position.

'Metallum Majoris,' Morie said at once. 'A facility singularly failing to live up to its name.'

'Indeed,' Vorspung agreed. I must have looked baffled,[97] because he immediately went on to explain. 'The largest mining facility on Eucopia, and among the least productive. Which accounts, in some considerable measure, for the shortcomings you were sent here to investigate.'

'I see,' I said, a very large coin beginning to drop. 'And you didn't think to mention that when I arrived here?'

'I didn't see the need,' Vorspung said, in what looked like honest bewilderment. 'We inloaded all the relevant data to your slate when you visited the Nexus control chapel.'

'Of course you did,' I said, as though I'd been aware of the fact all along. 'But you'll appreciate things have been a little hectic since then, and I must confess to being far from skilled in the interpretation of such technical detail.' Both of which were true, and neatly skated over my complete failure to have even noticed the new documents.

---

97  *Or Vorspung simply couldn't overcome the impulse to elucidate common to members of his order, who seem to think the rest of us ill-informed at best, and little brighter than the average ork at worst.*

'I see.' If Vorspung was at all put out he failed to show it; indeed, if anything, he probably relished the opportunity to show off again. 'Then perhaps a short verbal summary?'

'By all means,' I said, bracing myself for an avalanche of tedious detail, but once again Morie came to my rescue.

'We have extensive hololithic representations of the mine and its surroundings,' he said, 'which Commissar Cain is at liberty to examine should he so wish.'

'Very helpful,' I agreed hastily.

'You do?' Vorspung looked faintly surprised, and perhaps a little irked. 'Why is that?'

'We curate information about every significant installation on Eucopia,' Morie said, looking almost equally surprised at the question. 'In case our aid is requested to assist in their defence.'

'I see.' Vorspung nodded, evidently satisfied by the half-truth. I had no doubt the Reclaimers had just as many contingency plans to assault them as well – certainly any competent Guard commander would have put those in place in case of treachery, insurrection or Chaotic intervention, and Space Marines hadn't earned their reputation as the finest warriors in the Imperium by being overly trusting. 'Then I shall give you just the, ah, bolt points, as you so succinctly phrase it,' he continued.

'That would be helpful,' I said, hoping he'd get to the point some time before my ship departed for Perlia.

'Very well.' Vorspung paused for a moment, as if deciding how much of his prepared data might reasonably be discarded in the interests of greater efficiency. 'The initial surveys of Eucopia identified unusually high concentrations of many important raw materials in unusual abundance in a relatively small area. The importance of the site being so great, rather more of our resources were diverted towards their extraction than would normally be the case.'

He hesitated again, presumably to make sure I'd grasped this, before continuing. I nodded encouragingly, hoping he'd get to some kind of point soon.

'In effect, the entire mining operation was given a degree of autonomy unusual in an undertaking of this nature.'

'Basically, you just picked a team and told them to get on with it,' I said, with a quick glance at Morie, who clearly liked this idea no more than I did.

'Succinctly put,' Vorspung agreed, 'but essentially accurate. Magos Tezler was afforded complete discretion over the allocation of resources and personnel to the project.'

'Magos Tezler being?' I enquired, as the unfamiliar name meant nothing to me.

'A mechwright of great potential,' Vorspung said, 'with a reputation for efficiency second to none. They seemed the obvious choice for the role, despite some reservations among the more senior tech-priests.'

'What kind of reservations?' I asked, liking less and less of this the more I heard.

'Tezler was relatively young and inexperienced,' Vorspung said. 'A few of our number were of the opinion that someone more familiar with the ways of the galaxy and the tenets of the Machine-God would be a better choice.'

'I see,' I said. It sounded to me like the old guard were resentful of being elbowed aside by someone up and coming, instead of seeing a prestigious position going to one of their own. A trait not exactly confined to the Adeptus Mechanicus. 'Would anyone have objected strongly enough to have ensured Tezler's efforts were not as successful as we might have hoped?'

Morie nodded, grasping the point I was trying to make tactfully, and verbally bulldozing through the niceties. 'In other words, instead of wasting our time looking for genestealers and heretics, we ought to be looking into petty-minded rivalries within your own hierarchy.'

To my thinly veiled astonishment, Vorspung seemed to be considering this seriously, instead of exploding with indignation as I would have expected.

'There are frictions between members of the order, of course,' he conceded, nodding thoughtfully, 'and I'm bound to say Tezler earthed more than their fair share of static from time to time – their views on the perfectibility of humanity in the image of the Omnissiah by extensive augmetic upgrades are not universally approved of by any means. But the balance of probabilities are quite heavily weighted against animosity towards Tezler's stewardship of Metallum Majoris being the motivating factor behind the incidents we've observed.'

'How so?' Morie asked, palpably reluctant to have a new and promising line of enquiry so abruptly curtailed.

'Because it would be in the interests of such a group to facilitate the commissar's investigation, ensuring that he discovered evidence of Tezler's culpability, possibly even by fabricating it if none actually existed. Attempting to assassinate him, and us, would be entirely counterproductive from their point of view.'

Morie nodded. 'Your reasoning appears sound,' he conceded grudgingly.

'It does,' Vorspung said, allowing himself a second or two of self-satisfaction, before resuming his habitual sober mien. 'Unfortunately, that leaves us no further forward.'

'We do still have one option,' I said, trying to ignore the

painted Emperor on the wall behind me, whose expression of prissy disapproval seemed to be warning me that this was a really bad idea. I turned to Morie. 'I'll need to take you up on your offer of a look at the files on Metallum Majoris, and arrange some transportation.'

'Of course.' He nodded. 'A personal inspection seems the best way forward.' He exchanged a glance with Vorspung. 'We both look forward to discussing your findings.'

'Assuming I make it back here,' I said, trying to sound as though I was joking, and not think too hard about Magos Clode, who, for all I knew, had made the same connection before disappearing from mortal ken. On the other hand, I had Jurgen to watch my back, and some of the finest warriors in the galaxy just a vox call away. Surely that would be enough to ensure my safety.

I took another glance at the Emperor behind me, and found myself hoping He'd come along too, although, as usual, I was sure He had far more pressing concerns than keeping my miserable hide unperforated.

I'd just have to take care of that for myself, then; no change there.

# FIFTEEN

If I'd had any expectations of what Metallum Majoris would be like, based on the hololiths I'd studied before leaving the Chapter holding, the reality far exceeded them. I knew that a vast pit had been excavated, several kilometres in extent, but the static image in the viewing tank had done little to prepare me for the sheer sense of scale the sight of the real thing evoked as our Thunderhawk dropped towards it from the upper fringes of the atmosphere. Despite my less than happy memories of travelling in the sturdy attack craft decades before, I'd accepted Morie's offer of transportation with alacrity; the short suborbital hop would minimise Jurgen's discomfort at being airborne, I'd be able to get a good look at the reality of what awaited us before we grounded, and, far from the least important consideration to my mind, the blocky gunship carried enough firepower to put a dent in a Titan.[98] If anyone at

---

98   *Maybe a very small one. If its void shields were down, and the entire crew had disembarked for a picnic. Then gone to sleep.*

the mine really was involved in skulduggery of some sort, the clear message that disembarking from a Space Marine flyer would send might just turn out to offer me more protection than a set of carapace armour. (Which, to be honest, I'd have donned under my greatcoat like a shot if there were any sets to be had this far from an Imperial Guard quartermaster, and if the damn stuff didn't chafe so much.)

'Pretty big hole,' Jurgen said as the pilot banked, bringing the greater part of the mine into view on the pict screen in front of us. My aide paled a little at the resulting sudden shift in our inner ears.

'Indeed,' I agreed, as much to distract him from his rebellious stomach as anything else. 'And busy.' Even from this altitude, the bottom of the pit was clearly seething with activity, hidden from view by the ubiquitous shifting dust. As we descended, however, I was able to discern vast shadows moving within it, no doubt the mineral harvesters scraping the crater incrementally deeper with every pass.

'*On final approach, commissar,*' the pilot voxed, his voice muffled a little by the thick ear defenders Jurgen and I wore over our comm-beads to protect us against the bellowing of the engines, which would otherwise have made the journey intolerable. Jurgen's response was inaudible, but I caught the gist of it well enough – the sooner we were back on terra firma, the better, so far as he was concerned. '*Switching to tactical view.*'

'Thank you,' I said, as the pict screen in front of us flickered and began to return auspex imagery overlaid on the visible environment. The gigantic harvesters thus revealed, gorging themselves on the floor of the quarry, were far from the only things kicking up the dust down there. Contact icons erupted like mirepox blisters all around them, tiny scurrying vehicles collecting the scraps left in the harvesters' wakes, or carrying out ancillary duties in their service, like a shoal of pilot fish around a marine leviathan. Even more of them were ranged about the walls of the quarry, which, as our descent continued, proved to be composed of innumerable terraces, connected by wide, ramped roadways along which traffic streamed in both directions. The near-vertical walls between the terraces were riddled with tunnel mouths, which, according to the holos Morie had shown me, disappeared into the depths of the earth, crossing and diverging from one another to produce a labyrinth of bewildering complexity.

'That must be the shrine,' Jurgen said, an air of unmistakable relief entering his voice at the prospect of getting his boots back on solid ground again. A jumble of buildings was beginning to appear out of the murk, occupying a broadened-out terrace a few levels above the quarry floor; as we approached it, and the lines became clearer, its true size gradually became apparent. By no means as vast as the Nexus, it was still pretty impressive, only the cyclopean scale of the mine workings at the foot of which it nestled making it appear small at first glance. The central block must have been a couple of hundred metres tall at its highest point, the two flanking it around half as high, all three of them surrounded by a scattering of smaller structures barely distinguishable at this altitude from the larger chunks of debris tumbling intermittently from the higher levels. All three of the main structures were backed against the rock face behind them, into which further extensions undoubtedly burrowed, the roof of the central one reaching almost to the ground level of the terrace above.

'And there's the pad,' I assured him, noting the sudden paling of the few patches of skin visible through his habitual mottling of psoriasis, grime and facial hair as the retros cut in, sending a shudder through the fuselage. I straightened my cap and tugged my crimson sash into place. 'Better make ourselves look presentable, I suppose.'

Which in Jurgen's case was more of a pious hope than a realistic prospect, of course, but the remark did as I'd hoped, giving him something to think about other than his nausea; he began collecting up our kit, one eye still fixed on the steadily growing landing zone in the centre of the shrine's roof. It was larger than I'd realised, the scale of it only becoming apparent once I'd caught sight of a couple of parked Aquilas and a heavy cargo lifter, all in the ubiquitous russet livery of the Adeptus Mechanicus, widely spaced around the margins of the field. The irregularities protruding from the roof around the smooth, slightly scorched area, which I'd taken at first for the covers of maintenance hatches and air shafts, were the size of buildings in their own right, an impression confirmed by the windows and doorways beginning to become visible through the haze of billowing dust thrown up by the Thunderhawk's thrusters.

'We've been directed to pad seven,' the pilot informed us, as the landing field started to slip sideways beneath our slowly settling gunship. 'They'll be making a hard seal with the starboard hatch.'

'Good.' Jurgen stopped rummaging in the kitbag between his knees, and resealed it with a palpable air of relief. 'We won't be needing the breather masks then.'

'Works for me,' I agreed, appreciating the contrast with my arrival at the Nexus. Being able to breathe while disembarking would be a welcome novelty here. Out of habit, and a faint sense of foreboding, I checked my weapons as well, ensuring that the power packs of my laspistol and chainsword were both fully charged, and sufficiently loose to draw with the minimum of time and effort. Not that another attempt on my life so soon, and so publicly, seemed particularly likely, but I hadn't made it through to retirement by taking anything for granted. Come to think of it, I still hadn't, not until I actually set foot on Perlia, and the irony of being dispatched by an assassin so close to my lifelong goal of getting out of harm's way and staying there was one I was determined to cheat the universe out of.

'We're down,' Jurgen said, his voice suffused with relief, as the constant howling of the engines died back to an idling roar, and the deck plates beneath our feet stabilised, sinking slightly as the Thunderhawk's landing gear absorbed its weight. He adjusted his lasgun and melta across his shoulders, and bent to heft our kitbags, almost disappearing behind them – which was probably just as well as we were about to meet our new hosts. I hadn't spoken to Magos Tezler in person yet, but Vorspung had assured me that they were fully prepared for our arrival. A choice of words, I'm bound to say, which didn't exactly inspire me with confidence.

A loud *clunk* echoed through the passenger compartment, and the boarding hatch slid smoothly aside, to reveal a boarding tube clamped firmly to our outer hull. I led the way down it, our footsteps echoing from the metal mesh underfoot and the corrugated walls, faint puffs of gritty powder rising where our boots hit the deck plates. Evidently the ubiquitous dust being raised by the mine workings was sufficiently thick in the air around here for some small measure of it to have become scooped up by the corridor as it extended towards the Thunderhawk, and I found myself even more relieved not to have been exposed to the outside environment. A faint thrumming shook the whole structure, vibrations from the Thunderhawk's engines, and I picked up my pace a little towards the thick metal door sealing off the far end of the passageway. The pilot's eagerness to leave now his errand was over was obvious, and though I was sure he wouldn't take off again until we were safely inside the shrine, I saw no point in lingering.

Unlike the pristine surface of the Nexus, which had perplexed me at first sight, the portal we were approaching was as grubby as anything I normally associated with a Mechanicus facility. The incised cogwheel motif was choked with dust in which browns and greys mingled uneasily, contrasting with the dull bronze surface that was itself scored and pitted by decades of exposure to the airborne abrasives. Some of those had worked their way into the mechanism, judging by the muffled grating sound which accompanied its opening.

A second door awaited us a few metres beyond it, sealing the end of a short corridor floored and ceilinged with metal mesh, the walls of which were decorated with ceramic tiles creating an abstract mosaic of interlinked angular forms of staggering ugliness.[99] Glancing down, I saw the usual tangle of cables and ducting beneath the walkway, an arrangement repeated above our heads, with the addition of luminators at regular intervals.

'This looks cheerful,' Jurgen opined, without much conviction, as the portal by which we'd entered ground closed again, cutting off the muted grumbling of the Thunderhawk's idling power plant. Further clanks and clatterings announced the disengagement of the boarding tube, not quite masking the roar of the unleashed engine as the gunship took to the air again, effectively stranding us here. 'Think they've forgotten we're coming?'

---

99  *Or possibly representations of particularly venerated machine parts, or even binharic data packets, the Adeptus Mechanicus' idea of aesthetics being idiosyncratic at best by the standards of the rest of us.*

'I doubt it,' I said, as the door ahead of us began to glide open, a lot more smoothly and silently than its outer counterpart, to reveal a wider, more open area, with a higher ceiling, a few seats around the walls and more of the jagged mosaic. Several corridors radiated off from it, although the lack of external windows in most of them made it pretty obvious that the majority were part of the tunnel system riddling the ground around the main excavation.

A handful of tech-priests were waiting for us, clad, for the most part, in the russet robes of their calling. The single exception wore nothing, their body composed entirely of metal: the first tech-priest I could ever recall meeting without even the most vestigial portion of their original flesh being visible. Also unusual was the lack of any external mechanisms, like the mechadendrites most of the group sported, or the vox-grilles visible in faces or throats. Instead, their face was a sculpted human one, androgynous and bland, fixed in an expression of detached curiosity. The body it surmounted mimicked human proportions too, as smooth and genderless as its face, although it was somewhat larger than average, presumably to accommodate the mechanisms within, which whirred and hummed with every movement; I barely came up to its shoulder, and I'm not normally considered particularly short. (Unless you count the opinion of a Catachan commissar I spent a memorable, not to say pleasantly strenuous, couple of months with after she took a shine to me on the otherwise uneventful voyage from Coronus to Keffia back in my time with the 12th Field Artillery.[100])

'Welcome, commissar.' The metal androgyne took a step

---

100   *The first regiment Cain was assigned to, and from which Jurgen was detached to take up the role of his aide; an arrangement which seems to have suited their senior officers at least as much as the Commissariat.*

forward, raising a hand in greeting. In contrast to the even monotone I was used to hearing from the vox-units of most acolytes of the Machine-God, their voice was soft and lilting, almost melodic. 'Your arrival honours us all.' Which neatly skirted around the fact that it was probably a pestilential nuisance, even if no one was up to anything. An operation of this magnitude would require a formidable degree of oversight; I was beginning to see why some of Tezler's more conservative colleagues might have felt a bit happier with a more experienced hand on the tiller. Perhaps the shortfall in output really was down to nothing more sinister than administrative incompetence. But if that was the case, why would someone have spent so much time and effort trying to kill me, not to mention Vorspung, Norgard and Morie?

'A pleasure to be here,' I lied glibly, taking the proffered hand, and finding it just as unyielding as I'd expected. 'The view on the way in was even more impressive than I'd been led to expect.' Reminded of his presence by a barely stifled snort, I gestured to the ambulatory luggage pile behind me. 'This is my aide and amanuensis, Gunner Feric Jurgen. He'll be accompanying me on my tour of inspection.'

'Feric? An auspicious name,' the tech-priest piped, looking at Jurgen appraisingly over my shoulder. 'Though you'll find many of iron resolve at Metallum Majoris.' Their entourage did their best to show sycophantic amusement, but, like most tech-priests, it didn't come easily to them.

Jurgen's brow furrowed, clearly not getting it, and equally clearly damned if he was going to admit the fact. 'And yours is?' he asked, remaining, to my quiet relief, on just the right side of pugnacious. His position as a de facto Commissariat functionary, albeit a lowly one, allowed him a fair degree of latitude in situations like this, and he was never slow to take advantage of the fact when it suited him.

'Magos Hetrodyne Tezler, senior adept of Metallum Majoris,' the ferrous tech-priest responded, apparently unperturbed. 'My apologies for having neglected the formalities.'

'No apology necessary,' I reassured them, as diplomatically as I could. 'I neglected to introduce myself as well.'

Tezler emitted a reasonable approximation of a polite laugh, if articulating 'ha ha' like actual words counted in that regard, and tilted their head a little to mime amusement. 'That would have been something of a redundant courtesy,' they said, the liquid cadence of their voice still disconcerting in the extreme, 'given your unique position on Eucopia.'

'Not quite unique,' I said, keeping my voice casual. 'I gather one of your own order has a similar commission.'

'Young Clode, you mean?' Tezler didn't miss a beat, although their musical tones concealed any agitation they might be feeling just as effectively as the monotonous drone of the average Mechanicus voxcoder. 'I would have expected him to have completed his enquiries by now.' They turned to lead the way deeper into the complex, with a courteous wave to usher Jurgen and I ahead of them.

'He was here, then?' I asked.

Tezler's internal servos whined as they shrugged in well-simulated indifference.

'He was, although we didn't converse much. His interest was more in the practicalities of mineral extraction than the administrative details.'

'But he seemed satisfied when he left?' I asked, provoking another mosquito-like buzzing as Tezler shrugged again.

'I believe so. I did not observe his departure.'

'I'm sure you had far more pressing matters to deal with,' I said, choosing my words carefully. Appearing too interested would either shut down the conversation if Tezler really had something to hide, or, worse still, make me even more of a target than I already felt. 'Did he happen to mention where he was going next?'

'Not that I recall,' Tezler said blandly. 'As you say, my attention was elsewhere. I couldn't even tell you when he departed.'

'I doubt that it matters,' I said. 'But if I'd been able to talk to him, or read his report, I'd have been able to get out from under your feet a great deal sooner.'

'You overestimate the degree of disruption your presence will cause,' Tezler said, with another polite 'ha ha', an affectation I began to suspect would soon become irritating in the extreme.

'I sincerely hope so,' I said, responding with automatic pleasantries while my conscious, and reliably paranoid, mind began sifting their words for any implied threat. 'I have pressing business on Perlia, and the sooner I can get this little errand done and be on my way, the better.' Which, as well as being true, was calculated to foster the impression that I wasn't too keen to actually find any problems, hopefully lulling any conspirators within earshot into a false sense of security. On the other hand, if I was up to my ears in heretical conspiracies that's precisely the kind of thing I'd expect an investigator to say, leading me to keep an even closer eye on them in the future.

Either way, I reminded myself forcefully, there was no point in trying to second-guess everything; that way lay nothing but reliably sleepless nights.

'I trust you will find the accommodation to your liking,' Tezler chirruped, after a few minutes of twisting and turning through a maze of corridors a more suspicious mind than mine might have suspected was intended to disorientate unwelcome visitors,[101] accompanied by more inane prattle from the pair of us. A doorway in the wall slid smoothly aside. 'It was designed with the comfort of the non-augmented in mind. Not that we see many of those here, ha ha.'

Jurgen entered ahead of me, muttering something to the effect that he'd be the judge of whether the accommodation was fit for a commissar, thank you very much, which Tezler was tactful enough to pretend they hadn't heard, if they actually did.

'I'm sure it will suit us very well,' I assured them, as my aide assessed the small suite beyond with a grudging nod of approval, and disappeared into the nearest bedroom with my kit, leaving his own to form a trip hazard in the middle of the living area. Tezler departed after a further exchange of platitudes, and the door hummed closed, leaving me with a profound sense of relief.

'That was a creepy one,' Jurgen said, emerging from the master bedroom again and picking up his kitbag. 'Even for a cogboy.' His forehead furrowed with mental effort. 'There's something about them I can't quite put my finger on.'

'I know what you mean,' I agreed, a faint sense of unease worrying at the corners of my own mind. 'But I'm sure it's nothing to worry about.'

Which didn't sound true even as I said it, let alone in the light of what we were shortly to discover.

---

101  *A pointless endeavour in Cain's case, given his uncanny knack for finding his way through labyrinthine passageways.*

# SIXTEEN

If Tezler did have anything to hide, they were certainly not making it obvious. I spent the next couple of days being shepherded around the mine and its environs by tech-priests of sufficient seniority to maintain the polite fiction that I was a welcome and honoured guest, but without the authority to show me anything that hadn't been placed on my itinerary by someone a great deal further up the food chain. It was a routine I was familiar enough with from decades of Imperial Guard inspections to let pass without comment, merely making a mental note of everywhere and everything my hosts seemed to be politely deflecting me from.

In truth, the operation here was so vast, and so densely populated, that I'd barely seen a tithe of it[102] before Tezler dropped by our quarters to ask how we were getting on. To

---

102  *'Tithe' being used here in its literal meaning of 'one-tenth' rather than its more common associational one of a tax or an obligation due to a higher authority.*

my vague surprise they were unaccompanied, perhaps in an attempt to encourage me to speak candidly, although I, naturally, had no such intention – not least because of the high probability that anything I said was being recorded or transmitted elsewhere for later analysis.

'An unexpected pleasure,' I greeted them, while Jurgen, having ushered them in, faded into the decor as much as he ever could, an endeavour not exactly helped by the profusion of russet hues the tech-priests seemed to favour on most surfaces. Even the bed-linen was the colour of brick dust, which didn't exactly make for a restful night's sleep. 'I trust we're not proving to be too great a nuisance?'

'Not at all, ha ha.' Tezler inclined their head, and, to my vague surprise, seated themself in the geometric centre of the nearest sofa. 'Our intermediaries speak most highly of your discretion and attention to detail.'

'In my experience the detail's where the daemon is,' I said, dragging a chair round to face them, and sitting down on it with my best air of casual disinterest. 'And, of course, I need to show a degree of diligence if my report's to pass muster.'

'Of course.' Tezler inclined their head again. 'And do you think it will? As I've already explained, our shortfall in output is merely a temporary setback, soon to be remedied.'

I shrugged. 'It will if anyone actually bothers to read it. But I like to think it'll appear thorough enough for you to avoid any further inconvenience once it's been filed.' Thus neatly implying that I wasn't looking too hard for problems, and that if they were up to anything, their best chance of getting away with it would be to let me conclude my enquiries and depart without fuss – which would up my chances of survival considerably.

'That would be to everyone's advantage,' Tezler agreed.

'We're opening several promising new seams, and hope to be making quota again by the end of the year.' They held out a hand, the tip of their index finger peeling back to reveal a data key. 'I can inload the relevant data to your slate, if you wish.'

'That would be most helpful,' I said, picking up Jurgen's from the table and holding it out. I'd kiss an ork before I let anyone here gain unimpeded access to my own, although given how easily Vorspung had managed it on our arrival, I doubted Tezler would find it much of a challenge in any case. There was no point in making it any easier for them than it had to be, though, and if, as I suspected, their intention was to grab copies of whatever was already on the slate, then I wished them joy of my aide's extensive collection of erotica – I strongly suspected that after such extensive augmetic enhancement it would leave them baffled at best, if not reminded of what they were missing.

Tezler inserted the data key, emitted a short binharic chirrup and withdrew the digit, which immediately resumed its former smooth exterior. If they had attempted to rifle through the files already on the slate, they gave no sign of surprise or disappointment, however, merely composing themself on the sofa in an attitude suggestive of relaxation. 'There. I've placed it in the primary data node for ease of perusal.'

'Much appreciated,' I said, with a nod of acknowledgement. 'I'll be sure to read through it at the earliest opportunity.' I paused for a moment, as though struck by an idle passing thought, before adding, 'I don't suppose a copy of Clode's report has surfaced yet, by any chance? I don't see much point in duplicating our efforts, especially as there's so much of the installation here I still have to see.'

'Alas, no,' Tezler piped, looking about as forlorn as an

ammunition box, despite their words. 'But I gather he spent a good deal of time in the lower galleries. Despite repeated warnings of the dangers down there.'

'Dangers?' I caught the implied warning off, as I was clearly supposed to. 'You mean rockfalls and the like?'

'That sort of thing,' Tezler agreed. 'Also, firedamp, and a number of rockrat nests, not all of which have been found and eradicated.'

Jurgen caught my eye, behind the tech-priest's back, and pulled a face of extreme scepticism; an attitude I'm bound to say I shared. If I knew one environment above all others it was underground warrens like the one Tezler was describing, and in which I'd spent my earliest years not merely surviving but thriving.[103] Nevertheless, letting them know they'd piqued my interest would hardly be helpful, so I merely nodded.

'It sounds singularly unappealing. But if Clode's already examined it, and seemed satisfied when he left, I doubt there's anything down there worth the bother of another look. No doubt he'll present his conclusions when he decides to show his face again.'

'If he ever does,' Jurgen muttered, too quietly to be audible, though I saw his lips moving clearly enough to have got the gist.

'No doubt he will,' Tezler agreed, showing no sign of having heard, although given their extensive augmentation I would have been extremely surprised if they hadn't.

'Then let's assume I needn't bother with anywhere Clode's been,' I said. 'What other facilities would you recommend I concentrate my efforts on?'

---

103   *As noted before, Cain makes many references throughout his memoirs to having grown up in an underhive, without ever being specific enough to provide a clue as to which world it was on.*

'Primary processing,' Tezler trilled, after a moment's hesitation likely intended to mimic the flow of a normal conversation. 'That should afford you some relevant insights into the distribution chain.'

'Sounds fascinating,' I said, theatrically stifling a yawn. 'Perhaps if you could get someone to arrange it?' I yawned again, a little more blatantly. 'Tomorrow, perhaps?' I wondered if I'd have to repeat the trick once more, but Tezler had apparently taken the hint.

'I'll see that it's all taken care of,' they replied, rising smoothly to their feet, with another faint humming of servos. 'And if you'll permit me to make the suggestion, perhaps you should sleep and ingest nutriment. Your energy levels appear somewhat depleted.'

'I'm afraid they do,' I said, yawning more openly now. 'Perhaps if we start mid-morning? The extraction process sounds fascinating, and I wouldn't like to miss any of the nuances.'

'That would be a shame,' Tezler agreed, striding smoothly to the door. 'I will see to it that you remain undisturbed until then.' The door slid closed behind them, and Jurgen exhaled, releasing a degree of tension only someone who knew him as well as I did[104] could have spotted.

'Still gives me the creeps,' he commented. 'Shall I get your bed ready, or would you like some supper first?'

I shook my head. 'Neither. We've got about twelve hours while they think we're asleep.'

'To do what, sir?' One thing I could always rely on Jurgen to do was miss the obvious. Notwithstanding that, he was already checking his lasgun, no doubt inferring that we might be needing it.

---

104   *In other words, no one.*

'Take a look at these lower galleries,' I said. 'You heard the magos. They were doing everything they could to direct us away from them. And when I said I didn't think we needed to check them out for ourselves, they couldn't agree fast enough.'

'Maybe I'd better take the melta, then,' Jurgen said.

'Couldn't hurt,' I agreed, after a moment's consideration. Under most circumstances that wasn't the sort of thing one could carry around the corridors unremarked, but in a Mechanicus shrine no one was likely to bat an eyelid at the sight – assuming they still had any to bat. And, if challenged, I supposed we could always claim we were taking it to a chapel for a blessing of accuracy.

On the other hand, that excuse would wear progressively thinner the deeper we penetrated into the mine, and we were hardly going to be inconspicuous in the first place – Throne alone knew how many of the cogboys were connected by some form of techno-sorcery to one another, and to the torrent of data invisibly suffusing our surroundings; not to mention whatever imagifers might be keeping watch on the corridors. We were going to stick out like an ork in a chorus line, which made our chances of sneaking into the lower galleries unchallenged minimal at best.

Well, we'd just have to take our chances, I decided, taking a couple of steps towards the door before I managed to talk myself out of the whole thing. I took a final, regretful glance back at my bed, which was looking by far the more appealing option despite the colour of the sheets; then a potential answer to our most pressing problem suddenly presented itself.

# SEVENTEEN

'I feel like Tobit the Tallarn,'[105] Jurgen grumbled, pulling his hood a little further forward to conceal a bit more of his face – which I'm bound to say came as a distinct improvement. If it bulged a little where his helmet was, like the odd protuberances around his shoulders where the bulk of the melta and his lasgun were concealed, it only added to the effectiveness of his disguise; most tech-priests were so heavily augmented that the silhouette beneath their robes varied to some extent from the human standard. For that matter my own weapons had a similar effect, and I'd drawn back one of the sleeves to leave my augmetic fingers visible,

---

105   *A character in a number of mystery plays, a form of popular entertainment on worlds in and around the Damocles Gulf, combining inspirational texts from the scriptures with slapstick comedy and scatological humour. These are traditionally performed on holy feast days by an amateur cast who eagerly seize the opportunity to lampoon local dignitaries before drinking and eating far too much, ostensibly in the name of the Emperor, at their expense.*

which I felt would add an extra degree of verisimilitude to our imposture.

I have to confess to feeling more than a little ridiculous myself, but to my relieved astonishment our makeshift disguises didn't seem to elicit so much as a glance from any of the tech-priests we'd passed in the corridors since leaving our accommodation. It hadn't taken us long to fashion a rough approximation of the robes most of them wore from a couple of bedsheets, although the hems were distinctly ragged where we'd hacked through the fabric with our combat knives, and the joins were rather less than workmanlike, held together as they were with chirurgical tape from the primary aid kit Jurgen habitually kept squirrelled away in one of his utility pouches. (Something for which both of us had been grateful on far too many occasions.) Fortunately, the cogboys' taste for russet hues even on something as mundane as bed-linen made our deception relatively easy; I'd known a few acolytes of the Machine-God favour other colours over the years, chiefly white, but what that signified I had no idea,[106] and I'd seen none of them around Metallum Majoris in any case, so adopting any of those would probably have made us stand out almost as much as if we hadn't even bothered.

Despite our unexpected success, I must admit to a distinct sense of relief when we left the more crowded corridors for the comparatively lightly travelled passages of the mine itself. As I'd expected, they connected directly to the main

---

106   *Knowledge rarely explained by the Adeptus Mechanicus, but it may be summed up as doctrinal differences, expertise in a particular area of techno-theology, or an abstract representation of the forge world they call home. Most speculation from outside, however, boils down to 'No one knows, and no one really cares.'*

habitation area, funnelling us through a warren of utility zones filled with arcane mechanisms of quite stunning size and complexity on the way. Some of these I was familiar with from our tours of inspection, but many meant nothing to me at all, beyond the most tentative of guesses at what their purpose might be. I'd been paying enough attention on these earlier jaunts to be pretty clear where I was aiming for, though: a large and echoing cavern where the bounty from the lower shafts (or, to be more precise, a prodigious amount of rock fragments from which the bounty would later be extracted) reached the surface.[107] Warned by the increasing noise level we slowed our pace as we approached it, feeling the vibrations thrumming beneath our feet, and the booming roar of unloading rock plunging into the storage hoppers as an almost physical battering against our eardrums.

'This way,' I directed Jurgen, and he followed without question as I slipped down a side passage, content as always in an environment like this to let my instincts guide me. This wasn't the direction I'd approached the chamber from while being ushered around by a tour guide, but I was as certain as I could be that it would connect with it, and in this I was to be far from disappointed. The passageway, hewn directly from the rock, was evidently intended as a utility conduit rather than pedestrian access, judging by the number of pipes and cables running along both walls and the ceiling, its narrowness (it was barely wide enough for us to walk in single file), and the fact that it was unlit. The latter was a problem we solved easily by kindling the luminators we'd brought

---

107 *Relatively speaking; if Cain's description of the layout of the mine is to be trusted, and it does accord with the visual records in most particulars, this part of the complex would still be around a kilometre below ground level.*

with us. In some ways I'd have preferred to dispense with them, allowing our eyes to adjust to the pervading gloom, but time was of the essence, and the risk of concussing ourselves on a low-hanging pipe too great if we'd proceeded in total darkness.

We made good time, however, finding ourselves before too long on a catwalk suspended over the cavern I remembered: a vast space into which a number of tramway tracks emerged from irregularly positioned tunnel mouths. Far below us, tiny trains popped in and out, ministered to by artisans and tech-priests the size of my thumbnail, discharging their cargoes and scurrying back to their holes like startled rodents. Narrowing my eyes against the glare of the arc lights suspended below our vertiginous perch, and which, fortuitously, would render us invisible in the unlikely event of anyone down there glancing upwards, I was just able to make out the control chapel from which I'd watched the process a day or so earlier; in rather more comfort and silence than we were currently experiencing, thanks to the thick layer of armourcrys between it and the bustling junction.

'How do we get down there, sir?' Jurgen asked, and I pointed ahead of us, to where a gallery clung to the cavern wall. A series of staircases descended from it, several of the intermediate landings giving onto doorways leading Emperor knew where; we'd just have to hope no one emerged while we were passing. On the plus side, the ambient noise was so great there was virtually no chance of our footfalls being heard, even on the resonant metal mesh of which the treads appeared to be composed. He nodded, and fell in behind me, scanning our surroundings for any sign of a threat, although fortunately these seemed to be conspicuous by their absence.

We made it almost to the cavern floor before anyone noticed us – an unaugmented member of the workforce, who started climbing the staircase just as Jurgen and I began descending the second or third flight up. We slowed our pace, hoping the fellow would leave the stairs before we passed one another, and by the Emperor's grace he did, disappearing through the door on the next landing just before we reached it; though not without glancing briefly in our direction with a faint air of surprise.[108] He was carrying a data-slate in his grime-ingrained hands, the contents of which appeared far more interesting than my aide and I, for which I could only be grateful, and the closing door cut off the beginning of some remark about a blockage in one of the hopper feeds. A quick glance downwards was enough to show me that the little knot of workers nearest the foot of the staircase were moving away, picking up crowbars and sledgehammers, and I picked up our pace. We'd never have a better time to get down there unobserved.

'What now, sir?' Jurgen asked, looking around with mild curiosity at the scurrying trains, and stepping back hastily as one rattled past close enough for the wind of its passage to billow his makeshift robe around him like a banner in a gale. A human driver would undoubtedly have had a few choice words for us, but to my relief it was piloted by a servitor, apparently embedded in the power car as thoroughly and permanently as the ones which had directed the rogue skitarii walkers that had come so close to abruptly curtailing my commission from Zyvan, and it gave no sign of having even noticed our presence.

'We hitch a ride,' I said, as the last wagon trundled past,

---

108  Presumably because the simple courtesy of allowing him to pass unimpeded wouldn't have occurred to most genuine tech-priests in the complex.

already slowing, the head of the train clattering over a set of points a score or so metres ahead. It would take us a good couple of hours to walk to where we were going, not to mention back, and I was acutely aware that time was of the essence if we were to discover anything of use once we got there. The more time we could save, the better. I picked up our pace, using the slowly moving ore carriers to screen us from the control chapel's observation window, and any other workers who might be in the vicinity – although given the luck we'd had so far, our faux robes should have blended us into the background nicely.

'Very good, sir.' My aide nodded, despite the risks clearly inherent in such a plan, and fell into his accustomed place at my shoulder. 'How do we do that?'

'Still working on that bit,' I admitted. From what I remembered of my earlier visit to the control chapel, the process of dumping the collected ore was almost automatic. The trains pulled up next to one of several large holes in the floor, surrounded by waist-high metal barriers; then a pair of specialised servitors plodded down the line, lifting each wagon off the rails between them, inverting it, and shaking the contents into the receiving bin. At that point the newly extracted ore rattled down a chute to be crushed, graded and sent to the processing plant which, all being well, I would still be alive enough in the morning to be feigning an interest in.

And here they came, two hulking amalgams of metal and flesh, their footfalls sending vibrations through the rock beneath our boot soles that made the metal rails of the tramway whine with harmonic resonance. Relays clicked and hummed, hydraulics hissed, as they strode forwards, fully twice the height of a man, showing no sign at all that they registered our presence. Which hardly came as a surprise;

work units like these were built and optimised for one purpose only.

'Careful,' I cautioned, motioning to my aide to step back,
and we both did so, a trifle warily. I don't know how Jurgen
felt as the cyclopean servitors loomed over us like utilitarian Dreadnoughts, but I was certainly fighting the impulse
to draw my weapons.

Taking one end of the ore wagon each, the two servitors
lifted it off the rails and decanted its contents, which rattled
away in a gout of dust and a faint metallic booming as a
few of the larger rocks rebounded from the metallic enclo-
sure. A few seconds later they dropped it back on the rails,
and moved on to the next.

'Now's our chance,' I said, determined to seize it, and
scrambled up the side of the wagon, finding a plentiful supply of footholds among the dents and supporting struts. As
my head came level with the top of the bodywork I glanced
around furtively. No one seemed to be in our immediate
vicinity, so I hoisted myself over the lip and slithered down
into the bottom of the cart, which, predictably enough, was
coated in dust and gravel. A moment later Jurgen joined me,
accompanied as always by his distinctive bouquet, slither-
ing down the slightly canted internal side in a flurry of dirt
and profanity.

He glanced around at our surroundings, and the dust cak-
ing our improvised disguises, and his upper lip curled in
disapproval. 'Bit too grubby for my liking,' he said, oblivious as always to the irony. Anything else he might have said
was drowned out, perhaps mercifully, by an echoing metallic
clangour as the servitors replaced the next wagon in line on
the rails; a moment later our refuge shook as they recoupled
it, and moved on to the next. 'What do we do now?'

'We wait,' I said, hoping we wouldn't have to for too long.

As it happened, we didn't, although the minutes stretched alarmingly, my conviction that we were about to be discovered growing with every moment that we weren't. At length, however, the train jerked and began to move, picking up speed and all but loosening the fillings in my teeth as it rattled over a series of points.

'Here we go,' I just had time to say as the glaring lights and the echoing void over our heads was abruptly displaced by a ceiling of rock, and darkness enveloped us.

# EIGHTEEN

I've had more comfortable journeys, I have to admit; I had very little idea of where we were going, but wherever it was we were getting there a great deal faster than we would have done on foot. Though I'd decided against kindling our luminators again, in case any of the mine workers noticed the glow and halted the train to investigate, enough light entered the tunnel from side galleries to illuminate the rough stone ceiling just above our heads in intermittent flashes, revealing just how quickly we were moving.[109] Indeed, it was these flickering lights which most impressed me with the sheer scale of the mine workings. I soon lost count of the number of side passages we passed, although rattling around in a bone-shaking metal box during an aural artillery barrage wasn't exactly an aid to concentration in any case.

---

109  *Probably no more than twenty or thirty kilometres an hour, in reality, but the claustrophobic conditions and close proximity to the surrounding rock undoubtedly made it seem a great deal faster.*

One thing I could be certain of, though, was that we were descending quite rapidly, the growing pressure in my ears being more than sufficient evidence of that. I found myself having to swallow every few moments to relieve the discomfort, despite the way the gritty dust surrounding us kept insinuating itself into my mouth and throat, making the process remarkably uncomfortable. Jurgen, of course, ever the pragmatist, had filled our canteens with fresh water before we left our quarters, but there was no question of attempting to take a drink while we were being so comprehensively shaken around; any attempt to do so would only have spilled the contents everywhere, and we were bound to need it later. Not to mention the fact that we were now so thoroughly caked in dust and grit that any spillage would simply convert part of it into mud, which might impede the performance of our weapons just when they were most needed – something I hoped we'd never have to put to the test, although given my usual luck and past experience, that hope was tenuous at best.

It was only as the rattling and banging diminished in volume and the flashes of light from the side passages began to appear at less frequent intervals, indicating that we were approaching our train's final destination, that it occurred to me I had no idea what that might be. Or where, for that matter. My old underhiver's instincts were still good enough for me to have a rough idea of how far we'd come, and in which direction, but there were hundreds of sublevels down here, and thousands of galleries, which didn't narrow it down nearly as much as I'd have liked. One problem at a time, though: before I could address that question, there was still the minor difficulty of leaving the rail wagon unobserved. An issue which suddenly became a great deal more urgent as our eyes were assaulted by the glare of powerful luminators, and the echoes of our passage abruptly diminished, indicating that we'd entered a large cavern. We were being jolted around a good deal less too, as the train slowed even more, rattling over several sets of points. A moment or two later it came to a halt, the squeal of brakes against its metal wheels setting my teeth on edge.

I raised my head cautiously, peering over the side of the wagon. Though smaller than the chamber we'd boarded the train in, the cavern was still vast, swarming with servitors, tech-priests and miners; all, to my relief, almost as grubby as Jurgen and I had become rattling around in the detritus at the bottom of the ore bin. Despite the increasingly threadbare nature of our makeshift disguises, which had both developed a rip or two, they might just continue to serve us for a little while longer. As before, everyone seemed too engrossed in their own affairs to pay much attention to us, although I resolved to disembark cautiously – a resolution swiftly discarded, as a line of heavy servitors plodded into view and began to lift the wagons bodily from the tracks. These were even larger than the ones we'd seen before, fully the size of Space Marine Dreadnoughts, and equipped with handling claws of prodigious length. Instead of pairing off to handle the railcars, each of these cyclopean constructs was able to lift one, striding with it towards a shadowed area near the cavern wall.

Fortunately they began at the front, affording Jurgen and I the opportunity to scramble out precipitously while the activity shielded us from the view of most of the workforce. I must admit to wondering at the time if that was the wisest course, and whether it would have been more prudent to wait and see where the wagons were being taken in the hope of being able to disembark somewhere more secluded, but it was just as well I hadn't; we would both have been crushed to death almost at once, as the servitor bearing our former conveyance approached a heap of ore piled up in a corner of the cavern and scooped some of it into the wagon without so much as a pause.

'This way,' I said, raising my voice a little over the resultant clangour, and hoping I was right. I could feel the ever-present grit crunching beneath my boot soles, but the din around us effectively drowned such a minor noise. Indeed, I'd almost collided with the tech-priest apparently supervising the process before I even noticed he was there, standing between us and a patch of deeper shadow all my instincts for the subterranean were telling me was most likely a cleft in the rock through which we might make an unobtrusive exit.

Suddenly becoming aware of our proximity, the fellow glanced up from the data-slate he'd been perusing and emitted a chirrup of binharic, although whether that had been intended as a greeting, a warning or an irritated outburst I had no idea. Not responding at all would only arouse his suspicions, though, if our tatterdemalion appearance hadn't already done so, so I inclined my head in a creditable imitation of Vorspung.

'Malfunction,' I said, trying to keep my voice as uninflected as possible. 'Verbal only.'

'Commiseration,' the tech-priest said, in what sounded to me like a tone of complete indifference. 'Current production schedule now ready for inload.' His attention returned to the slate screen. 'Recommend corrective measures as soon as possible.'

'As would be most efficient,' I said, hoping that sounded cogboyish enough, and exerting a considerable amount of willpower not to pick up my pace as we moved away.

A rhythmic crashing began behind us as we reached the

tunnel mouth, the rolling stock being returned, piece by piece, to the rails. Inevitably, as we entered the natural choke point we began to encounter more of the workforce, but our luck and disguises seemed to hold; once again the people we passed seemed too engrossed in their own affairs to pay us sufficient attention to penetrate our imposture, something the decreasing light levels no doubt helped with immeasurably.

Finding a secluded fissure some distance from the nearest luminator, I paused for a moment or two and fished my data-slate out of my pocket, finding, to my relief, that it had come to no greater harm during our loud and uncomfortable journey than acquiring a thin patination of the ubiquitous dust. (Which both of us lost no time in clearing the worst of from our mouths and throats with a quick swallow of water, now that the opportunity presented itself.) A brief perusal of the map was enough to allow me to locate our current whereabouts with a reasonable degree of certainty, and I nodded in quiet satisfaction.

'We're here,' I told Jurgen, rather unwisely, as he leaned in to look, thereby giving me the full benefit of his halitosis. 'One of the lower galleries.' Which, according to Tezler, had been of such interest to Clode.

My aide nodded. 'Practically at the bottom,' he agreed, glancing round at our surroundings. 'And it doesn't look all that dangerous.' Which was something of a relative term, under the circumstances, but an assessment I was inclined to agree with. There was certainly no sign of any of the hazards Tezler had alluded to, and for a born-and-bred underhiver like me, they would have stuck out like an ecclesiarch in a bordello.[110]

---

110   *A circumstance not quite as rare as Cain seems to believe; for a man of the galaxy he can, on occasion, be quite endearingly naive.*

'Well, we're not quite there yet,' I said, an entire lifetime of unpleasant experience continuing to insist that the longer something bad didn't happen, the worse it would be when it did. Just quite how bad I still had no inkling, of course, which was probably just as well; if I had I would have run screaming for the surface at once, or just dug a hole with my fingernails to hide in until the local sun went nova and dealt with the problem on my behalf.[111] As it was, I simply shrugged, and memorised the shortest route to the lowest point in the mine, a handful of levels below where we were standing. 'Should only take us about half an hour, though, Throne willing.'

Which, a quick glance at my chronograph assured me, ought to give us an hour or two to nose around down there before heading back to the upper levels with plenty of time to spare before our prearranged tryst with Tezler. Hitching a ride on a surface-bound train would be a little more difficult with the ore wagons full, but we'd got away with it before, so I saw no reason why we shouldn't simply return the way we'd come – although leaving enough time to make the tedious trek on foot if we had to was only prudent.

To my relief, once we got away from the transport nexus the galleries we traversed were almost empty, and we encountered fewer and fewer workers the deeper we descended. The luminators we passed were spread out at ever-increasing intervals, which no doubt aided our rapidly degrading disguises on the rare occasions we still had to rely on them; if anything I welcomed the gradually encroaching darkness, not only for the concealment it afforded, but for the sense of familiarity and security it represented.

---

111  *Since this would take several billion years, it would be a less than optimal solution – as Cain was shortly to discover, time was very much of the essence.*

'There doesn't seem to be a lot down here,' Jurgen opined, after almost an hour of fruitless wandering, and I nodded, on the verge of giving up. Whatever Clode had been hoping to find was conspicuous by its absence, and I was beginning to doubt that it had ever existed at all.

'There doesn't,' I conceded. Perhaps it had only been coincidence that the mutinous skitarii had all served here after all. Perhaps Tezler had been telling the truth about the reasons for the fall in output causing the bottleneck in production I'd been sent here to look into, although there seemed to have been more than enough raw materials being extracted judging by the activity we'd seen. Perhaps the best thing I could do would be to sign off on the collection of bland platitudes I'd been compiling, get off this Throne-forsaken rock at the earliest opportunity, and palm the whole thing off on Amberley.[112] That's what the Inquisition were supposed to be for, after all, looking into things that threatened the Imperium from the shadows.

The only trouble with that idea was the time it would take. All my paranoid instincts were insisting that something was seriously wrong on Eucopia, even if exactly what that was hadn't quite come into focus yet, and by the time I'd got a message to Amberley and she or one of her colleagues had made the voyage from wherever they were, everything could have gone to the warp.[113]

Besides, if I'm honest, the idea that we could have gone to all that trouble for nothing rankled more than a little, making me determined to find something to justify our long and uncomfortable journey into the depths. I cast around

---

112   *Not for the first time, although, to be fair, his instinct for trouble was usually sound. Which was what made him so useful an informant.*

113   *Would have, in fact.*

hopefully, finding a bit more of nothing at all to attract my attention, yet still reluctant to leave without something to show for it.

'Mind out, sir,' Jurgen counselled, stepping to one side of the tunnel to allow a servitor to plod past us, pushing a barrow. Whatever it contained was emitting a faint greenish glow, which seeped out from beneath a shrouding cover, throwing diffuse shadows ahead of it. I followed my aide's lead, having no desire to be trampled by the single-minded construct, feeling a faint shudder of apprehension as it passed, although I couldn't have told you why at the time. All I knew was that it reminded me of something unwholesome, an association my forebrain was reluctant to dredge up from the depths of my memory.

'That's strange,' I said, turning my head to follow it, and feeling an odd sense of relief as that eldritch glow disappeared into the darkness of the tunnel. 'This is supposed to be a dead end.' According to the plan in my data-slate, the gallery we were in petered out a few hundred metres further on; we'd only entered it to avoid a party of miners heading for the main seam, and lingered a few moments to take the opportunity for a quick drink and a ration bar away from any more chance encounters.

'So where did the servitor come from?' Jurgen asked, as though I might actually know the answer.

I shrugged. 'Only one way to find out,' I said, leading the way deeper into the darkness.

# NINETEEN

Had I realised what was waiting for us at the end of that tunnel, of course, I would simply have turned and run as fast as I could in the other direction, but as it was, I just led the way deeper into the enshrouding gloom. After a few more moments had elapsed I began to feel a growing sense of unease, although I couldn't put my finger on why; only as we passed a side passage that shouldn't have been there did I finally realise what my subconscious was trying to tell me. Rather than the dead end I had expected, the gallery continued for some distance ahead, as broad and high as ever, if the echoes around us were any indication. When I reached out to run my fingers along the wall it felt almost smooth, broken only by the faint striations left by the tunnelling process.

Either the extension was recent, or the map I'd been provided with was inaccurate; most likely the latter, given that the passageway we followed was so long, and intersected by more side galleries. I felt my hands drifting to my weapons, but resisted the impulse to draw them. I could discern no immediate threat, but the potential of one hung in the air all around us.

'Clode was right,' I confided to Jurgen, in a voice barely audible even to me. 'They've definitely got something hidden away down here.'

'Not well enough,' my aide agreed, with a dismissive expectoration into the enshrouding darkness, although I must own to feeling a great deal less confident than he evidently did. All we'd discovered so far were some tunnels which weren't supposed to be there, and though that was undeniably suspicious, especially given the average tech-priest's horror at the very idea of falsifying data, that was hardly grounds for calling in the Reclaimers or Norgard's skitarii to raid the place. Not that I liked the idea of relying on the skitarii very much in any case – something here had apparently caused several of their fellows to turn traitor, and there was no guarantee that any sent in to cleanse the shrine wouldn't be equally vulnerable to whatever that was.

Such was my confusion, not to mention steadily increasing apprehension, that when I finally heard a faint echo of sound in the distance, my first reaction was one of relief. At last, it seemed, I was about to get some answers. Not that I expected to like any of them, and, I'm bound to say, that was an expectation in which I was to be far from disappointed.

At first the noise was too tenuous to discern anything comprehensible, but as it increased in volume I was able to make out the unmistakable sounds of distant activity – quite a lot of it, in fact. Which was something of a two-edged sword: it masked the sound of our footfalls nicely, but it meant that wherever we were going would be swarming with people, and I was under no illusion that our much-abused guisings could withstand much further scrutiny.

'Lights,' Jurgen said, a moment after I'd noted the slight diminution of the darkness surrounding us, and I nodded, becoming aware that the gesture would be visible to him by now. The glow in the distance was still very faint, but I could make out the walls of the passageway, and the mouth of one of the intersecting tunnels a score or so metres ahead of us. Up until this point I'd only been aware of their locations because of the way the echoes of our footfalls had changed as we'd passed them, but this one had become visible, and I couldn't resist turning my head to glance down it as we drew level. An impulse I regretted instantly.

'That doesn't look good,' Jurgen said, with commendable understatement, and I drew a couple of deep breaths before replying, determined to seem as calm about this unexpected development as he did – no mean feat under the circumstances, as I was feeling uncannily like I'd just been punched in the stomach by an ork. (Not an experience I'd recommend, on the whole.)

'Not if it's what it looks like,' I agreed, recalling the eldritch glow of whatever the servitor we'd passed had been transporting, and trying not to jump to the obvious conclusion. If the faint greenish refulgence in the depths of the side gallery was what I thought it was, and I'd seen enough of it on Simia Orichalcae to have little doubt, then pretty much anywhere in the galaxy would be safer than here, with the Eye of Terror a marginally possible exception.

'It looks like that necron tomb we found once,' Jurgen said, putting my worst fears into words with his usual lack of subtlety. Then his brow furrowed, dislodging some of the coarser pieces of grit which had been adhering to it. 'But they couldn't have found one here, could they?'

'Who knows?' I said. The one thing I was certain of, despite all my instincts telling me to run the other way as fast as possible, was that we had to find out for sure. Because if it really was what we both feared, the consequences would be catastrophic. I'd barely escaped with my life from necron tombs before, and was under no illusion about the severity of the threat they posed. The mere fact that we were still alive, instead of being scoured from the face of Eucopia along with every other living thing, could only mean that its inhabitants were still dormant. A state of affairs unlikely to last for long.

Palms tingling, my breath catching uncomfortably in my throat, I edged into the side passage, finding it rather more constricted than the one we'd just left. There was, however, just enough room for us to proceed side by side, which was something of a comfort; Jurgen had readied his melta by now, accompanied by a loud ripping sound as the unwieldy weapon finally did for the last vestiges of his disguise, and the knowledge that he could unleash a ravening blast of thermal energy powerful enough to check even a necron at a moment's notice was distinctly heartening. In fact I lost no time in following his example, discarding the remains of my own much-abused bedsheet with a distinct sense of relief, clearing the way to draw my weapons in a heartbeat if I had to. Come to think of it, why wait? My laspistol was in my hand before the thought was even completed, the familiar weight of it obscurely reassuring, despite the intellectual knowledge that if we actually found what I most feared down here, it would be about as much use against them as throwing rocks. (Which would at least be in plentiful supply, if the worst came to the worst.)

My chainsword I decided against drawing, preferring to leave my other hand free; the eerie glow ahead of us was still faint enough to make relying on it entirely to orientate

ourselves problematic at best, and touching the wall periodically could still tell me a lot about the tunnel we were in.
Like the way it had abruptly become less smooth under my
fingertips, the fissures and protrusions I could now feel an
eloquent testimony that this section had been dug in greater
haste – as if the orderly extraction of minerals had suddenly
been overtaken by another, more urgent purpose. Which,
knowing how methodical tech-priests normally were,[114] could
only have had one explanation. The sudden discovery of
archeotech, or some equally tempting prize. The cogboys
on Simia Orichalcae had been practically beside themselves
at the prospect of looting the necron tomb we'd stumbled
across there, though much good it had done them as soon
as its denizens had started to revive, and I could well believe
Tezler would have diverted every resource available to them
to follow up even the most tenuous of hints at such a discovery here.

'It's getting brighter,' Jurgen said, as if that were a good
thing, although I suppose from his perspective it was; lack-
ing my tunnel rat's instincts, he had only his eyes to go on,
and the more he could see, the more he could shoot.

'It is,' I agreed, with rather less enthusiasm, reflecting that
the same thing would also be true for any necrons wandering around down here looking for something to kill.[115]
I reached out to touch the wall again, and for a moment
felt the breath freeze in my chest. In the handful of paces

---

114  *Although a few exceptions do spring to mind.*

115  *Or perhaps not – the precise nature of necron perception, or
lack of it, is still far from clear; their habit of teleporting away with all
their casualties after losing an engagement has made research subjects
somewhat hard to come by. Which, given their propensity to regener-
ate from even a pile of scrap, might actually be something of a mercy,
come to think of it.*

since the last time I'd done so, the roughly hewn surface had become as smooth as glass. My darkest suspicions immediately became cold, hard certainty, confirmed a moment later as my fingertips found a small groove in the slick, chill surface. Despite the darkness, I knew immediately what it was: an incised inscription, in the curiously rounded sigils I'd seen before on Interitus Prime and Simia Orichalcae.

'Commissar?' Jurgen must have noticed my hesitation, a faint trace of concern appearing in his voice. 'Are you all right?'

'Far from it,' I said, feeling I might as well get all the bad news out of the way in one go. 'There are markings here. Definitely necron.'

'So it is a tomb, then,' Jurgen said, with his usual phlegmatic acceptance of the worst the galaxy had to throw at us. 'Do you think we should turn back?'

'I'd like nothing better,' I assured him truthfully, 'but that's not really an option, is it?' Which may strike you as uncharacteristically bold of me if you've read much of my reminiscences, but in truth it was the only pragmatic course of action. As I've often observed, quite literally on the battlefield, it's what you don't know that can get you killed. Simply knowing that there was a necron tomb down here would have been enough to get me on the vox to Morie and Norgard in a heartbeat if there was even the remotest possibility of a message getting through, but my personal comm-bead had far too short a range to reach either, even without the megatons of intervening rock. If we were going to get out of here in one piece, I had to know just how bad a situation we were in. Just turning round and running for it wouldn't do us a whole lot of good if all that got me was shot in the back by a gauss flayer. 'We have to know if they're still dormant.'

My aide nodded, a faint blur of movement in the greenish glow, which, Emperor help me, was growing brighter with every step we took towards it. 'If they are, they won't be for long,' he opined gloomily. 'Not with the cogboys swarming through the place, nicking everything that isn't nailed down.'

'You're right there,' I agreed, ignoring the irony as usual. The tunnel seemed to be coming to an end at last, and as the illumination grew to useful levels, I found my most pessimistic anticipations undeniably confirmed; it was indeed constructed of the eldritch black stone I'd seen before in necron tombs, into which light itself seemed to vanish like water into desert sand, the curious curve and stick sigils adorning it appearing simply as smears of even greater darkness. The sight of them stirred the hairs on the back of my neck, and I fought down the rising tide of hideous memories they recalled. If I was to survive this, I would need all my wits about me.

'Stay close to the walls,' I cautioned, as we reached the chamber itself, a lesson I'd learned well on the previous occasions I'd found myself somewhere like this. That way, if the worst happened, as I was morbidly certain it would before too much longer, at least we'd be able to get back to the tunnel mouth quickly. If we even made it that far; a thought I forced back down as soon as it formed. I'd learned a long time ago that the key to survival was simply to keep on surviving, and allowing yourself to doubt that you would could rapidly become a self-fulfilling prophecy.

'Right you are, sir,' Jurgen agreed, poking the muzzle of the melta round the corner, then turning to direct it in the other direction almost at once. He didn't pull the trigger, or get abraded out of existence by a burst of gauss flayer fire, so I assumed it was safe and edged out onto the cavern floor myself, drawing my chainsword as I did so. I no longer needed my other hand for navigation, and right now the more weapons I had ready for use, the better I liked it.

The cavern seemed both familiar and eerie beyond imagining. Familiar because I'd been in places like this before, where arcane mechanisms hummed quietly, leaking their sinister eldritch glow, and eerie because humanity had no business being here. Nothing living did. Even the echoes seemed freighted by dread, wrapping around my senses like a muffling shroud. The air was chill, permeated by odours I couldn't begin to identify, and I found myself keeping close to Jurgen, obscurely grateful for his own unique aroma, which at least partially displaced them from my nostrils. Cool as it was, the air also felt thick and hard to breathe. Distance seemed more difficult than usual to estimate, the strange geometries around us apparently distorting the very space through which we walked.[116]

Mindful of my earlier injunction we hugged the cavern wall, skirting the edge of the enclosed space, wary of venturing into the labyrinth of metal and refulgent liquid flowing through transparent conduits; normally I would have sought cover there, but in the strange, disorientating space I found myself, my normally reliable instinct for navigation in enclosed environments simply couldn't be trusted. Or, to be a little more accurate, I was unwilling to trust to it, which pretty much amounted to the same thing.

'What are these things for?' Jurgen asked, his voice muted by the peculiar air around us, and I shrugged, as much at a loss as my aide seemed to be.

---

116  *Cain mentions similar feelings of disorientation in his previous accounts of entering necron tombs – an experience apparently shared by others, though precious few of them have emerged again to ask.*

'No idea,' I said, slowing my pace a little to take a look at the one we were currently passing, 'but I doubt if it's anything good.' It was big, perhaps the size of a Baneblade, but more than that I couldn't tell you. Something about it seemed to repel my gaze, deflecting it to one side or the other, leaving me only with a vague impression of bulk and seething malevolence. As I drew abreast of the edge of it, though, I could see down the shadowed space between it and its neighbour, along a corridor of sorts lined with further engines of diabolical techno-sorcery. The dim, pervasive and sickly illumination made it hard to be sure, but I froze into instant immobility, my breath stilling in my throat.

'What is it?' Jurgen had come to a halt too, the instinctive rapport we'd honed over decades of campaigning together working as smoothly as ever, despite our unhallowed surroundings. He raised the melta, seeking a target.

'Movement,' I said, peering into the shadowed space between the machines, wondering for a moment if I dare believe I'd imagined it, before deciding that no, I most definitely had not; in a life like mine, assuming the worst at all times is the only safe option. Jurgen tightened his finger almost imperceptibly on the heavy weapon's trigger, peering intently through the sight.

'Got it. Just back there.' He slowed his breathing, preparing to fire. 'Shall I take the shot?'

'Not yet,' I cautioned, with what I still feel was commendable restraint under the circumstances. If the necrons were up and about, the last thing we needed to do was attract their attention. Not to mention the fact that there were probably cogboys poking around down here too, and potting a couple of those would reveal our presence in no uncertain terms, not to mention being hard to explain away to Tezler. 'Do you have the amplivisor?'

'Of course I do,' Jurgen said, sounding slightly affronted at having the request phrased as a question rather than an order. In truth I'd been in no doubt at all that he would have – my aide liked to be prepared for any eventuality, and his response would probably have been exactly the same if I'd asked for a frag grenade or an autographed icon of the Emperor. He lowered the heavy weapon to fumble in one of his extensive collection of webbing pouches, before holding out the device for me to take. 'Sorry about the jam, but it's not very sticky.'

'It'll be fine,' I assured him, wiping the 'visor carefully on my sash, before raising it gingerly to my eyes. The image seemed a little blurrier that usual, which I ascribed to the peculiar lighting conditions rather than the residue of Jurgen's mispacked sandwiches, and I froze into immobility again, steadying the image as much as I could. 'Frak, it's gone again.'

'I'd give it a moment,' my aide advised, bringing the melta back up.

I started to nod, in reflexive agreement, before checking the gesture as the magnified image swayed alarmingly. 'Seems best,' I said, as it steadied, then exhaled in relief. 'It's not necrons. Just cogboy looters with a death wish.'

A small group of robed figures had trotted into view, surrounding a servitor like the one which had passed us in the gallery. The swirl of figures around it obscured any sight I might have had of what was in the barrow it was pushing, but I hardly needed to see what I already knew: necron artefacts, without a doubt. And if the larcenous tech-priests kept on helping themselves, it would only be a matter of time before they broke or activated something vital, reviving the dormant occupants of the tomb. It could only be by the grace of the Emperor that they hadn't done so already – something I could be certain of now, as the scavengers in front of me weren't dead yet.

Not that that happy state of affairs was likely to continue for much longer. I needed to get out of there before the metal killers woke, call in Morie and Norgard, and find an astropath who could get a message to Amberley at once. Our chances of saving Eucopia were negligible now, but if we were going to do it at all we'd need the Inquisition behind us, that was for sure.

I was on the verge of lowering the amplivisor, and instructing Jurgen to pull back the way we'd come, when I caught sight of another flicker of movement in the distance. Humaniform, gleaming metal reflecting the sickly corpse-light which saturated this profane place, walking unhurriedly towards the little knot of tech-priests.

Jurgen tensed beside me, sighting the melta on the new and terrifying target.

'Necron!' he breathed.

# TWENTY

'Wait,' I said, raising my hand to forestall him from firing, and flinching from the sudden gust of halitosis as he let go the breath he'd been holding while remaining on aim. Something about the tableau in the distance wasn't quite right. For one thing, the gleaming metal figure wasn't carrying a weapon, the first time I'd ever seen one of the hideous abominations unarmed, and for another its gait was less smooth and fluid than the ones I remembered so vividly from the caverns of Interitus Prime and Simia Orichalcae. Even more oddly, the little knot of tech-priests weren't scattering in panic, even though they'd clearly seen its approach. I focused the image in the amplivisor as best I could, then exhaled myself, draining the tension which had gripped me at the first sight of the thing. 'It's just Tezler.' Now I came to look more closely, their mechanical body was more bulky than the xenos monstrosities it so closely resembled, and the sculpted metal face nothing like the death mask of the necron warriors.

'Tezler?' Jurgen echoed, his perpetual tone of bafflement even more pronounced than usual. 'What in the warp are they doing down here?' which was only the first and most insistent of the questions now flooding my own synapses.

'That's what we need to find out,' I said, as the metal magos began conversing with their subordinates. Whatever they were discussing seemed short and to the point, as the little group began moving away again almost at once, Tezler remaining with them. At least now the reason for the strange sense of disquiet I'd felt at our first meeting was obvious – their metal body was uncannily reminiscent of the undying warriors I'd encountered before, although whether that was coincidence or deliberate homage I still had no idea. More likely the former, I suspected, as the body they'd adopted had a recognisably human face, but the resemblance was still profoundly disturbing, particularly illuminated as it was by the sickly green glow I associated with necron techno-sorcery. 'Come on.' I gestured to my aide to follow me. 'We need to see where they're going.'

Moving away from the comforting solidity of the cavern wall, and its reassurance that at least we weren't about to be ambushed from behind,[117] was something of an effort of will, I don't mind admitting. As we started across the open space between it and the nearest bank of mechanica, I found myself darting glances in every direction, expecting to see movement at any moment, but we made it to the fresh cover of the labyrinth of arcane devices without any sign of hostile activity at all. Something my rational mind had been assuring me

---

117  *Other than by necron wraiths, which are capable of phasing through solid matter, of course – since Cain doesn't bother to mention these, and had certainly encountered them before, perhaps he was deliberately not thinking about the possibility.*

was the most likely outcome since my first sight of the scavenging tech-priests, of course, but under the circumstances I preferred to listen to my paranoia.

We made what haste we could to where I'd last seen Tezler and the tech-priests,[118] keeping to the shadows in the avenues between the towering machines; though given the diffuse nature of the ghastly radiance illuminating the place, those were few and far between. For the most part we simply skulked as close to the humming monstrosities as we dared, ignoring the way the sound set our teeth on edge, and their baleful, skin-crawling aura, as best we could. Our cautious progress took several minutes to cover the hundred metres or so, and I began to worry that the party of cogboys we stalked would be out of sight by the time we reached their previous position, but as it turned out I needn't have worried. Peering round the corner of some cyclopean pump, through which the foul, glowing liquid circulated lazily, adding grace notes of sloshing and gurgling to the migraine-inducing hum pervading the place, I caught sight of our quarry almost at once.

'Throne be praised,' I murmured, and Jurgen nodded, pious as always – he'd probably have made the sign of the aquila if he'd had his hands free.

'That light looks a lot healthier,' he agreed. Tezler and their chums were making for a gap in the wall a good deal larger than the one we'd entered by, and through which the reassuring yellow glow of Imperial luminators was seeping. Raising the amplivisor again, I could see that the wall must have been breached from the other side, though a lot more neatly than the tunnel we'd entered by had apparently been. The

---

118   And the servitor, although he doesn't bother to mention it again, *which would seem to indicate that it went with them.*

edges had been carefully squared off, partially obliterating an inscription, which terminated abruptly in a bisected sigil.

'Looks like they got in first the same way we did,' I said, 'then made this hole to get the loot out more easily.'

Jurgen nodded. 'Makes sense,' he said. 'Wonder what they're doing with it?'

'Nothing good,' I said, with complete certainty. Mucking about with necron techno-sorceries was about as sensible as joining a Chaos cult in the hope of having a friendly chat with a daemon over tea and florn cakes. I began moving again, keeping to whatever scraps of cover I could find, although I needn't really have bothered; none of the cog-boys so much as glanced back in our direction, intent on whatever conversation they were having among themselves. A lack of caution in these surroundings which struck me as verging on the suicidal. 'And there's only one way to find out.' See for ourselves, and hope to the Throne we'd be able to get out in one piece to tell the tale.

Despite my skin-crawling eagerness to be out of this hellish environment as quickly as possible, we slowed our pace as we approached the breach in the wall, keeping an eye out for whatever cover we could find. The welcoming light of normality was growing brighter by the minute, Tezler and their companions silhouetted against it, and obscuring our view of whatever lay beyond; but there was no guarantee that whoever or whatever might be waiting at the other end of the tunnel they were now traversing wouldn't be waiting to greet them, and notice a flicker of movement in the necrotic glow of the tomb beyond. There were certainly people there, of that I had no doubt; the babble of overlapping voices and the reverberations of heavy machinery were beginning to force their way through the muffling effects of the dead air surrounding us, and to be audible at this distance there must have been plenty of both.

'Sounds like it connects with where the other tunnel was going,' Jurgen muttered, and I nodded agreement, having come to the same conclusion myself. In so far as I felt able to trust my usual knack for remaining orientated in underground environments in this bewildering necropolis, I was reasonably certain that we were moving more or less parallel to the gallery we'd been following before our unexpected detour through the tomb. Certainly, the sounds and lights we'd noticed then were strikingly similar to the ones we could now discern.

'So let's see what that is,' I agreed, flattening myself against the frictionless wall of the tomb, despite a reflexive shudder of revulsion at the contact, even through the weave of my greatcoat. Despite knowing full well that it was already off, I checked the safety of my trusty old laspistol, and tightened my finger incrementally on the trigger, taking up any slack that a moment's inattention might have allowed to creep into my heightened sense of readiness; the activation rune of my chainsword was under the thumb of my other hand, the speed selector already flicked over to maximum.

I glanced across at Jurgen, who was mirroring my position on the other side of the passageway, the melta raised, ready to bring it to bear the instant we moved; catching my eye he nodded, almost imperceptibly, confirming his readiness.

'On three,' I said, mouthing the count almost silently. As I reached 'one' we moved together, pivoting round to cover the passageway, ready to fire at the first sign of any hostile activity. As it turned out, though, the tunnel was empty, and we both relaxed, glancing at one another. I suppose I should have felt a little foolish, but in all honesty all I really felt was a faint sense of relief – only a slight one, mind, as we still had a tomb full of dormant necrons at our backs, and Emperor alone knew what lying in wait at the end of the passageway.

So we advanced cautiously, the growing noise from up ahead masking the echoes of our boot soles on the floor, the increasing light levels allowing me to see more of our surroundings.

Within a handful of paces the sinister black stone of the necron tomb had given way to bedrock, and I felt a sudden rush of euphoria, as though a shroud around my soul had just been ripped away. I took a deep breath, inhaling the familiar odours of dry dust, dank air and Jurgen's seldom-laundered socks, and grounded myself again.

If ever I'd needed my wits about me it was now, kilometres beneath the earth, a potential army of relentless metal killers at my back, and an indeterminate number of unknown enemies ahead. And in case you're thinking I should still have been giving the majority of the tech-priests the benefit of the doubt, until I was sure how many of them were actually involved in the shadowy conspiracy Vorspung suspected, I suggest you avoid a couple of assassination attempts, find your hosts dabbling with the property of one of the most dangerous foes the Imperium has ever faced, and then tell me how trusting you feel.

The tunnel floor was smooth, carefully finished, but the walls were still rough, mottled with shadows from the light up ahead. Dug in haste, then, as I'd surmised the other one to have been, but intended to take a great deal more traffic. Too wide and high to be intended simply for barrow-pushing servitors, it implied that Tezler intended to move heavy machinery in – or out. You could just about have fitted a Salamander down here (although few drivers other than

Jurgen would have been willing to try it), so a small utility truck would have had little difficulty. Clearly the campaign to loot the tomb was about to step up a gear; and if that happened, any dormant necrons it contained would be certain to rouse. In fact, after my experiences on Interitus and Simia Orichalcae, I found it astonishing that its guardians hadn't already mobilised to repel the intruders, particularly given the amount of effort that had been spent on breaking into the place.

I suppose it was just possible that the sepulchre was empty, abandoned by its creators, but I didn't really believe that for a moment; and even if it was, that still didn't mean much. Both the tombs I'd entered before (much against my better judgement, I might add) had contained warp portals, and the denizens of the one on Simia Orichalcae had been revived by new arrivals from off-world.

'Oh, frak,' I breathed, as the implications of that particular memory began to sink in. Just because the other two had been directly connected to other necron outposts, that didn't mean this one necessarily was, but it was definitely the way to bet. Even if this particular tomb could be successfully cleansed, which was a distinctly dodgy proposition to begin with, Eucopia would never be safe until the portal was found and successfully neutralised.[119]

Definitely a job for Morie and his Space Marines, if you asked me, the Adeptus Astartes being the only Imperial troops capable of taking on necrons and having a reasonable chance of walking away afterwards. Not to mention being the only ones available: there were Norgard's skitarii too, of course,

---

119   Which is Astra Militarum jargon for 'blown to perdition with as many explosives as possible'.

but she would be loath to commit them until we could be sure there was no risk of any more having their minds warped by setting foot in the place.

That still troubled me. Despite Vorspung and Norgard's best efforts we still didn't have a clue what had affected the renegade units, or why, although I'd have been willing to bet a substantial chunk of my stipend that the presence of the necrons had something to do with it. (Which I would have been right about, as it happened, but not in any way I could have anticipated.)

The light and noise levels grew steadily as we made our way towards the welcoming yellow glow ahead, but I slowed my pace as we neared the tunnel's end, Jurgen doing likewise as always. As before, we flattened ourselves against the wall, peering out into the bustling cavern, and I began to regret discarding our makeshift disguises so casually; flimsy as they'd become, they'd have stood out a little less glaringly than our uniforms. Well, if there was one thing I was good at it was running and hiding, and I supposed we'd faced worse odds than this – at least we'd be trying to get past tech-priests and artisans intent on their own affairs, instead of dodging orks and genestealers like I'd had to aboard the *Spawn of Damnation*, and if the worst came to the worst and we had to fight our way out, I couldn't see them putting up much in the way of resistance.

'There's hundreds of 'em,' Jurgen said, as though pointing out some mildly interesting piece of scenery, underlining the observation with an emphatic expectoration. 'Do you want to go back the way we came?'

'I'd rather not,' I said, with what I felt under the circumstances to be a commendable degree of restraint. I scanned the echoing chamber in search of our quarry. 'Besides, we still don't know what Tezler's up to yet.'

'No, we don't,' Jurgen agreed, adding something like 'treacherous little gretchin-fondler' in a muttered undertone.

As I'd already surmised from the echoes reaching us down the tunnel, the cavern was vast, easily the size of the one in which we'd abandoned the train that had brought us here, what was beginning to feel like a lifetime ago. Unlike any of the ones we'd seen so far, though, it appeared to be an active mining face; the walls were a series of tiers, some five or six levels high, the miners and servitors swarming all over each one chewing away tenaciously at the precarious footing of their compatriots immediately above. Chunks of ore rattled down chutes and along conveyor belts, missing most of the toiling workforce most of the time, ending up in a heap in one corner. Several other tunnel mouths gaped around the chamber's perimeter, ranging in size from small ones barely large enough for a couple of people to have walked along abreast, to a couple even higher and wider than the one we were lurking in.

'This way,' I said, spotting a somewhat safer refuge behind a pile of crates someone had considerately stacked close to the cavern wall a handful of metres away; once we were behind those we could lurk unseen for as long as we liked, although that in itself was a far from attractive option – the more I saw, the more convinced I became that running for the surface and calling in the Reclaimers was the only sensible thing to do. Not that that was going to be particularly easy; we were quite literally off the map now, and while I was sure my innate sense of direction could get us back to the railhead, doing so unobserved with so many people about would be almost impossible. Not to mention the obvious difficulties of boarding a train again, given that the mineral wagons would now be full, leaving little space to stow away without the risk of being crushed by the shifting load.

To my faint surprise we made it to the refuge I'd spotted without being challenged or shot at, and I raised the amplivisor again, scanning the cavern for some sign of Tezler. Just when I'd given up all hope of spotting them again, my eye was caught by a gleam of metal, reflecting the overhead luminators, near the entrance to one of the larger tunnels.

'There they are,' I muttered. The metal magos seemed in no hurry to depart, loitering by the tunnel mouth, and occasionally glancing into it deeper than I was able to see from this angle. 'And they seem to be waiting for something.'

Something went *crunch* close to my ear, and I flinched reflexively, lowering the 'visor. Jurgen had prised one of the crates open with the blade of his combat knife, and was peering into it curiously, no doubt wondering if the contents might 'come in handy' at some point. His brow furrowed.

'What do you make of this, sir?' he asked, burrowing inside the receptacle for a moment before lifting a dull metallic ingot into view, which I stared at in equal perplexity.

'That shouldn't be here,' I said, checking the sigils on the crate. 'Processed materials are supposed to go straight to the manufactories, not brought back down to the mine workings.' I'd been quite diligent in maintaining my pretence of interest in such things, and had acquired a reasonable working knowledge of the procedures and protocols. If I was reading the stencilled information correctly, this entire batch should be in the process of becoming munitions for the Imperial Guard even as we sat here.

'That's why they're not making enough kit,' Jurgen said, with a contemptuous sniff. 'Tezler's been nicking stuff instead of sending it where it's supposed to go.'

'Evidently,' I agreed. 'The question is, why?' Personal profit didn't seem like much of a motive for a cogboy, even if they had managed to find some way of smuggling the resources they'd appropriated off-world. 'And how much of it they've taken.' Which must have been a hell of a lot, given that the shortfall in output their pilferage had created had managed to attract the attention of the lord general himself.

'Movement, sir. Over there.' Jurgen pointed in the direction of the tunnel mouth almost directly across the cavern from us, where the presumably larcenous tech-priest was still loitering, and I raised the amplivisor again. A quartet of cargo-8s, identical to the ones I'd pictured venturing into the tomb behind us, were chugging into the cavern, laden with more crates like the ones we'd taken refuge behind. The lead one halted, and Tezler approached it, apparently exchanging a few words with the occupant of the driver's cab; although, since they had no lips to move, the gist of the conversation eluded me, even if they had been considerate enough to converse in Gothic rather than their own twittering argot.

'Time we were moving,' I said, as the convoy started up again, and began edging its way across the crowded cavern floor. Its progress was slow and erratic, the leading vehicle having to halt or change direction periodically to make way for servitors oblivious to its presence, and the occasional miner too tardy or bloody-minded to get out of its path in time; not to mention the machinery and other obstacles impeding its progress. Nevertheless, it would be here in a matter of moments, and one of two things would subsequently happen: either my worst fears would be realised, and the trucks would sweep on past into the tunnel behind us, their drivers about to do enough damage to the tomb to bring the wrath of its occupants down on us all, or the crates they carried would be added to the pile behind which we lurked, leading to our inevitable discovery. Either way, somewhere else was beginning to look like the best place to be.

'Right you are, sir,' Jurgen agreed, following my lead as always, and glancing around for better cover. 'D'you reckon we can make it to the train over there?' I followed the direction of his gaze, and felt a sudden surge of relieved optimism. While my attention had been on Tezler, a line of tramway cars like the one we'd hitched a lift on before had coasted into the cavern, coming to a halt beside the ore pile. If we could get to it, it should take us back to the surface as quickly as we'd descended – with any luck we might even beat Tezler back to the main complex, and alert Morie to his treachery before the treasonous bag of bolts had a chance to respond.

'We can give it a damn good try,' I said, casting around for the next patch of cover between us and the tramway, and finally settling on a rattling conveyor belt running towards it no more than a score of metres away. No doubt if I were really the swashbuckling hero the picts and printsheets like to portray me as I'd have vaulted on top of the bloody thing and swept across the cavern in style, but if I tried it I'd be pureed almost at once by the tumbling chunks of rock bouncing around on it – not to mention making my presence blindingly obvious to an awful lot of people, many of whom quite possibly wished me dead, so on the whole my natural inclination to hiding behind it and sneaking along in its shelter seemed a great deal more sensible.

'You go first, while I cover you?' Jurgen suggested, and I nodded; if I attracted any hostile attention, the melta would discourage it a great deal more effectively than anything else we had with us, and if I didn't my aide could cross the relatively open ground with reasonable ease while I returned the favour with my laspistol.[120] As it happened, though, we both managed to make it to our new refuge without being spotted, crouching behind the rattling belt, and trying not to choke on the pall of dust being raised by its energetically bouncing contents.

And not before time. The trucks were drawing abreast of the heap of crates behind which we'd been crouching a few minutes before; there was no doubt about it, had we remained where we were, we would have been spotted within seconds. I raised the amplivisor again, and brought the lead vehicle into focus. For a moment I thought it was about to nose into the tunnel, and tensed, ready to flee for the ore train the moment the coast was clear, but to my heartfelt relief it slowed to a halt a few metres clear of the opening. It seemed no one was about to go and poke the necrons with a stick, at least until we'd had time to get out of here.

'Looks like they're delivering more contraband,' I said, and Jurgen nodded.

'Seems a daft place to put it, though,' he said.

'It does,' I agreed, a shiver of unease running through me at the thought. Cogboys are nothing if not scrupulously rational, and if Tezler had chosen to stockpile the crates there they would have had a very good reason. 'Maybe they're just hoping no one will disturb it away from the main ore face.' Now I could observe their movements more fully, the workforce did seem to be avoiding that corner of the cavern,

---

120 *Not quite as much of a disparity as it sounds – Cain was an exceptional marksman, and would have been able to take out a potential threat at a far greater range than most people equipped with a handgun. At which point he'd probably have attributed his success to sheer blind luck, claiming he was only hoping to keep their heads down.*

which I could hardly blame them for if they had the remotest inkling of what lurked at the other end of the tunnel; but on the other hand they seemed to be productively engaged in whatever tasks they'd been assigned. I doubt if I'd have been able to keep my mind on the job knowing what the darkness concealed. Perhaps Tezler had simply declared this part of the mine workings off limits, and that was that.

The drivers disembarked, accompanied by a servitor apiece, and the constructs immediately began to unload the boxes, adding them to the pile behind which Jurgen and I had so recently sought refuge. To my surprise, each of the drivers was a tech-priest, their russet robes and abundance of visible ironmongery leaving their identities beyond any reasonable doubt, instead of the minimally augmented artisans I would otherwise have expected.

'They're cogboys,' I said, and Jurgen nodded.

'Makes sense,' he said. 'They won't trust the workers to shift the stuff. Someone might talk. Or help themselves.'

'Good point,' I agreed, deferring to his greater expertise in the field of pilferage. I focused the amplivisor image as best I could through the clouds of dust being thrown up by the rattling conveyor belt in front of us. 'The fewer who know the better.' Then the driver of the lead truck, who'd stopped to converse with Tezler, came fully into view, and I felt the world take another lurch beneath me. It's a truism that all cogboys look alike once they reach a certain level in the Mechanicus hierarchy, in that the metal to flesh ratio moves decidedly towards the ferrous side of the equation, but there's a great deal of variety among them for all that; and this was a face I'd grown very familiar with, from its depiction in my briefing slate and my keeping a conscious eye out in the hope of glimpsing it since my arrival on Eucopia.

There was no doubt about it: I'd finally discovered the whereabouts of the disconcertingly absent Clode.

# TWENTY-ONE

'Are you sure, sir?' Jurgen asked, understandably enough when I voiced my astonishment, and I nodded, before refocusing the amplivisor on Clode and his companions.

'Certain,' I said. The more I observed the tech-priest, the more convinced I was of his identity. I must admit that, now my first rush of surprise at finding him still alive, rather than rusting away at the bottom of an abandoned shaft somewhere as I'd been assuming up until now, was diminishing, my predominant emotion was one of righteous indignation – accompanied by the impulse to march over there, grab him by the front of his robe, and ask him what the hell he thought he was playing at. An impulse, needless to say, which I was far too sensible to give into.

'Do you think he's joined the heretics?' Jurgen asked, and I nodded again.

'It's the only explanation that makes any sense,' I agreed, at which point my aide began to exude an air of smugness almost as dense as his body odour. It was just possible, of course, that Clode was playing some kind of double game, still sticking to his original commission from the magi on Coronus while worming his way into Tezler's confidence, but I didn't think so. If that were the case, he would have contrived some kind of meeting with me to pass on what he'd learned, rather than remaining hidden for so long. My presence here would be known to anyone with access to the blizzard of information constantly swirling around Eucopia, so he could hardly have remained in ignorance of it. Far more likely that he was up to his neck in whatever conspiracy Tezler seemed to be orchestrating, a willing participant in treason, no doubt as dazzled by the techno-sorcerous baubles they were hoping to plunder from the necrons as any other cogboy aware of what lay under their feet would be.

Or perhaps he was under the influence of whatever had corrupted the rogue skitarii. In which case trying to bring him back alive would be our best hope of finding some kind of defence against it; a prospect I was, as you can readily appreciate, less than enthusiastic about. I was confident that we could subdue him, along with all his companions if we had to; the real problem was what to do next. Getting him back to the surface, through thousands of potentially hostile miners and cogboys, would be tricky at best – we could hardly shove him in an ore bin and expect him to cooperate, which ruled out the train, and right now that was looking like Jurgen's and my best chance of returning to the upper levels unobserved and unopposed.

I took another look at the unloading operation. The servitors had been busy while I deliberated, emptying three of the trucks quickly and efficiently, and adding the crates from their flatbeds to the stack behind which we'd so recently been lurking. Only the first, Clode's, still had some of its load left, and that had no more than a quarter-dozen boxes remaining. The quartet of tech-priests seemed to be conferring among themselves, in binharic unfortunately, so once again I had no opportunity to try to follow the course of the conversation.[121] The gist of its conclusion was clear enough, though; Clode's hand gesture was unmistakably dismissive, at which point the other three tech-priests climbed back into the cabs of their cargo-8s and fired up the engines.

'They're pulling out,' I said, as they reversed, turned and began to make the same slow and meandering progress back towards the tunnel mouth they'd initially emerged from. Only Clode remained, supervising the stowage of the last of the crates.

An idea began to form. Ridiculous, far too risky for my liking, but undeniably sound – and, if it worked, it would not only get me back to a vox-set as fast as possible, but also potentially secure Norgard's skitarii against any further subversion. 'Do you think you can drive that other truck?'

'Of course, sir,' Jurgen said, his typically phlegmatic tone stopping just the right side of expressing exactly how stupid a question he thought that was. 'Doesn't look too different from the one we borrowed before.'

'Excellent,' I said, as the last of the crates joined the stack, and three of the servitors plodded away, apparently in search of whatever the next thing on their to-do list was. 'But we'll have to move fast.' Now there was no reason I could see for him to linger, I fully expected Clode to follow his compatriots.

'Right you are, sir,' my aide agreed, leaving our rattling refuge and sprinting for the cargo-8 as though he'd just spotted

---

121   *Not that it would have made much difference; he was an indifferent lip-reader at best.*

an unattended platter of finger food. I had intended being a little more cautious, retaining the element of surprise for as long as possible, but I certainly couldn't fault his enthusiasm. In the event it didn't matter; most people found Jurgen's appearance startling to some degree, even at the best of times. Clode simply stood there, boggling visibly,[122] as my aide bore down on him, brandishing the melta and bellowing something that might have been a Valhallan war cry, but which sounded to me more like an orkish insult.[123] With a quick glance round to make sure we were still unobserved, and thanking the Throne for the echoing din surrounding us, I followed hard on his heels, grateful for the additions to the rampart of boxes which concealed us from the workforce again within a handful of paces.

'What he said,' I snarled, waving my chainsword through a series of impressive-looking flourishes intended to convey that I was strongly minded to use it, and bringing the humming teeth to rest a centimetre or two from his neck. 'We've been looking for you.'

'Successfully, it seems,' Clode said, in the familiar even monotone of one of his calling. Both his eyes were augmetic replacements, but they blurred momentarily, as though blinking in mild perplexity. 'I take it you're Cain?'

'Unless you know of any other commissars on this benighted rock,' I said, and Clode shook his head, almost severing his chin as it passed my whirling blade.

---

122 *Quite a trick for a tech-priest, given the amount of metal in their faces.*

123 *Which, to be fair, makes up an appreciable proportion of their language. Like many Valhallans, Jurgen was reasonably fluent in orkish, and could read their runes after a fashion, a cultural legacy of the greenskins' unsuccessful invasion of his home world some generations before.*

'None are known to me.'

'If you know who I am, then you know why I'm here,' I said. Clode started to nod, thought better of it in the interests of keeping his face intact, and froze into immobility again. The servitor, its job done, and mindlessly indifferent to the drama unfolding in front of it, turned away, and began to follow its fellows into the maelstrom of activity surrounding our tiny, secluded enclave.

Jurgen watched it go, and hefted the melta. 'Do you want me to stop it?'

'There's no point,' I said. 'It's not as if it's going to tell anyone what we're doing.'

'And what are you doing, exactly?' Clode asked, with what seemed like genuine curiosity.

'You just said you knew,' Jurgen said belligerently, literally minded as always, 'so why ask?'

'I can infer,' Clode said, 'but confirmation is always welcome.'

'Then you can infer that you're coming with us,' I said, 'or that I'll drop you where you stand. Which is it to be?'

'Neither,' Clode said. 'It is highly improbable that you would kill me without gaining any information you believe I might have, and I most certainly won't betray the Omnissiah's divine purpose by divulging it. Which leaves only one rational option.' His eyes misted momentarily again, and I remembered where I'd seen the same thing before: when Vorspung had communed with the machine-spirits of the Nexus. He was transmitting the entire conversation to Emperor knew where, although I'd bet a year's tarot winnings that wherever it was, Tezler was on the other end. 'I had hoped to experience the transcendence for myself, but will no doubt observe it from the eternal data files.' His

body spasmed and went rigid, thin tendrils of blue lightning sparking around his exposed metallic parts. A thin,
teeth-aching whine began to sound from somewhere within
his torso, growing in volume and intensity with each passing second. I whirled round to face Jurgen.

'Take cover!' I bellowed, suiting the action to the word,
hurling myself to the cavern floor and rolling beneath the
parked truck. No sooner had I reached the flimsy refuge than
the tech-priest exploded, with a surprisingly muted *splutch*,
showering the immediate vicinity with shrapnel and viscera.

'Are you all right, sir?' Jurgen asked, emerging from behind
the nearest crates, looking no worse for wear than usual. I
rolled out from beneath the truck, which seemed to have survived with only superficial damage, its bodywork marred by
a number of pockmarks from the metallic fragments of the
erstwhile tech-priest, being careful to avoid the larger gob-
bets of the rest of him. Which, come to think of it, hadn't
done a lot for the cargo-8's paintwork either.

'I'll live,' I said, frowning at the mess in perplexity.

'What happened to him?' my aide asked, in tones of no
more than mild curiosity.

'Throne alone knows,' I said, still trying to work it out. It
had been self-inflicted, that much was obvious, although he
couldn't have been carrying any actual explosives – a proper
frag grenade detonating that close to us would have taken
Jurgen and I out along with him, cover or not. My best guess
was that he'd overloaded some of his internal systems somehow, intending to deny us the answers we sought, and that
any resultant harm to us would only have come as a bonus.
I shrugged. 'Maybe he ate a bad ploin or something.'

Jurgen nodded. 'Must have been well dodgy,' he agreed. He
glanced around, keeping the melta levelled in case Clode's

messy demise had attracted any unwelcome attention, but the workforce was still burrowing away at the rock face, oblivious to everything but their own concerns. True, the ambient noise would have drowned out a far bigger explosion than that, but their single-minded diligence was beginning to seem a trifle disturbing;[124] their relentless fixity of purpose put me in mind of a tyranid swarm, or the necrons themselves, who, now I was reminded of their presence again, were still far too close for comfort. 'So what do we do now?'

'We take the truck,' I said, considering the options rapidly. It was here, now, and the ore train was halfway across the cavern; getting to it would involve a lot of running, skulking and possibly violence. Besides which, if I'm honest, the prospect of repeating our loud, uncomfortable journey down here was far from welcome. The tunnel Clode had driven down must reach the surface somewhere, or at least connect to one that did – unless the sturdy little vehicle had been assembled down here, which I doubted. We were still off the map on my data-slate, but I trusted my sense of direction to get us back to *terra cognita*, and once we were I could plot us a route back to the open air and call for reinforcements. The lorry would afford us a welcome degree of concealment as well; Jurgen and I would stand out like orks at a cotillion on foot, but in general people only notice the presence of a vehicle, not whoever's driving it.

I resheathed and reholstered my weapons, and clambered

---

124   *In actual fact, this isn't all that surprising, given the degree of augmetic enhancement to their cerebellums most tech-priests seem to indulge in. This process of 'optimisation' undoubtedly allows them to access more information more quickly, but at the expense of more human forms of cognition, such as idle curiosity, and, in all too many cases, self-preservation.*

up to the passenger door. I was just on the verge of unlatching it when I froze, alerted by some primal instinct I couldn't quite put into words. From my elevated perch, I glanced down the dark, forbidding passageway leading to the necron tomb, the faint charnel glow still ominously visible in the distance. And it appeared to be flickering.

A spasm of pure terror seemed to douse my body in ice water – a sensation anyone who's spent as much time as I have serving with Valhallans, and been less than punctilious about checking the temperature of the shower before using it, will be intimately familiar with. There could only be one explanation.

'Jurgen!' I called, trying to keep an edge of panic from infecting my voice. 'Movement in the tunnel.' Something was partially blocking the sinister green refulgence, something which kept shifting its position. Lots of somethings. 'The necrons are coming!'

# TWENTY-TWO

When faced with the choice of standing my ground like a man, or running away as fast as possible squealing like a hrud, I've never hesitated – it's been running and squealing every time. At least when that's been a realistic option. All too often it hasn't, due to the presence of witnesses in front of whom I've felt forced to live up to my fraudulent reputation for unshakable heroism (or at least appear to, which isn't the same thing at all) in the interests of continuing to enjoy its benefits in the (often unlikely) event that we both survive, or the knowledge that making a run for it would only take me somewhere even worse.

On this occasion, however, there was no choice at all. Staying where we were with necrons on the move would be nothing short of suicide. Forget nobility of sacrifice, and all that other nonsense ecclesiarchs and front-parlour generals who've never seen a Guard uniform from the inside, let alone the myriad of unpleasant ways its contents can leak, like to pontificate about; once you're dead you're dead, and futile gestures which won't even slow the enemy down are nothing short of treason in my book. Every Guard casualty is a victory for the forces ranged against us, which is why, unlike so many of my fellow commissars, I regard the essence of my job as keeping as many of them alive and healthy as possible. That way there are more of them standing between me and anything liable to spoil my day, especially one of the unfortunate friendly fire accidents so common in the premature curtailment of promising commissarial careers.

'Get this thing moving!' I cried, swinging into the passenger seat, while Jurgen scrambled in through the driver's side door, swearing repetitively as the melta and his lasgun got snagged on the narrow frame.

I risked a glance down the tunnel again, and immediately wished I hadn't. The luminators in the cavern were striking glittering highlights from the tide of metallic bodies bearing down on us, by now no more than a handful of metres from the tunnel mouth.

'Got it!' Jurgen slapped the toggle on the dashboard which closed the doors, immediately cocooning us in a blessed bubble of relative silence. Only as it descended did I realise the true volume of the cacophony outside – my ears were ringing slightly, and both our voices sounded unnaturally loud in the confined space, despite the hushed tones we were conversing in. He poised a grubby thumb over the activation rune.

'Wait!' I said, just before he could fire up the engine. The gleaming metal killers were far too close by now. If we attracted their attention, we'd both be dead in a heartbeat. 'Stay very quiet, and very still.'

Which may seem completely counter to all good sense;

we were in a vehicle, after all, and could probably outrun them easily. But we couldn't outrun the guns they carried, and I'd seen what gauss flayers could do even to the armour of a Leman Russ; our light-bodied truck would give us about as much protection as a sheet of paper. On the other hand, as I'd observed for myself on our nerve-shredding journey through the necron tomb on Simia Orichalcae, they could be evaded, so long as you didn't do anything stupid to draw attention to your presence, such as shooting at them. With any luck, they'd simply register the presence of the parked vehicle[125] without bothering to consider that someone might be lurking inside it.

'What about the miners?' Jurgen asked, his whispering somehow enhancing the effect of his halitosis. In fact, crouching as we both were below the level of the windows and the dashboard, I began to be even more aware of his presence than usual; something I initially attributed to the stress of the situation we found ourselves in, before belatedly realising that the cabin of this truck was pressurised, like the one we'd used on our eventful little jaunt to the proving grounds. Which was something, at least; it pretty much confirmed that there was a route back to the open air, or as much of it as existed on Eucopia at any rate. If we managed to survive the next few minutes, our chances of getting somewhere I could contact Morie suddenly seemed a great deal higher.

'No way we can warn them,' I said, with a degree of regret which surprised me. The ambient noise in the cavern was so great that any attempt to cut through it would only attract

---

125  *If they even realised that was what it was, rather than simply an obstacle to be circumvented or removed; the precise nature and acuity of necron senses is still very much a matter of conjecture.*

the attention of the necrons, which, by now, must be surrounding us. Of course, once the slaughter began, the danger would be pretty hard to ignore, even for tech-priests, and a few of the work crews might cotton on to what was happening and escape down the side passages before it was too late, but I wouldn't give a lot for the chances of most of them.

I glanced up, catching sight of a pict screen in the dashboard. I'd seen similar things before, intended to give the driver a sight of the road behind when simply turning your head to take a look seemed like a bad idea, due to heavy traffic, excessive speed or incoming fire. (Or sometimes all three, when Jurgen was driving.)

'Can you get the screen working?' I asked, as quietly as I dared.

Jurgen nodded. 'Piece of florn,' he assured me, reaching up a cautious hand to flick the appropriate switch. After a moment of humming quietly to itself, and displaying a miniature snowstorm, an image appeared on the screen, and my breath stilled. The tide of living metal was already all around us.

Contrary to my expectation, however, it wasn't surging forward into the cavern, intent on massacre. Instead of the humaniform nightmares I remembered so vividly, we were surrounded by the giant metal spiders I'd seen in my previous unwilling incursions into necron tombs. Not exactly a reassuring sight, given the number of my companions they'd ripped apart on Interitus Prime, but unlike the plodding foot soldiers, these seemed to be more like the necron equivalent of servitors than war machines in their own right.[126]

---

126   *He's partially correct here, at least according to the most prevalent theories among the Ordo Xenos. The primary purpose of these constructs appears to be the maintenance of essential systems while the*

'Why aren't they attacking?' Jurgen asked, a question which, I must confess, was at the forefront of my own mind too. I shrugged, and took my best guess at the answer.

'Because they're here for the boxes,' I said. It was hard to make out much on the flickering pict screen, owing to the angle at which we were peering up at it, but a couple of the hideous things had moved past the imagifer, crates gripped in their mechanical mandibles like insects at a picnic making off with grains of sucrose. As I watched in horrified fascination, two of the things picked up a larger cargo container between them, and trotted off back in the direction of the tunnel.

'But how did they know they were there?' my aide rejoined, which was another good question, and one I very much didn't like the obvious answer to.

'They were expecting a delivery,' I said, everything falling into place at last. This could be nothing other than the collection of payment, Tezler and their fellow hereteks bartering the raw materials which should have been bolstering the defence of the Imperium for techno-theological trinkets. And, possibly, the lives of their subordinates, although I'd have been surprised if that had been much of a consideration. How they could have negotiated such an arrangement was beyond me, though, the necrons not being all that big on diplomacy.

At the time, however, those particular revelations were still to come; all I could do was attempt to control the anger and astonishment that swept over me at the realisation of the full extent of Tezler's treachery. This was clearly a long-standing

---

*inhabitants of a tomb remain dormant; which isn't to say that the tools they're equipped with don't make unpleasantly effective weapons under the right circumstances. And unlike Imperial servitors, these spyders, as they've inevitably been dubbed, can apparently be repurposed for any contingency, including combat, at a moment's notice.*

arrangement, given the extent of the shortfall in Eucopia's output, and I'd been a soldier for far too long not to real-ise how many lives, possibly even worlds, had been lost as a result. Vengeance for those souls would be exacted, I swore, at my own hands if possible.[127]

Jurgen nodded. 'Makes sense,' he agreed. 'Must be why they were stacked over here, out of the way.' He chewed his lower lip, thoughtfully. 'Wonder what they want it all for?'

'Nothing good,' I said, the reflexive shudder which chased itself down my spine at the thought at least dispelling the anger that had threatened to cloud my brain. The only way to get out of this with my hide intact, instead of being draped around the torso of a necron,[128] was with a clear head. I tried to estimate just how much material had disappeared into the tomb, given the length of time this deception had been going on, and the amount of it I could see the spiders swarming away with, but gave up almost at once – far too much was the only answer that mattered. And, as Jurgen had rightfully raised, for what foul purpose?

I was still pondering on that when the lorry lurched, with a faint groan of stressed metalwork. Before I could utter the curse which rose unbidden to my lips, let alone make a grab for the weapons I greatly regretted having stowed such a short time before, the motion was repeated even more strongly.

'We're moving,' Jurgen said, in tones of mild curiosity.

'We are,' I agreed, with a confirmatory glance at the pict

---

127 *A somewhat atypical outburst, to say the least, given his usual attitude of Horus take the hindmost. But it does illustrate the concern he genuinely seems to have felt for the trooper in the field, at least if his own survival wasn't threatened by their own.*

128 *Cain had observed some of the trophy-taking subcategory of necron warrior, dubbed 'Flayed ones' by those of my colleagues with a flair for the dramatic, on Simia Orichalcae.*

screen, wondering if it was time to panic yet, or whether things were about to get a great deal worse. A quartet of the automated arachnids had lifted the truck bodily off the cavern floor, and between them were bearing it towards the tunnel we'd so recently emerged from. Back into the tomb.

Well, that settled it for me, panic time it most definitely was, even though there was no time to give in to the impulse; I needed a clear head even more now than I had before.

'But why are they taking the truck?' Jurgen certainly wasn't panicking, his voice betraying no more than his usual bemusement at whatever was going on around him.

'I've no idea,' I said. 'Probably because it was right next to the crates. Maybe they thought it was just another unusually big one.' Which sort of made sense. If Clode had driven off as he'd intended before our unexpected intervention, the whole stack would have been left entirely on its own. Not the kind of mistake one of the servitors would have made, but the spider things were xenos artefacts; who knew what kind of machine-spirits animated them?

On the plus side, the mechanical monstrosities clearly had no idea we were crouching in the cab, or they would have chewed their way through the metalwork to dismember us a long time ago...

*'Vehicular unit two-zero-three, confirm location.'*

I jumped as a voice burst unexpectedly from a speaker grille just beneath the pict screen. Up until that point I'd assumed it had something to do with the imaging system, but it seemed the truck had some kind of vox-unit installed as well, presumably to facilitate whatever logistical requirements it was supposed to be fulfilling. And for it to be working this far underground, there had to be some kind of relay reasonably close by.

'Throne be praised!' I breathed, scanning the frequencies with my comm-bead, and picking up nothing but static for my pains. I was just on the verge of giving it up as a bad job when I chanced on a relatively clear channel. I assaulted it with all the override codes I had at my command: Commissariat, general staff and even a couple of Inquisitorial ones I wasn't entirely sure Amberley realised I'd picked up in the course of being her messenger boy.[129]

Tenuous as it was, the signal was fading fast; we were inside the tunnel now, the static growing louder with every jolting pace the tomb spiders took. There was no time for subtlety, or to worry about who else might overhear the message. Quick and concise was the only way.

'Morie!' I called. 'There's a necron tomb on the lowest level of the mine. Hostiles active, repeat, active. Over.'

Not that I actually expected a reply, of course, but I'm bound to say I was hoping for one, forlorn as the hope was, and was far from surprised to be disappointed. Within seconds the static had swelled enough to swamp any potential reply, then an eerie silence descended on all the frequencies I could reach. The bedrock tunnel walls had given way to the sinister black stone I remembered so well, cutting us off from the rest of the galaxy as thoroughly as though it had never existed at all.

---

129  *Of course I did – why else would I have made sure I used them in his presence?*

# TWENTY-THREE

Despite a distinct disinclination to do anything of the sort, I began to rise a little from my cramped position beneath the dashboard, leaning back against the passenger seat, and lifting my head to the level of the windscreen. The image on the pict was too small to get any real sense of our surroundings now, and if we were to have any hope of escaping the tomb alive, we needed to know exactly where we were being taken. I don't mind admitting that moving to a position where I might be visible from outside the truck took every milligram of resolution I could summon; although the arachnoid automata had remained oblivious to our presence so far, there was no guarantee that they wouldn't spot me the moment I poked my head above the dashboard.

Luck was still with me, though; perhaps the sickly, gangrenous glow, and the deep shadows cast by it, worked to my advantage – or perhaps, like the servitors I was familiar with, these wind-up abominations simply weren't programmed to notice anything outside the parameters of their assigned task. Our presence here certainly hinted at that – although I'd seen too many companions fall victim to their like over the years to take anything for granted where these hell-spawned mechanica were concerned.

Needless to say, the prospect before me looked just as unprepossessing as it had while Jurgen and I were traversing it on foot such a short time before; but this time we were being borne deep into the heart of the tomb instead of skulking round its edges, and a suffocating sense of despair began to settle across my spirits as the glow of the Imperial luminators receded into the distance. The long line of glittering spider things stretched out ahead of us, carrying their burdens at a brisk trot along a wide boulevard between towering mechanisms the size of buildings, into the very heart of the darkness surrounding us. What any of these cyclopean devices were, or were intended to do, I had no more idea of than before, but the malevolence they radiated was palpable.

'Coffins,' Jurgen said, indicating a towering construct down one of the side passages we passed, encrusted with innumerable sarcophagi. I nodded, immediately spotting more in the distance. I'd seen the like before, on Simia Orichalcae, crammed with uncountable thousands of dormant necron warriors, and shuddered at the memory. Something about these seemed different, however; an instant later, with a thrill of pure horror, I realised what it was.

'Empty ones,' I said. The warriors they'd contained were gone, already revived, and no doubt looking for something to kill.

'Then where are they?' Jurgen asked, not unreasonably under the circumstances. Apart from us, and the scurrying spiders, the tomb seemed deserted. Given the number of empty stasis chambers I'd spotted, there should have been some sign of activity, even in a space as vast as this one.

'Beats me,' I said, not liking any of the possibilities I could think of. Preparing a full-scale invasion, most likely. I glanced around, in the vague expectation of seeing some sign of movement, but there was nothing as far as the eye could see.

Which was quite some distance, the tomb easily as large as the ones I'd been in before (and left as quickly as I could). Strangely, however, I found the sense of disorientation I'd experienced on those previous occasions considerably diminished, perhaps because the solidly quotidian confines of the lorry cab insulated me from the full strangeness of our surroundings. At any event, I was reasonably certain that I knew how far we'd come, and the way back to the tunnel connecting the tomb to the mine.

How we were going to make use of that knowledge, however, was still a moot point. The only hope that I could see was that the arachnoid automata had been instructed to deposit their booty in a storage area somewhere, from which we could sneak away as soon as the coast became clear. A hope that was dashed almost as soon as the thought occurred to me.

'Seems to be getting brighter,' Jurgen remarked, having squirmed upwards enough to be getting the benefit of the view directly through the windows himself. He was right, too, the necrotic green glow up ahead increasing in intensity. It seemed to be pulsating, too, in a rhythmical fashion that stirred the hairs on the nape of my neck, although I couldn't have told you exactly why – but it reminded me of something, I was certain of that.

Only as we rounded the corner of another monolithic mechanism did realisation dawn, and with it a thrill of horror that pierced me like a blade. The spiders bearing their purloined supplies weren't stacking them neatly in some out-of-the-way corner after all; they were scuttling determinedly towards the one thing I'd known must be down here, and most dreaded the sight of.

'It's a warp portal,' I said grimly, as the spiders at the head of the column scurried straight towards the swirling vortex and vanished into it, still bearing their booty. 'And it's active!'

'At least we know where the rest of them went,' Jurgen said, somewhat inaccurately, as Horus alone knew what might be waiting on the other side of that obscene rip in reality. Something we were about to discover for ourselves, though, unless we did something about it in the dwindling handful of seconds remaining to us. I'd been through a necron portal before, and been fortunate to survive;[130] not an experience I was at all inclined to repeat.

'You'll be able to ask them in person if we don't get out of here right now,' I said, rising the rest of the way and dropping abruptly into the seat, either habit or my innate survival instinct impelling me to fasten the crash restraints as I did so.

Jurgen followed suit, shoving the melta out of his way with an alacrity which might have taken my eye out if I hadn't grabbed the clumsy weapon by reflex. 'Oops. Sorry, sir.'

'Don't mention it,' I said, as he stabbed at the vehicle's activation rune.

I held my breath for what seemed like a lifetime, but in reality could only have been for a second or so, then the engine rewarded me for my vigil (and fervent prayers to the Emperor) by roaring into life, with what sounded to me

---

130    *Quite possibly the only human in the galaxy able to make that boast – I've certainly failed to find any other instance on record of someone doing so, and being subsequently able to describe the experience.*

like a bellow of panic. Our wheels spun, suspended in the air between the spiders carrying us, and I cursed with all the vigour you might expect given the amount of time I've spent in barrack rooms and combat zones. If they were at all disconcerted by this sudden and unexpected development, the gleaming metal arachnoids gave no sign of it, simply scuttling towards the void in the air with the same mindless fixity of purpose they'd always shown.

'Sorry, sir,' Jurgen said again, pumping the throttle to no avail, unless you counted an excessive amount of engine noise a desirable outcome. I certainly did not, having no desire at all to attract the attention of the tomb's guardians, which must surely have been lurking somewhere in the vicinity, even though we'd seen no sign of any yet. 'Can't get any traction.'

Only the sheerest desperation could have impelled me to do what I did next, but given the situation any risk seemed worth taking. We were less than a score of metres from the portal by now, its gangrenous glow flickering as it threw out evanescent tendrils of cold green light, like some hideous aquatic polyp attempting to snare a passing morsel, while infinity swirled in its depths. By contrast, the black stone of which the arch around it was composed appeared to drink in all illumination, starkly framing the swirling dimensions in what seemed to be solid darkness.

'You will in a moment,' I assured him, and popped the door seal, swinging it open with a strange sense of deja vu, which disconcerted me for a moment until I realised I'd been reminded of doing something similar during our recent skirmish in the desert. This time, however, I wasn't potting ineffectually at our pursuers with my laspistol; the spider things were right outside the cab, and I still had Jurgen's melta in my hands.

I swung it round, manoeuvring the thing through the narrow gap with some difficulty, and, despite the urgency and danger we were in, somehow found time to wonder how my aide managed to carry and use the unwieldy weapon with such apparent ease.[131] I fumbled for the trigger, aiming hopefully at the spider supporting our nearside[132] front, and pulled it, closing my eyes against the familiar retina-stabbing flash. The burst of thermal energy struck home with satisfying force, severing a couple of scurrying limbs. The spider fell, the front of our truck followed, and by great good fortune the sudden lurch broke the grip of the three carrying the other corners, ripping our conveyance free of their mandibles. The cargo-8 slammed into the floor of the tomb, bouncing on its suspension, which, fortunately, seemed as rugged as the one fitted to the lorry we'd escaped the renegade Striders in. The butt of the melta smacked me hard in the face, but the seat restraints held, and against all the odds I remained where I was supposed to be instead of being tipped out of the cab.

'Go!' I bellowed, quite unnecessarily under the circumstances, as our wheels were already spinning; the second they touched the floor we were moving. Backwards, fortunately, our overstressed engine howling in protest, as Jurgen had had the foresight to engage reverse – had he not done so, we would certainly have plunged into the vortex under our own power, instead of being carried through it by the spider things. As it was, though, my aide swung the wheel

---

131   *Decades of familiarity and practice, probably.*

132   *Since driving conventions vary so widely from world to world, along with the vehicles to be found there, many seasoned travellers simply describe which side of a vehicle they're referring to as 'nearside', meaning the one nearest the edge of the road, and 'offside', meaning the one nearest the centre.*

from side to side, his eyes fixed on the pict screen showing the view behind us, his jaw clenched with concentration, missing the handful of spiders that had joined the cavalcade behind the ones carrying us by what seemed like millimetres. Finding the barrel of the melta still protruding from the passenger door, I pulled the trigger a few times as the bloated metal bodies flashed past, but what with the speed we were going and the blinding glare every time I did so, I doubt that I did much damage.

'Frak this,' Jurgen said, a sentiment I heartily endorsed, 'they'll be on us in no time at this rate.' And, indeed, the surviving spiders were rallying, dropping the boxes they carried and forming up in what looked uncomfortably like a battle line. They began to surge forward, two or three of them spitting bright lances of necrotic green light which sheared through one of the arcane mechanisms filling the cavern, releasing some glowing viscid goo – which promptly began eating its way through the bedrock floor. Jurgen spun the wheel, taking us into the cover of a side passage, then did something with the brake and throttle controls which sent us skidding round to face in the opposite direction. (I might have noticed what if I hadn't been so concerned with hanging on and not losing the melta, which was bound to come in useful again before too much longer. Not to mention the fact that if I'd let his favourite toy fall out of the truck, Jurgen would have sulked for days.) 'That's more like it.'

As he spoke, a surge of acceleration kicked me in the spine, and I pulled the door closed with almost unseemly haste. Those beam weapons the spiders had looked powerful enough to chew through whatever meagre protection the cab offered, but while they were doing that they wouldn't be chewing through me, and even a fraction of a second to react can make all the difference in a firefight. I glanced at the pict screen, and immediately wished I hadn't.

'Go right,' I instructed, hoping my sense of direction was still reliable enough to get us out of here. Jurgen swung the wheel in response, taking us up another passageway between the looming devices, just as another burst of fire sliced through the air where we no longer were. I just had time to glance back and see a tide of malevolent metal scuttling round the corner in pursuit, then we were away, and still accelerating, out of their line of sight once more.

'Take a left,' I said, then, 'right again,' and to my inexpressible relief I caught sight of the familiar yellowish luminator glow which marked the mouth of the tunnel back to the mine. 'Over there!'

'I see it, sir,' Jurgen assured me, powering us towards it at what under any other circumstances I would have considered an insane velocity in such cramped surroundings. As it was, though, knowing what was behind us, I found myself willing our screaming engine to even greater effort.

I glanced at the pict screen, seeing a glint of pursuing metal falling ever further behind, and exhaled, allowing some of the tension to drain from my body. A few of the things spat bolts of energy in our direction, but only one struck the flat-bed at our backs, punching a fist-sized hole in the tailgate, the others making a mess of the mechanisms around us. Perhaps wary of inflicting any more collateral damage, the pursuing spiders ceased fire.

'Nicely done,' I complimented my aide, beginning to dare to hope that the worst was over; a hope in which I was to be predictably disappointed. I began to consider our next move. Using the truck to get up to the surface somehow still seemed like our best chance of survival, but as soon as we were back in the mine, and free of the signal-dampening effect of the necron tomb, I could use the vox-relay I'd tapped into before to contact Morie and update him on the situation here. With any luck, by the time we made it to the outside world we'd be met by the Thunderhawk, and a squad or two of Terminators to hide behind.

Then, of course, I saw movement up ahead. Necron warriors this time, levelling their gauss flayers. It seemed my instincts were correct – not all the ones from the empty sarcophagi had escaped through the portal to Throne knew where. Forewarned of our presence, probably by the spiders, they'd moved as calmly and methodically as they always did to cut us off.

I just had time to shout a warning before Jurgen yanked the wheel over, almost overturning the truck in the process, and shot down a narrow side passage like a rat up a sump pipe. A volley of gauss flayer beams tore through the space we'd just vacated, a couple luckier or more accurate than the rest chewing some additional holes in our much-abused conveyance. Just how close they'd come to crippling it, and moving in for the kill, I became abruptly aware of as I noticed a sudden draught around my knees – the cab door had been neatly penetrated, an area of solid metal the size of a dinner plate having evanesced into nothingness. There went any chance of escaping to the surface, I thought, but waste not, want not; I stuck the muzzle of the melta through the makeshift firing slit, and waited for a target of opportunity.

Which didn't take long to present itself, another phalanx of the ghastly metal warriors appearing as soon as we reached the next junction. Jurgen swung the wheel again, dropping a couple of gears to keep all of our tyres on *terra firma* this time, and I triggered the melta, sweeping its beam across the whole formation. Not all of them were incommoded as much as I'd have liked, although at least one melted away into thin air in the disconcerting manner their casualties tend to do; we ducked as the survivors fired, just in time to keep our heads attached to our bodies as the cargo-8 cab began to more closely resemble a wreck I'd take cover behind on the battlefield rather than something I'd make a frantic escape in.

'Persistent frakkers, aren't they?' my aide remarked, accelerating up through the gears again. The truck shook, and bounced over the remaining necrons before they had another chance to fire. Which wouldn't slow them down for long; a quick glance at the pict screen was enough to show me that they were already rising smoothly to their feet, dents and scrapes along their torsos smoothing out as the living metal they were composed of flowed to repair the damage.[133]

'They are that,' I agreed, seeing the welcome light of the tunnel mouth ahead, and, by the grace of the Throne, nothing metallic and malevolent standing in the way of it. I jammed my cap, which was in imminent danger of being dislodged by the wind now howling through the thoroughly perforated cab, a bit more firmly on my head. Then I caught sight of a flicker of movement, yet another group of the indestructible warriors moving swiftly along the line of the cavern wall in an attempt to cut us off. 'Drive!'

'We'll beat 'em to the tunnel, sir,' my aide assured me, hunching low over the steering wheel, but the necrons were moving fast as well, running with a peculiar fluid grace, instead of the measured, relentless stride with which they

---

133   *Highly unlikely, given the probable resolution of so small a screen, and the fact that the truck was moving so fast – more likely he's extrapolating from what he'd seen in earlier encounters with the necrons in the interest of dramatic effect.*

usually advanced. Jurgen glanced in their direction with an air of mild curiosity. 'Don't often see 'em in that much of a hurry.'

'Not often they need to be,' I said. In my experience they tended to come on in waves, methodically eliminating everything that stood in their way, overrunning fixed positions as inexorably as the incoming tide. Fleeing survivors too quick to be shot in the back (which I have to admit has included me on more than one occasion) eventually tire and falter, while the relentless enemy doesn't, content to catch up in their own good time and complete the work they've begun. The only way to be sure you've outrun them is to find a shuttle, board a starship, and hope it gets into the warp before any of their own vessels turn up.

As it happened, though, Jurgen's driving skills proved equal to the challenge, and we reached the tunnel entrance just ahead of the necrons. I took another shot with the melta, downing one as we flashed past, flinched as another volley of gauss flayer fire riddled the bodywork of the truck even more comprehensively, then we were in blessed darkness, the welcoming yellow glow of the mine ahead of us.

# TWENTY-FOUR

After the eldritch half-light of the necron tomb, the welcoming yellow radiance of the luminators seemed almost dazzling, and I felt a surge of elation as we broke through into the cacophonous cavern, our ears assaulted once again by the noise of heavy industry. The truck lurched, taking another volley of gauss flayer fire, and faltered, the engine adopting a distinctly unhealthy rattling in counterpoint to the overstressed wailing I'd almost become used to. The whole vehicle was vibrating now, jarring my spine uncomfortably every couple of seconds, accompanied by a rhythmical thudding and a clattering like the last couple of stubber rounds in an ammo box. I shot an apprehensive glance at the pict screen, and found the tunnel behind us packed with our pursuers.

'Get us out of here!' I urged, probably quite unnecessarily, as I somehow doubted my aide felt like stopping for a friendly chat with them at this point, and gestured towards the tunnel across the crowded chamber from which Clode had emerged with our faltering transport what was beginning to feel like a lifetime ago. 'That tunnel over there!' It still seemed like our best route back to the upper levels at least, even if escaping to the surface no longer seemed like an option. Not unless we traded in our cargo-8 for one less perforated, anyway; but perhaps if we found where it had come from in the first place, the Emperor would provide – or, failing Him, Jurgen's propensity for acquiring things without the bother of filling out the appropriate forms in triplicate.

'Right you are, sir,' my aide responded, nursing the controls, and still getting a fair turn of speed out of our crippled conveyance despite, or perhaps because of, the distinctly un-tech-priest-like litany accompanying his efforts. He scowled at a couple of russet robes leaping for their lives as we passed them, and spat disdainfully through the gap where the top half of the driver's door used to be. 'Be a lot easier if these frakbrains would keep out of the way.'

Reminded again of the presence of the workers down here, I pushed what was left of my own door out of the way, and leant out of the cab, gesticulating wildly.

'Run!' I yelled, my voice completely lost in the racket surrounding us. 'Run for your lives!' A panic-stricken glance behind us confirmed my worst fears – the necrons had reached the cavern, and were fanning out, their sinisterly glowing weapons at the ready. But, to my surprise, they didn't immediately begin slaughtering everyone in sight; they simply plodded after us at their usual unhurried pace, apparently indifferent to the feverish activity surrounding them. That gave me pause, I have to admit – after their earlier sprint, the sudden change struck me as somehow confident, cocky almost. An emotion necrons definitely didn't have; though they didn't have any others either, come to that.

It was then that I noticed the most shocking sight I'd yet seen, in a day positively crammed with them. A necron a few paces ahead of the pack seemed a little different from the rest; as I watched, it turned its head, glancing at its surroundings with what seemed to be vague interest, before freezing into momentary immobility, like a tech-priest communing with the surrounding data flow. The others promptly changed direction, widening the skirmish line. This was the first time I'd seen anything resembling an officer among the living machines, let alone one apparently capable of something resembling independent thought instead of just following what seemed to be an instinctive drive to annihilate everything in its path.[134]

'Why aren't they killing everyone yet?' Jurgen asked, and I shook my head, equally baffled.

'Beats me,' I admitted, not really caring – so long as they weren't shooting at us, that was fine by me. I glanced back again, still scarcely able to credit what I'd seen, and the true horror of our situation suddenly became apparent. The necron leader was passing a couple of the local tech-priests, perhaps the ones Jurgen had almost mown down in our precipitate progress across the cavern; instead of fleeing, or simply staring at the metallic abominations in their midst in shocked incomprehension, both merely inclined their heads and made the sign of the cogwheel before going about their business.

---

134 *Some small percentage of necron warriors do indeed seem to have a kind of limited autonomy, although how much and under what circumstances still remains unclear. They are generally encountered in groups – a single one in charge of ordinary warriors appears to be quite unusual, unless Cain is simply misinterpreting what he was seeing, and all were of this type.*

'Holy Throne, the rank and file are in on it too!' Or a fair proportion of them, anyway. Which meant no one in the mine from Tezler on down could be trusted, and everyone we met was a potential enemy.

Well, you may think, no change there – I'd been working on that assumption since we first set foot in Metallum Majoris. But whatever I'd thought the conspirators we sought had been up to, this was far more heinous than my worst imaginings.

'That won't end well,' Jurgen opined, still fighting the controls as our battered truck bounced and slithered across the cavern floor, slaloming through the obstacles littering it far faster than anything I'd wager had been seen down here in living memory. (Or unliving, if you counted the necrons.) By some miracle we still hadn't hit anything, or anyone, but that didn't make us safe. On the contrary, the sinister metal figures I could see were clearly still after us, and I had no doubt that if they hadn't been instructed not to use their weapons where there was the possibility of evaporating a cogboy or two by accident, we would have been under fire the whole way. Why that seemed to be a consideration for them I had no idea at the time, but simply thanked the Throne for the brief respite.

Which I meant to use to its fullest advantage. Tapping my comm-bead, I tried to find the frequency I'd used before in an attempt to contact Morie, still hoping against hope that I'd be able to yell for help – or, better still, be reassured that my earlier message had got through, and that it was already on the way. Predictably, however, I was to be disappointed, finding only a wash of white noise so strong that the channel had to be being deliberately jammed.

'We're on our own,' I told Jurgen, as our much-abused

truck bounced over a set of tramlines, and entered a broad, high tunnel carved into the bedrock, sloping gently upwards. The engine growled and rattled, and the whole thing shook worse than ever. We seemed to be moving more slowly, too, I noticed, although I forbore to mention it, knowing that my aide was doing his best, and that hardly anyone else would have been able to keep the motile scrap pile moving at all.

'No change there then,' he responded phlegmatically, which, perversely, I found somewhat encouraging. We'd certainly been in enough dire situations together over the years, more often than not with no help to be had, and we'd managed to survive well enough.

'I suppose not,' I agreed, and took another glance at the pict screen. It was hard to pick out our pursuers from the rest of the activity in my narrowing view of the cavern behind us, but I was sure they were hard on our heels, moving metallic glints appearing intermittently, and worryingly close. Not for the first time I found myself reflecting how much ground a steady pace could cover in a frighteningly short period, unbroken by a single misstep or slowed by fatigue. 'At least we seem to be keeping out of range.' So far, at least.

Traffic in the tunnel was light, people on foot for the most part, interspersed with the inevitable servitors moving heavy equipment about, but there were no other vehicles in sight; something I found both encouraging and worrying in equal measure. Encouraging because Jurgen could keep his foot down without having to evade any significant obstruction, and worrying because the paucity of other traffic implied that it was relatively rare this deep in the mine, and a replacement for our labouring truck was going to be hard to come by if it gave up the ghost.

Which seemed more and more likely by the moment. We

were definitely losing speed now, Jurgen dropping down through the gears in an attempt to keep the wheels turning, while the jolting and buffeting was getting more pronounced than ever.

'Drivetrain must be damaged,' Jurgen said, as though simply exchanging pleasantries. He shrugged. 'Can't say I'm surprised, after all the holes the tinheads have put in us.'

'Looks that way,' I agreed, as if I knew what he was talking about; but whatever it was, I was inclined to take his word for it, given the number of vehicles he'd pushed to their limits and beyond over the years. 'Will it hold together long enough to get us to the upper levels?'

One of these days I'm going to learn to stop asking questions like that. Hardly had the words left my mouth than a loud *crack* echoed from the tunnel walls enclosing us, and the truck shuddered to a halt, its motor racing, and, by the sound of it, trying to shake itself to pieces inside the scored and perforated engine compartment.

'Don't think so, sir, no,' Jurgen said regretfully, reaching out to cut the power. Relative silence descended, as though he'd just granted the mortally wounded vehicle the Emperor's Peace.[135]

'So we're on foot from now on,' I said, clambering down from what was left of the cab, and drawing my laspistol, indifferent to the curious glances of a couple of passing artisans. I looked back down the tunnel. We'd come a little further than I'd realised, but our head start was being eroded by the second.

'Best get moving, then,' Jurgen agreed, jumping from the cab and scrambling for his weapons.

---

135  An Imperial Guard euphemism for the mercy killing of grievously wounded troopers.

'We had,' I said, striding out up the gently sloping tunnel as I spoke, Jurgen falling in at my shoulder as always. It receded into the distance, no sign of any side passages which might have afforded some measure of concealment, and my heart sank at the realisation. We couldn't outpace our tireless pursuers, that much was obvious; our only chance of survival would be to somehow give them the slip. Which would be far easier said than done.

Despite my apprehension I couldn't resist glancing back once more as we set off, and immediately wished I hadn't; sinister metal figures were already entering the tunnel, their hellish weapons glowing visibly in the reduced illumination of the widely spaced electro-sconces set into the walls every thirty or forty metres. At this rate they'd be in firing range within moments, and I picked up my pace a little, fighting the urge to run. Understandable as it was, giving in to the impulse would be fatal; Jurgen and I would tire quickly, especially as we were moving uphill the whole way, and as soon as we began to slow the gap would close. Almost by instinct we fell into the traditional infantryman's gait, which would eat up the kilometres as efficiently as possible, hoping that would keep us far enough ahead to find some kind of shelter or means of escape before our relentless pursuers came into effective range.

'Traffic's thinning out,' Jurgen said after a few moments, and I nodded.

'I noticed that too,' I said, not bothering to add that I'd hoped it had only been my paranoia imagining the worst. But he was undeniably right. The number of mine workers traversing the passage had dwindled perceptibly in the last few minutes – in fact we were practically alone now. And that could only mean one thing. Someone was diverting them away from this gallery. I could think of several reasons for that, and liked none of them. 'All we can do is press on.'

Which was becoming more and more difficult, I have to admit. We'd been down here for hours by now, don't forget, at a time when we'd expected to be sleeping, and our little adventures on the way had been strenuous to say the least. I was definitely beginning to flag, and although Jurgen remained as stoic as ever, I had no doubt that he too was feeling the strain.

I glanced back again, finding my worst fears realised. Our pursuers had gained a little ground, and their weapons were readied for use. Galvanised, I picked up my pace again, Jurgen following suit as always, but all too soon our footfalls became laggardly, the constant slope sapping our energy as though we were wading through a swamp. I began to feel uncannily as if we were trapped in one of those nightmares where something formless and evil is dogging your heels just out of sight, but in this case the evil was all too visible, and becoming closer every time I turned my head. My breath began to rasp in my throat, and I cast around desperately for any kind of refuge, even a discarded crate we could hide behind long enough to engage our pursuers, but fortunately, perhaps, there was nothing, not even an irregularity in the tunnel walls sufficiently large to provide a bit of cover. Fortunately, because attempting to stand and fight would simply have got both of us killed, and it was only the fatigue dulling my synapses which prompted the thought in the first place.

'Shouldn't we have reached a side passage by now?' Jurgen asked, as though the mine was somehow breaching etiquette by failing to provide one.

'Probably,' I agreed. We were still some way from the mapped portion of the complex by my estimate, but the lack of other galleries intersecting with this one seemed puzzling to me. The only explanation I could think of was that this tunnel had been constructed specifically to access the necron tomb, which could only mean in turn that prodigious amounts of refined materials had vanished through the warp portal in the last few years. Despite our immediate predicament, I found myself wondering what that could mean – why would the lifeless metal killers need so much of it?

'There's something up ahead,' Jurgen said, just as a beam of necrotic light struck the tunnel wall close to our position, punching a neat circular shaft in the bedrock deeper than I could easily see. It had probably been a ranging shot rather than a serious attempt to kill us, but we took to our heels anyway, all thought of conserving our energy forgotten. 'Praise the Throne, it's a door!'

'Looks like it,' I agreed, trying to focus on the metallic structure which protruded from the tunnel wall ahead of us. It was curved, like part of a pipe, and, as my aide had pointed out, a door had been set into it, following the shape of the cylinder. For a moment I couldn't make out what it was, other than a potential way out of here, then realisation struck. 'It's a transport tube, like some of the void stations have!'[136]

'I think you're right, sir,' Jurgen said, as though the matter were of no more than academic interest. 'Wonder where it goes?'

---

136   *An arrangement of branching pneumatic tubes, through which sealed compartments containing passengers and other items can be quickly and easily conveyed. The abrupt changes of direction are usually compensated for by localised gravity units; even so, they are far from comfortable, and a strong stomach is recommended. Not unknown on planetary surfaces, but far less common; where they are employed, most people outside the Adeptus Mechanicus prefer to take the stairs.*

'Who cares?' I asked, not entirely rhetorically, 'so long as it's deficient in necrons.' We panted up to it, and I slapped the activation plate, hoping the door would open. It didn't, but a panel lit up, counting down the time until the next piston arrived. At almost the same moment another gauss flayer beam ripped through the air between us, and I whirled round, bringing my laspistol to bear.

The hideous things were closer than even my most pessimistic estimate, evenly spaced across the width of the tunnel, advancing in lockstep, highlights from the electro-sconces glittering from their torsos and skull-like heads. I cracked off a couple of shots, which seemed to do little more than raise rapidly fading blemishes on the chest of the one I took for their leader. The automaton turned its head to look directly at me as though in mild reproof. Its weapon was bulkier than those of its subordinates, and although I had no idea what it might do, I instinctively regarded it as the greater threat.

'Aim for that one!' I called to Jurgen, who by now was already levelling the melta. Too preoccupied to respond, he merely grunted something I took for acquiescence, and squeezed the trigger.

The results were highly satisfying, at least for a short while. The burst of thermal energy struck its target, square on the peculiar weapon it carried, the backwash gouging a deep crater in the leader's torso. Then, to my dismay, it strode on regardless, ignoring the damage which should have felled it, and bringing the huge and sinister-looking gun to bear. As it did so its subordinates echoed the gesture, every gauss flayer being levelled at us with a simultaneous precision which would have elicited a grudging nod of approval from even the most exacting of drill sergeants.

For a moment I stared death in the face, squeezing the

trigger of my laspistol in the forlorn hope of getting off one more retaliatory las-bolt before my mortal frame shrivelled into nothingness; then the damaged necron weapon sparked, exploded and wreathed the entire squad in a storm of lightning bolts, which jumped from one to the other in a maelstrom of destructive energy. The air became acrid with the stench of ozone, and the leader dropped, the metal of which it was composed distorting and flowing like candle wax. The warriors nearest to it fared little better, staggering back, wreathed in eldritch fire, coming apart at the seams even as we watched.

'Lucky I clipped it,' Jurgen remarked. 'Wouldn't want to be on the wrong end of that.'

'Neither would I,' I agreed, with a faintly panic-stricken glance at the numbers still counting down on the door panel. The transport capsule was almost here, but was still taking a bit too long about it for my liking. 'Better stay sharp. These things take a lot to put down.'

Well, I wasn't wrong about that. As the lightning storm subsided, the leader and the most badly damaged of the soldiery accompanying it faded from view, the crack of air floating into the sudden voids they no longer occupied being drowned out by a last few electrical discharges. The survivors, however, resumed their relentless forward march, a volley of gauss flayer fire slicing the air ahead of them. A few of my laspistol bolts found their mark, having just as little effect as before, and Jurgen downed another by the simple expedient of vaporising one of its legs, leaving it scrabbling forward trying to shoot one-handed from the ground, but we were still outnumbered and outgunned – barring a miracle, we had only seconds left.

Then the door to the travel pod swung smoothly aside,

releasing a hiss of compressed air and a hymn to the Omnis-siah that sounded like somebody failing to juggle a pile of scrap.

'Get in!' I yelled, following my own advice, Jurgen hard on my heels. I smacked the closure rune, and the door thudded into place behind us, cutting off the resonant clatter of metal on stone, and sealing us in with Jurgen's distinctive odour and the cacophonous melody. An irritation I relieved us of almost at once by the simple expedient of putting a las-bolt through the speaker.

'Where to, sir?' Jurgen was studying the controls, which seemed to be displaying a bewildering array of potential destinations.

'Anywhere but here!' I snapped, as a resonant clang echoed through our surroundings. It wasn't going to take the necrons long to get through the doorway, even if they didn't bother just vaporising it with their flayers. I hit the activator, and a sudden surge of motion almost knocked me off my feet. If my inner ear could be trusted we were rising fast, which was fine by me. Now we were on the move, I joined Jurgen in peering at the read-outs. 'Looks as though we're just going to whatever the last destination somebody picked is.'

'Oh, right.' Jurgen scratched absent-mindedly at one of his larger patches of psoriasis, and shrugged. 'Don't suppose it can be any worse than where we've just been, anyway.'

Which was tempting fate if anything was.

# TWENTY-FIVE

As the transport pod lurched and rattled its way towards the surface, with a complete disregard for the comfort of its occupants which made me suspect that only senior tech-priests ever used the thing, I began to wonder who'd built the network and why. Given that no one had mentioned its existence to me at any point since our arrival, and that we'd boarded it in a part of the mine Tezler had gone to some pains to prevent me finding out about, I suspected it connected concealed sites crucial to the conspiracy; perhaps even harbouring more necrons. Which meant that, wherever we were going, we were likely to find ourselves among enemies when we arrived. I said as much to Jurgen, who nodded soberly.

'Don't suppose we're going to find many friends around here,' he agreed.

That reminded me of Morie again, and I activated my vox-bead, only to discover that we were still being jammed

on all the frequencies I could reach. Though I still hadn't
given up all hope of getting through to him, it looked as if
we'd be on our own for a while yet.

The pod jerked again, then came to a sudden halt. For
a moment nothing happened, then the *clunk* of disengag-
ing latches echoed around the enclosed space, followed by
another hiss of equalising pressure. I lifted my weapons as
the door slid open, but no enemies appeared, and I took a
deep breath.

'Time to find out where we are,' I said. All I could see
through the widening gap was a wall a handful of metres
away, which, from the ambient acoustics and the abstract
patterning adorning it, I thought was probably a corridor
somewhere in the main complex.

My spirits rose. With any luck I'd be able to orientate
myself now, and find a route out of here. If I'd been right
about Tezler monitoring our conversation with Clode, the
only sensible option would be to find a vehicle and make a
run for it straight away, before anyone realised we'd found
our way back to the upper levels.

I took a cautious step into the passageway, finding it curiously quiet – unlike the corridors I'd criss-crossed in my tour
of inspection, hardly anyone was around, the few exceptions
being russet-robed tech-priests hurrying along in ones and
twos, too engrossed in their own affairs to pay us any heed.
Or so it seemed; by this time I was unwilling to trust the
appearance of anyone or anything around here.

'Should we try one of these doors?' Jurgen asked, indicating
the nearest. There were several lining the walls, every dozen
metres or so, and I shook my head – there was no telling
who, or what, might be lurking behind them.

'Best keep moving,' I said, hoping to find some clue as to

where we'd ended up. The doors all had neat little metal plaques attached to them, so I squinted at the nearest, finding it embossed with a sequence of fine lines of varying thickness, and a couple of words in plain Gothic. *Magos Kathoed*. With a sudden surge of relief I realised where we were, and why the corridor seemed so quiet. 'We're in the cogboys' living quarters.'

'If you call being a cogboy living,' Jurgen added.

His cynicism notwithstanding, I felt a sudden surge of optimism. All at once the rare and unwelcome sense of disorientation which had been plaguing me ever since we stumbled across the necron tomb was lifted. I'd been paying, as was my habit, particular attention during my guided wanderings around Metallum Majoris to any potential lines of retreat in case I needed one in a hurry, and right now I most definitely did. There should be a loading area a few levels up, where vehicles were prepared for deliveries of raw materials to the nearest manufactories. If we could just make it there without further incident, we should be able to acquire one and be well away before anyone even realised we'd gone.

'Commissar. What an agreeable surprise.'

I spun round, raising my laspistol, while Jurgen brought up the melta, recognising Tezler's mellifluous tones before I even caught sight of them. The silver mannequin was standing a few strides behind us, next to an open door.

'I thought you must still be grubbing about in the bowels of the earth. Or dead, of course, ha ha.'

'Sorry to disappoint you,' I said, reining in the impulse to pull the trigger with some considerable effort. The las-bolt would probably do relatively little damage to the treacherous tech-priest's mechanical carcass, but Jurgen would follow my lead in an instant, and gratifying as it would be to see them reduced to a puddle of slag, there was still too much I didn't know. If I was going to get out of here with my hide intact, the more information I had the better. And I could always kill Tezler later; Throne knew they deserved it.

'Disappointed?' the piping voice responded, while the body emitting it adopted an attitude indicative of polite surprise. 'Quite the contrary.' They stood aside, indicating the doorway behind them. 'My guest was most impressed by your resourcefulness, and would like to make your closer acquaintance.'

I gestured towards the open door with the laspistol. 'After you.'

'By all means, ha ha.' Tezler turned, and disappeared through it. Jurgen and I exchanged glances.

'Are you sure about this, sir?' Jurgen asked, and I shook my head.

'Far from it. But if we're going to find out exactly what that heretical boltbag's been up to, I don't see we have a choice.' I glanced up and down the corridor. 'Stay here and cover our line of retreat.' I'd have preferred him to accompany me, of course, the melta being a reasonable assurance of Tezler's good behaviour, not to mention that of whoever else might be lurking in their quarters, but leaving him on overwatch made better tactical sense. Besides, after some of the horrors I'd faced over the years, I felt confident of being able to hold my own against whatever Tezler and whoever they'd been conspiring with were capable of throwing at me.

My aide nodded. 'I'll keep you covered from out here,' he said, taking up a guard position opposite the door, where he could see into the room, and both ways up and down the corridor. He tapped the comm-bead in his ear meaningfully. 'And I'll listen in. First sign of trouble, I'll be there.'

'I don't doubt it,' I said, feeling reassured, as always, by his vigilance. So I followed our host into the room, checking each side of the doorway for potential lurking assailants as I entered, although I didn't really expect them to try anything so crude or obvious.

'Please, make yourself comfortable,' Tezler said, gesturing to a well-padded couch in the centre of the room. I approached it, keeping the laspistol in my hand, taking in the rest of their quarters as I did so. I hadn't visited many tech-priests in their own personal space before, but much of it was as I'd expected: the plain metal walls, embellished with abstract designs reminiscent of machinery and circuit boards; the utilitarian furnishings, and votive icons of the Cult Mechanicus scattered about on shelves and small tables. Pride of place was given to a large and competently executed painting of the Emperor in His aspect of the Omnissiah, a metallic figure enthroned on a pile of what looked like scrap to me, but which probably represented specific pieces of junk of particular theological significance to His acolytes. After what I'd seen in the last few hours, the gleaming humaniform figure seemed positively sinister to me, though Tezler must have liked it, because a statue of the same image, about half again as tall as I was, stood in one corner. 'Some refreshment? I recall that you're partial to these, although I'm sure you'll forgive me for not joining you. I lack the requisite biological functions these days, ha ha.'

I regarded the tray on a small table next to the sofa dubiously; it held a pot of recaff, a finely wrought steel cup and a plate of florn cakes, still warm from the oven. The recaff was still hot, too, I noted, and glanced around for a door it could have been delivered through, though I failed to see any sign of one. Which didn't mean there wasn't a concealed entrance somewhere, of course; the guest they'd alluded to was nowhere to be seen, and they could hardly have evaporated, so they must have sneaked out some other way. As I sat, I angled myself to keep my back to the door Jurgen was covering, relieved to see his distorted reflection still on guard in the polished metal of the recaff pot as I lifted it to pour, alert for any sudden movement in the rest of the room.

'You shouldn't have gone to all this trouble,' I said, determined to seem as much at my ease as possible. Tezler was impossible to read, but I wasn't going to make things any easier for them than I could help either.

'It was no trouble, I assure you,' Tezler said. 'If you survived your visit to the shrine below, your most probable point of emergence would be the one you took. I simply ordered the refreshments on the off-chance. And I'm pleased to see the effort wasn't wasted.'

'Quite,' I said, taking a sip of the bitter liquid, and replacing the cup on the table to pick up a florn cake. I was prepared to play the game of good manners, but I wasn't foolish enough to put my laspistol down while I was doing it. I took a bite, finding it considerably more palatable than most of the food I'd had since my arrival there; it did cross my mind that it might have been poisoned, but I couldn't see why Tezler would have bothered, since they'd already had plenty of opportunities to kill me if they'd been so inclined. 'That would have been an inefficient use of your resources.'

'Precisely,' Tezler said, inclining their head in agreement.

'But I have to admit to some confusion,' I said, having disposed of the cake and lifted the cup again. A strange sense of deja vu floated across my synapses for a moment, until I realised what the conversation reminded me of: the superficially civilised chat I'd had over the tea table many years before with Killian, the deranged renegade inquisitor who'd hoped to win me over to his cause.[137] That had ended in a bloodbath, of course, and I could scarcely hope for a better outcome on this occasion; but Tezler was evidently gripped by a similar compulsion to have someone admire their cleverness, which meant that by playing suitably impressed I could probably find out exactly what had been going on here. Whether I'd survive long enough to report it back to Zyvan, or Amberley, was a moot point, but I'd certainly give it my best shot. 'I've never heard of anyone brokering a truce with the necrons before.'

'Probably because their potential partners fail to grasp the wonders to be gained by co-operation,' Tezler said earnestly. Though they spoke in the same piping tones as always, I had no doubt that their original voice, had they still possessed it, would have been suffused with the same insane fervour that Killian's had taken on at about this point in the conversation. 'Not to mention their essential divinity.'

'Divinity?' I echoed, almost choking on the recaff.

'Of course.' Tezler gestured to the painting on the wall, which, now I came to observe it more closely, looked more like a necron dressed up with a few Imperial votive symbols than the Machine-God as an avatar of the Emperor. Though I've never been all that pious, finding the average Emperor-botherer tedious company at best, the sheer depth of the blasphemy that implied practically took my breath away. 'Are they not the perfect embodiment of life purged of all organic imperfections, the very state the Omnissiah teaches us to aspire to?'

---

137   *Already described in exhaustive detail in an earlier volume of his memoirs.*

'It's a point of view,' I conceded, as politely as I could, 'although it's one for the theologians as far as I'm concerned. I'm just a soldier, who's only ever seen them as an enemy.' The plain-speaking warrior was a persona I'd grown adept at hiding behind over the years, and it's served me well. Tezler seemed to be buying it anyway, as they responded with another carefully modulated nod.

'Only to be expected,' they conceded. 'But you do see what we're hoping to achieve here by enlisting their aid?'

'Not exactly,' I said, meaning not in the slightest. Nothing good, though, of that I was certain, but I kept my voice as neutral as I could, with the ease of decades of practised dissembling.

'Transcendence,' Tezler said, as mellifluously as ever, though I thought I detected a tremor of eagerness beneath their even tones. 'The uploading of human consciousness to perfect, imperishable bodies, formed in the very image of the Omnissiah!' Their sculpted metal head tilted slightly in stylised ecstasy. 'Can you even imagine it?'

'Not easily,' I admitted, concealing the sheer horror which coursed through me as the full import of their words sunk in. 'And this would be all humans, would it?'

'All those who desired it,' Tezler said, with the complete tunnel vision of the fanatic. 'The Cult Mechanicus would lead the way, of course, but who wouldn't embrace immortal perfection given the chance?'

'A good question,' I said, meaning 'practically everyone if immortality meant turning into a bloody necron', although putting that thought into words would hardly be politic under the circumstances. I pretended to think about it for a moment. 'But how can you be sure that it's even possible?'

'Because the necrons achieved it,' Tezler said, with perfectly circular logic. 'They must once have been mortal, vulnerable to all the frailties of the flesh, just as we are.' I looked at their mechanical body with, I must admit, some degree of scepticism, though I suppose they must still have had a few squishy bits sealed away inside somewhere. 'But they transcended. We can do the same.'

I considered this. In all my previous encounters with the necrons I'd thought of them as entirely mechanical constructs, like homicidal CATs, only bigger, simply following preprogrammed instructions to wipe out every living thing they encountered. The notion that they had once been living creatures, voluntarily discarding their humanity (or xenosity, or whatever their equivalent had been) was a profoundly disturbing one.

'It's a heady vision,' I said, playing for time. 'I take it Clode discovered what you were up to, and signed up on the spot?'

'Indeed,' Tezler said, inclining their head again. 'It would, perhaps, have been better had he returned to Coronus to report all was well here, forestalling your intervention, but he was eager to remain, in order to transcend as soon as possible.'

'So this is all happening soon, then?' I asked. Tezler nodded, with a fair pantomime of eagerness.

'So we are given to understand,' they said. 'The preparations are complex, and require prodigious amounts of materials. But our new bodies are being constructed even as we speak. Soon we will transcend. Then humanity will be safe forever from the depredations of Chaos and the xenos breeds.'

'I see.' I nodded. The psychotic boltbag may not have had any of the subtle tells I was used to reading in the course of more human interaction (and which I'm so adept at suppressing in myself), but I can tell when someone wants to

*Sandy Mitchell*

believe something so much they'll wilfully ignore any and all evidence to the contrary. The necrons were stringing them along, I was certain of that. 'And the skitarii you suborned? I take it they were all for this transcendence lark too?' That was pure speculation on my part, of course, but it seemed plausible, and I'd jolted enough admissions of infractions out of defaulters over the years by pretending to know what they'd been up to already, so it seemed worth a try.

'Regrettably not,' Tezler said, with another carefully modulated shake of their head. 'Although you are correct in your inference that a few of the security details assigned here have stumbled across evidence of the shrine below from time to time. Unfortunately their loyalty to their commanders was hardwired into them, which made them immune to all attempts at persuasion. And that left us with only one option.'

'Killing them?' I suggested, pretending to be slower on the uptake than I actually was. Doing that would have attracted far more attention to Metallum Majoris, and dead skitarii wouldn't have been able to turn on us at the proving grounds. As I'd hoped, however, my apparent obtuseness provoked Tezler into explaining in more detail.

'Of course not. We merely modified their cortical programming to remove the memories. And took advantage of the situation to install a few datanomes of our own, ha ha.'

'Forcing them to turn on their own comrades,' I said, failing to keep all of the anger I felt at that entirely suppressed. Skitarii were hardly like the normal human soldiers I habitually served alongside, but I knew they must still feel loyalty to their comrades and the causes they fought for; a forced betrayal like that struck at everything that made them who they were.

'Exactly,' Tezler confirmed, as though expecting to be congratulated on their cleverness. 'The behavioural modifications were activated by a simple signal.' Perhaps they belatedly read something of the tenor of my thoughts, because they produced a prolonged musical note I suspected I was supposed to interpret as a sigh. 'Quite regrettable, but by that point you had already survived three attempts to prevent your interference, and seemed to be forming an alliance with an alarmingly high probability of disrupting our plans. We had hoped to foment distrust between Praetor Norgard and yourself. Not to mention the Space Marines, of course. An escalating confrontation with them would have covered our tracks until the transcendence was fully under way. And once that happened, naturally all true followers of the Omnissiah would have joined us, including Norgard and her skitarii.'

Well, if they truly thought that, they had a very tenuous grasp of both the woman herself and the troops she led. But I nodded anyway, as though they'd scored a substantial debating point.

'A clever stratagem,' I said, and Throne help me if Tezler didn't nod in evident satisfaction, as though I'd just paid them a compliment. 'Which I assume you've applied to the current security detail?'

Tezler shook their head. 'Not as yet. It seemed unnecessary, given that they remain ignorant of our true purpose.'

'Very wise. Why take the risk of attracting Norgard's attention now that she's wasting her time investigating her own men?'

'Precisely,' Tezler said. 'I can see that you understand all of the essentials.'

'Not entirely,' I said, coming to the nub of the matter at last. 'I can see what you're hoping to gain from this alliance, but I don't really grasp what the necrons are getting out of it.'

'My success and elevation,' a new voice said, in impeccable Gothic, though delivered in an echoing monotone which set my teeth and inner ear on edge. I sprang to my feet, bringing my laspistol up and drawing my chainsword in one smooth motion, as the statue in the corner took a leisurely pace forward.

# TWENTY-SIX

If I'm honest, I expected to die before I even pulled the trigger, but I fired anyway, placing two rounds squarely in the middle of the thing's chest. Instead of retaliating, though, the towering figure simply stopped moving, and raised a finger in what, in a human, would have been a gesture of mild reproof.

'Really?' it said, in the same sepulchral voice as before. It turned to Tezler. 'You said this one was intelligent.'

The tech-priest shuffled their feet in what I took to be an indication of embarrassment. 'He has a reputation for considerable acuity,' they said. 'And he's already demonstrated his resourcefulness by infiltrating the tomb.'

'The disruption he inflicted is of no consequence.'

'I'll try harder next time,' I said, deciding that I heartily disliked this specimen even more than the average necron, which at least had the courtesy to kill you without making disparaging remarks beforehand. Come to that, I'd never previously encountered one which had shown the slightest interest in conversation, or, indeed, the ability.[138]

'Commissar.' Jurgen's voice was in my comm-bead, hushed and urgent. '*I can't get a clear shot. Stand aside.*'

The metal figure turned its head towards the door. 'I'll kill your pet unless he relinquishes the weapon.'

'Jurgen,' I said, 'stand down. I don't think we're in any immediate danger.' Which was something of an exaggeration, but there was no point in appearing too concerned. I didn't doubt that the towering necron could make good on its threat, but the fact that it hadn't yet meant that for some reason it was reluctant to, and if I could find out what that was it might give us some advantage.

'Very good, sir.' My aide complied as readily as he always did with a direct order, although the tone of his voice and the glare he bestowed on the metal giant as he lowered the melta left me in no doubt as to what he thought about the wisdom of that. 'I'll keep an eye on the corridor, then.'

'If you wouldn't mind,' I said, then glanced dismissively at Tezler before returning my attention to the necron leader. 'I take it you'd rather your own pets were left intact as well?' The tech-priest didn't exactly bristle, but the attitude of their head altered a little, as though they were considering the full implications of the remark, and not liking any of them.

The necron nodded. 'I would prefer it,' it said, turning its

---

138   *Records of necron encounters tend to the fragmentary, given the low number of survivors, but the Ordo Xenos has begun to draw some tentative conclusions about the matter. The vast majority do indeed seem essentially devoid of intellect, but the leaders among them are clearly of a higher order, and have been observed communicating among themselves. Occasions on which they have conversed directly with members of other races are not entirely unknown either, although such exchanges tend to be rather on the terse side.*

own head to look at Tezler with an air of what seemed suspiciously like disdain. 'You must have something useful to do.'

'Of course.' Accepting the clear dismissal with a creditable display of good grace, the treacherous tech-priest slunk out of their own quarters, sidestepping the immovable obstacle of Jurgen in a somewhat dignity-puncturing shuffle.

'You heard our host,' I said, more to rub it in while Tezler was still in earshot than because I thought he needed the instructions, 'no shooting anyone unless you have to.'

'Quite so, sir.' Jurgen nodded, adjusting to the situation far more readily than most men in his position would, his singular lack of imagination proving as useful as it always did. 'Good manners cost nothing.'

'Couldn't have put it better myself,' I said, and turned back to the towering metal figure in front of me. 'And speaking of which, I'm afraid we haven't been properly introduced.' Quite where that came from I had no idea, but I'd learned a long time ago that the appearance of being at ease put me in control of a situation, however much my mind was scrabbling around like a rodent in an exercise wheel gibbering in panic, and the occasional non sequitur went a long way towards keeping an antagonist off guard. Naturally, I had no idea what kind of mental processes a sapient pile of genocidal scrap might actually have, but it couldn't hurt to try. To my surprise it inclined its head, in a parody of sociability.

'How remiss. I am Aznibal, overlord of the Hapset Dynasty, suzerain of the Vodik Expanse.' None of which meant anything to me, naturally.[139] 'Your name and reputation I have been apprised of.'

---

139  *The necrons have their own names for worlds and regions of the galaxy, not all of which even exist any more.*

'Of course.' I nodded too, and decided against offering a hand to shake, in the interests of keeping it. 'A demesne you're clearly expanding. You'd hardly have let Eucopia be colonised if you'd already owned the place. I'm guessing you came through the portal once the tomb was discovered and its systems activated in response.' Which was more or less what I'd seen before on Simia Orichalcae, so it wasn't all that much of a stretch.

'Astute.' The metallic monstrosity looked down at me in a faintly ruminative manner I found far from comforting. 'Perhaps Tezler didn't overestimate you.'

'I'm sure they did,' I said, more from the habit of maintaining my undeserved reputation for modesty about my equally undeserved one for selfless heroism than anything else. 'But they do seem remarkably easy to fool. You have no intention of giving your dupes here necron bodies, do you?'

'Of course not,' Aznibal admitted. 'It would be an honour far greater than they deserve, even if it were possible.'

'So you never were mortal?' I asked. To my astonishment Aznibal laughed, an echoing, hollow mockery of amusement.

'That part is true. But we were not the ones who performed the transference. That was done by the old masters, before they were sundered and the shards became the slaves.'

'I see,' I said, entirely untruthfully. Elaborate metaphors have never really worked for me, although the gist of it seemed clear enough. The necrons had been turned into whatever they were by someone or something else, which was no longer around to perform the same trick. 'And the resources you've cozened them out of are being used for…?'

'This,' Aznibal said, making a strange gesture in the air. An image suddenly appeared, floating in the space between us, as crisp and clear as a t'au hololith. An asteroid, seen from some distance away, rotating gently in the void between the stars. There was little to indicate its scale at first, our viewpoint moving in towards it, the refulgence of the spiral arm behind it striking glittering highlights from its surface. These, on closer inspection, proved to be the locations of metallic structures protruding from the regolith, weapon emplacements of prodigious size for the most part, bestowing a palpable air of menace on the benighted rock. Only when a starship, an image I remembered all too well from the destruction of the *Omnissiah's Bounty*,[140] drifted into the field of vision did I realise that the void station must have been several kilometres across.

'Once it has been restored to its full capabilities, my elevation to phaeron will be assured.' The parody of laughter echoed around the room again, raising the hairs on the back of my neck. You never can tell with xenos quite how sane they are, especially a specimen like this, which, by its very nature, lacks the usual subtle clues of facial expression and body language, but I was pretty sure that if I'd been having the same conversation with a human, I'd have been keeping a wary eye out for medicae with sedatives and straitjackets by now. 'Then those who mocked and patronised me will acknowledge my power or be annihilated.'

'How very nice for you,' I said, masking my astonishment that even necrons seemed to get embroiled in petty rivalries. 'But I don't see why you didn't simply send your warriors to take what you need instead of resorting to subterfuge. With the element of surprise, you could have taken this world easily.'

---

140　*The vessel which had conveyed him, and the ill-fated Mechanicus scavenging expedition, to Interitus Prime.*

'Indeed I could.' Aznibal was looking at me again in the same appraising manner. 'But holding on to it once your Imperium responded would have required a bit of effort, and delayed the completion of the battle station. Once it's mobile that won't be a problem, but some work still remains to achieve that.'

'Mobile?' I repeated, hoping I'd misheard, but knowing I hadn't. I'd seen the files on the necron World Engine which had ripped its way through the galaxy at the beginning of the century, and my blood ran cold at the memory. Stopping it had required the sacrifice of an entire Space Marine Chapter,[141] not to mention innumerable Navy vessels and personnel. The asteroid station Aznibal had shown me was nothing like the size of that, thank the Throne, but the amount of damage it could wreak if it became operational was incalculable.

'Of course.' The hollow voice took on a tinge of smugness, although that could just have been my imagination, I suppose.[142] 'There would be no point in having a weapon that potent if it couldn't reach something to destroy.'

'I suppose there wouldn't,' I said. An awkward silence descended, like one of those moments at a formal reception when you've both run out of conventional platitudes to exchange, and are wondering how to go and find someone else to bore without appearing to be rude. 'Was there anything else you wanted to tell me?'

---

141   *The Astral Knights, whose heroic last stand is still commemorated and revered throughout the Imperium. There were, of course, a few survivors, chiefly detached units too far from the conflict to rejoin their battle-brothers in time, but too few to continue their Chapter's traditions; they were absorbed into the newly founded Sable Swords as a veteran training cadre, with, apparently, great success.*

142   *Almost certainly correctly.*

'Only that now you know I'm here, I'm claiming the planet,' Aznibal said. 'Keep the tribute coming, and you get to live. Otherwise it will be taken, and everyone will die. The first option is marginally preferable, because the battle station will become operational sooner, but another few years are neither here nor there to an immortal.' He raised a hand, and I suppressed a reflexive flinch, before realising the gesture was one of mocking farewell. 'You have seen the extent of my power. Choose. Spend your momentary flicker of existence serving a purpose greater than you can possibly imagine, or be annihilated by it.'

Then he vanished, with the familiar *crack* of imploding air left by a displacer field.

'Neat trick,' Jurgen said, in a tone which implied it had been anything but. 'Do you think we were supposed to be impressed?'

*Editorial Note:*

*Since Cain, predictably, skips over much of what hap-
pened in the next few days in the apparent belief that
anything which didn't concern him personally can be
disregarded as of little interest to anyone else, I've inter-
polated another extract which touches on most of the
essentials.*

From *In Blackest Night: The Millennial Wars Appraised*, by
Ayjaepi Clothier, 127.M42.

The revelation of the true nature of the foe which had
so insidiously corrupted the weaker-minded among the
Adeptus Mechanicus on Eucopia was to have far-reaching
implications, not just for that world, but for the entire sector. The arrest of the conspirators was only the first step in
mitigating the harm they had done, but, as ever, Commissar
Cain remained undaunted, conceiving a plan remarkable in
both its daring and its effectiveness. That it worked as well
as it did can only be considered a result of his inspiring

leadership, and the unparalleled martial expertise of the Adeptus Astartes.

Not that the outcome was by any means assured...

# TWENTY-SEVEN

The conference room in the Reclaimers' Chapter holding was pretty much as I remembered it, other than the presence of Vorspung, who had arrived in a Rhino a few hours before and seemed a little uncomfortable so far from his habitual haunts. Even though the back of the conspiracy had been effectively broken with Tezler's detention, there was no telling how many of their associates had so far escaped the net Norgard had thrown over the Nexus, and no one wanted to take any chances with the magos' safety; after all, he'd been the first to suspect that something clandestine was going on, found the courage to confide in me, and been instrumental in bringing the perpetrators to book. The last thing we needed was a stray traitor deciding to kill him in a fit of pique, especially as it felt as if we were going to need his intellect more than ever now.

He looked up as I entered the room, making a beeline for the samovar of tanna as soon as I arrived, and finding it full, to my intense relief. Though the afternoon seemed like it was going to be a long one, it should at least be more tolerable now.

'Magos,' I greeted him. 'I'm pleased to see you so well.' To my vague surprise I found I actually meant it; despite my initial doubts at our first meeting he'd proved to be a valuable ally, and at least there was a bit of flesh left on his face, which, after Tezler's blank robotic visage, seemed positively homely. I finished filling my tea bowl, and, more from the dictates of good manners than anything else, indicated one of the surprisingly delicate pieces of ceramic beside the samovar.[143] 'Can I offer you some refreshment?'

To my surprise he nodded. 'Thank you. I require the ingestion of thirty-seven millilitres of fluids within the next day or so to maintain peak operation of my biological components, and doing so now would be an efficient use of the time while we wait for the others.' Which for a tech-priest was being positively sociable. I handed him a full bowl of the fragrant liquid, which he sipped at, apparently indifferent to its tongue-scalding temperature, then nodded again. 'Remarkably flavoursome.'

'Not many non-Valhallans seem to like it,' I said, 'but I've picked up a taste for the stuff over the years.'

'Remarkable,' Vorspung said, though I wasn't sure whether he was referring to the flavour again, or the fact that I found it palatable.[144] He took another sip. 'Although efficiency dictates that taste is an irrelevance where nutriment is concerned.'

'Perhaps so,' I agreed diplomatically, 'but sometimes it

---

143   *Perhaps some of the battle-brothers dabbled in pottery as well as painting.*

144   *Having been persuaded to try it once, I strongly suspect the latter.*

helps.' Fortunately, I was spared any further attempt at small talk by the arrival of Morie, who strode into the room like a force of nature, visibly chafing at the delay in carrying the fight to the necrons. Though my attempt to contact him from the depths of the mine had been too garbled to make much of, enough of the message had got through for the Thunderhawk to be dispatched on a recon sweep, and the squad of Tactical Marines it had brought with it had proven more than helpful in rounding up Tezler and their confederates – especially since the treacherous tech-priest had been kind enough to inadvertently vouch for the loyalty of the skitarii garrison there during our earlier conversation, and the red-robed warriors had joined in with alacrity as soon as they realised what was going on. 'Brother-sergeant. Some refreshment?'

'Thank you, no.' Morie took his place at the head of the table. 'Time is of the essence.'

'Of course it is,' I said, taking my seat, and leaving Vorspung to manage as best he could on one of the oversized ones. As it turned out, though, he merely glanced at the nearest and remained standing, which seemed sensible under the circumstances, especially as he was the one with the augmetic legs. 'With Tezler out of circulation, Aznibal's bound to realise we're moving against him sooner rather than later.'

'Indeed.' Norgard came bustling in, her robes flapping around her mostly metallic carcass, and came to rest next to Vorspung. 'Tezler's still refusing to cooperate fully with the interrogators, but has indicated that they're in communication every few days. And Aznibal will no doubt be waiting for some indication of how we intend to respond to the ultimatum he gave the commissar.'

'So the longer we can keep him guessing, the better,' I said. Which is why we hadn't simply flooded the lower levels with skitarii and Space Marines, and committed mass suicide by storming the tomb straight away. Aznibal was bound to have expected precisely that response, and I was certain that the hellish place would be swarming with necron warriors by now. 'By not mounting an immediate assault, we've given him the impression that we're considering capitulation.' Which, of course, we weren't. But Aznibal seemed arrogant enough to believe that we might, and that arrogance might just be the weakness we could use against him.

Morie nodded. 'Which is buying us the time we need to formulate a strategy,' he said, activating the hololith. 'Although taking the tomb by direct assault will be far from easy.'

'I concur,' Norgard said, reaching forward to highlight the cavern Jurgen and I had driven across so precipitately, the missing portions of the map having been restored to the records almost as soon as the conspirators' interference with them had been discovered. Both entrances to the tomb were marked, but the space beyond them appeared only as a vaguely defined void. 'Our forces will be pinned at these choke points, and butchered as they attempt to force entry. Whereas the necrons not only outnumber us already by a considerable margin, but can also reinforce their defences through the warp portal at any time.'

'That's the thing that most worries me,' I said, partly because it was true, and partly because I thought I ought to show that I was paying attention. 'So long as it's operational, Aznibal can launch an attack on the entire world through it. He said himself that he'd be willing to do that to grab the resources he needs to finish building his toy World Engine.'

Norgard and Morie exchanged concerned glances.

'Which would be a far greater threat in the long run,'

Vorspung put in, somewhat unexpectedly. 'If the battle station is as large and well armed as the commissar described, it could render a world uninhabitable in a matter of hours. Sooner, if it encounters no significant resistance.'

'I'm afraid I wasn't exaggerating,' I said. 'And I rather suspect that he'll choose targets incapable of putting up any resistance, at least to begin with. It's what necrons do.'

'In my experience,' Morie agreed.

'Then the logical course of action would be to disable the portal,' Vorspung said, before stumbling to a halt, his augmetic voice box somehow managing to take on a trace of embarrassment. 'Of course, I don't mean to impugn your expertise in this area, which far exceeds mine.'

'I couldn't agree more with your assessment,' I said. Morie and Norgard nodded too, and Vorspung suddenly looked a great deal happier. 'Destroying it has to be our highest priority. It's the only way to secure Eucopia, deny Aznibal the resources to complete his war machine, and restore the flow of materiel the whole subsector so desperately needs.' Which would still leave us an army of necrons to deal with, most likely, but the chances were I'd be dead by then, so it'd be someone else's problem anyway.

'Easier said than done, unfortunately,' Morie said, returning his attention to the hololith. 'Attempting to force either of these tunnels would simply channel our forces into a killing ground. By the time we forced a breach, our casualties would be too great to press our advantage.' Which seemed to me to be an unwarrantedly optimistic prognosis. More likely, bearing in mind both the Astartes' and skitarii's propensity for pressing the attack even in the face of overwhelming numbers and superior firepower, both of which the necrons undoubtedly possessed, they'd simply be wiped out to a man before gaining so much as a toehold in the tomb. Given the way the metal horrors' gauss weapons vaporised their targets, there wouldn't even be the dead of earlier waves to provide some rudimentary cover, allowing subsequent ones to make a little more ground.[145]

'Perhaps a kill team,' Norgard suggested. 'A sufficiently determined-seeming attack on the main access point could draw the defenders away from the secondary one, allowing a small force of specialists to infiltrate the tomb unopposed.'

'A fine idea in theory,' I conceded, 'but I doubt that the necrons will fall for it. And they must have thousands of warriors available to defend the place.' Unbidden, the memory of my own desperate attempt to infiltrate the tomb on Simia Orichalcae on a similar mission years before rose up in my mind, and I shuddered – the entire Tempestus squad I'd gone in with had perished before we'd even got near the damn portal, and I'd been lucky to get out with a whole skin myself. I took a sip of my rapidly cooling tanna. 'It was only the merest fluke that Jurgen and I got close enough to see it, and if those spider things hadn't mistaken our vehicle for part of the delivery in the first place...' I broke off, an idea suddenly taking root in my mind. A ridiculous, impossible, probably suicidal idea – but Throne help us all, it was the best I'd got. I braced myself for the inevitable chorus of derisive incredulity, and turned back to Norgard. 'I don't suppose Tezler's mentioned when the next delivery's due?' I asked.

Norgard shook her head. 'As I said, they're being singularly uncooperative. What little useful intelligence we have been able to glean has largely been inferred from their bluster and

---

145   *A tactic more often adopted by orks than anyone else, although desperation has its own impetus, especially when facing foes like the necrons.*

threats. They still appear to believe that Aznibal will liberate and reward them for their service.'

Vorspung emitted a short burst of static from his vox-coder. 'I'm sure they'll be disabused of that particular notion as soon as the Inquisition arrives,' he said, with a most un-tech-priest-like degree of relish.

'I'm sure they will,' I agreed hastily, before anyone could start asking awkward questions about who'd called them in. 'Not to mention the task force from Coronus.' Pretty much the first thing I'd done after emerging from that Emperor-forsaken hole was find an astropath and make sure Amberley and Zyvan were both brought up to speed, and both had responded with commendable rapidity – although I'd been careful to create the impression, without actually saying so, that it was the lord general who'd dumped the matter in the lap of the Ordo Xenos. Of course, I'd have liked nothing more than to simply sit back and wait for the reinforcements to get here, but the warp currents were fickle at the best of times, and unless we dealt with the matter ourselves, all they'd be likely to find when they arrived was our eviscerated corpses and wall-to-wall necrons energetically looting the place.

'Why do you ask, anyway?' Morie asked, his curiosity piqued. 'It might give us a better idea of how long we've got, but other than that I don't see the relevance.'

So I told him, and, in all honesty, the reaction of everyone present was pretty much exactly what I'd expected.

# TWENTY-EIGHT

As it turned out, we didn't have to waste any of our time trying to persuade Tezler to give us the schedule for the next delivery of tribute to the necrons; Vorspung plunged eagerly into the archives, and after a couple of hours of paddling around in the ocean of information generated by the vast array of cogitation engines we'd seen back at the Nexus, was able to produce a chart which he lost no time in disseminating to the data-slates of everyone else.

'This is conjectural,' he cautioned, while the rest of us stared at the devices in our hands, trying to look as though we understood any of the information they were displaying. 'But given the movements of material, and the insultingly rudimentary attempts to obfuscate them, I've been able to extrapolate a pattern. The intervals vary from around three days to two months, with a mean frequency of seventeen point two-eight-seven standard days.'

'Which would be far too long to wait before taking action,' Morie opined.

I nodded agreement. 'Throne knows how much damage Aznibal could do in more than two weeks,' I said. The last thing we needed was to give him enough time to formulate an effective plan of action against us. 'Especially once he realises Tezler's out of the picture.'

'Quite.' Norgard nodded too. 'We need to retain the initiative. Act before he does. But let him think he's setting the agenda.'

'Exactly,' I agreed. I shrugged. 'It goes against the grain, but I think our best chance is to let him think he's won.' I shot an anxious glance at Morie, expecting a speech about honour and glory, and loyalty to the Throne, but to my surprise he seemed to be in full agreement.

'Scruples are for theologians,' he said. 'More battles are won by subterfuge and pragmatism than principle. And deceiving the enemies of the Emperor is holy work in itself, is it not?'

'Works for me,' I said, heartened by the ripple of approval around the conference table.

'Then it's decided,' Morie said, standing with impressive speed for a man of his bulk. 'We adopt the commissar's plan with all due dispatch.'

Which is how come I found myself, a couple of hours later, at the head of a convoy of cargo-8s uncannily similar to the one we'd fled the tomb in, rattling down the ramp to the cavern below. As we passed the transport tube, I found myself looking out for the wreck of the lorry the necrons had shot to pieces, but there was no sign of it, beyond a faint patch of discoloration where fuel and lubricants had leaked. Which shouldn't really have surprised me – no doubt it had been swiftly removed to restore unimpeded access, and sent off to make some unfortunate enginseer's life more complicated than it needed to be.[146]

'Didn't expect to be back here so quick,' Jurgen said, his familiar presence at the wheel as quietly reassuring as ever.

'Neither did I,' I said, trying to sound a lot more casual about it than I felt. We were taking a huge gamble, even by my own standards; everything depended on whether Aznibal really was as arrogant and overconfident as I suspected. I hoped so, but I couldn't be sure. Over the course of my long and discreditable career I'd faced most of the enemies of humanity, even parleying with them on occasion, but even xenos species and Chaos-corrupted loons had something like facial expressions I could make a reasonable stab at interpreting. Aznibal's blank metal visage, on the other hand, had left me nothing to go on but his words, and I was all too aware of how easily they could be twisted to deceive.[147]

No use worrying about it now, though, I told myself; we were committed.

The cavern was less busy than I remembered, with fewer tech-priests and artisans hacking away at the rock faces, moving the spoil or directing servitors than on our previous visit. As Jurgen steered us across the cavern floor, at a far more sedate pace than the last time we'd been here, a russet-robed tech-priest raised an idle hand in greeting – recognising Norgard, in a disguise rather more convincing than the ones my aide and I had adopted on our last little jaunt to the lower levels, I returned the gesture, and nodded. Everyone in sight

---

146 *Quite unlikely, in fact: if it really was as badly damaged as Cain describes, it would simply have been rendered down for spare parts and the metal it contained.*

147 *After all, he'd had plenty of practice.*

was a skitarius, their weapons concealed beneath their robes, or among the mining tools they wielded with surprising expertise.[148] There were a few more servitors around than I remembered too, ignoring our presence as always, but most of the ones I could see appeared to be wandering aimlessly rather than engaged in any purposeful activity, parts of their bodies shrouded in tarpaulins, or concealed by boxes or bundles they were carrying to nowhere in particular with the single-minded diligence of their kind.

'Looks like the cogboys are ready, anyway,' Jurgen said, and I nodded.

'Let's hope the Astartes are too,' I added, as my aide rolled us gently to a stop in almost exactly the same place Clode had parked such a short and eventful time before. I took a deep breath, steadying my nerves, as the rest of the trucks came to a halt behind us, and clambered out of the cab.

The sense of deja vu was almost overwhelming. There was the line of parked lorries, packed with crates of all sizes, from standard ammo box to taller than I was; there were the servitors plodding forward to unload them; and there was the mouth of the tunnel leading to the necron tomb, its sinister, sickly glow seeping through from the far end. I swallowed, my mouth dry, and was unexpectedly heartened by a familiar odour as Jurgen killed the engine and jumped down to join me. His lasgun was slung at his shoulder, the melta tucked away neatly in the cab. I would have been no less happy to see it in his hands than he would have been himself, but this was a calculated risk – we needed to look relatively harmless, but if we'd turned up appearing to be

---

148    *Which had presumably been uploaded to their cortical processors, in the interests of verisimilitude.*

completely unarmed Aznibal was bound to smell a rat. However arrogant and conceited he might be, he was evidently far from stupid.

'So what happens now?' Jurgen asked, with a seemingly casual glance at the disguised skitarii in the cabs of the other trucks. All were remaining where they were, with the limitless patience of those with augmetically enhanced cerebellums,[149] although I had no doubt they were assessing everything around us for signs of a threat.

'We get this lot unloaded,' I said, 'withdraw and wait. See if those spider things take the bait.'

My aide glanced down the tunnel again, the slight narrowing of his eyes the only indication that he was anything other than his normal phlegmatic self. 'Something already is,' he said.

He was right, too. The necrotic light in the distance was flickering, intermittently obscured, while shimmering highlights danced against metal. Several somethings were on the move, heading towards us, and I fought down the impulse to draw my weapons. If I did, I was confident that I'd be dead before I even completed the movement.

'*We have you covered,*' Norgard said, cutting in on my vox-bead, and I inclined my head a few millimetres rather than responding verbally. All that probably meant was that my murder would be swiftly avenged, but I preferred to think that the overwatching sharpshooters would be quick enough to take down any threatening necron before it completed its attack.

The handling servitors had reached the lorries by now,

---

149   *Some of them, anyway. Mott, my savant, can get distinctly tetchy on occasion.*

and begun to unload. One crate in particular, about a metre long, wide and high, caught my eye, and I found my fingers closing around something small and hard in my greatcoat pocket – realising what I was doing, I let go of it hastily. The servitor holding it froze in place, like its fellows, waiting to be instructed where to put its burden.

Before I could point to the spot where the last stack had been, however, a flicker of movement caught my eye, and the first of the metallic spiders I'd been expecting scuttled into the cavern. Ignoring everything else it approached the servitor, plucked the box from its handling claws, and skittered away back down the tunnel. Taken by surprise I just had time to squeeze the activation stud on the little device in my pocket, and hope for the best.

'Commissar. Again you surprise me.' Aznibal strode out of the tunnel mouth, gazing down at me, his eye sockets glowing like a guiser's daemon mask,[150] reflecting the eldritch energies of the staff in his hand, which I took to be some kind of symbol of his office. It glowed, in the same way as the weapons I'd learned to be so wary of, so I wasn't about to take it on trust that it was harmless, though; if nothing else, it looked heavy enough to inflict a lot of damage if used as a polearm. He turned his head to take in the line of lorries, and the servitor, which had turned away to retrieve the next crate from the flatbed. 'I was not expecting gifts so quickly.'

'Well, you know,' I said, determined not to show my

---

150   *Guising is a custom on several worlds in and around the Damocles Gulf, where holidays marking the Emperor's protection are celebrated by the populace dressing up as His most fearsome enemies before eating and drinking too much. Inevitably, the combination of relative anonymity and overindulgence creates difficulties for the local law enforcers, particularly as mutants and the Chaos-touched are able to mingle with the crowds without attracting as much attention as usual.*

surprise at this unexpected development. I would have bet a substantial sum that he was through the portal and back on his battle station by now; if he was still hanging around on Eucopia, that rather implied that he was preparing for an all-out invasion sooner rather than later. 'You told me to choose, so I did. Might as well start as we mean to go on.'

'Good decision,' Aznibal said, his voice as hollow as ever, although I hoped I detected an undertone of smugness. 'Though I haven't communicated my requirements to Tezler yet.'

'Magos Tezler is indisposed,' I said, in my best diplomatic voice. 'For the time being I suggest you liaise with me, or Magos Vorspung.'

'Killed the turncoat, did you?' Aznibal asked, as though the answer was both obvious and of little interest.

'Not yet,' I said, 'but we don't trust them as an intermediary. We feel happier dealing with you directly.'

Aznibal nodded. 'Of course. Once a traitor...'

'Quite,' I said. 'And since it was important to let you know we've accepted your terms, we thought you'd appreciate an immediate gesture of good faith.'

'I do.' Aznibal stared down at me again. 'You have a reputation for trustworthiness, I'm told. I assume that's why you were selected to lead this delegation?'

'I'm a pragmatist,' I said. 'I don't like your deal at all. Quite frankly, it sticks in my craw. But I can't stand by and see a world full of innocent civilians massacred, especially when you'd get what you want anyway. This is the least bad option from where I'm standing, so I'm living with it.' For a moment I wondered if I'd overdone it, but Aznibal's posture suddenly shifted, to one I read as a little less wary. Maybe he was buying it after all.

'I see.' The sepulchral chuckle resonated from his chest for a moment. 'If you'd given me pledges of fealty, I'd have killed you where you stand. I know a liar when I see one. Lesser creatures could never serve us as equals.' His head turned, taking in the growing pile of crates beside the lorries.[151] 'What did you bring?'

I shrugged. 'We weren't sure what your requirements were, so Magos Vorspung made an educated guess, based on the records of what you've had before. Just leave anything you don't need, and let us have a shopping list for the next delivery.'

Aznibal's voice became a little more resonant. 'Do not presume to anticipate me. Everything on this world is mine, and will be duly claimed!' Which was exactly the reaction I was hoping to provoke. He raised a hand, and a moment later a swarm of the mechanical spiders boiled out of the tunnel mouth.

'As you wish,' I said, trying to sound as though I was attempting to mollify him. The spider things picked up everything the servitors had unloaded, and scuttled away into the tunnel, while still more scuttled over the lorries, picking the flatbeds clean. As before, some of them carried the larger crates between them, while others grasped the smaller ones in their mandibles, occasionally steadying them with their front set of forelimbs. As the last of the big crates disappeared down the tunnel, I turned back to the cab of the truck and prepared to mount, carefully keeping a triumphant smirk from my face. He'd actually fallen for it.

'What I wish is for you to accompany me,' Aznibal said.

---

151 *Presumably Jurgen or one of the drivers had instructed the servitors where to place them while Cain had been talking.*

'Really?' I turned back, looking up at him, and tried to project an air of polite confusion. What I was actually feeling, of course, was rather more akin to blind panic. 'By all means. I haven't anything urgent to be getting on with.' Which wasn't entirely true. The timer I'd activated with the vox-pulse from the tiny transmitter in my pocket would be counting inexorably downwards by now. If I'd estimated the delay correctly it would be through the portal and well out of the way before it reached zero, but knowing my luck it was entirely possible that this batch would be stored somewhere within the tomb, and if that was the case, I very much wanted to be a long way from here when it did.

'As I allow you to continue to exist,' Aznibal said, 'you may bear witness to the glory that awaits this part of the galaxy.'

'If you mean the tomb, I've already seen it,' I said. 'And a couple of others, come to that.' I didn't think it was politic to mention that I'd been instrumental in the destruction of one of them, though, the last thing I needed was to give Aznibal the idea that I might be some kind of threat.

'Really?' the towering necron asked, and with a sudden flare of well-masked apprehension I realised that I'd piqued his interest. 'I would hear what little you may have understood of the secrets of inferior dynasties.' He turned to the mouth of the tunnel, where a couple of stray spiders which had arrived too late to collect anything were milling around uncertainly. He dismissed them with an irritable gesture, and they scuttled back into the enveloping gloom. 'Walk with me.'

'By all means,' I said, and with every appearance of ease I could counterfeit, strode after him into the darkness.

# TWENTY-NINE

After a few paces I became aware of the echo of Guard-issue combat boots a few paces behind me, and a familiar odour, and breathed a heartfelt sigh of relief. Though he would have had to leave the melta behind, I felt a good deal more confident in my ability to get out of here in one piece with Jurgen watching my back. I glanced at Aznibal, waiting for him to react to my aide's presence, but he made no sign of having even noticed him, which was fine by me. I tapped the comm-bead in my ear.

'I'm accompanying Lord Aznibal into the tomb,' I said, keeping my voice casual, and hoping that the eldritch stone of its construction wouldn't block the transmission. Norgard would have seen me enter, but Morie wouldn't, and would no doubt appreciate my services as a forward observer if he'd been able to pick up my vox. No way of telling if he had, of course; if our stratagem was to work, he had to maintain vox silence for as long as possible.

'Who are you talking to?' Aznibal asked, his head turning to look at me in the manner of one of my old schola tutors suspecting (usually accurately, if I'm honest) that I'd been up to something if they could only just work out what it was.

'Vorspung,' I said. 'If my vox-bead works down here, I can pass on your requirements more quickly.'

'Such crude devices are beneath my notice,' Aznibal said, as we reached the end of the tunnel and entered the tomb itself. 'That would be a matter for the crypteks to resolve.'

'Of course,' I said. 'That's what you have them for in the first place I suppose.' Although I hadn't the faintest idea what he was talking about, the gist of it – that he was too important to bother himself with the little details – was clear enough, and I thought a bit of extra flattery wouldn't go amiss. That was why I'd added the honorific to his name. I glanced around, orientating myself. The line of spider things was following the same course it had taken before, and I breathed a little easier, as sure as I could be that the crate with our little surprise in it was well on its way to the portal. In fact, by my estimate, it would probably be through it in another few moments.

'Exactly,' Aznibal said, and raised an arm in an expansive gesture which took in a vast echoing chamber, in which decorative gilding was rendered necrotic by the all-pervasive sickly green glow. Several large statues of my host were scattered around the place; a few of the plinths were vacant, the scoring of their upper surfaces strongly hinting that they'd previously held effigies of the previous suzerain. And, to my complete lack of surprise, he ascended a couple of steps onto a dais before seating himself on a throne carved from the ubiquitous black stone. 'Behold the power of Aznibal!'

'Very nice,' I said, glancing around at our wider surroundings through a series of arches in the enclosing walls. There were certainly more of the humaniform warriors about than I remembered, their gauss flayers glowing sinisterly, striking highlights from their metal torsos as they patrolled the wide boulevards between the ever-whining machines. I looked towards the side passage Jurgen and I had first stumbled in here through, and saw two or three squads[152] of the things lurking in that corner of the cavern, although I had no doubt that there were probably more. Our tactical assessment had been right, then: attempting to force a breach by that route would have been fatally futile. Glancing back at the tunnel through which we'd just entered, I saw a similar number guarding that one too, and I fought down a shudder of apprehension. It looked like there was no way out the way we'd come, either. Then I shrugged. 'But I suppose when you've seen one...'

As I'd expected, this stung our host's pride, and he leaned a little in my direction, apparently affronted.

'There is nothing to equal it in this portion of the galaxy, apart from the chambers of the phaeron himself!'

'I don't doubt it,' I said, trying to sound as though I wanted to conciliate him, rather than keep his attention on me and away from what was about to happen. 'To be honest, the last time I was somewhere like this I didn't have much time for sightseeing.'

'Of course not,' Aznibal said. 'The guardians would have reacted to your presence.'

'They most certainly did,' I said, 'but they were rather more concerned with some orks that had got there first. Which was

---

152   *Presumably he means groups of around the same size as that Imperial Guard formation, which would mean twenty or thirty.*

lucky for me. My comrades and I were able to flee the planet before they had time to deal with us.' Which was almost true, other than the bit where we'd blown the whole tomb to perdition and buried it under megatons of rock as a parting gift. Mentioning that would have been a bit tactless, however, not to mention planting doubts about my ultimate intentions.

'Unexpectedly wise of you,' Aznibal said, then seemed to consider for a moment. 'This world remains in necrontyr hands?'

'For all I know,' I said. 'No one seemed all that keen to go back and check.' If anyone had, they were Inquisition agents, probably reporting to Amberley, and she'd never mentioned any follow-up expeditions to me.[153]

Aznibal leaned forward a little more, with what, in a human, I'd have interpreted as eagerness. 'Where is this world?' he asked.

I shrugged, playing for time. The last thing I wanted to do was point him at any potential allies.[154]

'I don't know your name for it,' I said. 'If you show me a star chart, I can point it out.'

'By all means,' Aznibal said, making the same peculiar gesture he'd employed before to invoke the image of his battle station. A star field suddenly appeared between us. I frowned, pretending to be trying to orientate myself.

'Let's see,' I said, waving a finger vaguely over the Damocles Gulf. 'If we're here...'

---

153  *No necron activity has been observed on Simia Orichalcae to date, but that doesn't mean they're not still burrowing away beneath the surface. Given the sheer scale of the destruction Cain triggered, it seems unlikely, though not impossible; in recent years growing numbers of orks have been detected from orbit, presumably descended from a few who survived the cataclysm, so the possibility cannot be entirely discounted.*

154  *Or possibly rivals, considering his earlier remarks in Tezler's living quarters.*

To my immense relief I was suddenly interrupted by an explosion, which shook the ground beneath my boot soles, and left my ears ringing with the violence of its detonation.

'Treachery!' Aznibal expostulated, leaping to his feet and swinging the sinisterly glowing staff at my head. I ducked by reflex, drawing my chainsword and blocking the downward motion instinctively. Sparks flew as the whirling adamantium teeth met aeons-old metal, cleaving deep, and the shaft buckled.

The familiar *crack* of ionising air told me that Jurgen had his lasgun out, firing short, precise bursts; for a moment I feared for my own safety before, in the act of pivoting out of the way of Aznibal's initial strike, I realised he was shooting at another set of targets entirely. The warriors which had been guarding the entrance had turned away from it, and were bearing down on us, the close-combat blades attached to their gauss flayers flickering ominously as their keen edges caught the ambient light. One went down, a hole blown through its chest, but kept twitching, the living metal beginning to knit back together even as I watched. Quite why they didn't simply shoot us, I have no idea; perhaps they were afraid of hitting their boss by mistake.[155] Whatever the reason, though, they'd be on us in moments.

'*Primary target destroyed,*' Morie said, his voice attenuated a little by my vox-bead's tiny speaker, and whatever effect the tomb's peculiar construction might be having. '*Commencing withdrawal.*' The louder bark of bolters, and a couple of

---

155  Given the average necron warrior's lack of emotion, highly unlikely. Going by what little we understand of their limited intellect, they were probably inhibited by an innate prohibition against firing on their own kind, and, like a servitor faced with an unexpected contingency, simply reverted to the next most applicable instruction.

explosions slightly quieter than before, echoed through the eldritch cavern.

'What have you done?' Aznibal demanded, taking another swipe at me, which I evaded by stepping inside the swing, and slashing my blade across his upper thigh. A mortal opponent would have found the strike crippling, but again I was rewarded with nothing more than a shower of sparks, and a gash in the metal of his leg which began flowing together as soon as I'd inflicted it.

'*Acknowledged,*' Norgard said, her voice even fainter than Morie's had been. Jurgen fired again, taking down another of the implacable metal warriors, even as his first victim rose to its feet and resumed its advance.

'Done?' I said, forcing a laugh, hoping to provoke Aznibal into something fatally reckless. 'What I set out to do.' I ducked another swipe which came uncomfortably close to taking my head off, sending it on its way with another parry from my chainsword which left the haft of his weapon looking even more chewed-up than ever. Sparks began spitting from it. 'Remember you said you could spot a trap?' I drew my laspistol and gave him five rounds rapid square to the face, more in the hope of distracting him than because I thought it would make any difference. 'Really don't think so, do you?'

If he said anything coherent in reply, I missed it, the sound emerging from his voice box battering my ears as a roar of sheer inchoate rage. Before he could take another swipe at me, though, the phalanx of warriors bearing down on us were torn apart by a storm of crackling energy, sparking from one to the other as though caught in a maelstrom of lightning. Fast-moving servitors on tracked chassis roared into the cavern from the tunnel mouth our would-be assailants had so recently turned their backs on, ravening energies pouring from the heavy weapons fused to their torsos.

'I will take this world!' Aznibal roared, the volume of his voice raised by some eldritch means to echo from the towering mechanica surrounding us. 'Leaving nothing but blood and bone!'

'You and what army?' Jurgen taunted, emptying the clip of his lasgun into the towering necron's back now the immediate threat was collapsing into a puddle of liquified metal and shorting circuitry.

'My legions wait beyond the portal!' Aznibal boasted. 'In numbers greater than you can possibly imagine!'

'Oh, the portal,' I said, taking advantage of the distraction to open the distance between us again, with an opportunistic swipe at the arm holding the staff; which, I'm bound to say, was about as effective as the by now almost invisible cut I'd inflicted on his leg a few seconds before. 'I think you'll find that first explosion was the sound of it being destroyed.'

'It was,' Morie confirmed, materialising at my shoulder, and emptying the clip of his bolter into Aznibal's chest. The hail of explosive projectiles seemed to have hurt the towering necron for the first time, ripping a ragged hole deep into his chest. From within it, some thick, viscid fluid began to ooze, glowing as unhealthily as everything else around here. 'Reduced to rubble, and the connection to wherever it was going completely cut.'

The servitors were coming under return fire now, as other necron warriors emerged from the shadows to engage them, several falling victim to the gauss flayers and some kind of lightning gun; but reinforcements were already pouring into the tomb, Norgard at their head, wielding an axe so large that only someone as extensively augmented as she was could even have lifted the thing. In her other hand was a pistol of some kind, spitting remarkably destructive energies which felled every necron she hit. Equally deadly beams lanced from the weapons of the onrushing skitarii, and tech-priests in the raiment of common artisans chanted litanies of power, wreathing themselves in crackling shrouds of lightning which burst against the metallic bodies of their foes, leaving them blasted and even more lifeless than usual.

Other Reclaimers were becoming visible now too, Tactical Marines taking down necrons with precisely aimed bursts of bolter fire, and plodding Terminators, their storm bolters roaring, ripping them to shreds before trampling their remains into the cavern floor. Not that we were getting things all our own way, of course; in one quick glance I saw a battle-brother vaporised by a clean hit from a gauss flayer, and an entire squad of skitarii consumed by a lightning storm, but the battle was undeniably turning our way.

'Jurgen!' I called, holstering my pistol again. 'Krak grenade!'

'Commissar.' My aide glanced up from snapping a fresh power pack into his lasgun, and rummaged in one of his collection of pouches. Finding what I'd requested, which I hadn't doubted for a moment, given his propensity for squirrelling away anything which might come in handy, he lobbed it across the intervening space, then resumed potting necrons with his usual phlegmatic deliberation. I caught the small armour-piercing charge in my free hand, almost fumbling it in my haste, and primed it.

Aznibal's head turned, taking in the carnage being wreaked on his unliving retinue, then returned to meet my gaze. When he spoke again, his voice was even more sepulchral than ever, positively quivering with malice.

'I will return, and scour you all from the face of the cosmos!' he said.

'No, you will die and be forgotten,' I riposted, and thrust the grenade deep into the hole in his chest cavity, which was already beginning to fill with liquid metal. The small explosive charge disappeared even as I watched. As belated realisation dawned, Aznibal scrabbled helplessly at the fresh metal scab.

'My vengeance shall be the terror of–' he began, then the armour-piercing grenade detonated, turning his chest into a blizzard of shrapnel, which might have inconvenienced me considerably had Morie not seen the danger and darted forward, shielding Jurgen and I with the bulk of his ceramite armour. Bits of Aznibal clattered and pinged against the brother-sergeant's chestplate, leaving a number of scores and pits in it, none of which appeared to have penetrated.

'Liked the sound of his own voice, didn't he?' I said, as the eldritch glow in the ruined necron's eyes faded, and Norgard pelted up to us, swiping Aznibal's head from his shoulders with a single swing of her battleaxe. Which might strike you as a little theatrical, but believe me, with necrons there's no such thing as overkill. 'Praetor. Good of you to join us.'

'My pleasure,' Norgard assured us, before darting off to dismember a few more necrons before they all vanished into thin air and spoiled her fun. There were still more than enough around for my taste, though, and I began moving towards the tunnel mouth as quickly as I could without looking as though I was making a run for it.

'I must confess I had my doubts about your stratagem,' Morie said, falling into place at my shoulder, evidently intent on continuing the conversation. 'But it was undeniably effective. The spider things carried us straight to the portal. We were able to place the charges as soon as we broke out of the crates, while the Terminators eliminated them.'

'I noticed none of them examined their loads when Jurgen and I got carried inside here,' I explained. 'So the chances of discovery were remote.'

'Especially after you manoeuvred Aznibal into taking the whole shipment to preserve his sense of superiority.' Morie chuckled, which I have to say took me by surprise, particularly under the circumstances. 'I see your years of playing the diplomat on the general staff haven't been entirely wasted.'

'Everything's a weapon in the service of the Throne,' I quoted,[156] popping off a couple of laspistol shots at a scuttling metallic beetle, which crunched most satisfyingly a moment later under Morie's heavily armoured boot. 'Even your enemy's ego.'

'That's why Astartes aren't allowed one,' Morie said, showing another unexpected sign of a sense of humour. We gained the relative sanctuary of the tunnel, and I felt my spirits lifting as we left the unhallowed precincts of the tomb forever.

'Now for the difficult part,' I said. 'Persuading Vorspung to destroy all that archeotech.'

---

156   From Inspiring Thoughts for Simple Minds, *a Schola Progenium primer for commissarial cadets; whether he actually remembered this from his own education, or had whiled away the journey from Coronus preparing for his new pedagogical role, remains unclear.*

# THIRTY

Which actually turned out to be surprisingly easy. Unlike Tezler and the other necron dupes, Vorspung seemed to regard everything in the tomb as blasphemy incarnate, and began urging its destruction almost as soon as I'd broached the subject.[157] The upshot of which was that by the time Amberley arrived in-system aboard the *Externus Exterminatus*[158] all the machinery had been reduced to its component parts by judiciously placed melta bombs, and the roof brought down

---

157    *Though, like the Ecclesiarchy, the Adeptus Mechanicus likes to keep its internal divisions private, this does seem to be one of the major schisms within it; some tech-priests being eager to study alien technologies and artefacts, while others apparently consider their very existence an affront to the Omnissiah. Vorspung, perhaps fortunately, fell into the latter camp.*

158    *The starship I commandeered for my personal use almost a century ago – the life of an inquisitor tends to the peripatetic, and it's nice to have somewhere to call home. Particularly if it has a couple of lance batteries and a torpedo bay to discourage unwanted visitors.*

to bury the remains by equally carefully deployed mining charges. I had been a little apprehensive about her reaction to the news that I'd dragged her halfway across the Gulf to inspect a filled-in hole, but fortunately she took it in good part.

'You did the right thing,' she confirmed, over a light supper in her private quarters, the curve of Eucopia visible in the viewport behind her. 'You can't be too careful with those things.'

I nodded. 'Especially the clever ones, it seems.' Now I'd had time to reflect on it, I'd found the implications of my encounter with Aznibal profoundly disturbing. Up until then I'd always considered the necrons to be nothing more than murderous automata, blindly following instructions given aeons before by some long-extinct creators. 'Is it true they were once living creatures?'

Amberley placed her empty goblet beside her plate, and regarded me thoughtfully. 'Some of my colleagues have long thought so,' she said. 'I preferred to keep an open mind. But in the light of your experience... I'd be inclined to agree with them.'

'And Tezler wanted the same,' I said, suppressing a shudder. 'Eternal undeath. I almost think they deserve it.'

Amberley nodded, soberly. 'And speaking of Tezler...'

'Have you got them to talk yet?' I asked.

'Oh yes.' She reached for the decanter, refilled her goblet, and leaned over the table to top mine up as well. For a moment I caught a faint whiff of hegantha blossom, a perfume she'd always favoured. 'Or, to be more precise, Vorspung did.'

'Vorspung?' I made no attempt to hide my surprise. 'That man has hidden depths.' And was no doubt about to find himself inducted into the same loose network of her agents and informants as Jurgen and I because of it. If he hadn't been already.

'He has indeed,' Amberley said. 'Once we knew Tezler and their confederates had suborned the skitarii who attacked you by modifying their neuroware, Vorspung was able to reverse engineer the technique by examining the cortexes of the bodies recovered from the proving grounds.' She shrugged, as though discussing something a lot less terrifying than hijacking someone's entire being. 'Sauce for the grox, and all that. With their brains hacked, the conspirators you'd already rounded up were falling over themselves to betray the rest of their network.' She arched an eyebrow at me. 'Including, you'll be pleased to know, the ones who tried to kill you on Coronus by hacking your transport ship.'

'So what happens to them now?' I asked, more in the interests of politeness than because I actually cared.

Amberley smiled, without any trace of good humour. 'They wanted new bodies, and they're getting them. Norgard lost a lot of her forces, as well as a large contingent of combat servitors. Replacing them's the least we could do.'

'Sounds fair,' I agreed. 'Particularly now she's having to mount a permanent guard on the lower levels of the mine. Just to be on the safe side.'

'A wise precaution.' Amberley rose from the table, and stretched. 'I gather output's more or less back to what it should be.'

'It is.' I nodded, rising too. 'And so's production by the manufactories. The weapons are flowing again.'

'Zyvan will be pleased to hear that. And the admiral too, I suppose.' She glanced at me, a hint of mischief in her eyes. 'I'm sure the Navy won't begrudge you the loan of a plasma torpedo.'

'Just the warhead of one,' I said. The scent of hegantha was back in my nostrils, and her head was resting against my shoulder. 'With any luck it made a real mess of Aznibal's battle station when it went off.'

'Yes, well. That.' She raised her head, nailing me with her eyes. 'Where a threat that potent's concerned, we can't rely on luck. We need to find it.'

'I suppose so,' I agreed, a quiver of apprehension beginning to manifest in the pit of my stomach. 'Good luck with that.'

'When I say we, I mean we. You, me and Morie. I've had him seconded to the Deathwatch.' Her voice remained light and conversational, although I knew beyond doubt that this was an order, with all the authority of her office behind it. 'I'm afraid the schola on Perlia is going to have to manage without a commissarial cadet programme for a little while longer.'

'Of course,' I said, bowing to the inevitable. If I'd known how long it was going to be before I took up that appointment, and the horrors I'd have to face before I did, I suppose I might have protested a little more, but I already knew it wouldn't make any difference. I sighed. 'When do we start?'

Amberley smiled again, the one I always liked to think was real, and slipped an arm around my waist. The stars beyond the viewport shone hard and cold, but for a moment I felt neither of those things.

'The morning will do,' she said.

[Though Cain continues for several more paragraphs, these concern themselves entirely with matters of a personal nature unconnected with events on Eucopia, so I have chosen to terminate his account at this point.]

## ABOUT THE AUTHOR

**Sandy Mitchell** is the author of a long-running
series of Warhammer 40,000 novels, short
stories and audio dramas about the Hero of the
Imperium, Commissar Ciaphas Cain. His other
stories include 'A Good Man', included in the
*Sabbat Worlds* anthology, and several novels set in
the Warhammer World. He lives and
works in Cambridge.

An extract from
*Outgunned*
by Denny Flowers

I cannot tell you when war began on Bacchus.

I could provide the date that Imperial forces were dispatched to the once prosperous agri world to combat the mounting ork threat. But greenskins emerged from the swamps years prior, local forces suppressing their numbers for almost a decade before their sudden plea for assistance. Many had already lost loved ones or limbs before official records decree the conflict even started. Their war began early.

My war began in a dingy cabin nestled deep within Orbital Station Salus, the monolithic space station suspended above Bacchus. I awaited authorisation to depart for the planet below, and had for over a day. There were either atmospheric irregularities or hostile forces operating in the area, depending on whether one believed the official account or overheard whispers in corridors.

With my meagre possessions and ample equipment already stowed, there was little I could do but wait. My time was occupied watching a tiresome recruitment pict, even though I had already endured it a dozen times or more. It was, after all, the reason I was there. The holo-display projected a grainy image of an ork warrior. A wiry creature, clad only in a scrap of loincloth, the greenskin was nevertheless imposing, its tusks bared in a snarl, a crude spear brandished with intent. It sniffed the air, like a bloodhound, before roaring and surging forward, intent on its prey.

'On the agri world of Bacchus, vile xenos beasts threaten the loyal citizens of the Imperium!'

As the narrator's voice crackled into life, the panned shot revealed an Imperial citizen fleeing, dragging a child behind her. Their attire was not in keeping with Bacchus, for the image had been cut from a far older pict and crudely spliced into the more recent footage. The work was sloppy, either that of an amateur or someone who cared little for their subject or reputation.

The woman stumbled, falling just as the ork loomed behind her, its spear poised for the killing blow. She tried to cover her child with her body, even as the boy glared at the ork with undisguised hatred.

I paused the playback, the image freezing.

The footage presented some classic archetypes: the mother embodying noble sacrifice, her child angry and defiant despite the xenos threat ably represented by the ork. I could see the intent. But the seams between the cuts were painfully apparent, noticeable to even the most dull-witted menial worker. The footage of the ork was genuine from what I could tell; the way its feet sank into the burnt-orange swamp would be difficult to simulate. Conversely, the woman had been deposited on a convenient stretch of rock in a crude attempt to disguise the pict-seam. She was beautiful in a restrained way, and I was sure I had seen her in a previous vid. *Beware the Foul Mutants!* perhaps, or *All Heretics Will Fall.*

'Restore playback,' I murmured.

The ork raised its spear, poised to impale both mother and child.

*'But the God-Emperor protects the faithful. Look to the skies!'*

The narrator's intransient optimism was grating. But at his words all three figures raised their heads, glancing upwards as if on command. Cue the roar of an engine, the pict zooming in on a distant spec hurtling through the sky.

The ork barely had time to raise its hand-hewn weapon before a las-bolt sheared off its head. It stood a moment, despite the absence of cranium, before pitching forward, the focus of the vid shifting to the mother and child. Both stood proud, her arms crossed in the sign of the aquila, her son offering a salute crisp enough to satisfy even the most stringent commissar.

*'No matter how craven the xenos or foul the heretic, we need not fear. The brave pilots of the Aeronautica Imperialis are our impenetrable shield!'*

An aircraft zoomed overhead, the shot cutting to the pilot, who returned the boy's salute even as his Thunderbolt fighter hurtled over the swamplands. The fighter's top speed is over one thousand miles per hour, and the pilot would barely have seen the child, let alone been able to plant a tank-piercing las-bolt between the ork's eyes. But here he was, finding time to make nice with the citizenry during his fly-by.

It was galling.

Of course, my peers would shrug and say, so what? The purpose of these vids is to reassure the masses, or inspire fresh recruits to enlist. It does not matter whether they are accurate, as in all probability none of the menial workers who join the Imperial Navy will ever get the chance to fly; that is the preserve of the nobility. All that matters is that the audience leave the vid flush with conviction and a desire to serve, and that enough enlist to fulfil the roles of ground crew, indentured workers and mechanicals.

But I maintained that such a poorly crafted vid could only encourage ridicule. And the recruitment figures suggested I was right.

The aircraft now swept over the swamp, its Avenger bolt cannons scything down an ork horde – a weapon that the standard fighter variant previously shown should not have had. Amateurs.

The orks' response was to hurl spears and insults, whilst the narrator continued to extol the inevitability of humanity's victory and the inferiority of the greenskins. It seemed the recruitment drive was focused on portraying the war as a thrilling adventure that could conclude at any moment, urging citizens to enlist before it was too late and the fighting ended. Not an inaccurate assessment, if one were to listen to some of the whispering in the corridors, but not for the reasons suggested in the pict.

By the Throne, it was tiresome. But I persisted, for what followed was the only shot in the pict worth a damn.

A second craft lurched into view, wobbling above the swamp at barely a walking pace. It was constructed from wood, though the rear-mounted engine looked to be assembled from scrap metal. It belched thick black clouds, the holo-display struggling to depict the smoke as anything more than static. Its pilot was a haggard-looking ork who appeared to be missing an eye and more than a few tusks. As the Thunderbolt fighter soared overhead, the ork attempted to fire a crude cannon mounted beneath its craft, but the recoil pitched it off balance and subsequently into the swamp. A rather impressive explosion followed, but I found myself winding back the footage until the ork flyer was visible again.

I had first thought it fake, the wooden aircraft spliced in to lighten the pict and ridicule the greenskins. But there were no seams. It was real, though the precise age of the footage was impossible to determine.

I frowned. I am no tech-priest, but it seemed impossible that such a craft could fly; I have used field latrines that were more aerodynamic. Yet somehow the orks found a way. There was something almost admirable about their ingenuity.

Admirable, and troubling.

The vox suddenly whined into life. I shut down the playback, opening the channel.

*'Propagandist Simlex?'* said a voice.

'Yes?'

*'We are ready to depart, sir.'*

'Thank you. I will be there shortly,' I replied, closing the vox-channel and rising to my feet. I should have felt elated, for finally my work would begin. But I found myself dwelling on that primitive ork aircraft. It was disconcerting seeing such a savage creature achieving powered flight. Humanity mastered the skies millennia ago, and our fighters and bombers have changed little since then, for the same sacred designs are portrayed in picts and murals stretching back centuries.

The orks on Bacchus began cobbling aircraft from scrap a few score years ago. Yet recent reports suggested they now possessed something akin to an actual air force.

As I departed, I found myself wondering if the greenskins' aspirations ended there.

The flight sergeant stood at the corridor's end, rigid as a sabre, his hair seemingly welded in place, his uniform unmarked by stain or crease. He was the model of an Imperial soldier, except for his face. Somehow, even when attempting to appear stern and sombre, he looked poised to break into a smile. As I hurried closer, he threw a salute so earnest it risked a head injury.

'Propagandist Simlex?' he asked.

I nodded.

'Flight Sergeant Plient, sir!' he said. 'Well, Acting Flight Sergeant Plient. Field promotion, sir, though I'm not sure the paperwork has been filed.'

He already sounded apologetic.

'My pleasure to make your acquaintance, acting flight sergeant,' I said, bowing my head. 'I take it we are ready to depart?'

'Yes, sir. I have your cases secured and stowed aboard the Arvus lighter. Just awaiting some last-minute clearance.'

I nodded, my gaze already drawn to the viewport behind him. From it, I could see a tapestry of glittering stars, each a priceless gem in the God-Emperor's Imperium. The scale was terrifying, but also strangely comforting. Suns blazed and planets progressed along predestined paths, ambivalent to the follies of man. It all seemed so ordered from such a vantage point, as though the galaxy were on the cusp of peace. The rim of the planet Bacchus was barely visible beneath, framed by a halo of violet light.

'Sir?'

I glanced round, having almost forgotten Flight Sergeant Plient.

'I've just been informed we have an opening, sir. Need to depart.' He gestured to the launch bay.

I nodded, following him through to the vessel. I had never ridden an Arvus lighter, nor even seen one before. It was a stub-nosed cargo shuttle, unarmed and seemingly unremarkable. Plient opened the rear doors, revealing an interior hastily refitted to transport human cargo. A trio of flight seats were bolted to the floor. My cases lay beside them, secured in place by mag-clamps.

'Please take a seat, sir. We will be departing soon,' Plient said, smiling as he slid the door shut behind me.

I glanced at the three identical chairs and, after a couple of false starts, opted for the seat on the left, closest to my cases. The flight harness was unfamiliar, and seemed intent on slicing through my shoulder. Plient's voice crackled through the vox-channel.

'*All set, sir?*'

'Yes, acting flight sergeant,' I said. 'Ready as I will ever be.'

'*Nervous, sir?*'

'A little. Though more excited. I've never made planetfall in a craft like this.'

'*Understandable, sir. Though I should caution you that the shift between gravitational fields is disconcerting. Some nausea is not uncommon.*'

'I'll try not to make a mess of your vessel,' I said, smiling. 'I suppose for a pilot such as yourself atmospheric re-entry is just another day's work?'

'*That's what I should say,*' Plient replied. '*But, between you and me, I never get used to it. It's magical, sir. Awe-inspiring. Except for the nausea.*'

'I wish I could see the way you do.'

'*I can arrange that, sir. You are not the first passenger to make such a request.*'

Ahead of me, just above the cockpit door, a shaded pict screen lit up. I craned my neck, cursing myself for picking the wrong chair. My reward was a view of the now-familiar stars. They looked smaller on the pict screen, less significant.

'The ship has external viewers?' I said. 'Is that standard?'

'No, sir, but this vessel regularly ferried dignitaries before the war. Some of them enjoyed a view.'

'Thank you, Acting Flight Sergeant Plient.'

'I'm here to help, sir. Stand by for launch.'

My nails dug into the armrests. I willed myself to relax, taking a deep, slow breath, trying to unpick my apprehension. I had reservations about the journey, of course, but that was not the root of the unease. Nerves were not unknown to me; I felt positively queasy before arriving on the shrine world of Sacristy. But the pict I'd produced, a biopic of the life of Brannicus the Thrice-Maimed, had been received as my finest work. The infamous scene of the saint beating three hundred sinners to death armed only with his own severed leg is still regarded as a cinema-pict masterpiece.

But this was different. This time I would be on the front lines, obtaining live footage from an actual conflict, whilst balancing the whims of at least two masters. My unease was driven as much by the political pitfalls surrounding my work as it was by the prospect of imminent death on the surface below.

The craft shuddered, breaking out of the gravitational pull of Orbital Station Salus. A vast shadow blotted out the stars as Bacchus loomed into view. The moderately prosperous agri world was known for the quality of its wine but precious little else. Viewed from the shuttle, its surface was a dirty orange, with little indication of habitation or geographical variance. A casual observer might assume that deserts lay beneath them, the sands devoid of life.

They would be sorely mistaken.

A lurch. It was subtle now, for we were between gravities. But I felt my back press into the flight seat as the orange sphere swelled to fill the screen.

'*Stand by, sir. It is about to get dicey.*'

The screen flashed white as we commenced re-entry, flames lapping at its rim and seemingly consuming the planet below. They were purple, the tips edged in magenta, presumably a by-product of the atmosphere. A small sliver of me, the eternal propagandist, wondered how this might affect the project, whether I needed to adjust the lenses to minimise light diffusion, or should embrace the conditions to make my pict visually distinct.

The remainder of me was focused on holding down my breakfast, with mixed success.

'*Enjoying the ride, sir?*'

'It's a unique experience,' I replied, wiping my mouth on the back of my hand. The limb felt extraordinarily heavy, the craft's systems unable to fully compensate for the acceleration. 'Though I confess I am used to larger craft, where I suspect the ride is smoother.'

'*True enough, sir. But a larger craft makes for a bigger target. Our re-entry is less likely to be spotted by the orks.*'

There was something in his tone. A seriousness. But I assumed he was merely focused on his duties. I still pictured the greenskins as spear-brandishing brutes flying flimsy wooden planes, despite more recent reports. I could not conceive them posing a threat to a void-worthy vessel.

I would learn otherwise.